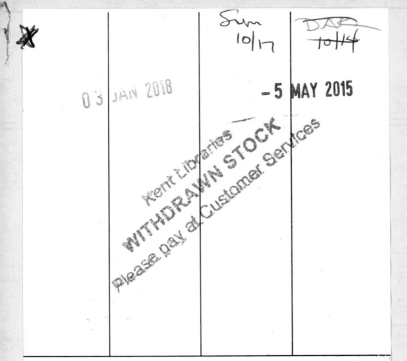

freeway, turn left at Sexy Street, right at Scandal Boulevard.
Your destination is Victoria Fox's Hollywood.'
—*dailyrecord.co.uk*

POWER
Games

Victoria Fox

HARLEQUIN®MIRA®

Harlequin MIRA is a registered trademark of Harlequin Enterprises Limited, used under licence.

Published in Great Britain 2014
by Harlequin MIRA, an imprint of Harlequin (UK) Limited,
Eton House, 18-24 Paradise Road,
Richmond, Surrey, TW9 1SR

© 2014 Victoria Fox

ISBN 978-1-848-45309-8

60-0714

Harlequin's policy is to use papers that are natural, renewable and recyclable products and made from wood grown in sustainable forests. The logging and manufacturing processes conform to the legal environmental regulations of the country of origin.

Printed and bound by
CPI Group (UK) Ltd, Croydon, CR0 4YY

ACKNOWLEDGEMENTS

Thank you to Maddy, my agent and my friend, for more with every book.

To my brilliant editor, Sally Williamson, for drawing the best out of this novel, for her fabulous ideas, and for always pushing me to potential; and to the superb team at Harlequin UK: Mandy Ferguson, Tim Cooper, Nick Bates, Alison Lindsay, Donna Hillyer, Jenny Hutton, Ali Wilkinson, Elise Windmill and Helen Findlay.

To Cara Lee Simpson for her excellent notes on *Power Games*, and to Oliver Rhodes for his publishing prowess. To the guys at Cherish PR, especially Rebecca Oatley, Sam Allen and Shane Herrington: you make my dreams come true!

To Jo and Jeff Croot for helping straighten the plot; to Kim Young for Kevin and the Little Chasers; to Louis Boroditsky for his fantastic support; to Toria and Mark for going Bear Grylls; and to Rosie Walsh, Jenny Hayes, Vanessa Neuling and Kate Wilde for their friendship and writerly advice.

For Madeleine Milburn

PROLOGUE

I

Koloku Island, Southeast Asia, the Palaccas Archipelago
July 1, 2014

The jungle comes alive at night.

In the darkness strange shapes creep and fold. Liquid shadows are black as ink and the undergrowth moves. Things shift unseen, slipping beneath leaf-silk. The air quivers, hot and clenched. It smells of the colour green, fragrant and private; and the purple sky, glimpsed in diamonds through a trembling canopy, is bursting with stars.

There is no safe way to arrive on these shores. The water is shark-infested, the land crawls and seethes. It is a forbidden paradise set apart from the world, and it does not welcome visitors. Peril lurks in swamps. Cat snakes drip from trees. Leopards prowl with silent intent, eyes gleaming gold at the scent of the kill. On a far-off branch, the panicked screech of a proboscis monkey rips through the pregnant heat, high and taut and violent. Fruit bats clap leathery wings.

It is impossible to see in the depths of the rainforest. Dense threads thick as rope are damp and fat and scented like rot. Enquiringly they finger the skin, coiling around wrist, knee or ankle, tethering any who trespass into the sucking, clinging earth. This is no place for humans. The wilderness took over a long time ago.

Beyond a wall of jade, the beach is torn into view. Cliff shards soar, rugged and sheer, their lofty peaks silhouetted against star-crust, prehistoric and bone-sharp. Rivers thread vein-like into the slithering jungle and grottos are sliced out of the rock, interiors caked in salt. Palm trees rise like swords against the sky, a hundred feet up, maybe more. The indigo lagoon shimmers like silk, kissing the pink crust of the reef, beyond which spreads the wide, dark Aralanda Sea. Water whispers onto sand, sighing as satin over pale shoulders. It brings secrets from the far-off Pacific, drifting them onto the shore like shells, for nobody to hear and nobody to pick up.

Everything is still.

The jet appears at first like a silver comet. It is small, a moving star, but to blink will draw it into focus, its clean, light contours and the tipping line of its wings. It falls closer, glinting against the lilac clouds. Too quick it is eating up distance, eerily noiseless as it falls and falls over glittering black, reaching for the moonlit bay.

Smoke trails from the rear, dissolving into the indifferent dark. There is a flash of hot orange, close to the tail. The sky begins to growl.

With a crash the body plummets through the canopy. Profuse thickets resist its mighty onslaught, breaking the descent. Thunder blasts as the fuselage guillotines through trees. The forest shrieks. There is an explosion of birds' wings.

The captain has a second to think before the windshield bursts and a jagged shaft breaks through, neat as a splinter, impaling him through his chest. His lungs are demolished; his breath is crushed. He is surprised. He wasn't meant to die today. The last person he thinks of is the woman who sold him his coffee that morning in Jakarta, her light, smiling eyes and the sweetness of the liquid on his tongue. Blood spills from his mouth and he slumps forward, chin on chest, and stops living.

It is a peculiar quirk of fortune that prevents the jet from slamming into hard ground: later, those on board will realise that the forest saved their lives—and curse it for it. Instead, the stricken plane shudders through foliage, hell-bent on its manic detour, battered by rocks and the thump of knotted branch. Parts fall away. The mammoth trunk of a chengal tree severs one wing, flipping the missile. It breaks up, an eagle in the skies but down here little but haphazard pieces of fractured metal. In the cockpit the overhead panel collapses, knocking the first officer cold.

What is left carves a giant wound through the under-growth. Despite the broken plunge, the impact is severe. The aircraft groans to an uncertain, injured rest, slashed with mud and green. The moon bathes it in light, like a pearl.

Of the seven passengers who boarded that morning, three are men and four are women. It is unclear who is left.

One is smeared with red, her face and neck sticky with salt and iron, though she cannot decipher through her terror if it is her blood or another's.

One is trapped beneath something solid. He doesn't know if he is alive or dead. He must be dead, he thinks, because everything is dark.

One is the first to move. She gropes into the black and detects the outline of her hand, tentative and ghostly, and knows in that moment she has made it.

Half a mile behind, the remainder of the cabin is suspended in a tree seventy metres from the ground. It hangs between moss-covered creepers and is tilted on one side, caught in a nest of fronds. The ribbons strain: they cannot hold it.

Inside, a woman opens her eyes. She can hear her breathing, fast and short, and the furious blood in her veins.

There is a final, desperate moment before somebody screams. The animal cry flies into the jungle like spitting fire, a red warning: there are survivors.

II

Nine thousand miles away, in an ancient fortress buried deep in the woodland, the telephone rings. Its chime echoes through sprawling gothic caverns, lonely and stark.

Billionaire Voldan Cane receives it.

Anticipation climbs in his throat. 'Is it done?' he rasps.

The voice makes him wait. Eventually, it comes.

'Yes. It is done.'

Voldan exhales. A wheezing moan escapes where the skin between his top lip and his nose has ruptured. His bruised heart burns.

It is done.

The call is terminated. Voldan tries to smile but it is hard. The movement tugs at his ruined features, his sallow skin pitted as fruit peel. Normally he avoids his tortured image—mirrors have long been banished from these rooms—but here, in the high, arched windows of Szolsvár's Great Hall, he catches a flash of the man he used to be: handsome, wealthy, coveted…happy.

One out of four isn't bad.

The panes are faded and cobwebbed with age. Only

Voldan's eyes betray the depths of his satisfaction. *It is done.*

He backs away from his reflection and the shadows swallow him whole.

PART ONE

Six months earlier

I

New York

Angela Silvers was being fucked from here to infinity.

At least, that was how it looked. In the mirrored dressing room of Fit for NYC, the bijou latest addition to her chain of sought-after fashion boutiques, her image was fractured and repeated, chasing replicas of her naked body to vanishing point. Angela was flung against the sweat-slicked glass, her arms wide and her blood racing.

The man between her thighs was forbidden.

Noah Lawson.

Movie star, heart-throb, teenage crush—the man she wasn't allowed to have.

Noah's tongue circled with exquisite precision, tracing around, between and beneath, everywhere but the place she knew would ignite her like dynamite.

She grabbed his hair, tilting her hips, and gasped as fireflies swarmed in her belly, rising and rising until the world and everything in it diminished to the pure, clear pleasure of her approaching climax. Oh, how she had tried to forget him. Noah was her lover, her best friend and her constant: he was the magic in her heart.

She couldn't help the rebellion. It had been in her since she was fifteen.

'Keep going!' she begged. 'Don't stop!'

Drawing her to him, Noah plunged deep, finally giving her what she wanted where she wanted it, and in a delicious, delirious flash she was there, slave to the surge, electric ripples tearing her apart. He kissed her lips, her neck, her collarbone, and whispered in her ear those three sweet words he saved just for her.

If only she believed them.

'Ms Silvers?' There was a knock at the door: a female voice, summoning her for the launch. 'They're ready for you. Is everything all right?'

Angela closed her eyes, throwing her head back to gasp her admission: 'I'm coming!'

Fit for NYC was a walk-in wow-fest of everything retail could and should be.

The gallery was spectacular. Silhouetted mannequins were draped in lace and crepe. Champagne glittered on diamond plinths, embossed with the golden FNYC logo. The air was spritzed with an aroma of privacy, of secrecy, even of conspiracy. Couches sat plump as raspberries, their Milanese fabrics shimmering with hand-gilded leaf, and goblets of fizz drifted along with zingy morsels of antipasto: juicy baby figs, Parma ham as light as silk, salty *pepperoncini* and fleshy artichoke. The pieces were one-offs, painstakingly selected from the fiercest new collections; if not by Angela then by her trusted clique of buyers. Personal assistants were on hand to advise. Designers were commissioned for bespoke tailoring. Caskets housed the chicest of gems. Fit for NYC was set to become *the* shopping mecca of the super-rich.

Heads turned as Angela moved across the floor. Hers was

a potent sensuality that combined feisty Italian beauty with the self-assurance and class of an elite Bostonian heritage. In a tailored trouser suit with deep V neckline and heels that put her at a fraction under six feet, Angela Silvers was bracingly attractive.

She smoothed her curls. Sex hair. Her cheeks were still flushed, her knees weak.

Already she ached for Noah, her skin dancing from his touch and his kiss still alive on her lips. Why did they have to hide? Why couldn't he be here, at her side?

Some days Angela convinced herself to throw it all to hell and stand in defiance of her father; others, it was career suicide. Donald Silvers was a powerful, domineering man, and he would not be moved when it came to his precious only daughter: if he found out she and Noah were together, he would take from Angela the one thing she had always craved—that one day, the family business would be hers.

Her heart or her ambition… Why did she have to choose?

According to her father, despite Noah's fame and riches, he wasn't one of them. He wasn't from her stock. Girls in Angela's position were expected to see and be seen with the right sort of man, to date wisely, to marry correctly.

She ignored the sliver of doubt that told her that wasn't the only reason. Doubt that looped through a hole in her heart; a hole Noah himself had made years before.

The thing was, no one else matched up. No one looked at her in the way Noah did. No one listened, and cared, and made her laugh. No one held her hand and kissed her like it was the last kiss on earth. No one made love to her like he did.

'*I'll call you*,' she had told him, as he'd slipped through the doors and into the night. His strong arms around her, his voice in her ear: '*Not if I call you first…*'

'Where've you been?'

Orlando, the elder of her two brothers, swiped a chalice of Louis Roederer and drank lustily from it. At thirty Orlando was a polished, complacent kind of handsome, as if his looks and status were assets he had won on merit, not by chance.

'Shouldn't you slow down?' Angela commented. Unable to resist stoking the fire of sibling rivalry, she added wickedly: 'Anyone would think you were jealous.'

'Jealous?' He snorted. 'Hardly.'

But she didn't believe it. Orlando and Luca existed on the soft plush pillow of their father's wealth like cats in the sun, safe in the assurance that they had to do very little to merit his attention. Angela, on the other hand, had had a fight on her hands since day one—and it had forced her to succeed. As the only girl and third in line to the Silvers throne, she was long accustomed to a role in the shadows. Why should a world-famous heiress to immeasurable fortune be getting involved in the tough stuff when there were more frivolous things to be doing, like getting her nails done, or partying, or visiting their private Hawaiian retreat for a week of sun and spa?

Angela didn't give a shit about any of that. She had the balls and the brains of any man—bigger, better—and had demonstrated she could easily trounce her brothers when it came to business. Setting up Fit for NYC by herself was testament to that.

'You're drunk,' she said, switching seamlessly to a smile for their guest of honour, supermodel of the moment Tawny Lascelles. Tawny was blonde, wide-eyed and sultry. She was four years younger than Angela but the gap felt wider—the way Tawny behaved in the press was naïve to say the least, snorting coke, flashing her knickers (or lack of them), creeping into cabs with married men… It hadn't stopped her snagging contracts with Burberry, Mulberry and Chanel—and her attendance tonight was surely to make certain that Angela's brainchild was next.

'Tawny, how great to see you, thank you for coming…'

The model delivered a tight air-kiss, sniffed the air and moved on.

Orlando smirked. 'Why are models always baked?'

'Yeah, well, at least one of us is on top of our game.'

'Which is why you've been AWOL for the past half hour?'

Angela conceded that her pre-party dalliance with Noah hadn't exactly been the height of professionalism. She couldn't help it. Snatched moments, hidden trysts, each second savoured to carry them to the next encounter, always an eternity away. Both public figures, a glimpse would be splashed across the web in a nanosecond—already rumours simmered dangerously. Noah had implored her, but still she said no.

Damn! She could not live beneath her father's jurisdiction for ever.

'Well?' Orlando pressed. 'Gonna let me in on your vanishing act?'

'It's none of your damn business.'

He raised an eyebrow. 'Want me to tell Dad?'

'Tell him what?'

'You know what.'

'I know you can fuck off.'

'You're a shitty liar, Angela.'

She wanted to hit him. 'And what makes you such a saint?'

Orlando shrugged. 'Nothing. Guess I'm better at hiding it than you.'

It had been too much to hope for her brother's support. Only Noah had believed she could do this. Only he'd had faith. Despite the way her family had treated him in the past, Noah had been adamant that victory was in her blood—and if the men could do it, why couldn't she? Ever since her great-grandfather had founded a modest Boston department store, through the decades growing it from strength to strength, winning had been the name of the game. On the crest of success her father had expanded into wider markets still: hotels, casinos, fashion labels; on to the Middle East, Tokyo and Singapore…

Today the Silvers brand was a worldwide lifestyle force. Angela was dead-set on running the ship one day. In the meantime, if her father wouldn't stake her a role, she would simply go up against him. She had to prove herself one way or another.

Gianluca joined them. Together, the Silvers brothers reeked so strongly of a Harvard Business degree it settled like fog.

'Dad's got an announcement,' said Luca, with his irritating I-know-something-you-don't-know pout. Luca's wide, thick-lashed eyes and high brushstroke cheekbones were trademarks of the family. Women went crazy for him.

'Isn't it obvious?' Orlando took another drink. 'He's retiring—and you know what that means. Silvers is coming straight to me, baby.'

Luca arranged his jacket. 'Yeah?'

'I'm the eldest.' He swigged. 'But hey, don't worry, I won't fire you.'

Luca smirked. Then he said: 'May the best man win.'

'Or woman.'

'Forget it,' Luca dismissed, waving a hand about, 'haven't you already got this…sideline?'

'Which is a damn sight more than you've got,' Angela shot back.

A tinkling glass put paid to the dispute. Angela seized the platform, welcomed the sea of guests and press and recounted her journey, from a teenage summer in Paris that had ignited her passion for couture, to the first flame of her Fit for NYC idea; from the funding she'd secured—independently from her father—to the glory of this opening night. She imagined Noah next to her, encouraging her and urging her on.

When the applause died down, echoes of light still dancing from the raft of cameras, she invited her father, as arranged, to offer his congratulations.

As Donald Silvers approached, she fixed her determined gaze on his.

In spite of it all, Angela knew that he believed in her. She had never been the daughter he'd anticipated—she'd been more.

He shook her hand, equal to equal.

Now was her chance to prove it.

2

Los Angeles

Kevin Chase was watching his manager's mouth. He noticed for the first time that it was a small mouth, the teeth crowded, and the jowly cheeks bolstering it brought to mind a yapping dog wedged between two cushions. The mouth was moving, but no sound was coming out. In the years since becoming America's biggest solo artist—scratch that, the world's—and the definitive pin-up for a squillion screeching tweenies (when was his fan base going to *grow*?), Kevin had honed the art of appearing to concentrate while actually not listening to a single word.

'Kevin, are you paying attention? C'mon, buddy, this is serious.'

'Yeh.'

'Well, what have you got to say for yourself?'

Kevin slumped further into the squishy leather couch in Sketch Falkner's downtown office and grudgingly lifted his shoulders.

'Dunno,' he grumbled. 'One of those things, I guess.'

Sketch contained his exasperation and came to the front of the desk. He had been in this game thirty years. He had seen it all. As the industry's top talent spotter and head of the board here at Cut N Dry Records, he knew how to handle his clients.

'What in hell were you thinking?' he encouraged.

Kevin folded his arms, stared ahead and refused to reply. His gold FNYC cap was wedged on sideways. His slouch jeans were massive, gangsta style despite his suburban upbringing, and strapped partway down his ass. He wore a white vest adorned by hefty chains, and on his feet were his cherished purple SUPRAs, one of which was jiggling up and down as if he needed the bathroom. Several tattoos were splashed self-consciously across his upper arms, the biggest depicting his ex-girlfriend, pop princess Sandi—and, as if having Sandi's image branded onto his skin for all eternity wasn't bad enough, the artist had given her some weird-ass dangly skirt that made it look like Kevin had a thing for chicks with dicks. His frame was slight despite rigorous gym sessions, and the wisps around his chin refused to mature beyond fuzz. The overall impression was one of a junior who had raided his big brother's closet, or else a snowman that had melted in the sun, leaving only a jumble of clothes behind.

Eventually he said: 'I want another Coke.'

'*Please*,' put in his mother Joan, seated at his shoulder like a parrot.

'Please,' Kevin grunted.

The truth was that a kid in Kevin's position didn't *need* to pay attention. Not really. Kevin Chase had three platinum albums to his name. He was the most talked about performer of his generation. He had scooped a raft of awards: Best Artist, Best Male, Best Single, Best Pop Act, Best Dance Act, Best Video, even Best Hair, which was only right because he took fucking good care of his hair, damn it. He was the ultimate twenty-first-century poster boy. He had close to sixty million followers on Twitter. His adoring fans, referred to as the Little Chasers, treated him like the Second Coming of Jesus. He blew up the media. He played sell-out gigs across the globe. He had his own fashion line, his own fragrance and produced his own movies. He had waxworks of his image in five major cities. He owned a chopper and a mega-yacht and so many properties that half the time he didn't even know what countries they were in. He was a phenomenon, a philosopher (who could forget the profound opener to 'Touch My Kiss'? *Girl, this life can get so serious*) and a poet (*You make me so delirious; I'm on this like mysterious*). He owned a dachshund named Trey.

At nineteen, Kevin Chase was the biggest superstar on the planet. He couldn't go for a dump without Security producing the toilet roll.

The Coke was brought over. '*Thank you...*' prompted Joan.

'Whatever.'

Sketch nodded towards the paused plasma screen mounted above his desk. On it, Kevin's image was frozen onstage at the Chicago United Center, mic to his lips, hips strutting, his metallic suit and dark shades part of the Raunchy Robot theme. In the front ranks, a sea of eager Little Chasers grasped for their hero.

'Joanie,' tried Sketch, who knew that bringing in Kevin's mom usually achieved the desired result, 'what do you think?'

'Well, I—'

'I can answer for myself, can't I?' Kevin scowled. 'It's a fucking hand gesture, what's the big fucking deal anyhow?'

'Kevin!' admonished Joan. 'Language!'

'You have to understand that this isn't what the fans expect.' Sketch laid it out. 'Kevin Chase is *boyfriend* material, OK? He's about puppy dogs and first dates. He's about Valentine's cards. He's about cookies. He's about…abstinence.'

Kevin gulped. Recently, he had run an interview with a British tabloid, in which he had happily blasted sex before marriage. Ha! That was some laugh. At this rate he wouldn't be getting sex until…well that was the fucking funny bit because he couldn't even think of when. Christ! It wasn't as if he was short of offers. He was Kevin Chase, for God's sake; by rights he should be nailing any girl he wanted.

Except he couldn't… *Physically.*

That was why Sandi had called it off. The label had tried to salvage it, but Sandi had a fire in her knickers and Kevin's hose was officially out of order.

Kevin started picking the skin around his thumb. Loneliness swept over him in a silent tsunami. His management had control over every other aspect of his life, so he sure wasn't about to hit Sketch with a confessional on his sexual problems.

Sexual problems! Him! It was enough to make him throw up.

'What Kevin Chase *isn't* about is this.' Sketch gestured once more at the still. 'Pelvic thrusting. Cursing. Rubbing his crotch like a… I don't know, like a dog with his balls in a knot. Telling girls he wants to,' Sketch consulted his iPad and inhaled sharply, '*grind you up against the wall where your mom and dad can't see.*'

'That was part of the song.'

'It wasn't.'

'It should've been. It's not my fault I've got to sing like a pussy. I told them I wanted the lyrics to reflect my personality.'

Sketch put down his pad. He assumed his *I'm listening*

face, tempered by a twinge of fatherly concern. When all was said and done, he was the closest thing Kevin had to a father—hell, maybe that was where it had gone so wrong.

Abandonment issues: oldest fuck-up in the book.

Of course the record company was doing little to alleviate it.

Forget it. It's for the kid's own good.

Sketch contained a gruesome shiver. *You just keep telling yourself that.*

He straightened. 'What *would* reflect your personality, Kevin? Tell me.'

But Kevin didn't know, or else he couldn't articulate it. He didn't even know if he *had* a personality, outside of what everyone else told him it was. Lately he had started gazing in the mirror and not recognising the person looking back, half expecting the other Kevin to do something he hadn't asked it to, like stick its tongue out, or burst out laughing at the punchline his life had become. He might laugh too, if he could remember the joke. Instead, every day was a circus of grabbing bankrollers, snatching and pawing at his fame like rabid dogs. He had no real friends.

He scratched at a mark on the knee of his jeans and tried not to cry.

'Listen to Sketch, honey,' Joan crooned, leaning forward in her chair. She wore ill-fitting Prada and too much make-up. 'He knows what he's talking about.'

'Yeah right,' mumbled Kevin. Sometimes he wanted to throttle his mom. She was happy to tag along for the ride but she didn't appreciate how much work he had to put in, what this job took out of you, how much stress he was under. She should try being Kevin Chase for a day and see how she liked it!

'Not good enough.' Sketch ran a hand through his hair. 'If

this was an isolated incident, buddy, then maybe I'd buy it, but the fact is it's not. You want me to lay it out for you? Turning up three hours late to the Seattle concert. Telling an audience of schoolkids that if they didn't like it, they could *bite me*. Flicking the bird to that pap outside your crib. Rocking up drunk to that book signing and breathing vodka fumes in a nine-year-old's face—it was a treat to see that splashed across *USay* the next morning, let me tell you. Trying to get that pregnant ape at the California Zoo Convention to drink a can of Kool beer. Forgetting what song you're meant to be singing. Messing up your routines. Speeding. Swearing. Trashing hotel rooms…and don't get me started on taking a leak in that plant pot at Il Cielo—'

'All right, all right, I get it,' Kevin supplied bitterly.

'And what's with the attitude? That dance troupe you worked with on the last video said you gave them hell. Cursing at reporters, telling press where to go, slamming out at that photographer in Berlin. I mean Jesus H., Kevin—'

'I never trashed any hotel room. I told you. The sound system exploded.'

Sketch took a breath.

'And I needed a leak! What do you want me to do, pee in my fucking pants?'

'You could visit the toilet like everyone else.'

'I'm not *everyone else*, though, am I?'

'Think about it,' Sketch said. 'You've got a reputation to uphold.'

'I'm sick of having a reputation.'

Joan put a hand on his shoulder. 'Honey…'

He shrugged her off.

'I've cancelled your commitments this afternoon,' offered Sketch. 'Go home, rest up, get looked after; watch some cartoons—'

'Cartoons?' Kevin flared. 'What am I, *five*?'

'Relax.' Sketch put his hands out. 'You've been under a lot of strain and it's starting to show. My job is to look after you, and this is what I'm prescribing.'

Along with the rest.

Sketch swallowed his conscience like a bad oyster.

'I'll call you in the morning. Sound good, bud?'

Kevin allowed himself to be ushered through the door. Joan was fussing over him, picking threads from his back. 'Ugh, Mom, piss off, will you?'

They took the elevator in silence. Kevin knew he was being an asshole. He wanted to say sorry but he didn't know how. He just couldn't help how *angry* he felt the whole time. That was the only word. He felt like a bomb about to blow off. The slightest word sent him plummeting into a rage. A throwaway comment made him fly off the handle. Right now he hated everyone and everything and he didn't, for the life of him, know why. All he knew was that he couldn't sustain it much longer.

Kevin was going to snap, and it was going to be soon. He couldn't say what would happen when he did, but one thing was certain: it was going to be bad.

3

London

Regardless of how many celebrities she interviewed, Eve Harley would always be amazed at the scale of their egos. Supermodels were the worst.

'I guess I kinda *always* knew I was beautiful,' Tawny Lascelles was saying from her position in the make-up girl's chair, angling her face as the blusher brush swept across a pair of immaculate cheekbones. Tawny had a lilting, Texan drawl, and a flush of softness to her voice that betrayed what Eve was beginning to suspect was a core of gritty ambition. She was the magazine favourite of the moment, sweet as candy but sharp enough to be interesting, with a well-publicised streak of rebellion.

'Can you remember your first shoot?' Eve asked, adjusting her position on the uncomfortable stool alongside Tawny's cushioned throne. In the portrait awarded by the bulb-lined mirror she accepted the uncrossable distance between prettiness and beauty. Eve was attractive enough, with her neatly cut shoulder-length brown hair, green almond eyes and petite, bright features, but next to Tawny's Cara Delevingne vibe anyone was going to look like a sack of potatoes.

'Oh, yes,' Tawny's blue eyes widened, 'a girl never forgets.' She pouted to permit a rose-pink liner to caress the contours of her perfect, bee-stung lips. Ravishing wasn't nearly enough for tonight's parade: she had to be flawless. 'I was so nervous. I mean, I'm actually totally uncomfortable with this whole "look at me" thing.'

I bet you are, thought Eve, tapping keynotes into her tablet.

'So, lucky for me,' Tawny went on, 'it was on this paradise beach…and d'you know what the *really* weird thing was? Like, totally surreal?'

Eve took the question as rhetorical, but when Tawny's sapphire eyes at last deigned to meet hers in their joint reflection, she shook her head.

'I'd been there before! On vacation.' The make-up girl tilted Tawny's chin, lifting it like a petal so she could add a hint of gloss. 'And as soon as I walked out on that sand,' Tawny managed to keep her mouth totally still while she spoke, 'I was, like, Whoa, this is cosmic, y'know? Like it was *meant* to happen that way. I was *meant* to do this. I was *meant* to be a model—and no one was going to stop me!'

Eve highlighted the section on her pad. She had it all on Dictaphone but, when it came to revisiting a piece, she liked to know which bits had jumped out at the time. This was one of them. Tawny's tone had slipped. An edge of bitterness had crept in, of having earned her place in the celebrity tree through more than a few strokes of luck.

'So you believe this is your calling?'

Tawny's eyes were closed against the delicate application of mascara. 'Oh, absolutely,' she said. 'I can't think of anything I'd rather do.'

'Don't you think it's an empty sort of profession?'

There was a pause. 'Excuse me?'

'Well, good as you might be at it, it's not really changing the world.'

'It depends which way you look at it.'

'Which way do you look at it?'

'I'm helping people feel better about themselves.'

'How?'

'Modelling gives regular people something to aim for.'

'Even if it's not attainable?'

Tawny's eyes opened a fraction, snake-like. 'What?'

'The impossible dream, for most women: size 6 and wearing Karl Lagerfeld.'

Tawny batted the make-up girl off. 'So I should leave them to stew in their fat, sad little lives watching re-runs of *America's Got Talent* and stuffing potato chips in their pie-holes?' Catching herself, she clarified somewhat more demurely, 'What I mean is, I'm giving them something to aspire to. Beauty… Well, it inspires.'

'Are you an inspiration?'

'Yes. In a way.'

'What way?'

'Girls want to grow up to be just like me.'

'Even if they can't?'

'Why can't they?'

Eve thought it was a joke, but Tawny appeared serious.

'Beauty is a construct,' she pointed out, 'right? It's subjective, prone to change, evolution? In twenty years' time, will girls want to look like someone else?'

Tawny's expression was blank.

'Do you see modelling as philanthropic?'

'I'm sorry,' answered Tawny, 'I don't know what that means.'

But Eve suspected she did. 'To enhance the world, to make it a better place.'

'Then, yes, I suppose I do.'

'Why?'

Tawny's eyes opened, flashing danger. The make-up girl's brush stumbled. 'Where exactly is this going?' she demanded. 'Why, why, why? How, how, how?'

'It's an interview.'

'Well, it sucks.' Tawny gestured for her assistant. 'Jean-Paul! Here!'

'You'll admit not much is known about how you arrived on the circuit,' Eve threw out. 'Maybe something from your childhood made you feel this way?'

'What, like making the world *a better place*?'

'Allegedly you've said of your family that—'

'I'll stop you there,' Jean-Paul intervened, 'I think that's time. Did you get everything you need?' But he turned away, not bothering to hang around for an answer. Tawny's hair crew were next to descend, rattling bottles of spray and cooing over their darling's fragrant mane as if it were the last head of hair on earth.

'Get me my grapes,' came a bad-tempered bark from somewhere inside the melee. 'I need sugar, JP. I'm dizzy.'

Jean-Paul scurried off to obey.

Eve Harley was frozen out. The interview was over.

The evening was a showcase of upcoming designers, each teamed with an established name in a kind of *haute*-glitz mentorship programme. Opposite Eve in the ranks sat a prim arrangement of fashionistas, editors, rock musicians and royalty, anyone whose image was regularly splashed across the London society pages—a colourful tableau of elaborate hairstyles, sharp suits and sleekly crossed legs, all with that slightly self-conscious way of sitting, as if these VIPs' entire lives had become a public display and a lurking photographer could be about to jump out at any moment.

A new collection spilled onto the runway. Tawny Lascelles strutted down the walk, glossily gorgeous and all too aware of that fact, in a Japanese-flavoured drape dress courtesy of a breakthrough artist. But for someone who was all too happy to disclose the finer points of her colonic irrigation regime, or how many egg whites she consumed for breakfast, Tawny was ferociously private about her past.

Eve would get the story, no matter what it took. She always did. She would hunt down the facts and she would hunt them her way. She didn't do failure and she didn't do backing out. Her column in the UK's biggest tabloid relied on it.

The show over, she made a swift exit. January in London was bracing and chill, shining red buses sliding past, their windows clouded with condensation. The River Thames glittered beneath a chain of bridges, snaking down to the golden crust of Westminster, whose peaks were obscured by shifting mist.

Eve checked her phone. It was the usual address, the one he used whenever he visited town. Hailing a taxi, she climbed in. The city rushed past, a blur of lights and sounds, and she spritzed perfume onto her wrists and between her legs.

She couldn't suppress the wave of butterflies that came with the inevitability of their meeting. It wasn't as if there were feelings involved—just sex, always sex—and the cold, efficient transaction of it somehow made it more of a thrill.

The cab dropped her at Marble Arch and she walked the rest of the way. Down a moon-frosted lane, away from the crowds, she arrived at his townhouse.

Tapping in the security code, the gates parted, a fairytale twist of black iron.

Orlando Silvers was already on the porch. The door was open, spilling yellow light.

They didn't say a word. He drew her into the warm and pushed her against the kitchen counter. She went to speak and he crushed her with a kiss, hooking her knee and flipping her round, strong thumbs tearing down her knickers. She felt them rip and he spread her wide and in a second he was inside, hot and deep and thick, her face pressed against the cool steel surface as he pounded, his hand snaking beneath her blouse and freeing her tits.

Eve let him drive against her, her skirt up over her back, one shoe kicked off, her hair pulled and grabbed and her lipstick smudged, until the calm, composed journalist of thirty minutes ago was all but obliterated. Only when Orlando was ready to come did she ease off and draw him to the floor. He was flat on his back, his dick straining beneath the crisp white fabric of his shirt. Slowly she mounted him, unbuttoning her top with tantalising leisure, and he groaned and reached for her as she backed away, peeling off her bra and watching his eyes feast. Making him wait, she finally sank onto him, feeling him fill her up, easing him in and out, right to his tip and down to his base, wetter and wetter each time as his cock became stiffer.

She rode him hard. Only through sex could Eve feel this way—like all the anger and hurt was set free, existing in some separate universe, and all she had here, now, was the intensity and blaze of their combat.

She collapsed against him, their explosions colliding.

Afterwards, Orlando lit a cigarette. They spilled onto the couch, naked and spent. Eve leaned on his chest, running her fingers across his torso, the skin olive-brown and scattered with dark hair. Orlando was the opposite of what she normally went for, serious-faced journos who smoked roll-ups and read satire. He was a cocky Wall Street boy, a glossy Starbucks American—not to mention one of the richest men on the planet. She felt him inhale, heard the crackle of cigarette paper.

'Is it true your father's retiring?' she asked.

Orlando laughed. 'That was a record.'

'What?'

'Fifteen seconds before you went for the story.'

Playfully, she smacked him. He grabbed her, kissed her again.

He was right, though. Eve had worked in this business ten years, yet she never tired of the buzz; what it was to chase a scandal. Today, millions across the globe read her work. Her biting appraisals were infamous. She took no prisoners, she refused to sugarcoat and her allegiance couldn't be bought—she wrote what she thought and she was faithful to her instinct, whether her subject liked it or not. Over the years she had gained a fearsome reputation. Eve wasn't out to hurt these celebrities, or to sabotage them, but she believed that if you were going to put yourself up for scrutiny, to use the media to your own ends, then you had to be prepared for it to use you back. Stars who crowed on about privacy didn't seem to mind so much when they were summoning paparazzi to the opening of their new perfume, or when they had a hot date on their arm or a radical new look to unveil.

Teen superstar Kevin Chase was a prime example. His success was so closely entwined with his courtship of the press that it was impossible to separate the two, yet when Eve had challenged him on the issue of sex (Kevin's stance had, until recently, been emphatically chaste), he had fumbled his way through a confused, tetchy, half-baked response before barking at her to fuck off because it was none of her business.

None of her business… It was a red rag to a bull. Eve intended to make it her business, whatever it was, and she would stop at nothing until she got there.

'So?' she tried again.

Orlando ground out his smoke.

'Don't want to talk about it,' he said. 'It's complicated.'

'Come on,' she urged, 'give me something.'

'I'm forever giving you something.'

'And I'm not?' She raised herself up on one elbow. 'What about that exclusive I kept back on the Mitzlar Brothers—?'

'You were planning to hold fire anyway.'

'I wasn't. My editor would kill me if she knew—sex dens, strippers, a world-class banking family…'

'We needed their sponsorship. This story would have ruined them.'

'Exactly.' Eve trailed her fingers down his stomach, felt him harden once more. 'So what do I get in return? I did it because you asked me…'

'You don't do anything you're asked.'

'That depends who's asking.'

He threw her off the scent. 'Tawny Lascelles just signed for my sister's label.'

Eve leaned over, reached into her bag and pulled out her pad. 'And?'

'And what?'

'D'you know Tawny?'

'She was at the launch a couple of weeks back.'

'Yeah, I figured that part out. Who was she with?'

'No one, I don't think.'

'Does Angela run checks on models before she employs them?'

'Why?' he scoffed.

'Tawny's press people are like Rottweilers, she's giving nothing away—but I know, I just *know* there's something there, if I could just…'

Orlando touched the end of her nose. 'You never let up, do you?'

'I came from the gala,' she explained. 'Tawny and I chatted.'

'Why didn't you ask her?'

'Don't be facetious.'

'Don't use long words.'

She stuck up her finger. 'That short enough for you?'

'Cute.'

Eve got up. She fixed herself a drink, raised the carafe in question. He nodded.

'Come on,' she said, leaning back against the mahogany dresser, 'I already had it in the bag about Tawny and Fit for NYC. What else?'

Orlando narrowed his eyes. 'What if I just wanted to see you?'

'Crap. I know you see other women.'

'Do you see other men?'

'What's it to you?' But she didn't see other men. She didn't have time.

And I don't want to.

He pulled her back to the couch.

'For chasing other people's secrets, Harley,' he murmured, 'you've sure got some mysteries of your own.'

Orlando held her down, his tongue tracing its practised route down her neck and across her breasts. She didn't answer, but then he didn't require it.

Suffice to say, there was a good reason why Eve did this job, and she wasn't about to compromise for anyone. Not even for him.

4

Tawny Lascelles took the red-eye back to LA. She was tired and crabby, pissed off at that bitch reporter for sticking her fat beak in where it wasn't wanted and then later at some piglet-faced model she had never worked with telling her she'd gone too fast down the catwalk. The nerve! Tawny wanted to slap her. The last thing she felt like doing now was getting stuck on an airplane for hours, but such was her schedule these days that she seemed to spend half her life zooming back and forth over the Atlantic.

Everything in the supermodel's first-class cabin was as requested, which helped soften the blow. Tawny's rider went everywhere with her—road, sea or air, she was never without her essentials: chamomile and echinacea tea, a cashmere blanket (silver, never grey), three bouquets of lightly scented peonies, a bottle of Coco Mademoiselle, her music station (Gaga for when she needed to hype up, Taylor for when she needed to wind down), and the only food she ate with any frequency, or indeed with any relish, a jumbo-sized bag of Haribo Sours.

Two thousand miles across the Atlantic, she stuck her arm above the parapet.

Immediately a glass of water was brought—carbonated but with just the right amount of fizz: Tawny hated to get burpy. She sipped carefully to avoid bloating, then without saying thank you settled back in her recliner booth and flipped open a magazine. A stinging flick brought the page open on a column by Eve Harley.

Prying tramp!

It was all Tawny could do not to rip the paper to shreds. She scowled at the reporter's name and at what unsuspecting prey had been targeted this time.

Kevin Chase.

The article accompanied a picture on stage during his latest World Tour.

> My opinion? Kevin Chase is an out-of-control teenage brat. So he's young, so people make mistakes, so we should cut him some slack—but the fact is there are countless young kids out there with nothing, no money, no job, no support, no future, and still we're supposed to feel sorry for this guy? A nineteen year old who set fire to a stack of hundred-dollar bills last week as a PR stunt? Give me a break…

It was a shame about Kevin, Tawny thought, assessing the superstar's dwarfed yet rippling torso—it was like all the ingredients were there, like he had the *potential* to be hot, only everything about him was so…well, *small*. It was as if he had gone through a photocopier and been reduced by forty per cent.

Give him a few years, she decided. The handsome part wasn't nearly as important anyway, since there was only room for one truly beautiful person in any relationship and Tawny would *always* win that crown. She had no interest in competing, even if there was competition to be had (which there wasn't).

Tawny was the worshipped, never the worshipper. And oh! Imagine how Kevin would worship her. She was tempted to bag him, just for the fun. Tawny loved it when a man fell under her spell—there were at least six out there right now who would take a bullet for her if she flashed them her tits and offered a BJ. Ha!

She folded the mag, trying not to think about the lashing no doubt hurtling her way courtesy of that British cow. It wasn't Tawny's fault women got jealous. She was everything they wanted to be and they simply couldn't handle it.

Eve Harley would never get the truth, anyhow. Tawny had buried her history so deep that she wasn't even sure *she* knew where to find it. No way was she going back there, not ever, and she would happily top herself before anyone else did.

Her manager called.

'Everything all right, my diamond girl?' he crooned.

'Fine.'

'I'm in the mood to spoil my favourite client. Breakfast at Clementine's?'

'I'd sooner die. I've got a date with a spa, a hot masseur and my bed.' Tawny paused, allowing herself a smirk. 'Maybe his.'

'Lunch, then.'

Tawny cringed. Food after sex always seemed a grim proposition. The idea of filling herself up on cock and then cramming in Eggs Benedict on top was disgusting.

'I'll call you later,' she said.

'Oh, and babe? Remember your slot on *The Bianca Show* tomorrow night.'

'Ugh, hell, I forgot about that.'

She hung up.

There was never any reprieve, but in her heart Tawny loved the attention. Wasn't this what she had prayed for, ever since she was a girl? To be admired, to be revered—above all, to be adored! She had been granted her wish.

Tawny smiled. Tucked into her Silvers tote was the other item she could never leave home without: the inscribed hair straighteners gifted to her by a legendary Italian designer at the beginning of her career, when she had been an upcoming starlet and named as his muse. The lemon-yellow tongs were her lucky charms: she insisted on using them for every shoot and every show, and they were emblazoned with the immortal line: 'TO THE FAIREST OF THEM ALL, WITH LOVE & ADMIRATION'.

Tawny Lascelles really was the fairest of them all. She always would be.

She would rather die than have that crown taken.

Satisfied in that knowledge, she fell fast into a deep and dreamless sleep.

5

Boston

Angela Silvers hated to fly. She had always possessed an irrational fear of airplanes. She hated the roaring take-off, the jumps of turbulence and the way that every sound and shudder convinced her they were about to fall out of the sky.

She closed the blind, shutting out the sprawling blue and floozy clouds.

'Excuse me?' She smiled at a passing attendant.

'Yes, Ms Silvers?'

'Would I be able to get a drink, please? A martini?'

'Coming right up.'

Noah would tease her. Angela had a fleet of jets at her beck and call—why not make the trip in luxury? But there was something ugly about jumping on a plane for one as easily as if you were hailing a cab. Besides, her father's aircraft were way too light for her liking: at least on a 737 it felt as if there were *something* between her and the ground. Her drink arrived and she threw it back in one.

She hoped the liquor might knock her out, but while it took the edge off it wasn't enough to relax her completely. The knack was to focus on something else, anything to detract from the fact they were 35,000 feet up in the air in a rattling tin can. Normally the promise of landing was enough to pull her through—thoughts of arriving at her hotel, taking a long soak in the tub, ordering room service, slipping into bed and Skyping Noah—but today, the flight was just the beginning.

Angela was heading to company HQ, the house in Boston where she had grown up. She intended to thrash it out with her father once and for all.

'*I'm taking this moment to announce my retirement,*' Donald had proclaimed at the FNYC launch. '*As of tonight I plan to step back from the front line and apportion duty between my two gifted sons, Orlando and Gianluca...*'

Two weeks after the event Angela still couldn't believe it.

Never mind the fact that her father had stolen her thunder—this had been her night, her project, her *triumph*, and instead of crediting her as he should have done he had snatched the attention right back onto the boys—his words had shaken her to her core. The injustice was breathtaking.

My two gifted sons? It had to be a joke. But as Orlando and Luca had paced proudly up to claim the prize, the grim reality had become clear.

All the while Angela had worn a rigid smile of congratulations, bitten her way through countless toasts and declarations of, 'Yes, they will be wonderful, won't they?' and crushed wave after wave of hot, irrepressible anger.

In the days that followed, Angela had turned Donald's decision over in her mind. Forget about it being unfair, it was simply illogical to give the reins to her brothers. She had stepped up time and time again to work alongside her father, drawing up proposals, putting forward solutions, re-organising budgets, but none of it came to any use: she was, and always would be, at a disadvantage because of her sex.

She would stand for it no longer—and her father wouldn't know what hit him.

The pilot's voice came on the PA system. They had begun their descent.

She braced herself for impact.

Logan International was packed. Angela was escorted through Arrivals, her head bowed against the burst of attention her appearance sparked, and was relieved when they emerged into fresh air. Paparazzi surged as she approached the BMW. In black Ray-Bans, skinny jeans and a coral blazer, her spike heels punching the tarmac, it was clear this was no pleasure trip. Angela Silvers had landed on business.

Eternally the paps fished for a bout of reckless behaviour that would give them the money shot and cement her role as spoiled heiress—a bad attitude, a crabby pooch or, best of all, a wardrobe malfunction, anything to prove she had succumbed to type. But with Angela it never came. She understood her position and carried it with grace, stopping to sign autographs for fans, which she delivered with a flourish and a smile. If the press weren't so desperate to capture the first fall—for surely at some point it would come, it did for the best of them—they would have given up long ago.

As her car joined the Mass Pike, she tried calling Noah. He was on location, shooting a romantic comedy whose script they had giggled over in bed.

'Hey,' he'd kissed her tenderly, 'so when are you gonna be my leading lady?'

She wished it were that simple. Noah was Hollywood royalty, the industry's most sought-after bachelor. Every project he took he was ambushed by female co-stars, and while it wasn't Angela's style to be jealous it couldn't help but sting.

'I only want you,' he told her every time, and while she wanted to trust him, she was no idiot. Noah had been a player from the moment they'd met.

She was scared of getting hurt again. Giving herself to him totally, risking it all. At the same time, he wouldn't wait for ever.

After her father's revelation, she wondered why she bothered concealing it from him at all. Donald had no intention of empowering his daughter with muscle in the business, now or ever. What difference did it make who she dated?

But the itch remained: *Tell him this and it's over for good.*

Donald hated Noah. He hated everything Noah stood for. He hated Noah's past. He hated Noah's family, where he had come from and where he had wound up. Countless times Angela had promised her father that the friendship was at an end.

To confess the betrayal would be kamikaze.

Noah's cell went to his machine. She listened, just to hear him; her heart lifted at his voice but she decided against leaving a message. In any case, he'd advised her against the Boston trip—he himself never returned to their childhood ground, the place owed him nothing and the memories were raw—and would be frustrated that she'd come. Donald needed time, he had promised, to realise the mistake he'd made. Angela was amazed at Noah's reluctance to take sides, at his fairness. After all Donald had thrown against him, still he didn't resort to cheap shots.

'I love you, and you love your father,' he said. 'That's all there is to it.'

She ended the call as they pulled onto Bourton Avenue. Hers was a majestic neighbourhood, lined with giant Victorian brownstones, grand porticos and gated driveways. Sunshine glinted on the Charles River. There was the Amity Street Church where Angela had spent reluctant Sunday mornings as a child, the Preston Historical Institute where many a school trip had wound up, and the Clemency College of Dance, where she had made out once on the steps with Henry Lambert. So much was unchanged, yet Angela didn't feel the same. Boston was her heritage, but now its magnificence seemed outlandish and silly. Coming in past the flagship Silvers Hotel, its peaks like turrets on a castle and its doormen tipping their caps, and the inaugural store her great-grandfather had founded, here, at least, they were royalty.

Commonwealth House was the most splendid on the street. The car eased through and Angela stepped out, thanking her chauffeur and breathing the old air.

She was home.

'Hello?'

Inside, the hall was vast. Her enquiry echoed, bouncing off the marble chequered floor. A staircase that wouldn't have been out of place in the world's most celebrated museum divided beneath a portrait of her great-grandfather, stern in his suit, his black walking cane in one hand. Cabinets housed relics from their schooldays—sporting trophies, certificates and photographs. In one portrait, a teenage Orlando and Luca were suited for their aunt's wedding. Angela stood between them, scowling because Orlando had told her she couldn't come camping at the weekend. Another was a still from Angela's tenth birthday party—she'd been a pain in the ass in those days. All the guests were in pink frilly frocks apart from the birthday girl, who wore a *Back to the Future* T-shirt and denim shorts, and was sticking her tongue out.

'In here!' Her mother's voice drifted through from the kitchen.

Angela emerged into a bright, richly scented space. The kitchen faced out onto rolling lawn, at the foot of which shone a serene lake, a rowing boat tethered in the reeds. It smelled of warm bread and rosemary and the spice of a cooking oven. Isabella was prepping salads, joined at the counter by Angela's *nonna*, and on the veranda a bunch of her extended family were drinking wine and mingling.

Angela kissed the women. 'You know I'm not staying for dinner?'

'Of course you are,' said Isabella.

'My return flight's booked—it leaves at nine.'

'And your father isn't home until this evening, so you'll have to cancel.' Isabella slapped her hand away from the just-baked ciabatta. 'Eh, *smettila*, Angela!'

'Is Orlando here? Luca?'

'No.'

'Good.'

Isabella clicked her tongue. 'I wish you three would not fight all the time.'

'I wish for a lot of things, Mom.'

'Life is too short to argue. Respect your father's decision.'

'I do respect him. If only he'd extend me the same courtesy.'

'He loves you very much.'

'That isn't the same thing.'

Angela bit her tongue. Isabella didn't understand her wish to take the spotlight. As far back as she could remember, whatever her fathers and brothers were doing had been infinitely more exhilarating—the closed doors, the hushed voices, the secret conversations, the covert business trips. Angela didn't care about baking and flower-arranging and the correct way to iron a suit shirt, and while she adored her mother, as women they couldn't be less alike.

Home wasn't enough.

Angela wanted more.

She preferred the south steps to taking the main stairs. '*Why?*' her girlfriends used to pout, as they flounced prettily down the banisters like Cinderellas at the ball. '*It makes me feel like a princess!*' Which, Angela saw now, was precisely why.

Her old room was on the second floor. The bed, immaculately made with peach sheets and silky fat pillows, was against the window. A stack of plump, fresh towels was arranged at its foot. Angela pressed one to her face and inhaled.

She settled on the linen, listening to the delicate *tick-tick* of a carriage clock and the occasional flutter of birdsong. In her bedside drawer were a collection of journals (ANGELA'S DIARY: KEEP OUT!), trinkets, postcards and jewellery.

Inside one of the diaries was a photograph. Her fingers traced its familiar edges. Slowly, she drew it out. *Noah.*

Her favourite picture of him, on that first summer they spent together.

Scruffy blond hair, bronzed skin, mischievous blue eyes…

He'd been the neighbourhood bad boy: bad family, bad schooling, bad all over. They had come from different ends of the earth.

But Angela hadn't cared. Not even then.

Everyone else had treated her like a queen—but not Noah. Noah had treated her like a friend. They had both been outsiders, in their way. He had been ostracised by the rich for failing to meet their standards, while Angela, wealthy beyond reason, harboured her own kind of leprosy: ordinary people were too afraid to touch.

She leaned on the windowsill, her chin resting in the heel of her hand, and looked out at leafy Bourton Avenue. She remembered waiting here on sultry nights, waiting for Noah to arrive on the steps so that they could exchange dreams with each other long into the dark. Outlawed by her father, they had held the secret of their friendship, and Angela had longed to be able to reach down and take his hand. Noah had written her poems, thrown the words up to the open window like whispered confetti.

She touched the silver band she wore on her first finger.

She knew what she had to do. She had to set the past to rest. *Noah, I'm yours.* She would tell her father tonight.

Donald Silvers' library was rich with leather and the scent of wood. Behind him, through the arched portico, Italianate lawns were aglow in the glare of the outdoor lamps, the fountains on, spraying the grass with diamond dewdrops. Their empire stretched as far as the eye could see: her father's, Orlando's, Luca's...but not hers.

'Skip the bullshit.' Angela cut to the chase. 'Why not me?'

'The boys are ready.' Donald eased back in his chair and steepled his fingers. 'It's time they stepped up to the plate.'

'It's time you credited me. I know why you did it. It's because I'm a girl.'

'It's because you're the youngest.'

'Orlando, fine—but Luca? You saw what a mess he made of the hotels—'

'Luca requires discipline. Management will give him that.'

'So Luca fucks up and you reward him, is that how it works?'

'I'm not discussing strategy with you, Angela.'

'Maybe I should require discipline too; then I'd get a break. Or else it would give you an excuse to get rid of me altogether—'

'Calm down.'

Nothing fucked her off more than being told to calm down. She met the wall of her father's inscrutable glare and every frustration she'd ever had against him boiled over. 'I'm through,' she lashed. 'I've done *everything* to earn my place.

I've achieved twenty times what they have and if you're too blind to see it, if you still make this decision, it isn't my issue. I'm done.'

'Good.'

'That's it? *Good?* After letting me lose sight of what's important—my friendships, my relationships? Because there's something you should know—'

'Yes,' Donald cut in, 'you are through, Angela. And you are done.'

She fought to get her words in a line. 'I don't follow.'

'You are ready. I've known it for a while.'

'Then why—?'

'What I want you to do for me is vital. It's more important than anything Orlando or Luca could offer.' He spoke slowly, each word measured. 'They're not capable of this, Angela. Only you are. You and I have serious business to share.'

She waited, sceptical and excited. Her father watched her, curiously, gently, and, in his eyes, she saw something that was new to her: a need, nascent and afraid.

'I want you to listen very carefully,' said Donald Silvers, 'for if you choose to accept, our empire is yours. Everything. You take over. But be ready, Angela: because what I am about to propose will change your life for ever.'

6

In a hotel suite across town, Kevin Chase woke suddenly, his skin dripping with sweat and his heart hammering wildly. The room was pitch black. He had no idea where he was. His breath rasped dry and painful, as if he had swallowed razor blades. Groping in the dark, he fumbled towards a switch. When the room flooded with light, it was painfully bright. Images from the nightmare were still scorched on his mind: the red flames engulfing the jet, and the descent…the horrifying, inevitable descent towards death.

Briskly he patted around to make sure he hadn't wet the sheets. Mortifyingly, it had happened in the past. Joan had even gone through a phase of laying diapers on top of the mattress, until one day Kevin had lost it, yelling at her so loud and for so long that she had whined about tinnitus for a week—and Joan knew how to whine.

Apart from a patch of hot perspiration, it was dry.

Trembling, he closed his eyes. It seemed important to pick out the details.

The nightmare had been *real*—real enough to touch, as if he had been there, as if it had happened! They said you couldn't dream your own death; you woke before it ended that way—and Kevin was certain, *certain*, he had been about to die. Dark sky all around, thick black dark, and the ground rearing up to meet them—or rather the sand, for it had been a beach, yes, a beach, the contrast stark even in moonlight between the thick water and the alabaster shore. Kevin grasped at the people he had been with, for he had not been alone, but their outlines were dissolving, leaving only ghosts. All that was left were the screams of panic ringing between his ears.

Fear swamped him.

He was never setting foot on an airplane ever again.

But even as Kevin thought it, he knew it was an absurd notion. International commitments meant he got thrown about the globe like a coin in a pinball machine.

What choice did he have? What choice did he have about anything?

The phone rang. It was Sketch.

'Ride's outside, buddy.' His manager's voice was drizzled thinly over a nub of hysteria. 'You're behind time. Again.' He cleared his throat. 'Everything OK?'

Shit. Kevin checked the time. Double shit. He had a show at the TD Garden in an hour. These days his power naps were turning into induced fucking comas.

'Be right down,' he snapped, hanging up.

A freezing cold shower slapped him to his senses. Afterwards, in the foggy mirror, Kevin grimaced at his reflection.

Come *on*. Why did he look so goddamn *young*?

Miserably he plucked at a single chest hair straining from his diaphragm. It was like a blade of grass in the middle of a barren desert. What the *fuck*? Where was his chest rug? Couldn't he sprout just a few more?

He was nineteen, for crissakes, and yet he had the torso of a ten year old.

The grimace deepened. That wasn't even the worst part.

Glancing down, Kevin loosened the towel around his

waist. He assessed the feathery covering of pubic hair scarcely concealing his miniature prick, and howled.

It was a worm dangling between two berries. *Shrivelled* berries. The whole thing was shrivelled. Why wouldn't it fucking well *grow*?

Was he balding? But how could he be balding if he'd never had hair there in the first place? Kevin howled some more, and the phone resumed its grisly summons.

Despite turning up ninety minutes late to the arena and enduring a cacophony of boos, the gig went down OK. Kevin knew how to charm his Little Chasers. Normally he refused to venture into the crowd—he didn't want their sticky fingers pawing all over his designer outfits—but to appease the irate parents, and on Sketch's counsel, tonight he made an exception. At one point, during a rendition of 'Fast Girl', he thought he was about to get torn limb from limb, his white suit strained into a crucifix by a pie-faced chick pulling him one way and a blubbing pre-teen the other.

The noise was thunderous—'*Kevin! Kevin! Kevin!*'—and the venue alight with the glitter of camera phones. When he crooned his mega hit 'Adore You', the sparkle swayed back and forth, arms in the air, kids at the front crying into their Kevin Chase T-shirts and gripping, white-knuckled, crudely assembled banners that bore confessions of their undying affection: KEVIN CHASE PLEASE BE MINE; SARA & KEVIN 4 EVER; I LOVE YOU KEVIN; I'M YOUR NO. 1 LITTLE CHASER…

After a hundred-minute set and two encores, he was beat.

Backstage, Sketch congratulated him with the unwelcome announcement that they were expected at a children's charity gala downtown—there was a galaxy of names attending and it was a wise gig at which to be seen. Kevin wanted badly to creep into bed and had to suppress the familiar flare of upset at this fresh injustice.

He wished he had someone he could call, a buddy, a friend, anyone who'd listen and tell him it was OK, just to keep at it, all this was bullshit anyway and it didn't really matter. He wished someone out there thought that *he* mattered—not his records or his hairstyle or the new mansion he was bought to live in like a fucking Ken Doll—just him, the real Kevin, the regular kid. But Kevin saw now that he would never be a regular kid, and he'd never have regular friends. What even *was* a regular friend? He'd watched movies about them, read about them as if they were exotic, elusive creatures prowling a distant landscape, but he'd never had one of his own. Kevin had the starring role in the movie of his life, and everyone was an actor.

In the beginning, it had been fun. Signing the contract in Sketch's old office on Santa Monica, then in the weeks that followed, a storm of crazy parties, premieres and photo shoots—but nobody had told him then what was being sacrificed. No one had said, OK, Kevin, it's this or it's this: which life do you want?

He didn't want this one.

'They're loving you on Twitter,' reassured Sketch as Kevin changed out of his clothes. Sketch omitted to mention the burst of hostility that had accompanied the star's fifth late arrival this season, trending worldwide as #KevinsLosingIt. Not ideal.

Outside, bodyguard Rusty was waiting with a yapping, wet-nosed Trey, cradling him because Kevin didn't like Trey to have to sit on the ground. The dachshund was clad in a blazer, baseball cap and sneakers to match his owner's—they'd had a whole wardrobe tailored bespoke. Snatching the pooch, Kevin was swallowed up by the car's interior. He felt like a vampire, if not confined to the night then confined to the *inside*, skulking around behind closed blinds, hiding beyond a tinted window or crawling about in the endless dark. He held Trey's fur to his mouth and quietly kissed his neck. *You're the only one who understands.*

Kevin demanded to drive the Audi R8 and Sketch hadn't the strength to refuse—after all, the kid had his licence, even if he did kangaroo-hop the vehicle into gear, the exhaust exploding behind them.

'You take your vitamins today?' asked Sketch as they whizzed through the city. He caught Rusty's eye in the rear-view mirror.

'For fuck's sake, course I did,' Kevin lashed. 'Don't you trust me?'

They approached a red light and the brakes shrieked.

'Sure I do, kiddo.'

'I want a lion,' said Kevin, out of nowhere.

'What?'

'Like that one we saw at the zoo. Get me one.'

Sketch chuckled. 'It ain't that easy, pal…'

'I'm Kevin Chase, course it's that fucking easy.'

'Why a lion?'

'Why not? They're cool, aren't they?'

'They're dangerous.'

'Yeah, but they're cool.'

'You won't be able to go anywhere near it.'

Kevin swigged from a can of energy drink. 'Sure I will, if it's tame.'

Sketch bit his tongue. What on earth was his client *talking* about?

'Rusty,' Kevin nodded into the back, 'what do you think?'

'Whatever you want, boss.'

The Audi took a corner at speed. 'It's king of the jungle,

y'know?' said Kevin. 'Manly. Like, the ultimate manly animal. And hairy. Really hairy.'

'You want a hairy animal I'll get you a guinea pig.'

'Now you're taking the fucking piss.'

'I'm trying to be practical.'

'Well, don't. There's no point doing what I do unless I get what I want, got it? You're supposed to be my manager—so manage stuff, dickwad.'

Sketch gritted his teeth. There was no point arguing. It was Joan's fault. Anything Kevin wanted, Kevin got. Anything Kevin demanded was produced. Any word Kevin spoke was law. By the time Sketch had discovered him, at the tender age of twelve, Kevin had already been nurturing an impressive Napoleon Complex.

You haven't helped. You've made him into the monster he is.

It was a relief when Kevin brought the car to a screeching halt outside the Guild Theatre. The entrance was a quarry of press. Stars drifted down the carpet, stopping to chat to camera, smiling and posing as they went. Hollywood king Noah Lawson, a coup for the event, was signing merch amid an adoring mass of women.

A band of Little Chasers had been tipped off about Kevin's arrival and, as the teen heartthrob emerged, their squeals reached blistering crescendo.

'*Kevin! OhmygodKevin! Kevin, I love you! Keviiiiiiiin!*'

Kevin waved, flashing his pristine teeth and criminally cute dimples. Sketch had to admit that despite Kevin's disastrous moods and fatal tendency to strop, when it came to putting on a game face he was up there with the best. The kid was a pro.

Kevin, meanwhile, was hitting his stride.

It was a dream, he reassured himself as a sea of hands

reached out to skim just a fibre on his blazer, *only a dream.* Nothing like that was ever going to happen. Plane crashes were the fate of old people, poor people, people who travelled on low-cost airlines in dirty foreign countries. No, a more likely end to Kevin Chase was total burnout, nervous break-down: a meltdown to end all meltdowns...

Imagine if he did it now! Just stripped naked and barrelled up to the gleaming gala entrance, blathering and drooling, maybe he could even deliver a steaming turd to the carpet to make absolutely sure? Instead he twirled for the crowd, performing one of his hallmark 360-degree dance moves, a splash of MJ mixed with Ne-Yo polished off with Usher, shooting one arm in the air as he sprung up on his ankles and released a high-pitched cry. Across the gangway he met Sketch's approving gaze.

Good little monkey, Kevin thought bitterly. *Monkey did good.*

At the end of the carpet, billionaire entrepreneur Jacob Lyle, one of the cooler guys on the scene, was draped around a gorgeous six-foot brunette.

What did it take to bag a woman like that? Kevin wondered sadly, absorbing her hip-hugging floor-length gown and the tight swathe of pastel-pink that barely covered her tits and ass. He imagined burying his head in those tits, plunging into her, making her moan, hearing he was the best she'd ever had, and having her admire the broad, muscled shoulders he yearned for so badly, working till he puked at the gym.

As if that was going to happen. *What was wrong with him?* Every time Kevin got to second base his cock fizzled and died. No wonder Sandi had run for the hills: she was probably screwing her way across LA this very minute, spreading her damning word as fast as she spread her legs. Kevin's erec-tions lasted mere seconds before they flaked, and even when his dick did get hard it barely amounted to more than a pickled gherkin. When he thought about screwing Jacob Lyle's Amazonian angel, the only image that sprang to mind was one of a naked child scrambling over a climbing frame. Even jerking off was like flogging a paper bag.

Jacob Lyle, on the other hand, had it down.

Jacob was a pussy magnet. Whatever *it* was, Jacob had it in spades.

Kevin wanted it too.

As he was ushered inside, his PR fending off the last of the requests, he resolved that a meeting with the entrepreneur was drastically in order. Maybe if he started affiliating with guys like Jacob, his luck might start to change.

Something had to—fast.

7

Los Angeles

In the back seat of a limo cruising down Sunset Boulevard, Jacob Lyle grabbed his girlfriend's hips and pulled her down onto his throbbing cock.

She was wet as fuck for him.

'Jake, oh, screw me, Jake, you feel so good!'

He knew he did. All the girls said it.

Jacob flipped her round so her palms struck the partition glass, soundproofed but who cared if they were heard; it only added to the thrill. In the tinted reflection it occurred to him how easily one hot cunt could be traded for another hot cunt. Creamy ass riding his dick like a jockey, swathe of glossy hair cascading down her back (he supposed the colour was a variant), the moans of ecstasy he could pretty much script by the book… 'Make me come,' she gasped, 'don't you dare stop till I've come…'

Once more, Jacob lifted her waist, supporting her so her drenched pussy was teasing the tip of his cock. He was making her wait, resisting her as she fought to plunge onto his length. Expertly he reached round and located her clit, deciding she was so wet she could put out a burning building, and proceeded to polish the silky bud like a button. Wetter and wetter she became, her moans reaching a mad cry as she bucked and thrashed on the head of his penis. Before he allowed her release, he reclaimed his finger and sucked it, tasting her, salty and sweet. She was wide on top of him now, open to his will, senseless in her desire, and with a growled, 'You ready, baby?' he pushed his finger hard into her asshole at the same time as leaning her forward and allowing the entirety of his cock to be consumed by her warmth.

Instantly she pulsed and shuddered on top of him, screaming like an animal. On and on she came, and again when he brought both hands up to clasp her tits, pulling the nipples sharply and whispering in her ear what a dirty sexy bitch she was.

It was the nipples that got him: he fucking loved girls' nipples. In a blinding burst Jacob ejaculated, slicing through her while he stretched the nipples flat, distending them to the point at which she shrieked in delighted pain, toying the hard plugs between his fingers as he crested the mount and the last waves ebbed into calm.

'Oh, my God.' Lilly-Sue, a wide-eyed wannabe actress he had been dating a month, dismounted. She was shaking. 'You just blew my mind.'

Jacob smirked. He was darkly sexual: dark hair, dark eyes, with the suggestion that he harboured dark intentions. Machiavellian in his appearance, he possessed pale, severe cheekbones and a cruel, yet handsome, line to his mouth. Women found him irresistible. He was the bastard they had been told to avoid.

'Your turn then,' he answered. 'Wanna blow my cock?'

Jacob Lyle was widely regarded as the savviest businessman of his generation. He had embarked on his first transaction aged twelve, when he had uncovered the clever knack of emptying his father's Lucky Strike filters and re-rolling the tobacco in cheap cigarette papers, bought for a dollar and sold on in the schoolyard for several times that amount. His dad never missed a pack or two, and one Strike stretched up to three smokes if he was careful—most of his buyers didn't know the difference anyhow. He remembered looking at the Strikes and thinking: *I could shift these at mark-up as they are, or I could make more by trebling my profit.* So Jacob did more, and the more Jacob pocketed, the more Jacob sold. At a young age he grasped that the world turned on the clean and straightforward principle that money, when channelled to effect, could make a shitload *more* money. It was simple when you looked at it right.

It was ever since his involvement with a world-changing social network site that his personal profile had rocketed. A young entrepreneur by the name of Leith Friedman had pitched his idea for an online hub whereby friends and followers could travel-share. It was smart, clean and most importantly green: a security-screened, 100% legitimised, twenty-first-century hitchhiking. Jacob had known how to make it fly: money and balls—and since Leith was lacking in both departments (especially the latter, but then he was a computer programmer), he had pushed for a sixty–forty split. OK, so he'd be getting more than half the business, but there wouldn't *be* a business without him, just some fat kid sitting in his bedroom jerking off into his babysitter's panties.

MoveFriends had been born—*Join the Ride*, ran the strapline—and both Jacob and Leith, in the space of eighteen months, had become billionaires. Since then Jacob had been invited onto every talk show, to attend every party, to speak on every panel, and last month had been summoned to the White House to meet the president. He had addressed a group of post-grad entrepreneurs in a scheme set up by the Republican senator Mitch Corrigan. After the show Jacob had nailed two blondes in the cleaning closet, both of whom had certainly known what to do with his rich investment.

'You totally messed me up,' Lilly-Sue purred as they arrived at Hollywood's Rieux Lounge, patting the back of her head and throwing him a naughty smile.

They exited the car and were hit by a barrage of sound.

'Jacob! Lilly! Give us a smile!'

Lilly-Sue primed and posed for the cameras, holding his hand and nuzzling his neck. Jacob decided he would dump her. She was a decent screw but way too clingy.

Kiss my cock and tell it you love it. Just don't tell me.

He dragged her through the doors. The Rieux was LA's number-one spotlight. Everyone who was anyone got photographed. Many a wasted selfie got tweeted in the small hours, only to be rapidly deleted by management next morning. Heavy beats thrummed. Bodies wound. VIP spaces were roped off, flanked by security.

Without warning Lilly-Sue pulled him into a toilet cubicle and gave him his second blowie of the evening. As Jacob watched her tongue attending to his hard-on, he leaned back against the marble and felt faintly bored. Truth was, he could only operate on half a tank unless there was a camera in the room. Shit, he knew it was wrong but he was a sucker for the buzz. He was as addicted to this as he was to the kick of investment. The one thing that turned Jacob Lyle on more than horny girls was watching horny girls fuck—more specifically, watching horny girls fuck him. As a result he had his personal cars, and several classified suites across town, rigged. He kept a record of every encounter. From Amy through Zara, the library grew and grew.

Was it legal? He wasn't sure, but Jacob showed them a fine enough time to not feel totally bad about it—always they left with dreamy-eyed avowals that they had never spent a night (or morning, or afternoon, or any time of the day, really) like it.

The girls wouldn't find out. Nobody would.

After all, he was Jacob Lyle—and Jacob Lyle was invincible.

Lilly-Sue stood, wiped her mouth and kissed his face off, which was kind of gross because she tasted of his come. They emerged from the bathroom and she spotted a friend, from here just a squealing flap of arms, and sprang off to join her.

Jacob headed for his booth, thinking the Rieux was at least a fresher vibe than that stodgy Boston gala. It had been worth it to get the Boy Scout points, but the whole thing had been a ball-ache. Pop embryo Kevin Chase had been up in his grill all night, and now it transpired Kevin's people wanted to set up a meeting. Was the kid gay? No big wow if so. Jacob affected both sexes. As it went he had dabbled with men, the odd hand job, the odd coked-up grope. One guy at Frat College had even sucked him off—he could still recall the sweat smell in the men's locker room, the sticky bench, the graze of stubble against his nut sac and the man's hot, strained breath, and, if he were honest, it still kind of turned him on. End of the day, though, he preferred pussy.

'Watch where you're going, asshole!'

Jacob held his hands up. The woman had appeared from nowhere, stepping straight into his path. Her hair smelled like coconut. Her blue eyes were scowling.

Whoa.

Instantly his cock stiffened. Who *was* that?

But, of course, Jacob already knew. Who didn't?

Tawny Lascelles. He had thought she was fine, but up

close the supermodel was unlawfully gorgeous. He had to have her. There was no question.

Long tanned legs in a pair of cute, butt-clinging shorts, killer black heels and a mane of blonde hair that tumbled round her shoulders. Her eyes were enormous.

Her blouse was loose and he could tell that she wore no bra. He wondered what her nipples were like, and imagined them to be pink and satiny, the sort of nipple that took up most of a small breast, until he tasted one in his mouth and licked till it hardened, shrinking and puckering between his teeth...

'Sorry,' he flashed a wicked smile, 'didn't see you.'

'Obviously not.'

She had thick, dark eyebrows and he wanted to know if she had a thick, dark bush to match, and if he asked her whether she'd slap him or let him eat it.

'I'm Jacob.'

'I know who you are.'

'Likewise. Wanna get out of here?'

He yearned to film her. Watch it again and again. Get her from every angle.

The scowl hardened. 'You think I'm easy?'

'Are you?'

'Bite me.'

'Love to.' He blocked her path. 'Come on,' he chanced, 'let me take you back to mine and I'll make you come so many times you pass out.'

'Thanks, I already have a date.'

'Lose him.'

'So you can continue charming me out of my knickers?'

'I don't think you're wearing any.'

Tawny was outraged. 'Fuck off.'

'Trust me. I'm the best you'll ever have.'

'I sincerely doubt it.'

He watched her, black eyes on blue, until she looked away.

'Hey, baby, what's going on?'

Jacob flinched as Lilly-Sue returned to his side. On seeing the famous model she raised herself a little taller. Tawny looked between them.

'Prick,' she muttered, before melting off and getting lost in the crowd.

Tawny posed for a flurry of photographs before ditching her date, vanishing into the Mercedes and zooming back to the Four Seasons. Her skin was crawling and she scratched furiously, nearly drawing blood, her manicured nails working so fast against her arm that her driver, normally too timid to speak, asked with trepidation: 'Are you all right, Ms Lascelles?'

'Mind your own fucking business,' she snapped back, tugging down the sleeves on her jacket, 'and keep driving. Isn't that what I pay you for?'

The dividing glass slid up.

Shit!

Jacob Lyle was a handsome bastard. Just the kind of man she had used to entertain—rich, pampered, polished rich boys with a lust for domination.

And a lust for the rest…

It's over! Don't think of it!

But she couldn't help it. Some men brought it rushing back. They reminded her of the bad times. Jacob Lyle was one of them.

Jacob's a cocky sonofabitch.

It was the look in his eyes—of greed, of ownership, of entitlement; Tawny had faced it more times than she cared to mention. Though admittedly that sort had been rare for her:

more often she would be landed with squalor; dirty, grimy vagrants who demanded all manner of degeneracy. Jacob represented those rare prizes they had all prayed for when the gates opened. *Bored money*, the girls used to tag them, sailing in after their city dealings and power lunches to splash a few bills on a stripper or three.

Dancer, remember? Not a stripper.

If only that was the worst bit. It wasn't.

The worst bit was the way Jacob had appraised her.

How it still had the power to turn her on…

Tawny hated herself, but it had excited her: that flash in his eyes, the spark of desire. She would never tire of it as long as she lived. The need for male approval was stitched into her fibre, as vital to her as blood. Where she came from, beauty equalled attention, attention equalled cash—and cash equalled the ultimate prize: freedom.

Was she free now?

Tawny recalled the crisp exchange of bills like it was yesterday, the loose tug of a tie and the hush of material as it fell to the floor. The scent of aftershave and cigars, brandy on breath; and the cold, clammy press of skin against hers…

Back at the hotel, she hurried up to her penthouse and ran a deep bath. She filled it with salts and lotions, syrups and tonics, anything to scrub the horrors away.

Tawny soaked in the water until she met the cusp of sleep.

Forget it.

Those days can't catch you now.

It was gone, it was over—and anyway, she never had to see Jacob Lyle again.

8

Rome

Eve Harley lifted her head from the toilet bowl in her suite at the Villa Maestro and groaned. Why did she feel so ill? All week she had been waking early, making a mad dash for the bathroom, and it was near impossible to keep food down.

Was it something she ate? Was she sick?

She ought to have consulted a doctor before flying, but couldn't bring herself to. It was a weak excuse, but still. She had seen too many of them, been inside too many hospitals. The antiseptic, the white coats, the plastic chairs in the waiting room while she and her mum had braced themselves to be seen, armed with a new tank of lies…

'Are you sure you should go?' her editor had asked the day before, taking in her waxy complexion and sunken eyes. *'You look terrible.'*

Eve was damned if a bout of nausea was going to stop her doing her job. She was yet to take a sick day in her life; she didn't believe in them. Often she got teased that she would be working on her deathbed. It was only half a joke.

If there was even a sniff of a lead then she wasn't letting anyone else reach the payload first. American senator Mitch Corrigan was one such assignment. Last month Eve had interviewed him on an imminent presidency campaign, and she remembered being seriously unnerved by his veneer. OK, so all politicians had one, but there was something about Mitch Corrigan's that sat more uncomfortably than most. Throughout their exchange Eve had noticed the splinters in his smooth disguise: eyes that darted, a twitchy knee, then the façade would slip seamlessly back into place and he would deliver yet another perfectly rehearsed answer. She didn't buy it for a second.

Now the senator had come to Italy, and it seemed he was doing all he could to keep the trip under wraps. Orlando Silvers had supplied the tip-off, in exchange for her spinning an effusive piece on Angela's new label (Orlando liked to make out that he didn't dote on his sister: Eve thought it sweet that he did). Corrigan's every move was publicised to the hilt ahead of his White House bid—except for this one. For some reason, the Republican didn't want them following him here.

The senator was intriguing, no doubt about it. Eve intended to find out why.

She cleaned up, took a brisk shower and snatched her bag.

No time to be ill. There was work to be done.

It was a struggle to keep the Jeep in her sights as they roared east out of the city.

The February sky was slate-grey, the autostrada darker still, throwing up spray from the vehicles in front. Senator Corrigan's Jeep was going at speed, switching lanes without warning and then abruptly ducking out on the exit to Ferentino. It was important Eve kept a safe distance—she did not want to give herself away.

They peeled off onto a winding, deserted road. She held

back, careful only to take a corner once the Jeep had a chance to move out of sight. Hulking trees dripped darkly and the sky thickened, bowed with the deluge it was set to unleash. Her hired Fiat's wipers jammed and momentarily she was blinded, the taillights up front her only beacons before the feeble swish resumed. She kept her headlamps dipped.

An animal shot out of the verge. Eve swerved, almost losing control, her nearside tyres scuffing the ridge of a ditch. She slammed on the brakes, the steering wheel spinning wildly in her hands, and abruptly came to a stop. The Jeep had vanished. Flooring the gas once more, Eve bombed along the slick road, determined not to lose her trail, and then, just as she was starting to fear Corrigan was long gone, a stain bled out of the mist: brake lights, far ahead. The Jeep was slowing, taking a turn into a bank of trees. As she came close, Eve saw it was a narrow dirt track, concealed behind a screen of leaves and just wide enough for the car to slip through.

Further up the road was another vehicle, a red Golf, parked at an angle.

She slowed and climbed out. The rain took seconds to soak through her jacket, matting her hair and chilling her to the bone. It was silent apart from the steady, gentle patter of rain-drops. A bird cawed. Dark wings flapped.

Eve picked her way along the track. It was tricky under her Converse and pimpled with potholes, rocks and foot-deep puddles, but she couldn't risk being picked up on the sound of an engine. At last, beyond a final twist, she caught the hush of a distant, murmured exchange. She tried to decipher what was being said.

There followed a mechanical scrape, like a gate opening.

Eve gave it several minutes before advancing. Concealed in the trees, she watched from afar. Wherever Senator Corrigan had come to, it was high security.

A hundred yards or so from where she hid, armed guards in military dress were pacing a mesh-wire blockade. Clumpy boots crunched on the wet ground. Every so often their radios crackled and a response was uttered. At each end of the barrier was a makeshift hut, housing further lookouts. The track continued beyond.

What was this place? No signposts off the road, no risk of pedestrians taking a stroll out in the middle of nowhere and stumbling across a hidden garrison.

And even if they did…

It was clear that nobody was getting past this—unless they had been invited.

Senator Mitch Corrigan had been invited.

Eve spent all afternoon trying to locate the building at Veroli. She scoped Google Maps, her own GPS, hunted any scrap that might get thrown up via a search, but according to the web the house did not exist. The only clue she hit on was a record, infuriatingly brief, connecting the Veroli Estate to the Casa Rocca in Rome. Eve knew of the auction house, had once met its famous jeweller Celeste Cavalieri, and she made a note to renew the contact. Her memory of Cavalieri was of a quiet, uncertain woman, a thousand miles from herself, and she was confident she could bleed enough from her to get her story off the blocks. *What had Mitch Corrigan been doing there?*

Lying back on her hotel bed, Eve tapped a pen against her teeth.

She was onto something big, she was sure of it.

Her BlackBerry beeped. She reached for it, taking news from her assistant of Kevin Chase's forthcoming trip to London, and stifled a ripple of disappointment that the email wasn't from Orlando. Why would it be? They never exchanged messages unless it was to plot their next encounter—and that had been her decision, remember?

Eve didn't admit the anticlimax, even to herself.

The first time they'd fucked she had been strict on the rules: it was physical, nothing more, and she wasn't getting into it for a boatload of emotional mush or sentimental phone calls. Orlando had laughed. Told her she was a tough cookie.

Eve allowed herself a rare moment of reflection and smiled, thinking of him. Normally she kept Orlando in his Orlando-shaped box, there when his body was joined with hers and gone when it wasn't. But sometimes, just sometimes…

They had met at an industry party three years ago. The attraction had been immediate, the kind of magnetism that Eve, a born cynic, had dismissed as Hollywood garbage. She hadn't known who he was, this arrogant man in Versace pinstripe and expensive aftershave, but it soon became apparent. He was *the* Orlando Silvers, successor to the empire: son and grandson to a legendary man, brother to heiress Angela. He was at the helm of one of the most powerful families in America.

After that first time, she hadn't expected to see him again. She had been taken aback when, a week later, he had got in touch to say he was in London, and did she want to meet? Orlando travelled as much as she did, and when they crossed cities it made sense to hook up, no strings, no commitment, just straight-up sex.

Before long they were exchanging more than sweat and kisses. He was useful to her, accessing as he did circles she could never hope to penetrate, and she useful to him, a muscle in the UK media that could change perceptions overnight. Never did they discuss anything deeper—Eve knew little about Orlando's life and he even less about hers. If they took other lovers it was never mentioned, if they made the mistake of falling asleep in each other's arms it went unsaid, and they never had a dialogue that began with anything like the words, 'So where do you see this thing going?'

It was the perfect arrangement.

Orlando Silvers was a stellar fuck and that was all there was to it.

What did it matter that he hadn't been in contact? Eve knew the clan was in Vegas; she had seen Angela pictured there at the weekend with her father. Orlando would be with them. She would ask him when they next met, and depending on Orlando's mood he would either elaborate or tell her gruffly, 'Business.' After three years she had learned to read him directly, knew when to push and when to leave alone. Maybe it wasn't so far from a real relationship after all.

Eve swung her legs out of bed and padded to the bathroom. She stopped at the door. *Just do it*, she told herself. *Then you'll know. You'll know it's a stupid idea.*

Her eyes fell to the rim of the bath, where the little white stick stared back at her, frank and unapologetic.

She did what she had to do, left it and returned to the bedroom.

Crazy girl. You've always been careful. It isn't anything, you'll see.

At the window, Eve parted the blinds. From high above the city she could see across the spires and rooftops and make out the bitten-down curves of the ancient Colosseum. The rain had cleared and tentative sunlight filtered through the clouds, soaking the amphitheatre in tender light. The bulbs in its arches were starting to come on, glowing hubs that grew against the stone with quiet, timeless dignity. In the violet sky, the evening's first stars were beginning to appear.

She returned to the bathroom and checked the result.

It didn't surprise her.

Fishing her phone from her bag, she dialled a number.

He picked up on the fourth ring, brusque voice announcing his name.

Eve took a breath. 'Hi. We need to meet.'

9

Szolsvár Castle, Gemenc Forest, Hungary

The attic was exactly as his son had left it. A narrow bed was pushed into the corner, the walls cobwebbed and stained with damp. A wooden table housed a heap of dusty books. Words were crudely scratched into its surface—terrible, heartbreaking words.

Voldan Cane read them. Misery swam in his throat.

He had not meant to come into the attic. The space had been out of bounds since Grigori's violent death, and Voldan knew to access it again would only spell fresh angst. Regret swilled in his stomach, bitter and black. He felt so alone.

Grigori, my darling son... Why did you do it?

'Mr Cane?' came a fearful enquiry from the bottom of the attic stairs. Janika. Her English was poor and so they conversed in Hungarian. 'Are you all right?'

Voldan cawed his response, a monotone bleat: 'Leave me alone.'

Unfortunate that it should come out that way, like a robot, with no more or less feeling than if he were reciting a shopping list—but the point was made. Voldan no longer bothered with pleasantries. Janika got paid, didn't she? And if she ever decided she'd had enough and went to tip him down the stair-case, well fine, he would welcome it. Things could get no worse.

He heard her scurry off down the hallway.

Oh, my son... Voldan wheeled himself across the desolate attic room. He hadn't counted on this compulsion to revisit Grigori's bedroom. It was a need to be close to his boy again, to inhabit the air he had breathed, to embrace the view he had seen, and always, above all, to seek the reasons behind the tragedy.

The reasons...

Grigori Cane had been a sweet failure, a weakling and a misfit from the day he was born. They had known it when they'd first held Grigori away from the womb, a scream-ing, wrinkled infant not two minutes old, and his dark eyes portals to a soul far older than they knew. Voldan had done everything in his power to integrate his child with normal youngsters, to give him a normal life. But Grigori had not been normal. He had been special. Shy and reclusive, with a debilitating allergy to sunlight and a stammer that made him a mockery, he had been helpless against a lifetime of taunts and rejections. The son of a tycoon, he should have had every-thing. He should have flourished. Instead he had carried the weight of his battered soul like a cross.

Perhaps his demise had been imminent.

Perhaps nothing could have stopped it.

It had been no easy feat getting up to the attic, in Voldan's decrepit state. Janika had lifted him, her solid Hungarian haunches straining under his load. The castle was vast, Vol-dan and his faithful maid the only inhabitants, and his recent consignment to a wheelchair worsened matters. Janika had deposited him on Grigori's bed while she brought the chair up—frailty an unwelcome admission for a man who had once been head of a worldwide banking corporation. Once, Janika had suggested he sell and move to a more manageable place. *Unimaginable.* Leave Szolsvár Castle, the home that had been in his family for generations? Leave the place where his wife had given him his only son, and in doing so had perished in childbirth? Leave the place where, twenty years later, Grigori had flung himself from the Great Hall mezzanine and splatted to his death? The ghosts here needed him. He needed them.

They were all he had left. His family.

After all, it was Voldan's own fault he was in this state. After Grigori died, there had been nothing to live for. His purpose had evaporated. His heart had ripped. He had attempted to follow in his son's footsteps and the results had been disastrous.

Deformed like a monster. Paralysed like a corpse.

And now he was trapped in this devil-sent machine, left with the use of only the thumb on his right hand. He was unable to speak save for a croaking voice box.

From the turret Voldan could see woodland, a blanket of green that stretched to the horizon. Grigori had returned here during the last few months of his life, scarcely leaving his room, refusing to eat or drink or accept visitors.

'*I am a failure, Father,*' was all he would say. '*I do not deserve to live.*'

Voldan's thumb twitched on the arm of his wheelchair. When he thought of his son he was filled to the brim with a restless injustice. He had been robbed.

Turning to go, he almost didn't see it. From darkness, a glimmer of light…

Voldan looked, and looked again.

If the wheelchair hadn't become stuck in the groove between two floorboards, he might never have found it.

'Janika!' he yelled—at least it felt like a yell, even if it did come out in that wretched, miserable, bionic drone. '*Janika!*'

'I am here, Mr Cane!' The maid came rushing up the stairs. She was middle-aged, with a frizz of mouse-brown hair, a flaccid chin and a sagging bosom. Seeing him stranded lop-sided in the furrow, she hurried over, flapping her arms like the wings on a nesting turkey. 'Oh, Mr Cane,' she cooed, righting him. 'What happened?'

The floorboard was loose. Voldan felt it give beneath the wheel. That was what had caught him. The monotone was back:

'There is something under the floor,' he said, the words betraying none of his excitement. He had thought he knew every inch of his son's domain, but no, here was more. Something Grigori had tucked away, kept to himself, a parting secret.

Something he had wished his father to find.

Janika removed the floorboard with a sturdy grunt. Inside was a wooden box.

'Lift it,' Voldan demanded. Janika did as she was told. 'Open it.'

Darkness fell across the turret window. Clouds brooded and in the distance came the first rumble of thunder. The lid prised open.

Janika tilted the box so that Voldan could see its contents.

He didn't understand. 'Who are they?'

Janika removed one of the photographs. It was a picture of a woman. Across her face was streaked a giant red cross. The red was smeared, turning to brown.

Blood?

The maid extracted another. This one was a boy. It bore the same red mark.

Angela Silvers and Kevin Chase. What had they to do with his son?

'The rest,' instructed Voldan electronically. 'Empty the rest.'

There were five more: seven in total.

Journalist Eve Harley... Model Tawny Lascelles... Investor Jacob Lyle... Senator Mitch Corrigan...and Celeste Cavalieri, the jeweller.

All defaced by that same blood cross: the mark of Grigori's plague.

'What is this, Mr Cane?' Janika whispered.

Voldan's eyes hardened. On the back of each photograph was scrawled a single word. BITCH. LIAR. THIEF. FRAUD.

'I don't know,' he replied, already tasting on the tip of his tongue the sweet, sticky nectar of revenge. 'But I intend to find out.'

IO

Las Vegas

'Angela Silvers! Just as pretty as I remember, hey, Don?'

Carmine Zenetti, casino boss and hotel magnate extra-ordinaire, greeted them in his palatial office above the Parisian. Angela remembered him from her childhood—a squat, stout man with a black monobrow and hands like bear paws. She knew her father hated being called Don. Her father knew she hated every minute of being here.

'No need to remind me,' Donald said amiably, as he accepted a cognac and they were encouraged to sit. The panorama looked out on the dazzling Strip, where in the spring sunshine tourists milled amid the peaks and spires of the replica city. Giant billboards screamed news of the hottest show in town while glittering hotels ushered through the next bout of spenders. The air was charged with the sharp tang of money.

Angela refused her drink. She had no appetite. Since her father's revelation in Boston, she had barely let a thing pass her lips.

'I gotta say, I'm glad you finally came around.' Carmine smiled fatly. 'All these years there I was thinkin' we were meant to be, but you had me wondering there for a time…'

Carmine waggled a heavily jewelled finger at her father, one of a handful of people in the world who was permitted to do so, and chuckled. 'But now you see it makes the best kind of sense. Zenetti and Silvers, united for the future.'

Angela clenched her fists in her lap.

'But hey,' went on Carmine, eagerly rubbing his palms, 'what are we waiting for? I know the guy you've really come to see.'

Another, younger, man stepped into the room.

'Meet Dino, my eldest.' Carmine clapped him on the back. 'Dino, you remember Don Silvers…and this, of course, is the gorgeous Angela.'

There was a long silence.

Dino was like something out of a catalogue—coffee hair, twinkling eyes, and a stacked body that was suited to perfection. He was an ad for mob fashion, gold rings glinting on his fingers, collar crisp, jacket pressed. Angela guessed he was in his thirties, indisputably handsome but so far from her type that even in a radically different context she could never have considered him a match.

It didn't matter who Dino Zenetti was. He wasn't Noah.

Her heart sank. *How am I going to tell him?*

She played out her defence, each claim more ridiculous than the last.

We can still see each other; it won't change a thing. Dino means nothing to me. I'm doing it for the business, a transaction, no emotions, I swear…

Even Noah Lawson's boundless patience wouldn't stretch that far.

'Aren't you kids gonna say hello?' Carmine boomed, breaking the tension with a guffaw. 'I tell ya, Donnie, this is like being back in the sixth grade!'

'Good to meet you,' said Dino, in a gravelly husk. He

put out his hand. Angela shook it. She said nothing. Every instinct recoiled. It wasn't too late, she could still back out of this; she could still change her mind.

'I guess you two're gonna want to get t'know each other, huh?' Carmine thrust a glass into his son's hand and supplied a wink. Their conspiracy filled her with horror. She wanted to run, never stop and never look back, until she reached his arms.

If only that was all there was to it…

'I want you to listen carefully,' her father had said that night in his office, 'for if you choose to accept, our empire is yours. Everything. You take over.'

The words Angela had waited her whole life to hear.

Her father's confidence, his respect, his finally recognising what she was capable of, a bond between them of trust and belief, nothing to do with her brothers.

But she could never have guessed at what cost.

'The business is dying,' Donald had explained. 'I've been shielding you from it. I haven't told Orlando, or Luca, or any of the board. I haven't even told your mother. I'm telling you, Angela, because you're the one I am counting on to help. We're in bad shape. Real bad shape.' He had wiped a hand across his face and she'd heard him swallow, a dry, sickening sound, coarse with regret. 'Twelve months ago I put money into a sideline I believed was a dead cert. I was wrong.'

Donald Silvers was never wrong. He had made a fortune on those grounds.

'But—'

'Let me finish. That's only the start.'

And then he had confessed the awful truth.

Her father had been diagnosed weeks ago. The doctors had

given him mere months to live. Isabella had been protected from that blow as well.

'No,' Angela had spoken with someone else's voice, tinny and strange in an upturned world, 'you won't,' she fumbled for sense, 'you can't—'

'I am.'

'They're wrong. You'll get through it—'

'The Zenettis can pull us out,' said Donald, matter-of-fact, no time for weakness. 'They're our last hope. They can give us back our future. *Your* future, Angela, should you decide to commit.'

Her chest tightened. 'Commit to what?'

He had laid it out in basic terms. The proposed marriage to Dino, the combined fortunes bailing them out of debt, the mutual interests to both parties as they embarked on a super-empire merging the last word in leisure and retail.

The Silvers would take a cut, thirty per cent against the Zenettis' seventy, but the brand would survive. Given time, it might even grow.

And she would be there to rebuild it. Her business. Her chance.

Her chance.

Carmine Zenetti wanted to make it official, cement the allegiance via a union with his son. Angela was the key. Donald hadn't been in a position to negotiate.

Her heart in exchange for her family—not just the dying wish of her father but her own wish, too: to step out from the wings and inherit the trophy.

She couldn't. She must. She wouldn't. She had to...

'Wanna take a walk?'

Dino lifted an eyebrow. Everything about him was suggestive. His knuckles were peppered with hair and he wore a signet on his pinkie. His nails were clean, his hands smooth, as if he had done nothing more in his life than to change a light bulb.

Angela stood. She could feel her father's gaze drilling into her but she could not return it. She could not look at him. Any other disclosure she would have welcomed, but not this. Never this. She was running on autopilot, ignoring Noah's attempts to make contact, cancelling his calls for fear she would lose control as soon as she heard his voice, trying to find some space while she figured out what on earth she was going to do. Every way she looked at it, there was an impossible penalty to pay. Refusing her father was unthinkable.

So was sacrificing Noah.

Selfish as it was, it came to this: Angela did want the title. She did want the job. She did want to claim what was hers because she had earned it.

'C'mon,' encouraged Dino. 'Let me give you a tour of our little hotel,' he put the emphasis on *our*, 'see if you like it.'

Angela followed. She could hear Carmine preparing to pop the champagne, the murmur of approval that passed between him and her father. She felt trapped in a nineteenth-century drawing room; engaged to be married against every belief her heart held true. Her head told her different. Her head told her this was a done deal.

Perhaps Noah would understand. Perhaps he would let her explain and then he would see that this was the only way. They could still be together—they were already forced to meet in secret, what real difference would it make?

One promise she could make him utterly: that she would never be with Dino Zenetti in the proper way. Their partnership was for show; that was all.

Noah would understand. She would make him.

Dino led the way. It reminded Angela of a walk she had taken a long time ago.

A boy she had fallen for, and nine years later still unable to set him free.

Boston
2005

'*Noah, oh yes, right there, that's it!*'

Noah Lawson obliged, driving deep into the woman who was lying spread-eagled across her expensively upholstered sunlounger. He was sixteen, nailing his boss's wife in the pool house he was meant to be cleaning, and what's more he was getting paid for it. Getting paid for getting laid... What boy wouldn't?

Mrs Mason wasn't bad either, tall and buxom with the greatest pair of tits this side of Vermont. Noah dipped his head to them, licking and grazing as she arched beneath him, grabbing tufts of his corn-blond hair and raking her scarlet manicure down his back. He tucked one hand behind her knee, pushing his cock harder and harder until she screamed. Mrs Mason's lipstick was smudged, her mouth parted in ecstasy.

'*You make me so hot,*' *she moaned.* '*Where'd you learn how to do this stuff?*'

As if to reinforce the point, Noah drew out, hovering his dick millimetres from Mrs Mason's sweet spot. She groaned, thrashing her head from side to side.

'*Now! Take me now!*'

He rested his thumb on her swollen clitoris, wondering when Mr Mason with his bald head and stuffy suits and perspiring brow had last done this, and began to tease, dipping his thumb inside her, drawing out her wetness.

'Noah! Please! Take me!' She was delirious, her hands reaching up to maul his chest before sliding down to clasp his proud, rock-solid erection. Noah rode through her fingers, his balls ready to burst. Mrs Mason's pussy was pink and glistening, her dark bush trimmed in anticipation of their weekly meetings.

Noah Lawson looked older than sixteen. Mrs Mason would have a heart attack if she knew. Truth was, he had bedded dozens of women and none of them had a clue. He had lost his virginity to a friend's older sister when he was twelve, a quick and strange fumble in the back seat of a vintage Cadillac, where he had panicked and pulled out and spunked all over her hand. He had come a long way since then.

'You asked for it,' he breathed, and in a single stroke he plunged into her, collapsing onto her tits. Mrs Mason was yelping, rocking so hard beneath him that he had to grab her wrists to hold her down and she was pulsing and writhing and biting his neck and only then did he let himself come, a series of white-hot electric spasms.

Noah rolled off, panting hard, his bronzed stomach rising and falling. He gazed up at the whirring ceiling fan. Mr Mason would be back soon.

'I gotta split.'

'Don't—' She sat up, starry-eyed. 'When can I see you again?'

'Soon.'

'When?'

'Keep this place dirty.' He grinned. 'Gives me more to do.'

As he exited the Masons' estate, summer sun shining on his back, it was panning out like any ordinary Friday: a couple hours at the Masons' and then on to Hank's Hardware for the rest of the day. Noah had quit school the year before—more accurately, he'd been expelled—and there was no one at home who gave enough of a shit to place him elsewhere: his mom was a waster and his dad had walked out on them years ago. Life was down to him. There was only one way to escape this neighbourhood and that was with a shedload of cash in his back pocket.

Soon as he could, he was getting as far from this town as possible.

He grabbed a hot dog, ravenous after the morning's exertions. Mrs Mason had slipped him an extra fifty bucks, which he could have taken offence at but didn't. There was enough money floating about this joint and since he hadn't seen a dime of it since the day he was born, it was high time he cut a piece. The Lawsons were the embarrassment of Bourton. Everyone knew they had nothing. Everyone knew his mom was a bum and his dad had drunk himself to death in a ditch somewhere.

Everyone knew Noah had gone the way they'd expected him to, bailing on school and drifting the streets: a loser, a troublemaker, a failure, a lost cause...

And yeah, maybe they were right. Maybe all he'd end up doing with his life was fucking married women in their pool houses while their husbands went out to work. He'd be hauling crates for Hank the rest of his days, earning six dollars an hour and trying to remember the name of the last girl he'd slept with.

Noah lost his appetite for the hot dog and tossed it in the trash.

A van pulled up outside Hank's and began unloading a delivery. Noah grabbed a couple of crates and headed through the door, colliding almost instantly with the most incredible-looking girl he had ever seen in his life.

The crates went smashing to the floor.

'I'm sorry!' The girl dropped to her knees, attempting to gather the mess.

'Don't,' he knelt, 'it's glass.'

'Ow!'

A prickle of blood flowered on her index finger. She sucked it.

For the first time in all his sixteen years, Noah Lawson was tongue-tied. The girl looked up at him, her eyes a deeper shade of green than he had known existed. Her skin was pale except for a flash of colour at the cheekbones.

'I'm Noah,' he blurted.

She took the finger from her mouth and inspected it. 'It's just a graze.'

'It was my fault. I wasn't looking where I was going.'

I was looking at you, *he thought.* Why haven't I been looking at you for every second of every minute of every hour of my life?

'Angela,' she said, with a tentative smile. 'Pleased to meet you.'

'Me too.'

She stood. He joined her. They couldn't take their eyes off each other.

'Can I walk you home?' he asked.

'Aren't you meant to be working?'

'I can come back.' He didn't care. 'Let me.'

That shy smile again. 'OK.'

The exit chimed just as Hank, the store's owner, came through.

'What the hell's just happened out here—?'

But the door was already swinging shut behind them.

Noah Lawson did walk Angela home, that day and the

whole summer after. He could have walked her to the ends of the earth and back, and still never tired. He knew from that very first day that he would never be able to share her with anyone.

I I

London

It was Saturday night and Kevin Chase was performing live on *The Craig Winston Show*. He hated gigging in tight studio spaces, so close to the primly seated front row it felt as if he was screaming the lyrics in their faces. It reminded him of his audition with Cut N Dry: the panel of execs, Sketch looking on approvingly as he had sang and danced like a court buffoon until every muscle in his body hurt. It had gone to the wire between him and some stammering kid whose name he couldn't remember.

The choice, Sketch told him later, had been easy.

Tonight marked the unveiling of his new single, the coming-of-age 'Wise Up'. Recently commissioned by Cut N Dry in light of Kevin's refusal to continue playing the pretty-boy-perfect role, it was about crossing the frontier into adulthood—or at least that was how Sketch had sold it. It wasn't quite as sexy and edgy as Kevin had hoped for, but he supposed it was a start. At least it wasn't about cuddly fucking toys.

'*You say you wanna feel me, girl this is the real me, come right here and deal me, cos girl I wanna call ya, I swear I will enthral ya, baby take it all yeah...*'

The audience remained on their fat asses as Kevin charged the small stage, working his dance routines, the flaps of his knee-length Cavalli coat flying out behind him. A handful of Little Chasers had been admitted which prevented the whole thing becoming totally cringe-worthy, like he was an upstart kid flaunting his wares at a school assembly, and squealed their approval as he shuffled to the beat.

'*I swear girl you're so beautiful, you know I think you're beautiful...*'

At this the Little Chasers squealed some more, and Kevin noticed through the blaring lights that one of them was at least his age, if not a couple years older. That was a novelty. She was pretty, too, with a thick dark fringe and sparkling eyes.

'*Be mine tonight, the best night of your life...*' He stepped off the stage, an impromptu move, and claimed the girl's hand. Fingers snatched at him from all directions, mauling his clothes and tugging him close. But Kevin's gaze remained on the girl's. '*Don't put up a fight, let me hold you tight...*'

The girl stared back at him in open worship, her lips sweetly parted.

Kevin hit the closing high note, tipping his head back to belt it, and before the lights went down he twirled once, brilliantly, on the spot, punching his arm high into the air. The applause was ear-splitting. Kevin returned to the stage to receive Craig Winston's praise, and decided then that he would be banging that girl tonight.

'*Never go with a fan.*'

That had been one of Sketch's first nuggets of advice.

But Sketch wasn't here now, was he?

The girl was. His assistant had sorted it.

'I can't believe this is happening,' the girl told him, her

voice shaking wildly as she perched on a chair in his dressing room. Kevin was busy peeling off his suit.

'You don't mind...' he gestured to his bare, sweat-drenched torso, 'do you?'

She blushed and turned away. 'I, er...'

'What's your name?' he asked, relishing the power. This was a different kind of power to the power he felt on stage. Sexual. Potent. Animalistic.

It would be his first time. Great that she was older, she could steer him if he needed it, but his own pleasure would be paramount. It was the golden combination.

'M-Marie,' she faltered.

'That's a pretty name.'

Kevin kept his pants on for now. He was conscious that he hadn't yet got hard. When were you supposed to? Now? When she got her tits out? After it went in?

He stroked her hair. 'You like me, don't you?' he warbled.

'Yes,' Marie choked.

'I bet you never thought you'd be here, right?'

'N-no.'

He leaned down. 'I'm going to have sex with you,' he whispered.

Marie's eyes were pools of lust. She tried to kiss him.

'Not yet,' he told her. 'Take your top off.'

Her fingers trembling, Marie undid the buttons of her shirt. Underneath she was wearing a plain white bra. Her stomach was pale and smooth and she had a constellation of freckles on her chest. Kevin reached to touch them. Slowly his hand moved lower, cupping her breast. It felt heavy in his palm, like a balloon filled with water. He handled it enquiringly, as if he were testing the weight of a bag of sugar. He moved to the other one, and her nipple stiffened under his thumb.

Marie tucked her arms behind her back and released the clasp. Her tits sprang into view, full and white. Kevin registered a faint ripple of longing, obstructed before it reached his groin: a message that wasn't quite computing.

He continued to fondle distractedly, like a chef oiling a cut of pork.

'Do you like them?' Marie asked in a small voice.

He supposed so. 'Yeh.'

For Marie it was a green light. Quick as a flash, she was fumbling into his underpants, attempting to release his coiled-up dick.

'What's the matter?' she asked when he pulled away.

'Nothin',' he grunted. 'You done this before?'

Marie lifted her chin. 'Course.'

'Good.'

As if to prove it, Marie shuffled out of her skirt and knickers and stood before him in all her naked glory. Kevin watched the triangle of fuzz between her legs, warily, as if it were an animal about to pounce. Still he felt nothing.

Maybe he should speak to Sketch about increasing his vitamin dosage.

One blue pill, one red pill, every day like clockwork—he had to stay healthy, Sketch vowed, keep ahead of the competition. The pills were a special formula designed to soothe, relax and nourish. Kevin had been guzzling them for as long as he could remember. Given how out of control he had felt lately, he dreaded the thought of what he would be reduced to without them. Without them, he might die.

Joan had made sure in those early days that he never missed a pill. *Do what Sketch says, honey; Sketch knows best.* Of course Sketch knew best. Sketch always did. It was gruesome how much of a brownnose Joan was—all *yes, Sketch* this and *yes, Sketch* that. Her head was so far up Sketch's ass you could practically see her toenails in the seat of his pants.

'Can I give you a blowjob?'

Kevin looked down at his dangling appendage. Maybe once it got in Marie's mouth it would start doing something. But that never happened in porn. The guy's penis was already an upright, splendid spear—not a flaccid, starved little thing that resembled a gerbil at the bottom of a cage. He wanted to weep.

Kevin backed up. 'Actually, I don't think—'

Marie moved like lightning. She was a substantial size, the same height as him easily, and threw him against the dressing room door. Tits smashed against his chest and her glossy lips attacked his face. He could feel her warm, fruit-scented breath, and before he knew it she was clasping his dick, rubbing it with the flat of her hand, up and down, up and down, until the friction started to burn.

'Stop it.' He took her wrist. It hurt. 'Back off a second.'

'Let me, Kevin, *please*,' she begged. 'I promise it'll be good—'

'No—'

'I'll swallow. I promise to swallow—'

'*Stop!*' Kevin pushed her away. Marie stood, helpless, attempting to cover her modesty now the glow of their union was off the cards.

Her bottom lip wobbled. She was about to cry. Great.

'Get dressed,' he told her, as kindly as he could. This wasn't her fault.

'But…'

'Just do it!' he roared. 'Get dressed and get out. Now!'

With a series of whimpers, Marie took her time pulling on her clothes, waiting for him to change his mind and ask her to stay. When he didn't, she miserably hauled open the door and slunk outside, her eyes brimming with tears.

Kevin closed the door. He sank to the floor, his head in his hands, trembling.

He felt awful. What a fucking disaster.

12

Eve Harley paced her Kensington apartment and decided that she would do just about anything right now for a glass of wine. Scratch that, a bottle.

Orlando was due in thirty minutes. She was trying everything she could to distract herself, tidying things pointlessly, rearranging possessions, even attempting to settle down with her item on Mitch Corrigan, but nothing could train her mind.

Their encounter hurtled towards her like a nuclear explosion.

It wasn't Eve's style to be nervous. Her job landed her in dozens of compromising positions and she knew how to handle herself. But this wasn't work.

For once, her private life was centre stage. It was an uncomfortable spotlight.

Her anxiety at seeing him wasn't helped when she flicked on the TV and caught him live at his London engagement. Orlando was opening a restaurant in Chelsea with a popular TV chef, out on the carpet shaking hands, cameras scattering the night with stars, and his pristine, moneyed grin flashing white in the storm.

In the end, he was late. An hour passed before the buzzer sounded.

Eve had never invited him to her home before. Personal

space was off limits, always had been with her boyfriends (not that he was one of those), and the arrangement with Orlando was no exception. As if she was giving something away by letting him see where she'd come from. There wasn't a great deal of personal memorabilia about the place, and certainly no family photographs, but even so.

Predictably he grabbed her as soon as he walked through the door.

'I've missed you,' he said, gathering her into his arms and nuzzling her neck. He smelled expensive, of leather and cashmere scarves, of warm winter coats.

She pushed against him, went to begin, but he stopped her with a kiss.

'So this is new,' Orlando murmured, enjoying the game, 'calling me up out of the blue—what's going on?'

Eve stepped away. He mimicked her frown before realising she was serious.

'Is everything cool?' he asked.

'Not really.' A beat. 'We need to talk.'

'Sounds serious.' He kissed her forehead. 'OK if I take off my coat?'

She nodded, watching him shrug out of his jacket and hang it on the back of a chair. At last his eyes roamed over her flat, refined by nature of its postcode but still scant compared with the opulence to which he was accustomed. The entirety of it amounted to his en-suite bathroom. Nevertheless, he broke the tension:

'Nice place.'

Eve wanted to blurt it. Knew she shouldn't.

'Can I get you a drink?'

'A beer would be good.'

She returned with the bottle, cracked the cap and sat down.

'Look,' Orlando said, joining her, 'if this is about Angela

I can't help. I don't know what she's doing in Vegas and my father won't tell us a damn thing. So if it's that you want then you've come to the wrong—'

'It isn't.' Eve waited until he had taken a sip of his beer, wiped his hand across his mouth and then she said: 'Orlando, I'm pregnant.'

His expression didn't change.

Eve remembered his teasing on the phone. What was the deal? Couldn't it wait? He wasn't planning to be in town for a couple of weeks, couldn't she hold off having him till then? She would have to; she went in on the joke, acted like it was nothing but every hour since the news had been agony. She had consulted her GP and conception was cited as the New Year. That meant she was coming up for nine weeks.

Eve hadn't thought anything when she'd skipped her first period—she had never been one of those women who could count it by the day.

'Well?' she ventured.

His face was steady and she wondered if this had happened to him before. What was earth-moving to her was another pain in the ass for him. That stung.

'How?' Orlando asked.

'I've got a pretty good idea.'

He nicked his chin, the shadow of a beard. 'We've always used protection.'

'It can still happen.'

Eve looked down to her lap. She hated that she had to cut the apologetic figure. It wasn't Orlando making her feel that way, just the role the woman had to fill. This was happening to her. It was her body and therefore her problem.

The chair scraped back. Orlando stood. 'How long?'

'Nearly three months.'

'And you just found out?'

'I did a test in Italy. I called you straight away. I wanted you to know but I felt it was important to tell you face to face.'

'Why didn't you do it sooner?'

She chose not to react against the note of accusation in his voice. He was in shock, just as she had been. Just as she still was.

'First month it was nothing unusual. Second month, it was. That's when I did the test. The weeks add up. So do the days. Every minute that passes…'

'What next?' He turned to the window, put his hands in his pockets. His back was taut, the muscles beneath his shirt strained. She wished she could tell what he was thinking, but at the same time dreaded it. Supposing he wanted to keep this baby?

Eve wasn't ready to become a parent. Analysing it, she didn't expect she would ever feel ready. Her own experience had been enough to put her off for life. Her father had been a terrible, violent man. All her memories were riddled with his vile disease.

Who was to say that Eve wouldn't mess it up as spectacularly as he had? That the damage she had been subjected to wouldn't be transferred to her own child?

Who could promise, really promise, that that wouldn't happen?

She dreamed of her baby. It had the eyes of her father and she hated it on sight.

'Do you want me to come with you?' Orlando asked, turning to her.

At first she didn't understand. Then, when she did, relief hit—but it was tinged with an unexpected shiver of resentment. He had assumed, albeit correctly, that she was set on abortion. Was she that obvious? Could he read it in her face?

'No.'

'Are you sure?'

'Quite sure.'

She was definite. She didn't need Orlando tagging along, holding her hand and saying all the wrong things. It would be a cold contract, not dissimilar to their relationship, in and out in a day and she would deal with it by herself.

She couldn't think of it as a person, just a thing inside her that wasn't yet born.

What kind of life could she give it? She wasn't fit to be a mother, and as for her situation with Orlando—they could never provide their child with anything stable.

'I'm glad you feel the same,' she said. It sounded hollow.

Orlando nodded. Out on the street, car horns blared. Normal life continued; it was only their bubble that had burst. Eve didn't recognise the serious, dark-eyed man in front of her. Their relationship so far had been defined by sex and secrets, by the thrill of the chase and a no-strings respect that left both their consciences clean.

All that had been severed. Always a string would now bind them, the cord of this misfortune, and it would throttle anything they had.

The ending made her sadder than she expected.

'Is it mine?'

His question came out of the blue. It hit her like a slap, cold and sharp.

'Excuse me?'

'Is it?'

'How dare you. You arsehole.'

'I had to ask.'

'No, you didn't. You didn't have to at all.'

Orlando sat down, but she pushed her own seat away.

'You have to admit,' he said softly, 'we don't know each other. I'm checking.'

'You're insulting.'

'So there's been no one else?' His voice was quiet. Different.

To her mortification Eve blinked back the hot stem of tears.

Don't cry! She never cried. It was the sheer injustice of his accusation, this lead weight she had been carrying around, the fear she had faced all alone, no one to share it with until now—and now she had, he had treated her as little more than a slut.

'Yes,' she lied. She didn't know why. She wanted him to be jealous, maybe, or simply to prove him right, to drive him away for good. 'But it isn't his.'

Orlando stayed quiet a while before he said: 'Who?'

'It doesn't matter.'

'It does to me.'

'The timing's yours. It's definitely yours.'

But when she looked up she could see that she had lost him.

Fine—if that's what you think, think it!

She wanted him to hurt. She was hurt, why should he get off free?

'I need you to go,' she said.

Orlando looked like he was about to say something, then he changed his mind.

'You'll let me know?' he said, slipping on his coat and making for the door. His bearing was cool, professional, playing out the motions.

'Yes.'

'I guess that's it, then.'

'I guess.'

The door opened. 'Goodbye, Eve.'

Eve didn't say it back. She waited until she heard the door close, a soft, final hush, and his footsteps travel down the stairs. Only then did she let the tears fall.

13

Washington, D.C.

MITCH CORRIGAN: WHO IS THE MAN BEHIND THE MASK?

In spite of the blonde head plunging determinedly up and down in his lap, Republican senator Mitch Corrigan couldn't stop staring worriedly at the article that had landed on his desk that morning. He squinted at the byline.

Eve Harley.

Vaguely he recalled her. She had talked to him here at the Farley Senate Building, before he had left for Italy. Tenacious. Persistent. Borderline rude. And now she had published a piece on his 'hidden persona'. Exactly what he didn't need.

Mitch squeezed his eyes shut and concentrated on the mouth clamped around his dick. His wife's gem-laden fingers were spread across his thighs, her lips going methodically to work with as much eroticism as a fundraiser bobbing for apples.

Seated at his mahogany bureau, from the waist up Mitch Corrigan was any ordinary politician—tie neat, collar pressed and cufflinks polished. Only his flushed face was a clue to what was going on beneath: pants down by his ankles, shirt untucked, and his wife's tongue catching and flicking his struggling dick as if it were a melting ice-pop. Finally, Mitch came. It was a ragged, unsettled climax.

He couldn't stop staring at that venomous write-up.

Mitch Corrigan made me uneasy... He might have been a film star, but the time for acting is over... How can he convince a nation if he can't convince me?

Melinda sat back and flipped open a compact from her Louis Vuitton purse.

'Stop looking at it: it's just some witch out to grab a headline.'

Mitch tucked his shirt and zipped his flies. 'For a man in my position I'd say that headline was a substantial concern, wouldn't you?'

'Our marriage is also a substantial concern,' Melinda complained, shooting him her best martyred expression, 'but I don't see you caring half as much about that.'

Mitch gulped his guilt like a lump of cotton wool. He shuffled the papers on his desk, moving Eve Harley's *Examiner* piece to the bottom of the pile. The Melinda he had married two decades ago had been a sweet, innocent girl, unimpressed by money or fame. She had always kept his feet on the ground, stuck with him through the drugs, the drink, the partying and the depression. Now that girl was gone.

'Don't you care, Mitch?' she spat. 'Go on, have the guts to tell me the truth.'

Truth. The word shivered between them, a caped stranger.

The world would never believe the truth. It could never understand.

His phone buzzed. 'They're ready for you, Senator Corrigan.'

'We'll talk about this later,' he told Melinda, clicking his briefcase shut.

His speech went down a storm. Mitch was unsurpassed when it came to putting on a show. He was master of the persuasive address, the loaded pause and the witty riposte. His years in Hollywood had served him well.

He might have been a film star, but the time for acting is over…

Eve Harley was a clueless hack whose job it was to sniff out heat, even when there was nothing to back it up. Mitch was careful. The press would never get to him.

Afterwards, a posse of reporters was lobbying for a word. Microphones lunged as he paced through the foyer. 'What's next, Senator Corrigan? Is 2014 your year?'

Mitch turned at the door to his committee, winning smile resolutely in place. After feeding them their quota of practised lines, he slipped into his antechamber.

Checking there was no one else around, he located the bathroom.

Mitch had a diehard bathroom routine. He could not do the business unless any and all cubicles behind him were vacant. The stalls had to be open, wide open, so he could see into them. He refused to have his back to a closed door.

If you want my ass so bad you'll have to damn well find it first!

But they had found it last time, hadn't they?

No way was he laying his ruined rump bare. He might as well put a tablecloth under it, give them a knife and fork and invite them to pull up a chair. Christ!

Today, Mitch was in luck. The restroom was empty. After a quick inspection in the bank of mirrors, comprising a swift adjustment to his chestnut-coloured toupee and a reassuring thumbs-up, he unfastened his pants. As he emptied himself into the urinal, he prayed that Melinda had scarpered back to the apartment. Mitch was grateful for tonight's TV slot—with any luck his wife might have gone to bed by the time he returned. Occasionally she would grope for him in the dark, murmur something enticing like, 'Have you showered? If you've showered you can put it in me,' but if he left it long enough she would have her eye mask on and her earplugs in.

If Melinda only knew where he'd been, what he'd seen…

Images from the house at Veroli came rushing back: the elderly couple, the shed in the courtyard, the driving rain… Part of Mitch wished he had never gone, had never laid eyes on the terrible reality. But there had been no choice.

Now he knew beyond any shadow of a doubt that these creatures were out there, biding their time, preparing to strike, their skills and machinery eclipsing anything this planet had to offer. Rome had confirmed their existence once and for all.

The invasion was nigh—and Mitch was its target.

Signor Rossetti had explained. '*They want you, Senator Corrigan. You are a special man. You will soon run America, the most powerful country on Earth…*'

Mitch would never forget those words as long as he lived. *Them.*

One probe was all it took. Fiercely he yanked up his pants.

Trembling, Mitch Corrigan bolted for the door.

The car arrived on the dot of six to escort him to the studio. Mitch was due live on *America Tonight* in an hour. He couldn't be less set for a public airing if he tried.

'Remember our focus is the campaign,' Oliver, his PR guy, chattered, stabbing keys on his BlackBerry. 'I've briefed the producer on what we will and won't say. I'm not sitting through a *Who's Who* of Mitch Corrigan movies like we did last time.'

Mitch's knee started to shudder as the downtown traffic rushed past. 'It's what they're interested in,' he conceded. After eight years in politics, people still hankered after morsels from his showbiz past: instead of hearing his views on a proposed health reform or a controversial rule on education, what they really wanted was a rendition of a celebrated catchphrase from his best-known flick, nineties action-fest *A Good Day to Die*. In it, Mitch's character Blaine, a stunt driver, tells his arch-enemy to: '*Side with me if you want to ride with me.*' Those ten words had haunted him the majority of his adult life. They got yelled at him in the street, at party conferences, on beach vacations, in restaurants when he was halfway through his shrimp appetiser…

'Wrong,' corrected Oliver, '*we* tell them what to be interested in. Once we confirm our White House campaign, they'll soon see where our priorities lie.'

Mitch felt exhausted by the whole thing. Along the line he guessed he must have signed up for this demented full-throttle ride, first Hollywood, then Washington, then a fucking presidential bid. Why was he doing it to himself? Fame was a cruel mistress. She had brought him notoriety, but she hadn't brought him happiness.

In the vehicle's wing mirror he spied the same black car he had noticed trailing them on to the freeway. Mitch narrowed his eyes. His knee juddered.

Quietly he eased back in his seat.

'Everything OK?' asked Oliver.

'Fine,' he replied.

Mitch couldn't confide in Oliver. He couldn't confide in anyone. They would pour scorn on his revelations: *Too many drugs with the Screw Crew?* That had been the name of his actor clique, years ago when the A-listers had stalked Sunset for babes and tallied up their victories. Maybe he *had* taken too many drugs. Maybe he *had* lost his shit at too many parties. Maybe the whole thing *was* a delusion brought about by his longevity at the top of a precipitous fame mountain: a gradual decline.

Mitch could forget all about a White House campaign if the world uncovered a breath of what he knew. Who would have thought it? This was the man who, back in his heyday, had been king of the silver screen; he had wrestled crocodiles, battled felons, shot at hijackers from a swooping chopper and flown missiles into Vietnam...

Yet here he was, besieged and cursed, tripped and taunted in the endless labyrinth of his waking nightmare. His palms were sweating. He wiped them on his trousers. He checked the mirror again. The black car was still in pursuit.

'Here we are.' Oliver was all business as their vehicle pulled up at the studio. Mitch sank down in his seat. The black car slid past, its windows opaque.

'Senator Corrigan, it's an honour, thanks again for joining us.' A smiling producer led him through the rear entrance, and he was encouraged by Oliver to raise a hand to the waiting band of paps shouting his name. Ten minutes in Make-up and he was set.

Mitch had to wait backstage while Jerry Gersham's star billing took the stage. Noah Lawson was that rare concoction to which every actor aspires: looks, charm *and* talent. It was why he was Hollywood's hottest property. Mitch knew that while he himself had done an OK job, somehow garnering his handprint on the Walk of Fame, he had hardly been the most versatile of players. In fact, his acting was shit.

'*Side with me if you want to ride with me.*' Good grief.

The studio audience went crazy as Noah told a joke. The actor ran his hand through his blond hair and gave them an easy grin. So charming, so relaxed…

Mitch wished it could be that straightforward for him.

The studio lights burned. A trickle of sweat travelled down his neck and into his collar. His tongue bloated. His lungs squeezed. Panic rose in his belly.

The house at Veroli flashed terribly through his mind. *The thing…*

Mitch released a strangled cry. He could take it no longer. He felt his asshole begin to protest, that horrid twitching dance it forced him into whenever it recoiled against a further assault, as if still reeling from the penetration two years before, as if so certain it was about to happen again: his poor, vulnerable, *raided* asshole.

'And now, ladies and gentlemen, please welcome my final guest for this evening. *D'you want to ride with him?*' Cue roar. 'It's Senator Mitch Corrigan!'

But it was too late. The wings were empty. Mitch had already fled.

14

New York

Tawny Lascelles was partying in a club on Gansevoort Street, less with friends than with tolerable randoms who were out to get papped with anyone who was anyone and, better still, the most desirable supermodel on the scene. Who cared if the hangers-on were genuine, so long as they were the right level of attractive? Which basically meant attractive enough to act as a plumping cushion for Tawny's irresistible jewel, but not so pretty as to rival her in any discernible way. Tawny did not like to be rivalled.

It was survive on your own in this industry, or don't survive at all.

Tawny was fresh from this afternoon's FNYC shoot, her first for Angela Silvers' tag as it announced the launch of its hyped new range. Working with the upcoming label was her most envied gig to date. She treasured the bitten expressions on her fellow models' faces as yet another deal went her way. Tawny snagged *all* the major names. Why? Because she was outrageously stunning, she chilled with the right people and she flirted on that line between innocence and danger that, for all the hard work in the world, models either possessed or they didn't.

'Everyone in here's, like, *staring* at you,' teased her wardrobe girl, Minty.

Tawny sighed, sipping vodka as her blue eyes scoped the room.

'Check out Tess Barnes' sherbet drainpipes!' she purred. '*So* unflattering.'

'I know, sack the stylist.'

'I like her T-shirt though.'

'Not as cute as yours.'

'Serious?'

'Sure. She's too bony.'

'Or I'm too fat?' Tawny's retort was quick as a whip.

'Shit, no! God. You, fat? Come on, you're the only model that *exists* right now, far as the bookings go. Tess Barnes is so yesterday. You, babe, are *today*.'

Minty's deft brushwork, credited with awarding Tawny the most striking and replicated eyebrows of the decade, was almost as impressive as her charm offensive, which was subtle enough not to be noted by Tawny but sufficiently forceful as to make her utterly indispensable to her number-one client. Tawny, like most models, thrived on compliments. Minty was the best at giving them.

'I'm bored,' said Tawny, as Kevin Chase's new record came on and everyone flocked to the dance floor. 'Wanna get high?'

The girls vanished into the bathroom. Tawny took a compact from her purse. When she had first been snapped with halos of powder round her nostrils, her manager had freaked and several pussy brands had backed out of their contracts. Now, it was expected—even encouraged. She was a supermodel, not a role model.

Tawny clocked him as soon as they emerged.

'Great,' she said. 'There's that jerk-off I met in LA.'

'Who?'

Tawny flicked her mane. 'Jacob Lyle.'

'Really? Where?' Minty's voice dropped. 'Shit, he's sexy, isn't he?'

'If you say so.'

'Not for you?'

'He's so full of himself it's coming out his ass.'

Minty giggled. 'Should we go say hello?' she asked.

'No way—he's a fucking perv.'

But Minty saw how Tawny narrowed her eyes, checking that if Jacob Lyle were indeed a perv, then he would be perving exclusively on her. It was the same story wherever they went: Tawny had to be the most attractive girl in the room and, eleven times out of ten, she was. What was it with models? They had been given exteriors most girls could only dream of, yet however gorgeous or successful they became, the jaws of insecurity went eternally snapping at their Louboutin heels. Tawny was legendary for her constant appraisal of other women. Despite being tagged the World's Most Beautiful, the Sexiest American or the Most Significant Style Icon Since Marilyn Monroe, the supermodel existed in fear of her crown being snatched.

Other women were perpetual and dreadful threats. Minty recalled a gallery opening they had been invited to last year, from which Tawny had demanded to leave almost immediately. She never admitted it, but Minty knew. Another woman at the function had been enticing male attention: Celeste Cavalieri, the Italian jeweller. Celeste's allure was at the other end of the spectrum from Tawny's: she was thin and petite, with a pixie crop of sable hair and deerskin-brown eyes. Celeste's beauty was quiet. It did not shout from the rooftops and it did not flaunt or strut. It did not even know itself.

Celeste hadn't noticed the attention—let alone cared. Tawny couldn't bear it.

'Did Jacob come on to you?' Minty asked now, keeping their exchange on safe ground.

'Yeah.' Tawny polished off the vodka. 'Course.'

'What did he say?'

'I can't remember.'

But that was a lie. Tawny remembered every word. Sometimes she replayed it in her mind and it turned her on so much that she had to vanish into the nearest toilet cubicle and plunge her fingers into her knickers until she came.

'If you're so hot on Mr Lyle,' Tawny commented, 'he's all yours.'

It stank of bullshit. The thought of Minty Patrick receiving Jacob's attentions was unthinkable. Jacob had been enamoured by *her*, by Tawny; his tongue had practically been hanging out of his mouth. Tawny knew he was a blatant, shameless womaniser, the kind of arrogant that, while you sussed it, was irritatingly appealing, and she recalled the flutter of interest when it emerged he'd once referred to university campuses (Jacob's preferred haunts for checking out fresh talent, business or otherwise) as 'cam-pussies', for the sheer number of girls he bedded. This sort of thing ought to send women screaming for the hills, but somehow, with Jacob's swag, had them screaming in their beds at night with a dildo vibrating between their legs.

Tawny *was* the fairest of them all—and she planned to make Jacob work for it.

'We're going.' She grabbed her purse.

'What? Already?'

'Tell JP to send a car.'

After another toilet refreshment, the women took the elevator down to the street. It was a cold night and Tawny wrapped her fur tighter as they were ushered into a hovering car. Deliberately she faced away from the road opposite. The only downside to her beloved Tower Club was its neighbouring joint, the gritty, grimy Rams & Rude Girls Dancing Bar. As usual, the memories clung on, dripping poison.

Tawny had been a different girl when she had first arrived in New York.

Another life. One she could never, ever go back to.

She'd had nothing and no one. Running from Sunnydale, the hick town where she'd grown up, Tawny Linden had been an ugly duckling desperate to make something of her future. Maybe she would become an actress, or write a film script, or find a rich boyfriend. Instead, she had been picked up by Nathan, a man who made his living skulking the subway and collecting waifs and strays like old coins.

Beyond her lank hair, train-tracks and wide, trusting eyes, Nathan had seen Tawny's potential. *Bar work*, he'd sold it as. Good pay. The start of a new chapter…

She should go with him, he said. He would look after her.

Nathan certainly did—and then some. He looked after her every morning. Every night. Every hour in between, until she was sore and ragged and weeping…

Tawny Linden had been powerless to leave. She could not go back. The Rams was the closest thing she had to a home and, over the coming months, as her beauty surfaced and her duckling became a swan, she began to bat for the big league.

That was when the competition really got going.

It was always a question of which Rams girls the punters wanted that night, who was prettiest and who they were prepared to pay most for. That was how the girls earned their keep. From the beginning Tawny understood she *had* to be the chosen girl, always, every time—she *had* to be the hottest, the most willing, the sexiest and the best—in case the

Rams decided she wasn't bagging the dollars and fired her ass out onto the street. She'd have ended up a hooker, just another sunken-eyed junkie begging for dimes. OK, the work wasn't easy—the men she was forced to service, the things they had made her do—but it was a damn sight better than that.

Thank Christ she had gotten out when she did.

'You OK?' asked Minty. 'You look like you saw a ghost.'

Manhattan rushed past. The Mercedes was warm, the seats plush. Tawny lit a cigarette and opened the window, flicking the butt with red-painted talons.

'I'm better than OK,' she said. 'I'm Tawny Lascelles.'

Minty gave a nervous laugh.

'No kidding,' she said. 'Haven't you always been?'

But Tawny didn't reply.

15

Celeste Cavalieri held the diamond up to the light. It twinkled and dazzled between her fingers, a plum-sized explosion of brilliance. She angled it, examining the way it refracted and dispelled the gleam, her eyes trained to hunt out the tiniest imperfection. The clarity was superb, a fifty-two carat Peruzzi with faceted girdle. Bright white.

She would never consider lifting a piece such as this, but the magnetism was always there. It wasn't about the value, or even the object itself—it was simply the thrill of the steal. Once, Celeste had taken a comb from a woman's open bag, next to her at an exhibition. Once, she had slipped from a Paris department store with a silk scarf folded away in her purse. Once, she had removed a silver-plated espresso cup from a bistro in Bruges. It didn't matter what it was. It mattered that she took it.

'Are you nearly done?'

Celeste jumped. She turned to the museum overseer, who had popped his head round the door. 'Sorry,' she smiled, 'you startled me.'

'It gets quiet in here, huh.'

'Sure does.'

He returned her smile. 'Let me know when you're ready?'

Celeste nodded. The door closed behind him and she exhaled.

Never again! But every time was the last. Every time she swore she was through. Celeste Cavalieri was revered, a trusted asset to the world's richest families. As if she had to push that trust, a dare, to see how far it would strain…

She touched the bracelet on her wrist, ruby and silver. Her first ever steal, from a castle in Hungary. She could see it now: buried deep in the forest, its turrets rising like a drawing in a fairytale. The owner had been an ex-banker, living there with his son. Their names escaped her now. Strange people. The son had a stammer.

Celeste had been summoned to value a painting of the banker's deceased wife, commissioned to the finest artist of the decade. A portrait of a woman, hung dourly in the castle's Great Hall, the oil thick and dingy and the features encased in shadow…

A channel of cold seeped down her spine.

Carefully, reverently, Celeste replaced the museum diamond in its casket. The jewel shone as a nugget of treasure on the ocean floor, seductive and dangerous.

Exiting the building on Central Park West, she was met by a bustling hive of rush-hour workers and sky-facing tourists. As she hailed a cab, her attention was caught by a bizarre headline on a nearby newsstand. She did a double-take, scarcely believing her eyes. It read:

ITALIAN INDUSTRIALIST INVOLVED IN ALIEN HOAX.

Celeste approached. The accompanying photograph showed Signor Rossetti being escorted from the Veroli house she had run a valuation at back in February.

> Detectives stormed the financier's hidden-away mansion at the weekend and described what they found as 'a grave and bold deception'. Rossetti and his wife were arrested on suspicion of three counts of fraud, including extortion of money from a group of as yet unnamed conspiracy theorists. Claiming their estate to be a UFO crash site, the Rossettis' replica was 'impressive' and 'high-concept', prompting Rossetti to be tagged 'the Martian magician'...

Celeste was startled. No doubt about it, the Veroli house had been peculiar, even by the standards she was used to—these old money clans were invariably eccentric, their half-forgotten-about painting, battered coffer of Grandmother's gems or relic hidden in a drawer fetching enough to sustain any ordinary person for a lifetime.

But this?

She remembered something else, too—the truly unusual part. Among the clandestine meetings she had witnessed, one visit in particular stood out. Celeste had been locked in the Veroli library, stifled behind shrouded windows and permitted to leave the room only under escort. But she was trained to decipher nuance, it was her trade, and no detail escaped detection: a smack of footsteps drifting in from the gallery, a series of closed doors and an American accent, gruff and male, speaking with authority but at the same time deep unease. Celeste had placed it right away.

Republican senator Mitch Corrigan—movie star turned

government royalty. Family man. All-American hero. Toast of Washington. *What was he doing here?*

Rain spitting against glass, Celeste had dragged up a stool and peeled open the drapes. The Veroli courtyard spilled into view. Out on the cobbles stood a billowing structure, a shed draped in tarpaulin, flanked by two sentries in protective helmets and boiler suits. The visitors were given the same, and after a short dialogue were admitted. Twenty minutes later they emerged, faces ashen, eyes thick with horror.

Shocked, she'd stumbled down. What was in there? What had they seen?

Celeste thought no more of it. She wasn't paid to ask questions. Even so, she'd been intrigued when, a week later, reporter Eve Harley left a private appeal on her voicemail. As a rule, Celeste didn't liaise with the press and, despite further attempts, hadn't been in touch. Here, then, was why. *A group of as yet unnamed conspiracy theorists…*

Senator Corrigan would be wild with fear at the exposé.

'Hey, lady, you want a ride or not?' The cab driver leaned out of his window, chewing gum.

Hastily, Celeste bought the paper. People never failed to amaze her. Humans were more complex and subtle fakes than any gem she could uncover. She made her living from citing forgeries, from scratching the surface and finding what lay beneath. Knowing when something wasn't all it appeared. She herself was no exception.

Climbing into the taxi, she slammed the door hard.

Back at the Plaza, she undressed, folded her clothes into a neat, even-sided block and brushed her teeth, once, twice, a third time. Celeste spent minutes brushing, always did, before and after every meal and sometimes in between. It made her feel clean, and the fiercer she brushed the more she stripped away. She didn't need her shrink to tell her it was all connected: the theft, the OCD, the insecurities, the throttling habits, the damaging relationship she'd been in for five years now, so that every trip away she was counting the days till she could leave, just to get away from him…

Slipping beneath crisp white sheets, she flicked on the TV and landed on a biopic of Tawny Lascelles—*Rise of a Fashion Icon*. Tawny was gabbling into camera at a fashion shoot, chatting to reporters at a red carpet line-up then posing on the arm of her latest boyfriend, her dress split to the thigh and her scarlet lips pouting.

Celeste was ready to switch over, but something about the model held her in thrall. She had met Tawny once, a while back. Though she mixed regularly with the rich and famous, she still found their company challenging—all that show and glitz, it wasn't her thing. Discretion and caution were the hallmarks of her career and over the years she had honed them to perfection. In a crowd she could blend in, become hidden, and that was exactly the way she liked it. Anonymous.

The supermodel had been even more striking in real life than she was in pictures: goddess-like, with long, caramel legs and tousled blonde hair. Celeste had felt outshone by her in every conceivable way. On introduction she had extended the arm of friendship, warmly saying hello, but all Tawny offered in return was a sniff of disdain, as if an unpleasant smell had passed under her nose. She had scanned Celeste up and down, deemed her unworthy of comment—worse, offensive to her in some way—and proceeded to whip round and stalk off without a single reply.

'Models!' their host had feebly joked, thrusting another drink in her hand.

Celeste had been able to think of a few other words.

She killed the channel and lay back.

What must it be like to be Tawny Lascelles? Brazen, unapologetic, so absolutely sure in her own skin as to cease to care an iota for what other people thought? Her rudeness was so blatant it almost demanded respect. Celeste had been left open-mouthed, wondering what on earth she had done wrong.

She closed her eyes. Sometimes, when she was alone, she imagined she was a different woman—a woman like Tawny, contained and confident, wholesome and undamaged, resting in splendour like a china doll in a velvet-lined box. A woman like Tawny didn't harbour darkness. She was a golden girl, a perfect swan. Clean.

In comparison, Celeste was rotten. Soiled. Ruined. Broken.

Evil.

And so she should be. She didn't deserve to be happy, to have those accolades. Not after what she had done. Why should God look out for a thief and a killer?

Outside, street shouts drifted up to her window. Celeste glimpsed the moon through the panes, huge and bright.

16

Broadway's Gold Court Theatre was buzzing. Noah Lawson's star billing had attracted fans in their thousands, the production selling out within hours of tickets hitting the stands. On opening night, the atmosphere backstage was electric.

Angela dressed in jeans and a sweater, sneakers and no make-up. Managing to slip behind the elaborate fan tails of a bunch of chorus girls, she located Noah's dressing room and knocked. The seconds before he answered were endless.

She knew she shouldn't have come. Not tonight. It wasn't fair to drop this bomb when he was minutes from a performance. *Are you crazy?* Maybe she was. Maybe she had actually lost her mind. Maybe, despite her justifications, she was embarking on a foolish and terrible thing from whose consequences she would never recover. Since Vegas she had been running on empty. She was stupid and mad and selfish—and desperate beyond her wildest dreams. Turning up like this wasn't fair.

Neither was it fair to let him read about it in the morning papers.

Noah's face lit up when he opened the door. Elated, he ushered her through. 'Hey, this is a surprise!' He kissed her. 'What are you doing here?'

'I had to see you.'

'I have to see you too.' Noah's arms closed around her. Unable to resist, she kissed him back—a long, slow, important kiss. It felt like a goodbye kiss, though she could not bring herself to think it. 'I've missed you,' he said. 'God, I've missed you.'

'So have I.'

'What's the emergency? Couldn't stop yourself wishing me luck?' He held her tight. 'I'm crazy about the outfit, by the way. You catching a game after?'

'Noah, we have to talk.'

'You're going to tell me that the last few weeks have been the longest of your life? That you can't stand to be apart from me ever again? That you—'

'I'm serious.'

His smile faltered. 'What's wrong?'

Angela could sense it written across her face like a disease—betrayal, fear, cowardice—and she could not look at him. 'There's something you need to know.'

'Can't it wait until after the show?'

'I'm flying back to Vegas after the show.'

Noah leaned against his dressing table. He folded his arms and regarded her in that way only he had, right into her core, deep into her secrets and her soul.

'Angela, what's going on?' he asked gently. 'You've been blanking me for weeks. I wasn't going to say anything. I know you're busy in Vegas, but, shit, it seems like you're there twenty-four-seven these days, always on some project you can't tell me about, always avoiding answering the phone, then you show up here out of nowhere and I'm supposed to drop everything?'

'I know how it looks.'

'Damn right it does. This is opening night.'

'I'm sorry.' God, this was hard, harder than she thought. How could she express it to Noah when she couldn't find the words to make sense of it herself?

She stumbled, eyes trained on the floor. 'I was buying time,' she whispered. 'Noah, I wanted to explain this to you properly but they beat me to it.'

He held her wrists. His grip was warm and steady.

'Beat you to what?' he murmured. 'What do you need to say?'

Angela met his blue eyes. 'I'm marrying Dino Zenetti.'

Time stopped. Noah blinked. 'What?'

'I don't love him.' It seemed crucial to say that first. 'It's not like that. It's…'

'I didn't hear right. I thought you said you were marrying someone else.'

'I am.'

Another knife wound. Another stab. Angela hated how she sounded, as if she was in one of her meetings, setting clear a proposal or delegating tasks. She outlined the arrangement with the Zenettis, why she had spent so much time there, why she had to do it, why she *wanted* to do it if it meant her only shot. She didn't tell Noah about her father's illness. She still could not bear to say it aloud.

With every word she uttered, Noah's disappointment settled like the roots of a throttling plant, changing his features, hardening them. It was worse than his anger.

'I have no choice,' she finished.

'Yes, you do. Choose me.'

'I am choosing you. I'll always choose you. We can carry on, just as we—'

He laughed, a harsh, bitter sound: the laugh of a stranger.

'Now I know for sure this isn't you talking.'

'It is me. You know what we have—'

'I thought I did. Clearly I was wrong.'

There was a knock at the door. He turned, his shoulders stiff. She yearned to go to him and put her arms around him and bury her face in his back, his scent.

'Five minutes to curtain,' came the call.

'Leave, Angela,' he said hollowly. 'I can't look at you. Just go.'

'But—'

'No!' He rounded on her. Fury flashed in his eyes, the final frontier; the last vestige of his endurance smashed. 'This is it for us. This is where it stops. I can't do this any more.' She tried to speak but he stopped her with a hand. 'How fucking dare you turn up and say this to me? How dare you make this decision after all we've been through? After years creeping around because you've been too scared to stand up to your father—and now this? This is how you repay me? This is how it ends?'

'No,' she begged, 'that isn't it, I—'

'You think this is what I want from my life, an affair with a married woman? It was bad enough having to protect your family's precious fucking sensibilities. You must take me for some chump—but then you always did. You think just like your father and you always knew I wasn't good enough. I'd always be content for whatever scraps you'd toss because that's where I belong, down in the gutter.'

His words hit her like a punch in the stomach.

'Don't you throw that at me,' she said. 'I wasn't the one who…'

'What? You weren't the one who what? Go on, say it: *you're punishing me*, Angela. You never heard a single damn apology I gave you. I said sorry a thousand times and it was never enough. Shit, it was always going to wind up this way. You never got over it. You never forgave me. You said you did but you didn't.'

'It wasn't about forgiveness.'

'Yes, it was. But you can't let it go. Even now.'

'This isn't about that.'

'Like hell it isn't. Always telling me it's because you're afraid of your dad—it's been a good excuse, hasn't it? You never wanted to commit. You never intended to make this into a real relationship and now I know why. You probably planned this all along. String me on, make me believe, then rip my fucking guts out.'

'No—!'

'How does it feel? Is it worth it? Is it what you hoped?'

She went to touch him. He threw her off.

'Making me watch you with another man. I hope revenge tastes sweet.'

'Dino's nothing to me,' she said, close to tears. 'It's an arrangement, that's all—I'll never be with him—it won't be like that, I swear…'

'Why should I trust you?'

'Because once upon a time I trusted you.'

He stood back. 'But you didn't. That's just it. That's why we're here.'

'It's the truth…'

'The truth? I'll tell you the truth. I knew it the second I met you and all this time I was just kidding myself. You wanted your glory more than you wanted me.'

'Don't say that.'

'Why not? Afraid of the facts?'

'I'm afraid of losing you! I'm afraid of you opening that door and telling me to get out and never come back and I'm afraid of never being able to see you again. I'm afraid of feeling like I did all those years ago and I can't do it again, I can't!'

His eyes searched hers. 'You don't care about me,' he said. 'Not like I care about you. I fucking *love* you, Angela. I'm so in love with you I can't even say it.'

Language deserted her. There were no words.

'But that doesn't matter to you. So go on—go do Daddy's bidding, just like always. I'm letting you go, there, you're free. I'd suggest you do the same with the past, or one of these days it's going to eat you alive.'

She opened her mouth but no sound came out.

'Goodbye, Angela.'

The door closed and she was alone.

From the day they met, they were inseparable. Angela had never met a boy like Noah Lawson. He was everything she wanted to be: spontaneous, dangerous, and made to answer to no one. All the other boys were from rich, glamorous families, defined not by their spirit but by the wealth and opportunity that preceded them. Noah was free.

That summer they did everything together. Took walks, swam in the lake, went to the movies. Angela was fifteen. She had never kissed a boy but she wanted to kiss Noah. She could tell that he liked her. His friends from Hank's teased him about it; he didn't think she'd heard but she had. When they turned their attentions on her, commenting on her dress or her long legs or how she had worn her hair that day, Noah went for them, telling them to shut the hell up or they would live to regret it.

At the same time, she was afraid. Noah was experienced. She could tell in the way he behaved, oblivious to the girls who giggled on street corners or the women who stared brazenly at him while he was unpacking the van at Hank's.

Blond-haired and blue-eyed, he should have been angelic. Instead there was something off-kilter, propelling him from handsomeness to a violent sensuality. She wondered how many girls he had slept with. If he was still sleeping with them, in spite of their friendship…

Was that all it was, a friendship? Some days Angela felt certain of the spark between them, others she convinced herself she was in way over her head. What would Noah Lawson want with her? She was embodiment of everything he said he despised: money and privilege, an expensive education, a house fit for twenty families. Angela's destiny was clear: she would marry suitably and stay in the same Boston home she had lived in since she'd been born. Noah's wasn't.

Some days Noah borrowed his friend's car and they drove to the lake with the top down. Angela's hair blew in the breeze. She wanted to put her hand on his arm, strong and bronzed on the wheel, but she didn't dare. She wanted to keep driving, just the two of them, and never stop. She wanted to run away with him.

He was sparing in the facts he gave. Little was revealed about his family. Noah's mom was barely around—Angela never saw her. His house was small and rundown but she didn't care. She didn't care about things like that. The fact that Noah was from what her father would consider 'a different class' never occurred to her. He was her friend. It didn't matter where he had come from.

'One day I wanna act in the movies,' he confided, breaking into a smile. They sat cross-legged in the park, Noah rolling a cigarette, blond hair falling over his eyes.

'You'll make it,' she told him, believing it utterly.

'You think?'

'I know.'

'Not so fast being a pool cleaner.'

'You won't be doing that for ever.'

'Maybe.'

Angela wished he wouldn't feel ashamed by it. By the same turn she felt ashamed of her riches. She didn't mind what Noah did. Once, early on, they had been in the market and a woman called Mrs Mason had claimed to know him. Noah had made out like he had never seen her before in his life. 'You clean my pool,' Mrs Mason had prompted, observing him quizzically. 'Just yesterday, you...'

'You got the wrong person,' he replied, and had walked away, leaving Angela to follow. 'I didn't want to admit it,' he confessed later. 'Can we just forget it?'

Months passed. Summer turned to fall and winter turned to spring. The concealment of their friendship was an unspoken acknowledgement. Noah expressed no desire to know the Silvers family, and Angela didn't force it.

One weekend, her parents departed for Carolina. Orlando and Luca were out. Angela seized the chance to bring Noah home. She had to know he felt the same.

'This is nice,' he said, awkwardly perched on her bed.

She closed her eyes as she asked: 'Noah, are you seeing other girls?'

He didn't answer. Instead his face moved closer, his fingers rested on her chin. She could feel the tickle of his eyelashes when his lips met hers and the soft, strange heat of his tongue. He smelled of pinecones, fresh and green.

She surrendered to his kiss.

And then the worst thing happened.

The bedroom door slammed open. It was her father. Their trip had been called short. Donald went madder than she had ever seen him, yelling at Noah to get out and to never darken their door again. What had he done to her? Had he forced *himself on her? Angela had cried Noah's defence but it fell on deaf ears.*

Afterwards, Donald was pleased. 'You're better off without him,' he said gruffly. 'You don't need him.' Angela was grounded. For weeks she could not eat, could not sleep. Noah didn't visit. It was as if the friendship had never happened, their closeness blowing cold as the chill winds that came in from the harbour.

It was only when Donald told her the awful truth, the truth she had feared all these months but had steeled herself against, did she learn to harden her heart.

By the time she emerged, Noah Lawson had skipped town.

'It goes to show I was right,' Donald told her. 'At the first sign of trouble, boys like Noah Lawson run a mile. He wanted you for one thing and one thing only. When he realised I was in his way, he cut his losses and bolted.'

She cried and cried. Orlando teased her. Luca didn't notice.

'You're a Silvers,' Donald reminded her. 'You'll get through this. You're strong. And, when you do, there'll be a queue of eligible boys. Just you wait.'

17

London

One glance at the teen heartthrob told Eve Harley that Kevin Chase felt like running the interview about as much as she did. Kevin was in town promoting his new single and looked as if he had been asked to lick bathroom floors for a week.

The mini emperor was ensconced in an upstairs suite with his PR team. Lavish bowls of fruit adorned a wide table along with piled-high cans of energy drink, a vat of candy and a selection of herbal teas. Kevin's mother Joan was having her nails painted in a corner, a half-eaten croissant at her side. Trey, the dachshund, was being petted on a press girl's lap, his T-shirt bearing the slogan: LITTLE STICK CHASER.

'Hi again, Kevin.'

It wasn't clear if Kevin placed her from their previous collision (in which she had ticketed him as 'curiously asexual' and 'eunuch-like'), a fact unaided by his refusal to remove his Wayfarers for the duration of the interview.

'Girlfriend or boyfriend at the moment, Kevin?'

'Ignore that,' droned his PR, at the same time as Kevin lashed, 'Of course I don't have a fucking boyfriend, you moron. I'm fucking straight. What the hell kind of a question is that?' He scowled behind his sunglasses.

She tried a new tack. 'It's been a while since Sandi. Why did you break up?'

Kevin didn't respond, just sat there, seething.

'Is it true she said you were "physically incompatible"?'

Kevin's lip curled.

'What do you think Sandi meant? For a guy in your position—'

'*Can someone please do something?*' Kevin screeched hysterically.

'We're not talking romance,' PR intervened. 'Stick to the single.'

'What do you make of claims that you recently assaulted a fan backstage?'

PR held a hand up. Kevin said: 'I have no idea what you mean.'

'No comment,' said PR. 'Move on.'

'A fifteen-year-old girl, after *The Craig Winston Show*?'

'Those claims are completely unsubstantiated,' said the woman.

'Don't you want to have your say?'

'We have no comment.'

'Kevin?'

'No comment,' he echoed, adding for good measure: 'Fucking bullshit.'

PR shot him a barbed glance. Eve had no sympathy. Kevin was happy to reap the benefits of his position—just like all famous people. Just like Orlando Silvers.

'The single,' warned the woman, 'or we'll draw this to a close.'

And so came the predicted response. As Kevin wittered on, Eve took a bland set of notes. *Focus, goddamnit! Concentrate!* But her head was in pieces, negotiating the unanswerable night and day, a labyrinth of dead ends and wrong turns and twisted logic. Indecision plagued her from the moment she woke to the moment she slept.

'Yeah?' Kevin's enquiring mumble brought her back to the present. He had finished answering and Eve hadn't listened to a single word. She consulted her iPad.

'*New single / departure / maturity / fan loyalty?*' Her notes ran out.

'You got all you need?' asked Kevin's PR coldly. The dog barked, a shrill, piercing yap. Kevin continued to stare emptily at her through his shades.

'I think so,' she said. 'Thanks for your time.'

'Go suck on it,' she thought she heard him mumble.

Eve took the tube to Green Park, where she drank coffee at The Wolseley, so strong and black it made her teeth hurt. The café's lofty ceilings, gleaming floors and buzz of conversation brought to mind Orlando in his polished American world, dealing in money, fast cars and women, not giving her a thought as she wrestled alone with the biggest verdict of her life. Had he thought about her? Was he thinking of her now?

Angela's engagement had been announced the previous week. Money stuck with money: that was the way it went. Orlando was the same. The only place his and Eve's worlds had deigned to cross was in the bedroom. He had messaged once since their meeting with the stark words: *I'll pay.* The instant the cash had landed in her account—too much, a gross sum to assuage his conscience as much as anything else—she had returned it. She didn't need his guilt money. This wasn't about that.

Eve spread her reports across the table. Her vision swam. The words blurred. Her scoop on Mitch Corrigan and Rome was the piece to define her career.

But for once that meant nothing. How could it, when tomorrow she was booked into the clinic and the life inside her died?

She paid her bill and left.

In the park she sat on a bench, cold, her hands clasped between her knees, looking out at nothing in particular. A jogger came past, his feet pounding the stiff April ground. She remembered being here as a girl, with her father, before things turned sour. Sitting on his shoulders. Making a daisy chain. Happy memories. She must have been five, maybe six—before Terry Harley got famous and their lives went to ruin. Greed. Vanity. Pride. Ego. How different things might have been.

It was too late now. Perversely, her mother had loved him until the day she died. Eve could not extend that charity. She could not care any more.

In 1987, Terry Harley had enjoyed one-time chart success with the band he had been toiling with for years. Overnight, their lives were transformed. Terry became public property. He became an idol, thrust into the spotlight, the country's hero, not just hers. At first it had been fun, and he'd been happy, but when he stopped coming home she wished it would all go away and she could have her father back.

It's just a performance, her mum used to comfort her, *don't be frightened*. But soon the performance took over. The performance became his life.

He made millions—and lost them just as quick. Pissed away on alcohol, drugs and strippers. On his family's misery. Terry turned from the man they knew. He turned into a monster: fame-grabbing and desperate and hell-bent on ruling the world.

In the months and years that followed, his campaign of terror began.

Terry rolled home drunk every night of the week. He beat her mother black and blue. He locked them in cupboards, his own flesh and blood, starving and crying and battering the door as they begged through their tears to be let out. One night, Eve had listened at the top of the stairs. Terry was on the rampage; she heard her mother's pleas as he threw her across the kitchen, calling her a whore, a bitch—his wife, Eve's mother, how *could* he? Eve darted to bed, the sheets taut, trembling with fright, and heard his footsteps mount the stairs—*thump thump thump*. The handle turned. She had seen him against the light, a savage silhouette swaying queasily in the shadows. When he approached, horror set in, paralysing her, impossible to make a sound. She thought her heart might stop. She thought she would die. What was he going to do?

He had put his hand around his daughter's throat. Seconds passed. Eternity. Booze fumes filled the air. Eve blinked against the black veil of consciousness.

Next time, she knew he would kill her.

Terry Harley was the reason Eve did the job she did. Stripping it bare wasn't going to win her any fans, but that wasn't the point. The point was that when she was little she had wished for a miracle. She had wished for an angel who could see through walls, inside keyholes and under doors, an angel who could witness her situation as it really was, not as it appeared to be. Not how everyone else saw it.

She had wished for someone to explode the myth.

Today, she was that person.

Terry was a prime example of what happened when fame went wrong. People deserved to know. They deserved to see. Eve knew what it was like to live in the shadow of fame. She knew what it was to live in terror of someone powerful.

It was her war, and she meant every word.

'You'll never amount to anything!' he had thrown at her once. *'You'll never do anything important—not like me!'*

Eve put a hand on her stomach. Tomorrow was the right thing. It was.

Angela pulled up outside The Ritz. Her car almost collided with an auburn-haired woman crossing the road. She recognised her but couldn't think from where.

Scooping up her cell, she braced herself and dialled Orlando. 'Can you talk?'

Her brother was terser than usual. Orlando was in Boston this week, on the tail of a new resort franchise. 'No,' he snapped, 'I haven't got time.' Then: 'What is it?'

'I'd rather not discuss it over the phone.'

Her chauffeur opened the car door and Angela stepped out. Heads turned as she entered the hotel.

The time had come to tell her brothers everything: about Silvers, about the future, about their father's illness and the true nature of her engagement. She could carry the secret no longer.

'Where are you?' he asked.

'London. Investors.'

'Makes a change—I'm surprised that fiancé of yours let you out of his sight.'

'He doesn't tell me what to do.'

'That sounds like a real American love story.'

'Fuck off. Expect me Friday. Luca should be there too.'

'What is this? You ditching the mob and eloping with Noah?'

His name stabbed her. 'What?'

'Come on, Angela, I'm not blind. He can't be happy about Dino.'

'It's nothing to him. We broke up ages ago.'

There was a short silence. 'Are you OK?'

'I'm fine. Stay out of it, Orlando, I mean it. Have you heard from him?'

'Noah?'

'Luca.'

'The Hamptons.'

'Get him on a plane. And I don't want Dad knowing anything about it.'

'Why?'

'Just do it.'

'Damn,' he muttered. 'As if I haven't got enough on my mind.'

It wasn't like Orlando to admit liability. 'Need to talk?'

'It's personal shit—it's getting sorted. I'll deal. I always do.'

'Good. Then prepare to have some more shit thrown in. I'll see you at the weekend.'

18

Palo Alto, California

MoveFriends HQ was the greatest sight this side of LA. Jacob thought so every time he visited. The glass building buzzed with entrepreneurial spirit, mixing the finest minds on the globe: what it was to be at the inception of something.

Leith Friedman was a geeky curly-haired guy who spent hours plugged into his music system and tapping code into a machine. His lanky frame was splayed across a Perspex chair in the open-plan arrangement, and in true Leith style his pants were too short for his legs, offering a glimpse of mismatched red and blue socks.

Jacob put a hand on his shoulder. Leith removed the plugs.

'Yo,' said Leith. 'I wasn't expecting you.'

Jacob thrust his hands in his pockets. He sensed the eyes of every female on his back. It was the same as on his college jaunts, crashing a sorority party and being spoiled for choice. Sorority girls were horny. He'd done things with them he didn't dare repeat—unless he was watching it back, of course. Kathleen and Kitty, the two special Ks. That had to be one of the most viewed in his collection.

A chick in a pencil skirt walked past. Jacob undressed her with his eyes.

Leith was looking at him. 'What's up?'

'Do I need a reason to check in on my investment?'

'Knowing you, there's an ulterior motive.'

Jacob grinned. 'Always is. You got an hour?'

Jacob's business summits frequently took place in night-clubs. He liked to get drunk, shout ideas loudly over the music and get whoever he was with so soaked on tequila that he could extract from them precisely what he needed.

'You're here to persuade me,' Leith ventured. 'Aren't you?'

Jacob downed a shot. 'It makes sense.'

'Aren't we rich enough already?'

Jacob's reply was swallowed by the music. He repeated it: 'How rich is rich enough?'

'The money's a bonus. I never did this for the money.'

'Bull.'

'I did it to change how we access the world. To bring people together.'

'What are you now, Jesus fucking Christ?'

Leith wrung his hands. Jacob fed him another shot.

'Listen,' he straightened his jacket, 'this is win-win. You still *get* to change the world, Friedman—you get to change the world in a bigger way than you or I ever dreamed.' He dropped his voice so only Leith could hear. 'This is the Russian government we're talking about, man…do you get it?'

Leith pushed his glasses up on his nose. 'What if someone finds out?'

'They won't.'

'How can you know?'

'This kind of trade goes down all the time. Collusions, collaborations, the whole world gets built on it. D'you think we know the first thing about what goes on in our own government? Deals get made every hour of the day. Don't you want in?'

'It's sinister.'

'What isn't? This is business, my friend. Remember when we started out? Remember what I told you? You need *balls* to get ahead. *Big* fucking balls. Because everyone's out for a piece and most of these guys have got bigger balls than you. Only you know how big your balls actually are—the rest is pretend.'

'Can we stop talking about my balls, please?'

Jacob kicked back in his chair. The way he saw it, the proposal was a gift. Any growing industry would receive an approach for takeover sooner or later, and the only thing that made their situation extraordinary was the unusual nature of the bid. Russia wanted MoveFriends for reasons unspecified. If reports were to be trusted, they had been assembling an advanced global surveillance system for the last decade. Jacob believed MoveFriends would form part of a grid able to footprint where any individual was at any given time, combining all the personal data of Facebook with a geographical tracking of where in the world that person was. When you took it that way, their site was already doing the job: just because they wrapped it up as a non-obligatory social network didn't detract from the essential notes of scrutiny. Jacob had put this to his partner before. Leith had capitulated. The sale would make them richer than kings.

'We lose control,' shouted Leith, over a blast of Jason Derulo.

'Then we forge on. MoveFriends has grown. It's time to fly the nest.'

Leith accepted another shot. He removed his glasses and wiped them on the fabric of his shirt. Then he replaced them, lifted his drink and said: 'All right. You've got yourself a deal.'

By the time Jacob returned to his apartment, he was defiantly drunk. Leaps in business gave him the violent horn. He fumbled with his key card, forehead slumped against the door, and Tawny Lascelles swam into his head. He had to have her. He couldn't get her out of his mind. She was a super-fox. He was frantic to nail her.

He would contact his assistant about it in the morning. Nobody refused Jacob Lyle and got away with it. If Tawny didn't come to him, he would have to go to her.

Inside, he loosened his tie and flopped onto the bed. He grinned, the ceiling spinning, at what a ride life was: a multi-billion-dollar enterprise; a treaty with one of the most formidable powers on the planet; girls queuing round the block to suck his famous dick…

Jacob thought of all the entrepreneurs who had approached Leith and him in the beginning, pitching their ideas, anxiously crapping their pants for approval and praying that if a dash of the MoveFriends magic rubbed off on their own initiative they would be made for ten lifetimes. Some of the concepts Jacob had sat through had been nothing short of insane. These days everyone fancied himself as the next big breakthrough. Having the audacity was one thing, but having the means and the intelligence to carry it forward quite another. It was why he and Leith fit so well.

Before Jacob passed out, one such encounter crept into his memory. A couple of years ago now, a kid they had laughed out of the room. A kid they had made cry.

Dark hair, pale skin, a stammer…

That wasn't why they'd laughed; it was the kid's blueprint. Jacob would never forget it. A living doll, anatomically precise, fitted with voice recordings and a library of phrases, some soothing, some sexual, anything you wanted to hear, all you had to do was ask. The doll was a friend when there was nowhere to turn: a robot for the lonely and the lost. He couldn't decide if it was more spooky or tragic.

Jacob wasn't proud of his behaviour, but neither did he award it a great deal of thought. He hadn't got this far by making friends.

He hoped he hadn't made too many enemies either.

19

Szolsvár Castle, Gemenc Forest, Hungary

Voldan Cane was drawing his plans.

Slowly but surely, they assumed their dreadful shape. Night and day he strived. He researched every name on his beloved son's list. He found things out—the basics, the details, the obscure—and in doing so furnished himself with all he needed about the seven: where they lived, their families, where they had grown up, what they wore, what they ate, what they drank, who they slept with, their fears and phobias, their weaknesses, their strengths, their greatest loves and their greatest losses…

No stone was left unturned in Voldan's pursuit of knowledge.

Before the discovery of Grigori's box, his life had held no purpose. Now, he had been given a quest. Grigori had offered it to him from beyond the grave.

Avenge me, Father, he seemed to cry. *Make them pay!*

Wind and rain thrashed against the windows of Szolsvár's Great Hall. A whistling draught in the rafters cried a haunting cry, reminiscent of his lost wife's moans as she writhed in the throes of childbirth. The ghosts had returned.

Voldan brought his wheelchair to a halt in the centre of the stone floor.

Janika had done the best she could with the mess, but there remained a tell-tale stain if you knew where to look. The fifth slab from the arched window bore a faint, fiery hue. It was where Voldan had crashed, leaping from the same mezzanine as his son and breaking like china, the blood seeping thickly. Only, where Grigori had succeeded in making away with himself, Voldan had failed.

Voldan had been gathered up, a cracked doll, his spine snapped in two.

The wheelchair had been his penance—that, and the appalling beast that confronted him every time he peered into a mirror. For the plummet to stone had not been Voldan's first attempt on his life. In the early agonies of his son's demise, he had made an initial, idiotic attempt at suicide by chucking a bucket of acid in his face. His reflection had been too like his son's to abide—he could meet it no longer.

To be deformed and disabled, what point had there been to his life?

Now, at last, there was a point. The devil worked in mysterious ways. He had been spared in order to carry out this fatal assignment.

Seven deadly sinners...

How he despised them! They were the people who had wronged his Grigori, who had forced his son to see no way out of this cruel, unfeeling world but for the horrible exit he had taken. They had crushed his spirit. They had ruined him.

Mercy was not an option.

Vanity, pride, lust, greed—whatever their crime, one punishment fit them all.

The plot Voldan had conceived was outrageous. It was high risk, and it was high impact. It would rock the world and shock the masses. It was gloriously evil and resplendently clever. There would be no traces—nothing to lead them to Szolsvár.

He could hear Janika rattling around in the far reaches of the castle, preparing the summons he had so diligently worded, envelopes ready to courier at dawn.

Voldan closed his eyes and pictured the invitations in his mind.

The trip of a lifetime… A charitable cause…

The kind of publicity an emperor alone could buy.

Two months was all. Two months until it began.

20

Las Vegas

'Angela! Dino! When can we expect to hear wedding bells?'

A crowd of press jostled at the entrance to the Parisian. Even at public appearances, galas or business matters for FNYC, the attention had never been this extreme. News of the union had exploded across the media.

Angela Silvers and Dino Zenetti: the golden couple. Engaged.

She pictured the word on a locked bathroom door. ENGAGED. Click and then closed. Bolted in. Trapped.

'Hey, slow down!' revelled Dino, in a pressed Ralph Lauren ensemble that was in defiance of the Nevada sun. 'I only just managed to get a ring on her finger!'

'Angela, this got serious fast! Was it love at first sight?'

She knew what love at first sight felt like. This wasn't it.

'Dino and me,' she said, 'it was one of those things. Sometimes it comes right out of the blue and catches you when you least expect.'

It didn't matter what lies came out of her mouth. Angela was a puppet for these people, not a person. The cameras formed a glittering wall that she stared straight through, her smile a rictus, Dino's hand holding tight to hers, cold and clammy.

The Boston house had received bouquets and magnums, congratulations from Donald's associates and abundant gifts designed to secure allegiance with the world's newest mega-dynasty. Dino welcomed the attention, of course. As Carmine's only son, he had waited to step into his moment. Angela was the prize. Dreams came true.

So did nightmares.

Carmine and her father shook hands, prompting the barrage of press to surge once more. In the background, the spires of the Parisian rose majestically against a bright-blue sky, fountains spraying jets of silver. Tourists swarmed like bees to honey, drawn by the bonus of a rich heiress and her casino-boss fiancé.

'A happy day for us,' Carmine grinned wolfishly, 'and for Vegas.'

Donald supplied more formally: 'We are thrilled at news of this alliance, and wish these two the best for the future. I couldn't be prouder of my daughter.'

The festivities over, Dino escorted her back to her suite.

'Should I come in?' They reached her door and he leaned in.

'No. I'm tired. I'm going to bed.'

'I could keep you company…?'

Angela turned, faced him on a level. 'Dino, this isn't what I want. You know that. I will be civil, and discreet, and the nature of our treaty will remain hidden. But I will *not*—now, or ever—be entering a physical relationship with you. Good night.'

Instead of dejection, she met determination.

'You won't always feel this way,' Dino murmured.

'I know I will.'

'You can learn to love me.'

'My position will never change.'

'Give me six months… Tell me after six months that you don't love me.'

'I can tell you now and save us both the time.'

His eyes were hungry. 'You underestimate me.'

'This isn't a game. Try and force me into a corner and I will destroy you.'

He chuckled. 'Careful. You'll turn me on.'

'This conversation is over.' Slicing her card through the lock, Angela vanished inside her suite. *Bastard!* Who did Dino Zenetti think he was?

She applied the chain to the door, went to her case and removed her Ruger revolver. Men like Dino thought they were entitled to whatever they chose. If he thought for a second that she fell into that category, he could think the hell again.

Peeling open her balcony, she stepped into fresh air. Her hair blew in the warm desert breeze and far below the blare of car horns swam up on the thermals.

Angela gazed at the Strip hundreds of storeys below and wondered what it would take to jump. One foot on the ledge, arms spread wide, a leap of pure faith…

Stumbling backwards, she collapsed, her head in her hands.

What had their lives come to?

Luca had cried when she'd told him. The siblings had met in Boston, gathered at the table they had grown up around, fighting over their mom's dinners.

'I can't believe it,' Orlando had repeated, again and again, his face leached of colour. 'It's not true. I can't believe it, I can't believe it…'

Angela lay back. She wished, if only for tonight, to be anywhere else but here. She wished for dreams—dreams of Noah, of the past, of their love, before it all went wrong. *You never forgave me. You said you did but you didn't.*

Was Noah right? Despite the years and the promises and the regrets and the reasons, was she still caught up in a past she couldn't change? Was she afraid to give herself totally, unconditionally, because it meant too much, because it ran too deep?

It was easier not to feel. It was easier not to care.

She hugged her knees and closed her eyes. Suddenly it was cold.

Noah Lawson wasn't backing down that easily.

Angela Silvers was his thunderbolt. He had known it since the day he met her—but it wasn't that simple and he wasn't that stupid. A kid in his position had nothing to offer. He had to get out of town, make something of himself, get his shit together so he could bring a future to her door and tell her: Trust me, I've got this, we'll be OK. We don't need your father. We don't need anyone. All we need is each other.

That was why he'd been taking on the extra work. Stupid to call it that, but he had to make money somehow. Servicing Mrs Mason and all the other housewives, a buck-a-fuck stud who never failed to satisfy, it was all he'd known, the only thing he was any good at. Maybe he was kidding himself hoping to hit Hollywood some day and make an honest living. The more he visited their pool houses and holiday homes, their marital beds and Jacuzzi baths, the more the dream seemed to slip further away.

The women he slept with told him he was special. Noah didn't feel it. Unless he was with Angela, he didn't feel much of anything at all.

She would never understand why he did it. How could she? She had never wanted for anything. She had never looked in the mirror and wondered why the hell she'd even been born. And so he hid the affairs. They made him feel dirty, used, unworthy of Angela and her bright smile and her hair that smelled like apples. He wouldn't make his move until all that was buried and gone. He didn't deserve to.

Following the altercation with her father, Noah swallowed his pride and showed up at the mansion. The thought of seeing Donald again filled him with anger but he would do it for her. He had reached a decision. He was splitting town, and Angela was coming with him. He could offer her nothing but a one-way ticket and the promise of his heart. Maybe it would be enough. He hoped it would be enough.

But Donald beat him to it. Waiting on the porch was the man himself.

'I want to see her,' demanded Noah.

'She doesn't want to see you.'

'I don't believe you.'

Donald smirked. He folded his arms. 'Stay away from Angela,' he said, 'or face the consequences.'

Noah defied the threat. What did he have to lose? What did Donald have to take? Angela was the only thing of value in his life.

'You can't tear us apart,' said Noah. 'You can't break what we have.'

'I already did.'

Noah wanted to hit him. Balled his fists but resisted the urge.

'You forget I am a powerful man,' said Donald. 'I have contacts in this town: people who work for me. Nothing escapes my attention, boy—least of all a sex-crazed worm that thinks for even a second he deserves to touch a hair on

my daughter's head. I know what you've been up to. I know about Veronica Mason, and Cassie Wentworth, and Brenda Dowler, and all the rest. Now, so does Angela.'

Noah raised his fist, drew his arm to strike, but he wasn't quick enough. A crunch of gravel and Donald's bodyguard was behind him, gripping his elbow and locking it at his back. A bolt of pain and Noah was forced to the ground.

'Begging, now, are you?' Donald taunted. 'How apt. I'll give you what you want. Take this,' he thrust Noah a cheque, 'and never cross this threshold again.'

Noah was released. Through the shooting pain in his shoulder he absorbed the sum. It was incredible. Enough to forge a whole new life: to split town, to move to LA.

Without thinking twice, he tore it up. It meant nothing without Angela.

'Let me talk to her. I can explain.'

'She's not here.'

'You're lying.'

'Angela knows about the money. She asked me to give it to you. She never wants to set eyes on you again and I don't blame her. How do you think she feels?'

Noah could only imagine. Knowing he had hurt her was unbearable. More than that, he had lost her respect, her love, her trust. The terrible things she must think about him. Angela's opinion mattered to him above all others.

'Tell her I don't want it.' He stood.

Donald laughed. 'Can't you see? A girl like Angela would never enter into anything serious with you. She said as much. You were fun for a while but she wants more from her life. She wants money, and security. She wants a solid family name, not a useless band of heathens. She hates you. She wants you gone.'

'I have to hear her say it.'

'After what you've been getting up to, do you think she so much as wants to share the same air as you, let alone look you in the face? Think about it, Lawson. You don't belong with us. You can't give Angela anything she doesn't already have. You're wasting your breath. You're nothing compared with her.'

The words were a blow to his gut. For the first time, Noah's confidence faltered. Donald's tirade cemented what a part of him already knew but had been hiding from: that Angela would always be too good for him. Even if she did hear him out, even if she did get his reasons, it was only a matter of time before she wised up and saw him for what he was. Her prospects were sky high. She could do—and be—anything. He was a waster with a drunk for a mother.

Donald wrote a second cheque and forced it into his hands.

'If you truly care about my daughter,' he said quietly, 'you'll do the right thing and get as far away from Boston as you can.'

The door slammed.

Noah didn't quit town right away. He kept Donald's cheque in a drawer and despised himself for not being able to destroy it. He thought of everything he could use it to become—and that one day, maybe, that might mean he could earn back Angela.

One afternoon, he spent every dime he had made from the housewives on a silver ring. It would be nothing against the finery she was used to, but he meant every cent. He put it in her mailbox the next and last time he passed the mansion gates, together with a note.

At dawn, he left for LA. There was nothing to stay for. Noah hitched his way to California, where fortune decided he was long due a break. Inside a week he was signed with La

Lumière models. Inside a month, he had snagged his first TV role.

It was a year before she made contact. She had read his note, and against her judgement could ignore him no longer. It wasn't the women that upset her, she said. It was that Noah had taken the hush money, that covert exchange at the heart of all she despised, the tyranny and suffocation of her father's rule. Even now, Donald's stance was unchanged. See Noah Lawson and she could forget all about the Silvers Empire.

In secret they rekindled their love. Both felt it, brighter and more brilliant than ever before, but it was stained by the confusions of the past.

Noah Lawson never recovered from the suspicion that he had done the wrong thing all those years ago. That his whole career was built on a cheap trick for which he should never have fallen. That he should have torn up that second cheque, he should have torn up a hundred cheques, and run for Angela Silvers like his life depended on it. He should never have given her up.

Los Angeles

'She was *fifteen*, Kevin! *Fifteen!*'

In a bubbling hot tub that Cut N Dry Records had had specially installed in the studio basement for their number-one protégé, Kevin Chase reclined in the churning froth, ramped his arms across his chest and scowled dangerously.

'I didn't know that, did I?' he grumbled.

Shame engulfed him. He felt terrible about the whole thing: poor Marie with her quivering lip and big, trusting eyes, his failure to launch, his harsh dismissal…

Not that he was going to admit that to Sketch—or to his mom.

'What were you doing anyway,' Sketch raged, 'making out with a fan in your dressing room? Are you insane? These people go crazy for you. She could have been anyone; she could have had a fucking psycho boyfriend hanging out in the closet!'

'Whatever.'

'No, not *whatever*, Kevin: not this time, buddy. This time it's serious.'

'We didn't *do* anything.'

'That's not what's she's saying. She's saying you were all

over her. That she tried to get away but you forced her, and it was only when she escaped—'

'She's lying!' Kevin struck the roiling surface of the water with both palms, prompting an almighty splash to surge over the sides of the pool and splatter his manager in the face. 'It was her who was coming on to me—!'

'OK, stop right there.' Sketch ran a weary hand over his brow. 'That is not going to wash. That is not going to stand up in a court of law or with the biggest jury of all—the public. The *fans*. Christ! *US Weekly* has already got hold of it. *Life & Style* called this morning. *Star* wants your first interview on the matter. Do you understand what this means for the brand?' His voice skittered up two octaves. Kevin had never seen him like it. 'After this, there *is* no brand!'

'Quit overreacting,' supplied Kevin. 'I'll make a statement.'

'Do you think I trust you to do any such thing after this?'

In the background, Kevin's mother Joan was wringing her hands. At last she spoke up. 'The gala prize might help?' she ventured tentatively.

Sketch was too irate to string a sentence together.

'What?' Kevin exploded. 'Don't tell me I actually have to *do* that piece of shit day trip, do I?'

Two wealthy middle-aged sisters had bid for the honour of Kevin's company: a morning of shopping, lunch at Nobu Malibu and an afternoon of play at the dolphin sanctuary. The auction had fetched close to half a million dollars. The thought of going through with the pantomime made Kevin want to curl up in a tiny ball and die.

Quietly Joan began: 'It's been paid for, darling—'

'With those fat old crones?'

'It's one day, I'm sure you can rise to the occasion.'

Rise to the occasion... That would be a first.

'Sure, so it's one day here and one day there and d'you know the thing about days, Mom? Days add up to weeks, and weeks add up to months, and months add up to years, and before I know it my whole fucking life's been shot down the drain!'

'Kevin, please! Your language!'

'Mom, please! Your *face*!'

'Sketch! Do something!'

Kevin's manager turned. There was thunder in his eyes.

'You haven't been taking your pills,' he said menacingly. 'Have you?'

'I have so.'

'Every day, like we made you promise?'

'I said I was, didn't I? What more do you want?'

'Those pills are meant to calm you, Kevin.'

'Yes,' parroted Joan, 'they're meant to help—'

'*Well they're not fucking working, then, are they?*'

Unable to continue the conversation for fear of bursting into tears, Kevin pinched his nose and vanished beneath the water. The tub boiled and foamed. A pair of bony hairless knees broke the surface. Sketch and Joan looked at each other.

'Right—that's it.' Sketch leaned in and hauled his client out by his elbow. 'You're doing the gala prize and that's not all. Bethan?'

Sketch's assistant approached, her high heels click-clacking on the spa floor. She produced a square of black card and handed it to Sketch.

Kevin was drenched and sullen. 'What's that?'

'We received it this morning. If you want my opinion—and Jesus H., pal, I would urge you to take it—you accept this invitation without a backward glance.'

'Invitation to what?'

Kevin snatched it. His wet paw prints marred the edges of the card, making them damp. He scanned the text. It was written in gold script, with an official stamp emblazoned across the top: CANE ENTERPRISES—FOR THE BEST YOU CAN BE.

'What is this?'

'It's a call to arms. For the Salimanta crisis.'

'The what?'

It had been too much to hope that Kevin read the news. As patiently as he could, Sketch illuminated. In January, the Salimanta coastline in Indonesia had suffered a giant tsunami. Entire families, their homes and livelihoods, had been wiped out. The devastation was titanic, the suffering terrible, and the aid effort thwarted by bureaucracy. The solicitation was the first of its kind. Kevin would become part of a never-before-seen crew who would fly out to the region and, through a global-scale PR mission, break down those barriers. It was a humanitarian crusade of the highest order, and it was hoped that each of the seven personalities invited to take part would have big impact on the crisis and its recovery.

'We've checked it out,' said Sketch, 'it's legit.'

'Why don't they just hand over the cash?'

'With the right PR they'll treble their money. *You're* the PR.'

'I'm not doing it.'

'You have to.'

Kevin's head snapped up. He'd never heard his manager use that tone before.

'No, I don't,' he replied carefully, reminding Sketch who was boss.

'Imagine how it will look if you refuse.'

Kevin spoke slowly. 'I. Am. Not. Doing. It.'

Joan rummaged in her purse for a Valium. There was a pause, before Sketch crouched down, located the controls to the hot tub and turned off the foam.

The water became cooler, and clearer, and Kevin brought his knees to his chest, looping his arms round them. Still he sulked, but with less bravado.

'You will do this, Kevin, because there is no choice. Without this, you can consider your career at the beginning of the end. God knows, I have been patient with you. We have all been patient with you. But this is where it stops. This is time for you to give something back. Your image, as it stands, is nothing short of a train wreck. You want to salvage it? Then you bite this Cane guy's arm off for a piece of the pie. Stars just like you wait a lifetime for this kind of save. Wake up to the facts. The way we're seeing you right now at Cut N Dry isn't the best. We're close to the edge. We're working for you, Kevin, but you're not working for us. We *believe* in you. We always have. Only I don't know if you believe in you any more.'

Humiliatingly, Kevin's eyes sprang with tears. He felt very young and very old at the same time. Goosebumps prickled his skin.

'Show us that you still care,' urged Sketch. 'Do this. Say yes. And I guarantee if you perform well then we're back at the top. We're right back up there. It's this,' Sketch took a dramatic pause, 'or it's nothing.'

The inference was clear. Even Joan got it. Kevin had been thrown an ultimatum. Get flown out to Indonesia—or get dropped.

Kevin picked up the soggy card again. Beneath the summons was a list of six other VIPs. *Accompanying you will be...*

It was quite a selection. Maybe this was his chance. Maybe

this was where he got to put his stamp on the world, to do something meaningful, that mattered.

Take your place and make a difference.

He prayed for a difference to his own life. Get out of LA. Leave the fans. Leave the paps. Leave the commitments. Leave the airplane nightmares that roused him in a hot, sick sweat and had him reeling for days. Leave his mom. Leave Sketch.

Kevin was ready. Whatever was in store, it had to be better than this.

'Fine.' He hauled himself out of the water. 'When do we leave?'

22

London

Eve sat across the table from the father of her child. She said what she had to say and then she waited for his response. It was a long time coming.

'You're serious,' he said eventually, his fork hovering over a rare veal shank. Pink blood was leaking from the meat and staining his potatoes.

'I am.'

Orlando leaned back in his chair at The Ivy and wiped his mouth with his napkin. The waiter came to refill their glasses. The silence was brittle. Their date had been impromptu, a rare occasion for them to be out, but he had insisted. Maybe it was his way of making it up to her: take her for a meal, expensive food, expensive wine, buy her into forgetting, see if they could pick up where they left off…

'But I thought…' He stopped. 'Everything you said—'

'I'm not getting rid of this baby. I can't.'

Orlando's dark eyes were trained on the tablecloth.

'The other guy,' he said, 'are you still seeing him?'

The question, of all the questions he might have asked, took her by surprise. It was a second before she placed what he meant. That stupid lie she had thrown at him in her flat.

Cheap shots and petty vengeances—was that all they had become?

'No.'

He watched her. 'So where does this leave us?'

'Us?'

'We made this baby, didn't we?'

'It doesn't mean anything.'

Without warning he balled his napkin and slammed it onto the table. Heads turned, alert at the disturbance. Orlando leaned in, fighting to keep his voice down.

'Why does everything have to be so cold with you?'

'I'm not cold. I'm practical.'

'Then quit being practical for a second—don't you have feelings?'

Eve sipped her water. 'Feelings are what led me here in the first place. This isn't a decision I've taken lightly.'

'It isn't a decision I've had a say in at all.'

'Why should you have a say? We're not together.'

'You should have consulted me.'

'What would you have me do, Orlando?'

'Keep your voice down, for a start.'

'You wanted me to get an abortion, is that it?'

He flinched at the word. 'You inferred that was the plan.'

'I changed my mind.'

'Since when did you get rights to lock me in for the rest of my life?'

'Lock you in? Who's having this baby? Who's going to look after it every day, feed it, clothe it, hold it when it cries?'

'You, because you chose it.'

'Or you, because you *screwed* me?'

'And now you're screwing me.'

'Do me a favour and grow up. Aren't you some big-deal billionaire? Hotshot Director of the Board? I would have thought you knew how to deal with a crisis by now—if that's what this is. Sooner or later you're going to get sick of playing with Daddy's toys and want to realise something all yours, something that's more substantial than what money can buy. Wake up: this is it.'

She didn't mean it, but she hoped it stung.

'There's stuff going on with my family right now,' his voice was harsh, strained, 'stuff I haven't told you. I can't tell you. It's difficult.'

'When isn't it?'

'Everything's a riddle with you, Eve. Everything's about pushing me away.'

'You never said you wanted to be close.'

'Come on, I'm not a mind reader. We never tried. We never bridged the gap. That sort of thing takes—'

'Exactly. It would never work.'

Eve wasn't about to disclose her feelings about her own family. How every night she lay awake worrying she would recognise Terry Harley in her baby, and wouldn't be able to love it. But fear couldn't stop her. That would mean fear had won.

'It sounds like you've made your decision,' he said.

'You're not disagreeing.'

Orlando put his cutlery together.

'You barely touched it,' said Eve.

'I've lost my appetite.'

She looked down at her tummy, barely showing beneath a tailored silk blouse. Five months gone, the life inside her growing by the day. A baby. A world.

'This will change everything,' he said. 'It will change your life. And mine.'

'I'm sorry I didn't run it past you first.' She meant it sarcastically but, in saying it, heard what she should have done.

But what if he had tried to talk her out of it? What right had he to do that? Orlando didn't want this child so it was pointless.

'I don't require anything,' she said evenly. 'You'll concede you're in a good position financially so I would welcome a level of support, but as far as contact goes it's up to you. There's no obligation. I'm not going to force it.'

'And that's all you want?'

She met his gaze and held her nerve. 'I don't hold you to anything.'

Orlando shoved his plate away. 'I'm done.'

He got to his feet. As a parting shot, he threw out angrily: 'I cannot be associated with this child. Whatever you have to do, do it. I'll organise a transfer, but, as you say with such conviction, that's all. I don't wish to see it, or speak to it, or hear its name—and I forbid my name, or the Silvers name, to be connected to it, or to you, in any way. As far as the rest of the world knows, this child is nothing to me. Do you under-stand? This is your child. It's your responsibility. Not mine.'

'Fine. Just the way I want it.'

'And you always get your way, don't you?'

'You don't know the first thing about me.'

'I doubt anyone else does either. I hope you're less of a bitch to your child, Eve, or they might just turn out as fucked up as you are. Good night.'

Eve arrived home and slammed her keys onto the counter. She wanted to kick something, scream at someone, throw a chair at the wall. *Rich bastard!*

Why ever had she done it? Why had she slept with him? She must have been out of her mind. Orlando Silvers was an arrogant, fame-wrecked rich boy. She should have avoided him like the plague. She made her living from sussing these people, knowing what selfish mechanisms made them tick, so it shouldn't have come as a surprise. She had made the mistake of thinking one of them could break the mould.

How dare he say those things to her? What right had he to tell her what kind of a mother she'd be? Eve stood in the hall, breathing hard. She would prove him wrong.

Why? Who cares what he thinks?

But she did. Against all her reasoning, she did.

So fired up was she that she almost didn't see it, the envelope tucked inside the rest of her mail. Savagely she tore it open.

Eve Harley...invited to cover the trip of a lifetime...the biggest names for the biggest need...to faithfully report on the crisis and its repercussions...

Cane Enterprises. Eve didn't recognise the charity.

Absorbing the six accompanying names, she landed on Senator Mitch Corrigan. The tabloid had been chasing her for days. A politician who believed in little green men? A senator who was missing a sanity chip? A would-be president who thought ET was real? It was farcical. Outrageous. The story was sure to ruin him.

Corrigan would be sitting tight right now, praying Rossetti kept his mouth shut. This trip, a chance to spend time with the man himself, was the Holy Grail.

Kevin Chase, Jacob Lyle and Tawny Lascelles.

Her gaze rested on another. *Angela Silvers*: Orlando's sister. Eve resisted the urge to rip up the invitation—that or set fire to it.

She wanted nothing more to do with that family, now or ever.

She would sleep on it. Perhaps she would feel differently in the morning.

23

Milan

Applause rang in Tawny Lascelles' ears as she slinked off the catwalk and into the throng of the dressing room. Hearing the gallery gush their praise, Tawny mused on the point at which it had stopped being about the clothes and had started becoming about her. *She* was the attraction people had come to see. *She* would be the charm written about on tomorrow's blogs and in tomorrow's papers. *She* was the reason for a fashion show in the first place: the designers could suck on that and see.

She flopped into a chair. JP came rushing over, together with her hairdresser. Tawny released the knot on her head, her gold mane tumbling around her shoulders.

'Hot date,' she said. 'Do something radical.'

JP was proffering an envelope. 'This came for you. Marked private.'

Tawny snatched it. As she did so, she noticed her hairdresser heating up some Babyliss hair straighteners and screeched her objection.

'Excuse me, but what do you think you're doing? How many times do we have to go through it? *I will not be frazzled by any machinery other than my own!*'

On cue JP produced her engraved lemon-yellow tongs:

'TO THE FAIREST OF THEM ALL, WITH LOVE & ADMIRATION.'

'I—I'm sorry,' stumbled the hairdresser.

'You should be,' blasted Tawny. She would fire her tomorrow.

Taking a breath, she gathered herself. It wouldn't do to start kicking off when there were other models in the arena, fangs bared for the next opportunity to tear at some bitch-flesh. Tawny slid a nail down the seal of the black envelope and opened it.

She skimmed its contents and yawned.

'Another junket thingy,' she said, without reading it properly.

'I see Jacob Lyle's been invited,' commented JP, before Tawny's acid glance confirmed he had overstepped the mark. The mark was always a touch blurred with Tawny: some days she was his boss and some days she was his BFF. He was screwed if he knew what was coming. 'Sorry,' JP bumbled, 'it's none of my business.'

'You got that right.' Tawny snatched it back. 'So he has. How interesting.'

'Should we accept?'

A rival model drifted behind her, listening in. Tawny's pretty mouth pouted.

'I don't see why not,' she said loudly. 'Who doesn't want me for *something* or other these days? I can't say no to everything…'

'Especially when it's for a good cause.'

'For *such* a good cause,' agreed Tawny sweetly, in a voice better reserved for cooing over ickle-wickle kittens wearing bonnets and posing in a calendar. As soon as the model had passed, she tossed down the invitation and rolled her eyes. What a drag!

Although…

Jacob could be in for a good cause too, she decided, if he played his cards right. She smiled as the magic straighteners worked through her silky hair. Predictably he had been in touch, begging for some face-time. Her rejection had been swift. She intended to make him wait for it: he could do with a smack of discipline.

At least she had been truthful in the rebuff. She *had* started seeing someone new, and was damned if she was going to let Jacob think she was holding out on him.

The new man in question was red-hot in the sack, a croupier Tawny had seduced with ease on a recent jaunt to Vegas—or, rather, he had seduced her, trailing her all night before cornering her at the bar when he came off shift. Their exchange had been magnetic. Normally Tawny wouldn't have given the time of day to someone so far removed from her high-octane lifestyle, but the encounter was bizarre—it was as if he already *knew* her. Everything he said had been tailor-made, every compliment word-perfect. They had so much in common. No wonder they had ended up in bed that night, and every other night; and, shit, he was one of the most sensational fucks of her life! His cock was the size of the Washington Monument.

Minty Patrick joined them, an outfit slung over her arm. 'Aren't you headed home?' she asked, clocking the hairdresser at work.

Tawny raised an eyebrow. 'I'm meeting you-know-who.'

'You sure you know what you're doing?' Minty held the colour against her. 'He looks… I don't know, kinda *dangerous* to me.'

'What's wrong with dangerous?'

Minty lifted her shoulders. 'I don't trust him.'

'Whatever,' drawled Tawny, 'I like that he's rough round the edges. It's hot.'

'So long as you know you can handle it.'

Tawny bit the inside of her cheek. If Minty and JP knew how much she had been made to handle at the Rams & Rude Girls Dancing Bar, they would think twice before dishing out advice. She had seen it all! Fat, scrawny, coked-up and doped-down; those who wanted to hit or slap and those who wanted to sit on her lap, naked and weeping about their frigid wives or their flaccid cocks; those who required hourlong blowjobs, or wanted a thumb up their ass, or wanted to use dildos or handcuffs or leather contraptions; those who wanted to hurt and those who wanted to be hurt.

Nothing this new guy could throw at her would be any kind of surprise.

'I know what I'm doing,' she answered, thrusting the invite back to JP. 'Sort this,' she instructed. 'Clear my schedule for July.'

Tawny was determined not to think of the Rams…especially *that* client.

He had been a dark-eyed boy, thin, unsure, with an awkward stammer. She had been able to spot the virgins a mile off: those who came to rid themselves of that hated coil. But this client turned out to be the worst type of virgin, one who had no understanding of the female body or what caused it pleasure or pain.

The things the boy had asked to do…

'*Freak!*' she had yelled at him, and for the first time had struck the alarm.

The Rams boys had come running, hauling the weirdo off as he kicked and writhed in protest. His words stuck with her, that painful stutter:

'*I—I d-didn't mean it, p-p-p-please…*'

She felt no sympathy. Treating her like a plaything, a curiosity in a museum he could poke and prod for his entertainment. Then he had started talking about his dead mother, how he had never known a woman, and crying, crying so hard…

All the way out she had taunted him, trembling as she spat the words. She had joked about his body, his flimsy, stark white body and his cluelessness.

But at least the freak had given Tawny something. He had been the last straw, the final push she needed to get the hell out. Without him, she might never have left.

'All done,' ventured the hairdresser, replacing the lemon-yellow tongs.

'Good,' Tawny said. 'I'm outta here.'

'Have fun.' Minty smiled. 'Don't do anything I wouldn't do.'

Too late for that, thought Tawny, as she departed into the night.

24

San Francisco

Jacob listened as patiently as he could. He tried his best not to yell back at his partner because there was a whole office out there and did they want the world to know what they were up to? Goddamn Leith—if only he could keep his shit together.

'I don't freaking want them,' Leith Friedman said through clenched teeth, thrusting two solid gold watches into Jacob's hand and forcing him to stuff them in his pocket. 'It makes me feel like I'm part of the fucking KGB.'

Their friends in Russia had couriered the gifts to Leith's private address—a token between business partners. Leith was shaking, his glasses steamed up.

'Relax,' Jacob said, unconcerned. 'We're on terms. That's a good thing.'

'Is it? I don't want terms. I don't want hand-outs. I don't want anything.'

'Apart from twenty billion dollars,' Jacob muttered.

'This was your lead. You're the point of contact. Got it?'

For all his genius, Leith was an idiot sometimes. Jacob spent the next twenty minutes talking him down off the ledge.

But Leith was right about one thing: from here on in, Jacob was the port of call. Leith should continue to do what he did well, and that was code. Jacob strapped the watch to his wrist, only too happy to wear it: it was a handsome thing, and a pleasing reminder of the power now vested in him. What was a present between friends? He certainly had no objections.

Later that night, Jacob signalled the waiter and ordered another Armagnac. Whenever he came to the San Fran office they always seemed to wind up at The Red, the city's premier gay club. Jacob was relaxed enough in his sexuality not to care.

In any case, it was a sweet spot for picking up girls. The Red attracted straight, gay and everything in between, meaning the instant Jacob got recognised, chicks flocked like flies onto shit. He settled back on the couch, a blonde nibbling one ear while a busty brunette ran a hand down his chest and towards the ever-present bulge in his trousers. 'You're wild, you know that?' purred the blonde.

Jacob knocked back another. The girls squealed when he requested a magnum of Schramsberg—vodka chasers, too. He felt like getting wasted.

The afternoon had been capped by news of Tawny Lascelles' rejection. 'Thank you for your interest,' her PA had responded, after several voicemails had been left, a bouquet of peonies sent and even a diamond necklace that had cost Jacob more than his first ever Ferrari, as if he were enquiring after nothing more than a sale item that had run out of stock. 'Ms Lascelles is otherwise involved. We will notify you if this changes, if indeed Ms Lascelles returns your consideration.'

Returns your consideration? It was an outrage. Who the

fuck did she think she was? Women on every continent revered Jacob Lyle and now he had been made to feel like some second-rate jock doing all he could to bone the most popular cheerleader in school. It wouldn't be so bad if he could guarantee that Tawny—sorry, *Ms* Lascelles—hadn't been made aware of his intentions, but he felt sure given her stinking attitude and cool appraisal that she had taken great pleasure in this denial.

Now she was shagging around? There was a surprise. Tawny was the dime-a-dip bicycle of the fashion circuit. It never occurred to Jacob that he was precisely the same thing, because surely you needed tits for that.

After a spot of detective work he found she had hooked up with some croupier she had brought home as a souvenir from Vegas. What did that guy have that Jacob didn't? Fuck all was the answer.

Jeez, who *hadn't* had Tawny Lascelles?

He hadn't, and it pissed him the hell off.

'You wanna skip this joint?' the brunette purred. 'We're sisters, y'know…'

As the trio staggered out of The Red, Jacob spotted a face he knew, registering even through his drunken fog because the face was out of kilter. A well-known face, and it shouldn't have been there—one of Donald Silvers' sons, Gianluca, yeah, that was his name. The guy was partying amid a circle of admiring males. Jacob hadn't known he was gay. He wouldn't mind banging that sister Angela though.

Outside, the BMW was humming. The girls were on him like a rash all the way back. One of them sealed the privacy screen, whipped his cock out and embarked on a frantic and for the most part unerotic hand job. Jacob encouraged her to turn her attentions to the blonde. Within seconds both girls were topless, fondling and licking each other, and now the blonde was on his dick and this time it was slower, softer, her palms cupping his balls. He lay back, transfixed, and let them make him come.

It was a blur getting out of the car and up to the bedroom, his suit pants half done up. A truck drove past and the brunette flashed her breasts, giggling as Jacob bundled her inside. There was a package in the hall from his assistant, with a scribbled note: MAIL FROM OFFICE. He tore it open, the girls shedding his clothes, and discarded a heap of junk, including the photograph he had promised to sign for a fan who had won his company at the Boston gala: a cute redhead who had flirted with him the entire meal, let him squeeze her tits and then refused to put out.

The black envelope piqued his interest. He opened it.

'Come along, big boy,' whispered the blonde, enticing him upstairs. 'You got any candy cane? We're gonna go all night…'

The gold lettering swam before his eyes. Jacob squinted at it, swaying slightly on the stairwell, and started to laugh. What was this, some big party? With Kevin Chase and fat old Senator Corrigan and that evil Brit reporter everyone hated…?

And…

Jacob peered closer, just as the brunette grabbed his tie and yanked him towards the bedroom. There was her name, embossed, the forbidden fruit:

Tawny Lascelles.

She of the long legs, cute ass and dirty lip…

Tossing the invite aside, he flung the sisters onto the sheets and ripped off their clothes, stripping them naked and wrenching their legs apart. A pair of perfectly trimmed muffs, one fair, one dark, greeted him. Checking surreptitiously that the tiny red light was steadily blinking in the corner of the room, Jacob dipped his head to each in turn until they melted like ice cream on his tongue.

The party was a done deal.

Tawny was going—and in that case so was he.

25

The Midwest

There was no question that Mitch Corrigan would accept the invitation.

If he didn't escape soon, he would suffocate.

Standing in the office of his sumptuous aristocratic-style manor, Mitch put his hands in his pockets. Melinda had loved this place on sight but it would never feel like home to him. How could it? Since the night of the event—August 4, 2012: it would be forever scorched onto his memory—he could regard it as nothing but an elaborate trap. They had found him: it didn't matter if it was in a castle or a crap-hole.

Mitch's study walls were plastered with photographs. Snaps of his time as a movie star seemed an important reminder at least from his wife's point of view, and a gallery of famous directors and producers adorned the space. Mitch frowned in at his own face, searching for a clue. It was like looking at the image of a dead person.

One picture caught his eye and held it. It had been at the start of the political campaign and they had been testing the waters with a string of appearances. This was a workshop at a secondary school: ten years ago now? Mitch had lectured the kids on Great American Opportunities, the Land Where Dreams Came True.

He hadn't thought of the boy in years.

Now, in the background of the photograph, he absorbed the tall, dark-eyed vision, standing apart from the rest of the group. Heard the boy's trembling stammer.

Something about him was ghostly. So set aside was he that he appeared superimposed, incongruous, the kid who didn't belong...

The sound of Melinda's footsteps in the hallway made him jump.

Glossy as a Barbie doll, preened and primed as a prize greyhound, Melinda Corrigan was the model Senator's Wife. She would be the model First Lady.

'Are you ready?' she asked curtly. 'The babysitter's arrived.'

Mitch nodded. Friday night and the bi-annual Stewarts Dinner had assailed them again. The ritual, at its heart a competition between the women for which could out-chef the other, was hosted in turn between Mandy and Melinda. Mitch's part was to guffaw at his neighbour Gary's jokes while comparing notes on lawnmowers and whether or not Gary should install a gym in his garage.

'You're dragging your heels over the presidency bid,' Melinda said on the way over. Of course, he should have known she would go straight for the jugular.

'We're working on it.' He lifted a hand to smooth his toupee.

'Especially after that embarrassment on *America Tonight*.' Her heels scissored the drive. 'I bet Oliver's thanking God you got the summons to Salimanta.'

Mitch preferred not to consider his disastrous appearance

with Jerry Gersham. Oliver's ministrations had been kind, but not without sharp edges.

Throughout the Stewarts' meal his wife ate without appetite, her tight pink mouth lacerating tiny forkfuls and her eyes trained miserably on the table. Mitch, too, was struggling to swallow the elaborate smorgasbord. Mandy's melting cheese balls sat like lumps of coal in his stomach. Gary droned on, quaffing beer after beer.

'Melinda, that *is* a pretty dress,' commented Mandy, dolloping more fish tartare onto Mitch's plate. 'Very…figure-hugging.'

'Oscar de la Renta,' said Melinda through pursed lips.

'Marked down?'

'Oh no… But, darling, did I see your shoes on the sale rail at TJ Maxx?'

And so on. The only merciful thing about conversing with Gary was that Gary rarely asked a jot about politics. With his bulging biceps and blank expression, Mitch's neighbour sailed through life without worrying about much except where his next protein shake was coming from. A threatened revision of gun laws, or, as Gary put it, 'those chumps taking a dump on my constitutional rights', was the only topic in which he took any interest. Gary had several shotguns scattered about the house, something Mandy found 'so manly'—and here Melinda would shoot her husband a caustic glance—and deemed the protection of his homestead a top priority.

'How are the kids?' Mandy asked Melinda, presenting a platter of satay chicken before retracting it with an, 'Oops! Not if we're watching our weight…'

'Fine,' threw back Melinda. 'This house must be so quiet without any of your own. You know, for all the hassle I wouldn't trade it for the world—the mess, the noise, the laughter, someone to care for you when you're old...'

Mandy glanced away, tears in her eyes. Delicately, Melinda put her cutlery together, the food scooped cleverly to one side and buried beneath a serviette.

As Gary steered the conversation onto safer ground, Mitch looked grimly around the table. Suburbia: the graveyard of America. People going about their lives like androids. As if a chip was removed, as if the community had been lobotomised. The planet was being colonised, one unsuspecting neighbourhood at a time.

It was how he knew that Veroli was no hoax.

Signor Rossetti's arrest confirmed it. That was how conspiracy worked. Cover the truth, conceal the prize, tell the world it was nonsense—but Mitch knew the truth.

Was Mitch's name safe? Rossetti and his wife were the only people who knew he had been there. He had to pray it was. If this ever got out, he was better off dead.

Afterwards, at home, Melinda went straight to bed.

Close to midnight Mitch joined her. His wife lay next to him, stiff as a board. He was about to drift into uneasy slumber when, with a sinking heart, he perceived her moving across the mattress towards him. She began to kiss his back, slowly moving lower... Mitch tensed. His dick twitched, disorientated, as if being woken from a long dormancy. They hadn't touched each other since Washington.

'Let's try, Mitch,' she whispered. 'Please, let's try...' Her touch explored. It was on his ass now, squeezing his buttock. Her hand dipped inside his nightshirt. He could feel her nails on his bare skin. Her breath quickened as she fingered the trail of hair running from the small of his back into the crevice between his cheeks.

In a flash she was there, applying the slightest pressure to the place that had been violated—before, like a toxic worm, she wriggled inside.

Mitch yelped in shock and bounced from the bed.

'You used to like it!' Melinda cried desperately.

Staggering blindly, he bolted from the room.

They craved his ass! They craved it just as they had craved it last time. When they had hovered above his house and filled his bedroom with sickly green light, and next he knew he'd been powerless to move, laid face down on a cold hard slab, their strange shapes looming and their long fingers pointing, and then…

Their probes, rising from beneath…

Mitch reeled down the hall. Inside the guest suite, he slammed the door, backing up against the wall, anything to keep his ass out of sight.

Whimpering, he sank to the floor.

It was hours before he got any sleep.

Melinda waited until three a.m. It was torture, the nagging sensation demanding to be sated. In the house opposite, Gary's light was still on.

Bingo.

She padded across the courtyard. A sliver of gold escaped from beneath the patio shutters. Gary was waiting. Silently, he led her to the downstairs bathroom.

'Screw me,' Melinda instructed, once the door was closed. 'Right now.'

Gary didn't need to be asked twice. It was their usual role-play, the thrill of each other's bodies matched only by that of being discovered. Melinda arranged herself against the sink, her ass against the porcelain bowl with its neat rows of Lancôme soaps and Elizabeth Arden hand creams, and hitched up her silk robe. Her breath came tangled in short, desperate gasps. 'Take me,' she begged. 'Do it hard!'

Gary's mouth slammed against hers, his tongue tracing her teeth. She fumbled into his pyjamas and freed his eager dick. It was smaller than her husband's, but was stiff to bursting, the thick shaft pumping through her hands as she worked him into a sweat. She felt no guilt. She never had, even the first time. Mitch had shown her no interest in months: they were acquaintances these days, enduring a marriage of convenience. She had toughened her heart against it. No more tears.

Peeling off her gown, Melinda revealed the nipple-less negligee she had shopped for that morning. Gary's hungry grin descended on the peepholes, lapping like a kitten as his fingers searched below, up her quivering thighs and towards her drenched heat. At once he was on his knees, his tongue exploring the place between Melinda's legs that had been shut to these attentions for so long she feared it might have been cobwebbed. She ground against his lips, squealing as his tongue dissolved inside her, grabbing and pulling tufts of his hair as she fought half-heartedly to stifle her moans. Lace ripped as it met the angle of her knees. Gary grabbed one ankle and planted it on his shoulder, her slipper skating off and falling down his back.

'Hurry,' she rasped, 'we haven't got long…'

Obligingly he lifted her and turned her to the wall. Melinda's breasts crushed against the cool bathroom tiles and Gary reached to tear what little material there was still covering her. A moment's pause, the proficient slit of a packet, before he plunged victoriously into her, his palms gripping and lifting her pert white butt as he marvelled at how yielding she was, so unlike his neurotic wife who slept listening to 'Sounds of the Rainforest' and wearing a facemask and just as well a cage around her privates.

Melinda began to shriek, prompting Gary to slam a hand across her mouth, which she bit and gasped against, thrashing out her pleas for him to ride her faster, deeper, harder. She clutched the rim of the basin, watching the bathroom door and almost praying Mitch would open it; that he would witness her like this, with Gary, naked and wanton and still all woman! What would he do? What would he say?

The thought of it made her come. 'I'm there!' she garbled, smothered by her lover's hand. In an explosion she fell against the wall. Gary climaxed in tandem, pulsing through her, his shuddering chest hot and sticky as it sank against her back.

It was an efficient exchange. Gary pulled up his pants. Melinda corrected her nightie and fastened her robe. She smoothed her hair.

Gary went to reopen the patio doors. In a moment, she would follow. For now it gave her pleasure to stand in Mandy's bathroom, surveying her enemy's anti-ageing face products and miniature bottle of prescription Xanax. Melinda consulted herself in the mirror. She appeared flushed and healthy, easily ten years younger. Her kind of anti-ageing was a different cream altogether. He waved her through.

A brief kiss and she prowled back to the mansion.

26

Venice

Celeste Cavalieri received her envelope a week later. She was surprised that anyone should have obtained the Venice address, since she kept it private. She was returning from the *mercato* when accosted by the elderly lady who lived downstairs.

'*Per voi, senora*,' said the woman, holding out a letter.

'*Grazie. Mi scusi.*' Celeste thanked her and hurried upstairs.

Inside the apartment, Carl was waiting. Celeste's heart plummeted. Her boyfriend was short, his skin pockmarked from a youthful bout of acne. His cropped hair was slick. Annoyance glowed in his eyes like the embers of a dying fire.

'Where have you been?'

'I told you,' she said. 'To the market.'

He consulted his watch. 'For an hour?'

'It's raining. I got held up.'

For a second she thought he was going to hit her, but at the last moment he reached behind her and locked the apartment door. 'What's that?' he said.

She gripped the black and gold envelope. 'Nothing.'

'Let me see.'

'It's addressed to me.'

'I said let me see.'

She passed it over. Carl's thumb tore the seal and a card slid out. He read it.

'What does it say?' she asked, as he folded the card out of sight.

'Property agents.' He was lying.

'Can I look?'

'You don't believe me?'

'Of course I do.' She swallowed. 'It's just I want to look.'

'We don't always get what we want, Celeste.'

She shouldn't push it. All the warning signs were there. The way Carl's voice jumped a couple of notes; the muscle that twitched in his neck. He didn't try to be cruel; it was that she made him be cruel. He didn't mean it when he lost his temper.

He went to the trash can, opened the lid and tore the letter into quarters.

Celeste charged towards him. He caught her wrists. His aftershave was strong, catching the back of her throat, and a fleck of spittle flew in her eye.

'When are you going to listen to what I say?' he breathed, grabbing a clump of hair and pulling hard so she screamed in pain. He pushed her head down to the stove. *Click-click-click* and the ignition lit. Blue flames sprang up close to her face.

'Let go!' she managed. 'Please! Let me go.'

'You know I have to teach you these lessons, don't you?'

'Yes.'

'You know you give me no choice.'

'Yes.'

'You know you have to learn, and this is for your own good.'

'I know.'

He released her. She stumbled back from the flames, hands to her eyes, and the tears rushed quick and strong, but she held them in with all her might.

'I'm glad that's settled,' said Carl. He flicked on the kettle. 'Aren't you?'

He went to bed. Their altercations drained him, he said.

Celeste peeled off cold clothes and towelled her hair. She dragged on an over-sized wool sweater and curled up at the window to watch the deluge.

From here she could glimpse the Rialto Bridge, its stone passage mottled and dank. How she loved Venice: it was her refuge, a maze of concealed spaces, attics and cellars, shadows and shuttered rooms and places to hide, the city its own island, cut adrift from the world. Today, it was awash with rain. When the weather turned, it became a labyrinth submerged, the canals running high, the cobbled streets seething with tourists and the café awnings battered by the downpour. Rushing across the Piazza San Marco had been like skating on a liquid rink. Pigeons scattered from the silver ground and the dimmed glitter of the basilica shone molten in the pools.

This was the closest thing she had to home. Growing up, her parents had been eternal nomads, her French mother an artist, her Italian father a dealer, and neither contented with staying in one place. Friends were left behind and schools abandoned.

She had met Carl almost six years ago now, when he moved into her building. Whenever she returned from a trip she would find flowers waiting, a bottle of wine or a box of pralines—and then, on one occasion, an invitation to dinner. Carl had taken her to the Riva degli Schiavoni where they had eaten mussels and drank champagne.

Celeste hadn't felt the electricity other women talked about, but after years of believing she deserved to be alone, Carl's attention paid an unexpected dividend. Besides, love, proper love, seemed a risk too great and precarious; to adore someone utterly when, in a heartbeat, they could be snatched away. She should know.

At first, Carl treated her like a queen. But, as the weeks passed, his behaviour changed. He lost his job, was evicted from his apartment and slowly tightened his hold. He would explode at her for leaving a glass out. If she failed to arrange the cupboards in the way he liked, he would yell at her until her ears rang. Then came the first time he hit her: when she kicked off a pair of heels by the door and he tripped on them, spraining his ankle. After that, things got worse. Carl slapped her for the tiniest thing. He called her a stupid bitch, an ugly thief—and she regretted telling him her secrets because when things got bad he called her a murderer. Celeste could handle everything he threw at her, but not that.

Celeste stood. She eyed the trash can, listening for Carl. A footstep at a time, she approached and lifted the lid. She had to scramble for the last quarter, but finally she found it. Piecing it together, she read. *Tawny Lascelles... Mitch Corrigan...*

Salimanta. Indonesia. The crisis.

The invitation cited she had been summoned as 'an asset'.

Celeste flipped back through the years. Yes, she had visited this place before. She had valued an item for the Salimantan vice president at one of his homes.

Cane Enterprises. Dimly she recognised the name, a door in her memory creaking open on rusty hinges. Where from? How did she know it? *Cane...*

And how had they discovered where she lived?

Celeste held the card to her chest, concentrating. Rain

lashed fast and feverish against the windowpanes. Somewhere far off, a girl shrieked.

On impulse, she scribbled down the return email.

The group would leave on June 29. Three weeks, it promised, on the other side of the world. She wouldn't have to tell Carl, she could just board the flight without breathing a word.

Three weeks away from him, no email, no phone, no contact.

Celeste twisted the stolen bracelet on her wrist.

She felt the skin beneath, naked and vulnerable.

There was a storm coming.

27

Boston

The sky was slate and dense with rain. A dull wind blew through the trees. Donald Silvers' mourners were shadows against a bank of brooding churchyard firs.

Angela stood by her mother at the grave. Isabella's shoulders were stiff against the cold, her head bowed to hide her stricken face. Thunder growled.

'*The souls of the righteous are in the hands of God...*'

Donald's coffin was lowered. Words were said, empty shapes that swam over Angela like fog on a still lake. They could never achieve what she needed them to.

'You OK, baby?' Dino murmured, fumbling to take her hand.

She slipped from her fiancé's touch. The question was inane. Of course she wasn't OK—whose funeral was he at? It pissed her off that he had even come in the first place.

Last night he had tried to comfort her. She had been shocked at his arrival at the house, and at how greasy his attempts to slide into her family's grief. Instead of having the eve of the funeral to lament the loss of the man who had raised her, she had been forced to spend it fending off the one she had psychotically agreed to marry.

She had to be strong. She had done the right thing: for her father, for her family, for her. Through all this, that was the rope she clung to. It gave her comfort to know she was keeping their kingdom afloat, but, for all her life applying herself to this end, nothing could sweeten its bizarre reality. She quashed misgivings that it had all been a mistake: losing Noah, signing her life to Vegas, taking Dino's hand, a man she scarcely knew and who wanted more than she was prepared to give...

But now there was no turning back.

The Silvers' fortune had already been channelled into the Zenetti Group. It would remain under Carmine Zenetti's charge until the wedding day. Once the ring was safely on Angela's finger, their combined assets would be freshly divided under the terms of the contract. Angela was a walking, talking insurance policy. Until she made it down the aisle and accepted Dino as her husband, her family had nothing.

'*The righteous, though they die early, will be at rest...*'

Across the congregation, Luca's red-rimmed eyes were hard on the ground. Her brother deserved his guilt. The night Donald passed, they had tried repeatedly to contact him, but Luca couldn't be found: he was out partying, like he was every other night of the damn week. Things were going to have to change if they had any chance of extricating themselves from the Zenettis. For that was what Angela planned—and that was what she would spend every waking hour battling to achieve. If she could grow, she could buy her way out of Dino—but she needed her brothers' help.

The congregation joined in a response, that joyless vibration particular to funerals, and though Angela had been raised a Catholic she found religion, expressly in death, hard to reconcile. '*If I should walk in the valley of darkness, no evil would I fear, for you are with me...*' She didn't like the idea that she should be cast upon the mercy of another, judged against a set of rules that seemed to allow for no shades of grey. Take her marriage to Dino: it spelled dishonesty in the worst way, a sacred bond used for financial ends, and yet hadn't she been martyred by the deed?

Who decided what was right? Who cast judgement on her soul?

If she had sinned, what would be served as her punishment?

'*Then the Lord God will wipe away the tears from all faces...*'

She hoped that someone, somewhere, was looking out for them.

Back at the house, Isabella retired to her bedroom. She wasn't able to read the messages of condolence and so Angela set about filing them away. Flipping through the cards, one alone stood out. Noah Lawson had sent lilies, along with the note:

I'm sorry.

The sight of his name plucked a fragile string. It was the first correspondence that had gone between them since the theatre. Angela had replayed that painful encounter myriad times, rewriting it in her mind, wishing she had said everything differently, wishing she had kissed him again, wishing for another outcome, wishing she had held on tight and never let go.

She had to let go. It was survival.

Noah was her past. Dino was her future. She had committed to this contract and she was a woman of her word. Her heart would always bleed for the life that might have been, but it must do so quietly and invisibly, and never give itself away.

I'm sorry.

The card was not addressed to any one name. Who was Noah sorry for? Her mother? Them all? Was he sorry for Donald's death, or for the way it had ended between them, the words that were said, the mistakes they had made?

Angela put the flowers in a vase. She wanted to run. She wanted to escape. Vegas, Carmine, Dino—the trio stood at her shoulder, frightening and oppressive. Wherever she chose, wherever she went to, she knew that they would follow.

Except...

She turned. On the mantelpiece, the mysterious invitation remained: she hadn't imagined it. It had come through that morning. All other deliveries had been visions in pink and white, cream and blue, yellow ribbons and peach paper—and yet here it was, bold and undeniable, a black and gold envelope addressed solely to her.

Go, it urged. *Get as far away from here as you can.*

As soon as Angela had read it, she knew she would say yes.

It was the distance she needed. It wasn't here, or in Vegas, or with Dino.

When she returned from this trip, she would be over Noah Lawson. She would put him from her mind and train her ambition and her energies on what lay ahead.

She would be ready to embrace the life and career she had always longed for.

Three weeks. Six companions. A charitable cause...

What was the worst that could happen?

28

Szolsvár Castle, Gemenc Forest, Hungary

It was the first time in months that Voldan Cane had ventured outside.

Janika wheeled him onto the castle terrace. Ahead, the dark, dense forest was a smudged wall of green. Milky daylight strained through the mists that hung like a veil on the horizon. Szolsvár's gardens stretched for half a mile, the once disciplined and cared-for plots now overgrown and wild with neglect. Weeds throttled the soil.

On the balustrade, a crow cawed, black as night. Voldan manoeuvred his chair so he could look at it. Its liquid feathers gleamed ominously, its orange beak sharp and its eyes twitching. With a heavy flap of wings, it plummeted out of sight.

Voldan breathed the new dawn. In lands far from here his wicked plan was in action. It was sweet to picture the missives arriving at their destinations, the words he had considered with such care, for each recipient a different text that resounded with them directly. Be it conscience, image recovery, career advancement or sheer goodwill, Voldan felt certain that of the seven invitations sent, seven would accept.

Seven of the planet's most powerful people, eradicated overnight.

Would they repent? Would they beg for forgiveness? It would make no difference. Seven icons, missing presumed dead, in the worst private jet disaster in the history of aviation. Voldan turned to the surfeit of news screens, erected across a wall, a flashing hive from around the globe. He couldn't wait to see them spring to life.

His first step had been to trace a way in—how to plot the crash, to make it appear an accident, and to vouch it could never be traced back to Szolsvár. Tawny Lascelles had bitten like a worm on a hook. The model's latest lover, on the face of it a Vegas croupier, was in fact one of the city's deadlier thugs. He belonged to Voldan, had been paid to find Tawny and seduce her. Voldan's fortune could buy things people hadn't dreamed up yet: it acquired contacts beyond the realm of the ordinary.

'Mr Cane?' Janika appeared in the doorway.

'Come!' he instructed in his reedy monotone. 'So I can see you.'

The maid obeyed. Her mousy hair was plastered to her forehead, the quibble of loose flesh that hung from her chin shivering with exertion. She had spent all morning scrubbing the Great Hall floor. Voldan had commanded it be done.

'I am finished,' Janika said.

'Can you see your face in it?' came the robotic, mechanised response.

'Yes, Mr Cane.'

'You are lying to me.'

'No, no, I'm not—'

'*You lie!*'

The wheelchair lurched forward, ramming into Janika's

legs. She cried out, clutching her shin. Last time, Janika had fibbed on the matter, believing her boss to be incapable of checking, but by angling the mirror on his armrest Voldan had been able to prove her wrong. She had deceived him—and worse, she had underestimated him.

Although Voldan had inflicted no physical punishment, the weight of his disapproval hung heavy as a cross. Even in his withered state, Janika loved him as a husband. She took care of him, she bathed him, she dressed him and she fed him. It was impossible not to grow close. Not that she could ever confess her true feelings...

Sometimes, when Voldan fell prey to one of his fleshly urges, Janika could expel just a fraction of her passion. But that hadn't happened in weeks.

'I will do it again, Mr Cane,' she begged. 'Please! Let me clean it again!'

She scuttled off indoors.

Alone, Voldan calmed himself. So restricted was his movement that he was occasionally forced to lash out. Right now he wanted nothing more than to leap from the chair and stretch his legs—athletic as they used to be, not the crumpled sticks that brought him such despair—and run, run, run like the wind, across the lawns, through the bracken, down to the river and into the woods. He wanted to fling his arms wide and embrace the trees, the sky, to shout out his joy with the voice he used to own...

But here he was, still trapped in this device: a sitting, squatting corpse.

As soon as this project was completed, he would be demanding of Janika the ultimate sacrifice: to do away with this useless, broken shell once and for all.

Grigori...

Would his son be watching when the plane went down?

Would he be watching as they gasped their last breaths, as they drowned in a dark and freezing ocean?

Angela Silvers, bitch heiress. Kevin Chase, child star, pop prince, thief. Eve Harley, devil-sent hack with a soul of steel. Tawny Lascelles: supermodel, seductress, slut. Mitch Corrigan, coward, dictator, ultimate fake. Jacob Lyle, cutthroat capitalist. And Celeste Cavalieri: the heartless, coldblooded killer.

All had shown their cards. All marked tombstones in the path of Grigori's torment. Once they were removed, at last his son could be free.

'Mr Cane?'

Voldan's thumb activated the stick on his armrest, rotating his chair to the door.

Janika held her arms out. 'It is all done now. Are you hungry?'

With a malicious grin, Voldan trundled up to her.

All of a sudden he had a brilliant appetite.

29

New York

While Tawny Lascelles was in the bathroom, the man achieved his final task. He located the payload without difficulty: Tawny never went anywhere without it.

He inserted the device, a timer and thermostat, and set it, consulting his watch to confirm the date and hour. He checked it, checked it, and checked it again.

This was no practice run. This was the real deal.

The man worked smoothly and quickly. In the adjacent room the shower ran steady, her voice singing a tune beneath the hammering water. He gave no thought to her as a person. She was a target. He could have sex with her, laugh with her, kiss her, all the things lovers did, and never feel a thing.

His instructions were simple, as all the best were. When schemes got over-complicated, that was when fuck-ups happened. There would be no fuck-ups.

Tomorrow, Tawny would fly to Jakarta to meet her party of doomed VIPs. He gave no regard to those, either. They were names on a list, bullseyes, nothing more.

At Jakarta, they would board their jet. No official would challenge them. No handler would check the luggage. No security would forbid the gas canister inside Tawny's precious hair straighteners and instruct her to remove them.

To do so would be an insult. These celebrities lived by different rules. Rules that would cost them their lives…

The man could picture it now.

Halfway through the flight, the timer activates: it is a soundless omen, the bringer of the end. The straighteners start to heat, setting alight to materials, first to Tawny's clothes and then to her companions', a licking flare and then a galloping fire, devouring all in its path. In the cockpit, the cargo alarm sounds.

The pilots don't have time to panic; they have trained for this. Extinguishers are triggered in the hold. *Remain calm*, they tell themselves, *keep control*.

There is less than seventeen minutes before the hull is a loss.

Emergency descent procedures begin. Altitude evaporates as the jet falls through the sky. The captain terminates the oxygen supply. Smoke and fumes fill the cabin. The passengers are unable to make sense of it through their terror.

Ditching briefs begin. They are going to land in water.

The aircraft drops to sea level, slowing in a last attempt at salvation. Maybe there is hope. Maybe they will survive. Maybe their prayers are heard.

Maybe there is a God.

Maybe not…

Panic erupts. The fuel tanks at the wings ignite. Smoke flounders from the rear. The plane decelerates and the cockpit collapses, killing both pilots on impact.

Unmanned, the stricken craft pitches and yaws, rolling to its demise in the cold, cold dark, plunging deep into the purple night ocean, and then gone.

After that there is nothing. Silence. Still. Objective complete.

Drawing himself back to the present, the man checked his work a final time, calmly replaced the yellow straighteners and resumed his post on the bed.

He gazed up at the ceiling, and blinked.

Tawny emerged with a towel wrapped around her waist. She let it fall to the floor. Her body was golden, perfectly proportioned, and it seemed almost a shame that in less than twenty-four hours it would be lost and bloated on the sea floor.

'So…' she teased, coming to join him, 'are you going to miss me?'

30

Jakarta

Angela Silvers was fifth to arrive. Her flight from the States had been long and turbulent and she was relieved to reach the safety of the VIP suite at Jakarta.

Four of her companions were already there.

'Jeez, Mom,' Kevin Chase was muttering, 'as if I've never gone away before!' He was tapping at his phone, a violet baseball cap yanked down over his ears. His mother was fussing, patting his rucksack and suitcase to make sure he had everything.

'Hello, Kevin,' said Angela. 'Good to see you again.'

'Hey.' Kevin deigned to toss her a cracked, insincere smile—an aloof reception given he was clad in thousands of dollars'-worth of Silvers gear.

'I'm Joan,' said the woman, compensating with an obsequious handshake that, at the last minute, flattened into a curtsey. 'It's a privilege.'

Sketch Falkner, whom Angela had met at several industry events, was grappling with a miniature dog. The dog was wearing the same cap as Kevin's.

'He'll be fine once he gets there,' said Sketch, giving the pop star a playful slap on the shoulder. The slap could have been gentler, Angela thought.

Joan simpered, 'I know he's used to all this, but a mom can't stop caring...'

'JESUS!' Kevin exploded, with a scowl that chewed his eyes up almost completely. 'DO YOU HAVE TO BE SO FUCKING EMBARRASSING?'

'We'll look after each other,' said Angela kindly, thinking Kevin's screw-you attitude wouldn't welcome the slightest bit of looking after. The Kevin Chase the world knew was a spoiled teen tyrant. Every day, a new story got splashed across the web: Kevin smoking dope outside a police station, Kevin drinking too much and ploughing the rear end of his Escalade into a mini-mart, Kevin shouting obscenities from a hotel window and flashing his tiny white ass over the balcony...

She felt sorry for him. This was his life. Everybody wanted fame but fame was only tolerable if you knew how to handle it, and that meant preserving some iota of privacy, whatever the cost. No one had told this to Kevin, and so Kevin didn't know.

As Angela moved to greet the senator, she heard Sketch mutter, 'Now you're *sure* you have enough pills?' and Kevin's yapped, exasperated response.

Mitch Corrigan was casual in slacks and a shirt, a regular all-American golf dad, but his handshake was tense. 'And this is my wife, Melinda.'

A shrewdly assembled blonde extended fingers heavy with rings, palm down, as if she expected Angela to kiss the back of her hand. Angela cradled the limp offering in hers, a lifeless paddle. Melinda seemed to be only half there, gazing off into the distance and thinking, quite clearly, of something or someone else.

Mitch's smile was rigid. 'Not a great flyer,' he admitted. 'You?'

'Hate it.'

'They call it luxury but, jeez, these light aircraft rock about like crazy…'

Angela preferred not to consider the crossing to Salimanta. 'It'll be tough seeing the wreckage,' she said instead. 'All those people…all those lives. It's awful.'

Mitch seemed to think that should have been his line, instead of complaining about their lavish transport. 'If we can do anything to help,' he put in, 'right?'

An attractive woman joined them. Immediately the senator turned away. His abrupt departure struck Angela as odd for a man so versed in greeting new faces, and she wondered if he and infamous news-hound Eve Harley had locked horns in the past. It wouldn't be the first time the reporter had pissed off someone important.

'Hi,' she said, 'I'm Eve. Good to finally meet you.'

Finally seemed an odd choice of word.

'I know Orlando,' she explained. Eve had the inquisitor's manner of making a statement into a leading question, as if Angela should already know this information.

But Angela was surprised. 'You do?'

'Yes.' Eve looked as if she had been expecting a different response, and was relieved not to get it. 'He and I have met, a few times actually. You don't look alike.'

'That's the nicest thing I've heard all day.'

They smiled at each other. Angela knew straight away that Eve was pregnant, even though her bump wasn't yet obvious. The reporter's auburn hair and bright-green eyes gave her a likeable girl-next-door appeal, and Angela identified something else there, too: an edge of steeliness, of defiance, something not unlike herself.

'I didn't know about Donald,' said Eve. 'Not until it came out. I'm sorry.'

'Thanks.'

Angela didn't want to dwell on it, least of all accept pity.
She nodded across the room to where a dark-haired woman
was sitting alone. The woman was absorbed in her Kindle. A
thick fringe obscured her features.

'Celeste Cavalieri?' she presumed.

'That's right,' said Eve. 'She price tags for the super-
elite—art, jewellery, antiques. She's quite the enigma.
Doesn't talk much.'

'I doubt there'll be much work where we're going,' said
Angela drily.

'I did wonder when I saw her name. She's not like the rest
of you.'

'The rest of us?'

'Celebrities.' Eve smiled.

Angela laughed. 'Right…'

'Don't ask me, I'm just here to write it up.'

'And what a job that must be.'

'Like you wouldn't believe.'

Angela went over to the Italian and introduced herself.
'How was your flight?'

'Uneventful.' Celeste's accent was strong.

'Where in Italy are you from?'

'All over.'

'My mother's Sicilian,' offered Angela, wishing Celeste
would make eye contact. 'It's a great country. I don't get back
as often as I'd like.'

Celeste nodded, quickly returning to her tablet. Angela
couldn't decide if she was shy, or rude, or possibly both, and
so it was a relief when the door burst open and admitted their
penultimate member. The playboy had arrived.

'Well, hey,' said Jacob Lyle, cocky as ever, as he let an
enormous bag slip off his shoulder.

Kevin leaped to attention. Celeste glanced up briefly.

Angela remembered from society functions that Jacob was tactile to say the least, so it came as no surprise when he strode over and embraced her, giving her waist a light squeeze just to make sure. Jacob had propositioned Angela in the past, on more than one occasion. The temptation had never been there. He had bedded more women than she could count, and his attitude, while fun in small doses, was rooted in what she suspected was a nest of severely tangled morals.

'Where's the lucky guy, then?'

She didn't connect.

'Your fiancé?' He smiled. 'Hey, if you wanna forget he exists then that's fine by me.'

'Never going to happen, Jacob.'

'What? It's an innocent question.'

'Like hell it is. Dino couldn't come.' In fact, her betrothed had pushed so hard to accompany her that in the end she'd fibbed about her flight time just to get away.

'How you doin', man?' Kevin was quick to ingratiate himself, clapping Jacob on the back and grinning like he'd just met his hero. 'Didn't you get my calls?'

Jacob appeared taken aback by this best-buddy display but, to his credit, went with it. 'Yeah, er, sorry we didn't hook up yet, you know how things get…'

'Sure do!' said Kevin desperately.

Seamlessly the entrepreneur turned to Eve, raking her with his eyes. 'Hello,' he said. 'I'm Jacob.'

'I don't believe I've had the pleasure.'

'All you gotta do is ask.'

'Eve Harley,' replied the journalist coolly.

'Your reputation precedes you.'

'So does yours—I'm not interested.'

'Ouch.'

A final voice joined them. 'Sorry, sorry, they had to close Duty Free!' Tawny Lascelles' lilting pitch carried through the lounge, a burgeoning LV suitcase trailing behind her. 'It was a total *drag* trying to shop with people coming up every minute!'

Sympathy did not come quickly. Angela knew the model through her affiliation with FNYC, and couldn't help feeling that Tawny was a bad apple. She wore an artificial skin that was impossible to reach past. Nobody had a thing on her before she became famous.

'Well, Mr Lyle,' said Tawny flirtatiously, drawing to a stop directly in front of him. 'This is a surprise.'

Jacob lifted an eyebrow. 'Tell me about it.'

Another jet roared from the runway. Kevin's dachshund barked shrilly.

The supermodel slipped on her Gucci shades.

'So, are we getting this show started or what?'

They boarded in a private field. A stream of paps followed as far as was possible, snapping as the group climbed the air stairs and clicking wildly whenever an arm was raised in farewell. The sun melted behind a low horizon, orange and gold.

The Challenger 350 was elegance epitomised, its slender white body and powerful twin engines the latest model in luxury travel. It waited like a giant bird on the melting asphalt, the captain and first officer standing to greet them.

Before stepping inside, Kevin turned to the viewing suite, where his mother and Sketch were waving goodbye. Joan was holding Trey the dachshund, raising the dog's paw to help him join in. *Goodbye, Trey*, thought Kevin dejectedly.

He stepped into the air-conned interior. The cream cabin seats were soft and throne-like, plush leather, and arranged in pairs with a wide carpeted aisle in between. A screen could be drawn to award privacy. Media centres accompanied each station, complete with iPads, DVD players and Wi-Fi access, touch-screen controls and large Bose speakers. Towards the rear, a bar was replete with an array of drinks and snacks. Kevin decided he would get a beer as soon as they were airborne, now that there was no Cut N Dry to tell him he was acting irresponsibly, or Joan to feebly rebuke.

Amber sunlight streamed through the windows, bathing the furnishings in a warm, treacly glow. Tawny Lascelles was already seated, checking her reflection in a compact mirror before snapping it shut and replacing it in her Mulberry tote. Jacob Lyle chose the base furthest from hers, and Kevin followed, slumping down next to the entrepreneur. Jacob shot him a half-hearted smile, before tipping a couple of tablets out of a bottle and swallowing them without water.

'Takes the edge off,' he said. 'Want any?'

Kevin shook his head. He had endured the plane crash nightmare yet again—the deep ocean and the terrible screams of panic. Now was not the time to think of it.

So long as he kept gulping his pills, everything would be fine.

Angela and Eve took seats opposite. Angela wore dark shades, and faced the window. Up front, Mitch Corrigan was next to Tawny. Celeste completed the line-up.

'*Good evening, ladies and gentlemen, this is your captain speaking—and it is my pleasure and privilege to welcome you on board this Challenger jet bound for Salimanta. Our flight time tonight is five hours and sixteen minutes, and we will be cruising at an altitude of 29,000 feet. The local time in Salimanta is nine p.m. and the weather out there is a calm and comfortable seventy-Fahrenheit...*'

The jet eased from its moorings with a gentle tug and taxied onto the runway.

Kevin drew down his window blind.

The engines began to roar, louder and louder still, the force of acceleration pinning him back. Violently they raced to max throttle. Kevin jammed on his headphones, but even Jay-Z and Kanye weren't enough to eclipse the juddering throes.

Fuck, he hated this part. His teeth chattered with the motion. His knuckles strained on the armrest. To his right Jacob was nonchalantly chewing gum, staring out at the blur of runway as it rushed past; the airport turned to liquid. Eve Harley was reading a magazine. Tawny was sitting sideways, long legs spilling abundantly into the gangway. The top of Mitch Corrigan's head was a glossy chestnut arrangement. Their attendant faced them on a jump seat, her smile neatly in place.

In a surge, they were airborne. Far below, the ragged shoreline gave way to open sea. Clouds lifted them to altitude, the sphere further above a still, cool indigo.

The last thing Kevin saw was the fading sun glinting off a pearl-white wing, before he closed his eyes and drowned in sleep.

PART TWO

31

Angela Silvers opened her eyes to the sound of screaming. It was a raw, blood-curdling cry, and she couldn't fathom where it was coming from because her own position was uncertain. She was out of her body. The mind that was thinking this no longer belonged to flesh and bone. She did not know where she was, which way up she was, if she were here at all. She must be here, she thought, if she was asking.

The scream was not human. Then, in echoes, it was. She lay, or sat, or stood, or hung, or whatever it was she was doing, and listened, indifferently, as one might to an overheard dialogue, trying to pick out the parts that could be useful.

Sensation crept up on her, and with each advance she slotted a piece at a time back into her skin. Every part of her hurt, but the pain did not register on any scale she understood. It was a new kind of pain. Her bones stung. Her legs burned. Her lungs, as they dragged in and threw out oxygen, were tight as fists. Her lips were cracked and dry. She blinked and a dagger slid into her eyes.

If only the screaming would stop. Then she could think.

Think.

She asked her hand to move. At first it did not respond, but then, in the dark, she sensed it touch her neck, inside which her pulse fluttered fast and strong. She felt for Noah's silver band, his name beating as firm as her heart, *Noah, Noah, Noah*, never forgotten, not even now, and when she found it she wanted to cry.

With fear came adrenalin. Palms out, she groped into the purple pitch. The air was alive, hissing and shivering. It smelled extreme, a tangy wet leaf smell that was bitingly fresh and intimate, mixed with the acrid stench of died-out smoke.

She became aware of bodies next to her, heaps of still, black matter, and she did not want to touch them. Instead she encountered a jagged edge of metal and prised her fingers around it, using it to raise her bones. The movement prompted a searing blow to her stomach. She needed to see. She needed light.

Angela was inside something. Her eyes strained to decipher shapes and form, to separate the night out there from the one in here. The shell was not entire. It had been blown open and she found she could peer through into infinite dark. The world around her was unfamiliar, impossibly dark and whispering. There were trees. She was in a tree house. If she reached she could fumble through a nest of foliage, the huge leaves waxy and smooth, like plastic, and the coarse twist of twigs and shoots.

A tree house...

Funny the memories a panicked mind will throw up. Her tenth birthday party, Angela and her friends, high in the branches and laughing, and a boy on the ground, the boy nobody spoke to, trying to climb, his sad, pale face and his whimpering stammer...

A thing, big and dark, shot into the canopy. Animal shrieks exploded, a burst of vicious, witch-like cries, high-strung and hectic. The wall of leaves shuddered and Angela backed up, scrabbling for something to hold on to as the capsule lurched precariously from its station. They were still in the sky.

Can anyone else smell smoke?

There it was—something she remembered.

She couldn't figure out the context. An old conversation, one she had had in a previous life, with people she no longer knew.

Close by, one of the lumps moved. It was a subtle eclipse, black within black.

Angela dared not follow. Her head felt heavy, as if the thoughts inside it were lead-weights and somehow she had to shift them, clearing a door she had to get through. Down below, far away, the screams that had woken her died.

She waited, and waited, because she did not know what else to do.

Next it was light. The pain in her stomach was worse. Angela put her hands to it, thinking there might be blood. There wasn't. A hard metal buckle was digging in, and a distant part of her brain knew without hesitation how to undo it.

The catch released, and with a lurch she was falling, falling through nothing, falling up into the sky. Her leg slammed against something solid and she reached out to grasp it, to save herself, but she wasn't quick enough. The jaws of the tree canopy yawned open, the ground far below—too far to make it, too far to be OK—and she thought how stupid it was to die so quickly upon realising she had survived.

A hand landed in hers. Angela was brought up sharp, her

legs dangling out of the torn fuselage, seventy metres above the forest floor.

'Here,' said a female voice. 'Take it.'

A strip of coarse fabric hauled her back in.

She grabbed the arm of a seat and gazed down at the distant drop, soft dawn sunlight cast in shafts through the fragrant air, and back up at her saviour.

Eve Harley had blood slashed down her face. Her auburn hair was matted, her skin blackened by smoke and grease. Her eyes were alert.

Angela's voice, though she knew it to be her own, sounded unfamiliar. She sounded like she did on tape recordings, not how she imagined.

'We have to get down.'

Eve asked: 'Are we dead?'

The women stared at each other, in sight and breath and touch corroborating the second's existence, and the question, huge and strange, dissolved.

'I don't know what's holding us,' said Angela, 'but it won't hold for long. We have to get down. We have to get to the ground.' The simplicity of this goal, some objective they could recognise and understand, was vital.

Caught in the spilled intestines of the aircraft, it was impossible to decipher the cabin's former layout. Seats were shredded, clumps of plastic and metal strewn at random. Where the tail had been was a dense barrier of shivering khaki, through which sunlight could be snatched in white, dazzling glimpses.

Angela was thirsty beyond a desire to drink; it was a primal, essential urge. Her body needed water. The plane had flipped, the ladder of seat backs a climbing rung so she was able to clamber onto them and haul herself up. Towards the rear, a wreckage of glass gave up the suggestion of the

in-flight bar, words and vocabulary making shapes of the
ghosts, stickering her trauma with profile and contour. In a
smashed compartment she found a bottle of Evian and tore
off the cap, her fingers trembling. She drank it, cold, sharp,
invigorating. A warning sounded in the back of her mind, told
her to stop, to save what they had. She passed the bottle down
to Eve.

'He's dead,' said another voice.

This one came from behind. One of the mounds she had
seen in the night now had shape, features, and a crouched
look of terror in its milk-white eye.

'He's dead,' it said again.

Kevin Chase. His T-shirt torn, the sallow skin of his
chest visible beneath, inflating and collapsing. His face was
charred; grey, smudged rivers threaded across his cheekbones where he had wept until the tears dried out. Angela had
a flash of the last time she had seen him, grappling with the
mask that had fallen like entrails from the overhead compartment. *Can anyone else smell smoke?*

Kevin had vomited. Eve had crouched forward, her arm
latched across her stomach. Words in Italian, a pleading
whisper: Celeste Cavalieri's prayer.

Ave Maria, piena di grazia...

'Jacob.' Angela understood. 'Jacob's dead.'

Kevin's fingers were covered in blood. They rested across
the slumped back of Jacob Lyle. He nodded. 'I'm scared,' he
rasped, 'to look.'

Angela climbed down, finding her feet on the cracked back
of a skewered cabin table, and manoeuvred herself beneath
the sack-like body. Jacob's eyes were closed. His face was
thick with charcoal, beyond which it was difficult to assess
the extent of his burns—but it looked bad. He had been the
one to access the hold, when they had tried to put it out. The

luggage flap had seeped dense, billowing fog. Jacob had been thrown, crushed by a flash of aggressive, blinding smoke.

Fire.

She felt his wrist.

The fuselage groaned, its angle shifting so the pool of light beneath them tipped and swayed. With a stomach-flipping jolt, they dropped. Angela was thrown, her head smashing against plastic, and this time she caught a hanging belt, pulling the skin from her palms as it shot through her grip, but she managed to hold on.

Kevin screamed. The plane settled, creaking to a still.

Nobody moved.

'I need your help,' she told him. 'We must be quick.'

The hold was a graveyard. Angela found the remainder of her case, its ends charred to hard, gluey nodules. It brought to mind a picture she had once seen, of a woman who had burst into flames in her house, and all that had been left was a pair of legs, blackened at the knees, the shoes and socks still on, resting in a mound of ash.

In the front flap she found what she was looking for: a penknife.

Flicking the blade, she set about severing the belts.

'What are you doing?'

'Making a rope. You know how to tie it?'

Kevin began shaking, muddling the cords.

'Like this.' She wrenched the ends. 'Tight, like that, OK? Eve goes first.'

'I want to go first,' Kevin blathered. 'I don't want to die.'

'I need you here—to help me. We can't leave him.'

The plane squealed, plummeting once more.

Kevin lost himself to dread. 'I'm jumping!'

Angela grabbed him, surprised at her strength. A lifetime spent dragging boys into order, punching her brothers when they teased her, kicking out against them when they pissed her off. Same girl. Different place. 'You're not.'

'Let go of me!' His lip trembled.

'Pull yourself together,' said Angela. 'You can cry later.'

She picked her way back through the cabin, through singed remains and strewn belongings. Ignoring Kevin's snivels, Angela secured the harness first around Eve and then, her hands shaking, her heart full in her throat, convinced with every movement that the capsule was about to give and send them crashing to the ground, she strained to loop the other end around a tree trunk an arm's reach away, knotting it tight.

She was hot—dead hot. The eggshell cabin was heating up like a greenhouse. Sweat pricked her brow. Her vest stuck to her shoulders. Six a.m.? Seven maybe? No way to tell. Her watch was smashed.

They needed to locate their cells and find a signal—that would be the first thing. Rescue was on its way. Rescue would come. They would be found.

Short goals, Angela told herself. Get down. Use the phones.

Eve gripped her hand, squeezed it. 'It's not just me.'

'I know,' said Angela. She had known at Jakarta. 'I promise it will hold.'

She helped Eve unstrap herself. 'I won't let you fall. Keep your eyes on mine.'

Eve nodded. She betrayed no fear. She would not show Angela the naked terror that, despite what care they took now, she had already lost it.

'I'm going next.' Kevin rushed forward. 'Put me on next.'

Angela watched as Eve worked down the cable, holding the trail between her legs. Dappled light swallowed her, the top of her head growing ever more distant.

A bird cawed. There was a whistling, rattling sound. The plane moved again.

'Strap me in,' said Kevin. 'I'm next.'

With Eve safely landed, Angela hauled in the rope.

'The hell you are. Take this. Get it round him.'

'He can't do what she just did.'

'You and I are supporting him, got it?'

'He's half dead.'

'He's half alive.'

She shouted down to Eve. 'What can you see? Can you see anything?' But the return cry was muted in the heat. The fuselage groaned again.

Lowering Jacob was arduous. In a state of unconsciousness his body was brick-heavy, the belt scraping and chafing and shredding between their clenched fists. Each time the rope rushed, their load plunged, swinging dangerously, and Kevin would let go, crying in pain, leaving Angela splitting under the pressure.

Kevin followed, scrambling like a monkey, and when he reached the ground he curled up in a ball and started to wail. Angela went last. She was mindful of the frayed belt and ominous sounds from above, one hand after the other; gently did it. When her feet touched down, she was grateful for this small but significant victory.

She looked up. From the forest floor the wreckage was a gaping catastrophe. The cabin wheezed and whined a closing time before dislodging, snapping then finally falling. The creepers that had been holding it broke like twigs.

'*Run!*'

Dragging Jacob, they hauled him into the trees. Angela stumbled over knotted roots, blinded by flies, the heat so close and hard she could have bit into it.

Behind, the remains of the stricken aircraft crashed to solid ground. Its impact was booming. Creatures squawked and shrilled. The dense sky ruptured.

They turned.

A jagged, forsaken line of survivors, faces blackened and clothes torn.

'What now?' said Kevin.

Angela jammed her jack-knife into a tree. 'Now we find the others.'

32

America

On the morning the news broke, Noah Lawson woke up in his married co-star's bed. Normally he clicked on NBC while he showered and brushed his teeth, but today, foaming last night's tell-tale secrets from his body, he enjoyed the thrash of water in silence. It was summer in New York, and, for the first time since Angela Silvers had walked out on him, he didn't feel like drawing the blinds and shutting out the world.

He wrapped a towel around his waist. In the bathroom cabinet he caught his sleep-deprived reflection, sandy hair tousled, blue eyes weary but sated.

Old habits died hard. Screwing around, the same old story. He'd tried for a relationship with the woman he loved and look how that had wound up.

She was still naked when he returned to the bedroom, sprawled on the king-size, her long legs and pert breasts invitations to slip back beneath the sheets.

'Shouldn't you get dressed?' Noah teased, as she pulled him down, spreading her hands over his chest. Twenty minutes till her husband came home.

'It turns me on,' she murmured. 'Knowing any second we might get caught.'

Noah hauled himself off, dragging on faded jeans that sat uncomfortably on his erection. OK, sleeping with his Broadway leading lady wasn't the wisest idea, but he was discreet enough to keep it under wraps—so long as she was, too.

'Next time.' Noah leaned in to plant a kiss, first on her knees, then the tops of her thighs, her belly, her ribcage, and finally the delicate plane between her breasts.

She giggled, gunning the remote at the plasma TV.

'Whoa,' she said immediately, sitting up. 'What's this?'

The screen was filled with colour and chaos, wildly edited frames of a clip of an aircraft, a head-shot of Kevin Chase and a wrecked Asian coastline. A reporter was delivering urgently to camera, mic in hand, pressing her earpiece for updates.

Hysterical crowds churned in the background. Multitudes were sobbing. Signs were held aloft: *The End is Nigh*, *The Rich Must Fall*, *Apocalypse Now!*

Noah's first thought was terrorism.

The scene was one of panic and confusion: a montage of disaster. At the foot of the broadcast ran a crimson banner:

BREAKING NEWS—SEVEN MISSING IN JAKARTA AIR DISASTER, SENATOR MITCH CORRIGAN, TAWNY LASCELLES AND ANGELA SILVERS AMONG THOSE ON BOARD...

'Holy shit,' she said.

For a few seconds, Noah was numb. He watched, listened, waiting for the instant when something would click and he could take it in. He couldn't. He could not take it in. Even when Angela's picture flashed up, he could not take it in.

'Noah, are you OK? You look like you saw a ghost.'

'We understand the jet lost radio signal around two a.m. local time, approximately three hundred kilometres northwest of Papua New Guinea. It is believed to have come down in or surrounding the Palaccas Archipelago, a region of islands en route to Salimanta, the flight's intended destination. Sources have since confirmed that all seven figures were indeed on board the aircraft. At present we are unable to corroborate the cause of the incident. A search effort is underway…'

Noah tore open the door. Ignoring his lover's enquiries, he shot downstairs, half dressed, stumbled into the New York sunshine and started running.

In a suite at the peak of the Parisian's gold tower, Dino Zenetti was treating himself to an early-morning blowjob. It was his favourite time of the day. The broad was hot, a big-titted, red-haired stripper he had summoned to his den at two a.m. Her lips were plump and soft and sticky with gloss. Dino lay back against the pillows, arms folded behind his head, and watched as his cock drove in and out of her mouth.

What was a guy supposed to do? His fiancée sure as shit wasn't putting out—and now Angela had skipped town, leaving him high and dry. He had hoped Donnie Silvers' croaking might have made her putty in his hands, because there was nothing hornier than a sobbing broad, but sadly no. The heiress was proving a hard nut to crack; meanwhile Dino's own nuts doubted whether they'd ever get cracked again.

Until Angela came to her senses, he would get it elsewhere. He had to. Dino harboured a theory that if his balls didn't get quenched at least once a day, he'd wind up getting prostate cancer. He came fiercely, pounding against the girl's tongue. She would leave a happy customer. Getting to pleasure a Zenetti was a privilege indeed.

While he was in the bathroom, the phone rang. Mid-piss, Dino ignored it.

As he was dressing, it rang again.

'Yeah?' He snatched it up.

'That how you answer all your calls?' came a sharp voice. Carmine.

'Course not,' Dino said hurriedly. 'Thought you were someone else.'

'You seen the news?' asked Carmine.

'No.'

'Then get on it. Cos you and I just hit a big fuckin' jackpot, son.'

Joan Chase was giving Trey the dachshund a bath. Trey didn't like it, he was all shivery and quivery until she wrapped him in his best towelling robe and dried him good as new, but she was sure that if Kevin were here he'd be pleased.

She wondered how her son was getting on in Salimanta. Her own return flight had been interminable, especially when they got held up in customs because Trey lost his passport. She hoped Kevin was faring better.

Joan planned to stay in Kevin's pad while he was away. She would do his laundry, clean his bedroom (already she had unearthed his stack of pornography while changing the sheets—it was just like the old days!) and cook some food to put in the freezer. Also, Trey was happiest at home and it wouldn't do to disrupt his routine.

Lifting the pup from the tub, Joan rubbed a flannel across his soggy fur and adorned him in a bespoke robe, the letters TC emblazoned across the breast pocket, though what exactly Trey would keep in his breast pocket was beyond even her.

It was as she was fixing breakfast—pancakes and syrup for her; chicken Chewa-Bunga for him—that Joan registered that something was wrong. She could hear a faint, frantic din, and when she peeled back the blinds that opened onto Kevin's drive, she saw, down at the gates, a band of desperate looking people.

Joan frowned. She closed the blind. The din grew louder.

Trey blinked up at her, licking his nose.

The pan on the stove was starting to burn. Butter hissed and spat.

Joan went to the plasma. Her thumb hovered over the power. In the split second before the screen lit up, by some terrible thread of motherly instinct, she sensed that life, as she knew it, was about to change for ever.

Melinda Corrigan rose from yet another athletic night, picked her way downstairs and poured a huge cup of sweet white coffee. The kids had left for school and the mansion was blissfully quiet. Her body ached pleasurably from Gary's keen attentions.

Melinda bit her lip. She was being naughty. It was naughty to be sleeping with her neighbour's husband, and to be cheating behind her own husband's back. It was naughty the things they got up to and the positions Gary put her in. It was naughty to rent a motel room on the road out of town, and creep back here in the depths of night.

As far as she was concerned, Mitch could stay away as long as he liked.

The promise of the morning played out. First she would take a long, luxurious shower, then venture out for a lazy day of shopping. Maybe she would pick up those lilac panties, the ones with the crotch cut out, and treat Gary to the full works tonight.

Mitch had used to love that sort of thing—these days, he couldn't give a crap.

Humming to herself, she padded upstairs.

Her cell bleeped. It was Oliver.

Don't panic. Call me.

The coffee churned in her gut—panic about what?

Melinda dialled his number. He picked up straight away.

'Oliver?' Her voice was shrill. 'What's going on?'

Orlando Silvers got the call during a meeting with the board. Partway through his presentation on the year's profits, which would have been an uncomfortable analysis at the best of times, his secretary burst into the conference room without knocking.

'Forgive my interruption, Mr Silvers.'

Orlando bit back annoyance. 'What is it?'

'I'm sorry,' she was shaking, 'but this is urgent.'

The assembly shifted in their seats. Directing a smile, Orlando said easily:

'Please excuse me. This won't take a moment.'

Out in the lobby, his secretary's expression was one of abject horror. Orlando forgot his anger. He had never before seen, nor would he ever again, an expression quite like it. It was an expression too old for her twenty-six years.

'What is it?' The question tasted horrible. 'What's happened?'

'There's been an accident.'

For some reason, he didn't think of Angela. She was his

baby sister: nothing bad could happen to her. 'Is it Mom?' he pressed. 'Luca?'

He wanted to say another name, but it never reached his throat. His secretary wouldn't know anything about that anyway. Nobody knew about that.

Eve was his cross to bear: Eve, and the life inside her.

'I'm sorry,' his secretary began, 'I'm so, so sorry…'

33

Day 1

Eve Harley staggered into the thicket. She found a ditch and slid into it, pulling down her jeans, her fingers trembling. She checked her underwear. She felt her stomach.

She waited for the pain, but it didn't come. The scarlet gush of blood: the certainty that what had been made was lost. It didn't come.

You're still here, she thought, knowing it surer than she knew her name. *You're still with me.*

Her vision swimming, one eye stained red, stinging liquid when she blinked. Alone, she flinched at the sounds and snaps that crackled in the foreign, backwards world, frightened she had tricked her fate and it could still be stolen from her. She heard her father's voice seep out of the trees, Terry sighing her name as he had at her bedroom door all those years ago—'*Eve, are you in there...?*'—and she spun round, breathing hard. Only leaves, the vibration of heat.

Are you in there...?

Orlando's name sailed through her, a paper boat on a stream.

She remembered a night they had spent together; moon-

light spilling into his London townhouse, his gentle breathing
and the hand he had kept in hers all night.

So far, so faint: another universe.

I want you here. Why aren't you here?

She started to cry and hated herself for it.

Kevin Chase lurched through a fresh door in his nightmare—and it was a nightmare, no question, because he had
been here before. Only before it had never gone this far, it had
always ended, the smash but never the detritus, and now the
corridors were multiplied, the horrors doubled, new scenes
playing out with no end or beginning.

He squeezed his eyes shut and told himself to surface. It
was a dream, just like the others. The crash had been a dream.
The fire and the screaming and the plummet through the trees
had all been a dream.

Wake up wake up wake up...

No dream.

His bedroom, back in LA—curtains blowing, the radio
on...

Wake up! For God's sake, wake up!

Trey would be licking his face. Joan would be pissing him
off. Sketch would be calling, about another promo, another
gala, another junket... Kevin wanted it to be real so much that
it was a physical pain, a throb that only at the last moment
identified itself as an actual thing, the ache in his side where
Jacob's bulk smashed into his.

Kevin could not sustain the other man's weight for much
longer. He could barely stand himself. His feet tripped and
staggered, his arms stung, his head banged.

Angela, on the other side, heaved them both. Kevin wondered what she would say if he gave up and lay down, refused
to move from this spot, just sat and waited for his mom to

come get him: Joan, with her big hugs and her soppy kisses.

You are coming...aren't you, Mom? Please come.

For all the times he had wished her gone, he only wanted one thing.

Home.

Kevin's face crumpled in misery. Home. His people. The world he knew and hated and loved—living, sparkling, plentiful, safe. *Mom, I want to go home.*

Tawny was screaming. She didn't know how long she had been screaming, only that her screams weren't working, because normally if she screamed something happened—anything happened—to make the bad things go away.

Shapes were coming through the forest. Voices: a rescue party.

Even in her delirium, or perhaps because of it, the thought crossed Tawny's mind that one of them might be a hot guy. She hoped her mascara hadn't run down her face, that her clothes weren't too torn, that her tint hadn't smudged and her hair wasn't a total bush. She hoped there were no cameras. That no journalists that had gotten wind of it. Give her an hour, some time to reapply her lotions and potions because, right now, it wasn't Tawny Lascelles in the middle of the jungle.

It was something...*ugly*. Something like Tawny Linden.

The scream turned into a burble. She would sue whoever was responsible for this so fast their asses dropped off, the airline, the pilots, the fucking organisation that had invited them out here in the first place, she would sue every goddamn party that had come within a thousand miles of this sonofabitch trip and, once she'd sued them, she would sue anyone who dared ask her a single fucking question about it until she'd had at least a year in a recuperation spa and was feeling back to her old self.

Her old self…

Tawny had a habit of never quite engaging with the scene she was in, rather always observing it, as if she were a spectator to the movie of her life. Here, now, she saw one person and one person only: the girl she used to be.

She crawled towards voices, rescue, return, and reached out to the light.

Senator Mitch Corrigan used his upper body to lever himself free from whatever was holding him. He expected the feeling to come straight back into his legs but it didn't. He tried to move his toes. He had visions of a doctor, in a clean, pristine hospital back in Texas, knocking a spatula against a heel. *Can you feel that?* No. No, he couldn't.

Mitch hauled out into the open. Outside, the heat was intense. The light was faint. The air pulsed. Why wasn't he dead? Why was he still breathing?

The remainder of the cabin smouldered on the tangled, rotten floor. The supermodel was screaming, a constant alarm. The Italian was gone.

In the distance, three outlines were approaching.

Mitch strained to see. A woman and two men: an apparition, distorted beyond being human. Their movements were unnatural, the one in the middle taller, but stooped, his head lolling forward on his neck. Mitch had seen them before. Where from? Then he realised, and with it came relief, for there were no accidents.

These were the same creatures that had abducted him that night in 2012.

Blinking through the hallucination, Mitch backed up and slumped against a tree. *You found me.*

He waited to be taken. He always knew it would happen. Rossetti had known it would happen. If he would not go to them, they would bring him in.

'Mitch?' said a voice.

His addled brain told him it was Melinda. His wife, his best friend, as she had been on their wedding day twenty years ago, soft lips and warm hands, *Melinda*...

'Mitch, it's Angela, open your eyes.'

The dream evaporated. Reality hit.

34

The wreckage the others had been caught in carved an open space through the thicket. A hulking scar dashed back through the forest, a ghostly passage of flattened foliage and punched shrubs. Hazy, humid heat soaked the air. The surrounding wall of jungle creepers was dark as night, pockets of sun flashing through in winking bursts. So lofty was the canopy that it hurt to look up: a distant, dappled aperture to an out-of-reach sky. Down here, daylight barely penetrated.

Tawny's screams had guided them. The supermodel was hugging her knees to her chest, her mouth an open gash of despair. Angela shook her. She screamed louder.

Angela slapped her round the face, eliciting a shocked yet fleeting silence.

'Kill me,' whimpered Tawny. 'I'm begging you. Kill me now.'

'Like hell I will. You're stuck here like the rest of us.'

'I thought you were them!' Tawny cried. 'Rescue!'

Angela dragged a stick through the ground. Her mom, Orlando, Luca, Dino, did they know yet what had happened? *Noah.* Right then she would have given up all hope of rescue for the chance to tell him she was all right. She could not stand the thought of his distress or his grief, of losing his smile for just one second: of his unhappiness.

'They're coming for us,' Eve said. 'Any second. Rescue is coming.'

Minutes passed. The heat was fat and cloying, busy with insects.

'We need a plan,' said Angela. She tacked on, 'Just until they do.'

The cockpit was obliterated. Eve helped Angela lug the captain from the deck, reeling under his weight. She had never touched a corpse before and it surprised her how cold it was, even in the oven of the jungle. Across the clearing Tawny gagged, choking saliva onto the stinking ground.

They deposited the body behind a mound of earth.

'We have to find the other one,' said Eve. 'The co-pilot. He might still be alive. He could help.'

'How?'

'Radio. Flares. Emergency supplies. I don't know.' Stuff she had read, random lines and warnings, anything to keep her moving, keep her *doing*, even if half of it was from some idiotic daytime movie she might have once seen. It didn't matter. She was here. This was now. The others could do what they liked. They could scream and panic, they could freak out and fall apart, but not Eve. All she cared about was getting her baby home. She would take down anything and anyone who stood in her way.

'What about the attendant,' said Angela, 'the woman?'

'Her, too.'

Away from the others, Angela asked: 'Are you OK? Is everything OK?'

Her meaning was clear. Eve pretended it wasn't.

'I'm fine.'

She didn't stick around for the useless sympathy in Angela's eyes, the same Silvers eyes that had regarded her pityingly over dinner at The Ivy the month before. Instead she turned, felt her weight on the ground, her roots in the soil, and glared darkly into the trees. *We're in this together. We don't need anyone else.*

Why should she? Eve never had.

Time drained. It felt like hours, but they couldn't be sure. Eve's was the only phone they could locate and she grappled with it, hoping against useless hope, as if the crumpled lump of metal might miraculously fix itself.

She thought of all her contacts hidden inside, the conversations, the emails, the arrangements to meet; the one time Orlando had put a single kiss on the end of his text message and she hadn't commented on it, and anyway it had never happened again, but Eve had liked it and kept it where she deleted so many others.

She wanted her phone back to make those calls but she also longed to see those names, to prove she hadn't imagined those people and those lives and that her own life thus far hadn't been one long strange fantasy that was now at an end.

Across the clearing Jacob Lyle began to moan, turning his head, disorientated, as he broke into bursts of troubled consciousness. His injuries were severe. Angry red welts obscured his face, ragged wounds singed with black, the skin tender and raw. Celeste Cavalieri sat with him and took his hand. She spoke to him softly, in Italian. Gradually he returned to silence, a temporary peace.

Eve's heart did not bleed. Sympathy was energy and she needed all she could get. Besides, in a way, Jacob was spared. He did not have to see it. He did not have to meet the nightmare.

***

The heat was incessant, the jungle a sweltering snare. Angela brought water from the tail, but the bottles went dry and in the hottest part of the day it was impossible to contemplate a return trek. Thirst tortured them.

They waited for the sound of helicopter blades: the charge of the search and the reassuring buzz of human conversation, the safety of stretchers and the medical team that would carry them all back to civilisation.

The helicopter blades didn't come.

They waited to hear their names cried out.

Their names didn't come.

They waited for the call of a ship.

The call didn't come.

Kevin said: 'How long is it going to take?'

'I don't know,' said Angela.

But she did know, then, that not all of them were going to make it out of here. Not all of them were going to survive.

35

Kevin snivelled. He stripped off his T-shirt. His narrow, bare chest glistened with muck and oil. 'We'll die here,' he said. 'We're all going to die.'

'You might,' said Eve. 'I'm not. They're coming.'

'When?'

'Soon.'

'How d'you know?'

'We've got a US senator with us. This is going straight to the top. They'll throw everything at it. It'll be soon.'

Kevin swiped his tears away with the back of his hand. He wished he wasn't such a crier. Chicks were meant to cry, not tough guys like him! Still, he was only a kid. Joan always called him her *special boy*, her *baby prince*—technically he wasn't an adult till he was twenty-one, and that meant he needed looking after.

Mitch Corrigan was watching the forest. The senator reminded him of Sketch, only fatter and balder. Mitch's hair, so carefully arranged at Jakarta, was now sliding off the back of his head like a flattened animal. 'We should get out of the jungle before nightfall,' he said. 'It isn't safe.'

Nightfall. Kevin shivered.

'But they'll be here by then,' insisted Tawny. 'Before it gets dark.'

'We're in a remote group of islands.' Celeste spoke for the

first time, her voice quiet but her words deafening. 'Rescue might take days.'

'*Days?*'

'Maybe.'

Tawny started crying. 'Oh, what would you know?' the supermodel lashed. 'I mean, who the hell are you anyway?' A shape scampered in the undergrowth and she shot up, eyes bugging. 'I can't do it!' Tawny blubbed. 'I can't make it five minutes in this shit-pit—I can't make it *days*, I hate the outdoors. Rats and spiders; *snakes*—!'

'Snakes and spiders are the least of our worries,' said Celeste.

'What is that supposed to mean?'

'Leopards. Tigers. Orangutans.' A pause. 'Crocodiles.'

'OH MY GOD!'

Angela stood. 'This isn't helping,' she warned. 'Before we get carried away, we make a reasonable guess about where we are. OK? Then we do this one hour, one minute, one second at a time if that's what it takes. We'll make shelter. We'll build fire. We'll use what we can from the aircraft. People survive in worse conditions. Our best assets are each other and if we work together we can pull through.'

The group eyed one another suspiciously.

'We should explore,' said Angela. 'Find the highest point. That's what we should do. Who's coming with me?'

Kevin considered it. *No fucking way!* Who knew what was out there?

'I am,' said Eve.

'Not you.'

'Why?'

Angela challenged her with a gaze. 'Tawny, you'll come,' she said.

'Why me?' the model wailed.

'Fear is what you can't see. It's what you don't know. You're going to see and you're going to know, then there won't be anything to be frightened of any more.'

Tawny kept scrunching balls of her hair, as if she was scrabbling around in a crate of moss for something she had lost. Kevin thought of all the times he had tried to jerk off over her in magazines, locked in his mom's upstairs toilet or in the bathroom at Cut N Dry when he got bored halfway through a meeting.

Mitch volunteered. 'There should be three of us.'

'Four,' Eve insisted. 'You can't make me stay.'

'You're staying.'

'What are you going to do about it, Angela?'

The idea of a fight breaking out was somehow appealing, like a thunderstorm after a heat spell. Angela seemed ready to say something. A silent threat passed between them. Eve backed down.

'I'm not sitting round here doing nothing,' Eve muttered.

Jacob groaned. Tawny shot him a disgusted look and folded her arms.

'Stake out the fuselage,' Angela told Eve, 'there might be first aid. Keep Jacob clean, and hydrated. Don't leave him alone.'

'We should get moving,' said Mitch. 'While it's still light…'

Angela turned to the model. 'Tawny?'

'I don't want to.'

'There's no choice.'

'What about my heels?'

'Take them off.'

Reluctantly she obeyed. Angela seized them, and, with a swift flick to each sole, sliced the spikes off with her knife.

'Let's go.'

36

Scant breeze filtered through the tight vegetation. It was challenging; with no path to steer them every step was an effort, hands in front, parting the thicket, a foot at a time. Every so often they would stumble across a trampled route, studded with the imprint of hooves, and follow as far as it led.

Tawny wanted America. She wanted JP, and Minty, and her entourage. She wanted to brush her hair and wash her fucking armpits. She felt like a dog. Right now she ought to be luxuriating in her villa in the mountains, Adonis boyfriend beckoning her back into bed, the blue pool glittering and her fragrant skin bronzed in the sun. She couldn't remember the last time she had been this dirty, this soiled, this disgusting.

Yes, she could.

Come with me, sweetheart. I'll look after you...

She wondered what had become of Nathan. She hoped he was rotting in a ditch. *Little Orphan Annie*, he had called her. Bastard.

The burn in Tawny's calves, not dissimilar to the one she sometimes got after completing a runway show in eight-inch stilettoes, told her they were moving uphill. It was hard to decipher their position because the trees were massive, their shafts zooming to vanishing point hundreds of feet up in the air, eclipsing any stab at orientation. Even the sky eluded them. Claustrophobia seemed a perverse notion, but the vines were so close, the drench of the air so stifling, that it was hard to breathe.

Angela was up ahead, beating a stick through the under-growth, the back of her top a horseshoe of sweat. Mitch was responsible for keeping time, instructing rest or else pushing them on, even when ten minutes felt like two hours. Jacob's gold watch was the only timepiece to have survived the crash: he had forwarded the hour partway through the flight, and the watch appeared, at least, to be working properly, though there was no way of checking until they cleared the canopy.

Tawny lagged wretchedly behind, their route strewn with complaints that she could not go on, that this would surely kill her and that she was about to die of thirst. They were all thirsty. One bottle to share between them, sipped in small doses every twenty minutes. She craved her aloe vera juice, kept slipping into wild and brilliant daydreams about oceans so full of it that she could dive right in, become one with the liquid, cool and drenching.

The trio climbed higher. Tawny heard a distant, rhythmic sigh.

Angela picked it out too. She stopped. 'Listen.'

Unmistakably, it was the sound of the sea. The group faced each other. This was something they recognised, something that could take them away, something that could transport them home. Energised, they pressed on. Tantalising slivers of azure flickered through the leaves. Tawny pictured a life-guard rushing out of the waves and scooping her up in his arms, abs rippling and his dark hair windswept. Safety.

'The canopy's thinning,' said Angela. She wiped the back of her wrist across her brow. 'The higher we get, the more we can see.'

They kept walking. Every occasion the growth seemed to

break, the brow teased them by lifting again, revealing yet another chamber of crawling dark. Mitch took over at the helm, slicing a way through the branches.

All at once, they hit a plateau. It came upon them suddenly: a smooth table of grey and pink granite, sparkling in the sun. It was big, the size of a tennis court, and the sky above it was wide and bracingly blue.

Angela hauled herself onto the rock and spread her arms. Up here was a new kind of heat: a dangerous, blazing one that came from a raging ball of fire. At this height, the sun seemed close enough to touch. Its searing furnace bounced off the granite plinth, baking them from beneath. They felt it on their shoulders, their backs, biting into their arms and hands.

Tawny slumped down, her head between her legs. Her normally gleaming blonde mane was coarse and bedraggled. Her feet stung with blisters.

'We made it,' said Angela.

'We didn't make it,' said Tawny. 'This is just a deeper circle of hell.'

The jungle might be clammy, but at least it wasn't naked flame. Mitch squinted. It had to be midday, or thereabouts. The gold watch read 12:30.

'Over here.' Angela crossed to the lip of the rock. Mitch joined her. His shirt clung. His toupee was itching. Beads of damp prickled on his scalp. He scratched the hairpiece, felt it dislodge and self-consciously patted it back into position. Not that he should care, but by some faint constancy to what had brought him here, he still did. As if the removal of the toupee signified more than a creeping baldness. It was the façade he had been wearing all this time. The one he couldn't do without.

From this vantage point they had a better view of their territory. They were on an island, a small one, maybe a couple of miles long, and in the shape of a lozenge whose ends have been pinched and drawn out of form. To the east, the direction from which they had come, the landscape was serene. Beyond the jungle canopy was an arc of flawless white beach. Its sand was alabaster-pale and impossibly smooth, at its widest point dissolving into a shallow, emerald, crescent-shaped lagoon. Half a mile out, a ridge of red coral broke against the ocean. Wavelets lapped over the reef, beyond which the water was deep cobalt, sprawling as far as the eye could see.

Mitch scanned the horizon for signs of life, another rock, someplace like theirs, a dimple however distant or minor, to break the faceless curvature of the Earth. Nothing. The horizon was a melting, liquid line, the definition between sky and sea dissolved because both were the same colour, equally still and equally indifferent.

The air quivered like a plucked string.

To the west the picture was more hostile: a jagged line of cliffs that petered out into the immense ocean, dimpled with caves and grottoes. A jutting cluster of crags splayed out like a serpent's tail, and harsh clusters of rock were beaten by the crash and froth of waves. Dark, swirling water threw up white spray.

There was no sign of life—no settlements, no boats.

They could make out the smash in the trees where the jet had entered, not far from the coastline. 'We'll set up camp on the beach,' said Angela. 'It's safer there.'

'Safer?' Tawny baulked.

'We don't know what's out there.'

Mitch thought: *I do. I know what's out there.*

'The beach makes us obvious,' said Tawny. 'People will see us!'

'There are no people,' said Angela.

'How do you know?'

'Because I have to go on what I can see, and right now I can't see anyone.'

'What about later, when it gets dark?' Tawny envisaged a line of torches dancing in the night, through the forest, coming to get them, and Jacob's crispy body impaled on a spit, turning amid a circle of shadowy hungry faces! *Cannibals!*

'If you want to take your chances in the jungle,' said Angela, 'be my guest.'

'I'm not doing anything by myself.'

'Being obvious is what we want. We want people to see us, don't we?'

'Not if they're cannibals!'

Angela lost patience. 'Shut up, Tawny, or I'll slap it out of you again.'

Tawny sulked. Angela returned to the trees. Dejectedly, the model followed.

Mitch went to go after them. As he did, his eyes travelled down to a hidden inlet beneath the line of the cliffs. It had to be close to the crash site.

He peered, not quite trusting himself the first time.

But there it was.

A spread of ivory shore, pristine and unscathed, the sand smooth as silk—apart from a trail of human footprints threading across it and into the slit of a cave.

37

He woke up because his stomach lurched.

Another lurch. A surge then drop. The seatbelt sign pinged on. 'Sit down, sir.'

Jacob careened through the listing cabin. Gulfs of air vanished beneath them.

'Sir, please sit down. The captain has asked that you all remain seated—'

A scream as they plummeted; the jet shuddered and shook. Somebody started crying. Faces transformed by fear. 'Can anyone else smell smoke?'

Black night outside; panic within…and that bitter, mushrooming stink.

'What's going on? What's happening?'

Oxygen masks dropped from the ceiling, a mess of tubes and plastic.

'Ladies and gentlemen, this is your captain. We are experiencing an issue in the hold and are doing all we can to resolve it. Until that time I ask you to please remain calm. Air supply has been withdrawn from the cabin: this is what your masks are for. We are descending altitude to enable you to breathe more freely…'

From Jacob's window they all saw the inevitable. Orange flames, bright and angry, lashed at the underside of the wing.

A murmur of prayer: 'Santa Maria, Madre di Dio, prega per noi peccatori…'

*The fuel tanks—*We're done for. *They thought it. They knew it. Unless he could get back there, do something… Access to the hold was a feature of this plane, a convenience, a luxury, and now the only shot they had at survival. The heat was intense. Only a fool would go in.*

They would die anyway; he may as well die trying.

It was a strange fusion: the prickling burn as vivid as sunshine, yet behind his damaged vision rolled an abyss black as night. In blindness, he was alone.

The pain was out of this world. He dared not raise his hands to his face, certain it would extinguish all hope.

Jacob had reached the summit of terror. He had reached it twenty thousand feet in the sky on a night a century ago. If he had been able to see, he would have looked it straight in its bright, evil eye, and maintained for the rest of his days that he had met terror on that dark path and knew what terror looked like.

Blindness incapacitated him: the vision he had taken for granted all his thirty-two years, this engine that enabled him to see the world, incidental and imperative.

His mind threw up remembered images. Years of watching his conquests, the women's bodies, their skin, their smiles, their breasts and legs, mouths soldered to his and each other's, limbs entangled as he gazed on, drinking in pictures, eyes gluttonous for more.

Now he sipped only at a dead screen, blank apart from an insistent red winking, a pulsing star that flashed amid the void, some faint anchor of the old world, some point of reference. A blinking light, yes, and the cameras were rolling—only there was nothing to see. It occurred to Jacob that he was simultaneously filming and viewing his own suffering.

Serves you right, a small voice said. *This is karma.*

Eve explained what happened, in words that made no sense.

Jacob recalled their exchange at Jakarta: details about the reporter's face, her brittle English accent, distant and detached. Without the nuances he had spent a decade learning, those giveaways in a person's expression—traces on which he had built the relationships of his career—there was nothing to connect. As Eve described their trek through the forest, what had brought them here and how Kevin and Angela had lowered him from the wreck, Jacob heard swishing fronds, the brush of the boiling air, and the way the shade moved, a fiery spectrum behind his lids. Messages to his brain were confusing and mistaken, self-deceiving and self-preserving. He deciphered the occasional liquid shape. There was only one thing he cared for.

'Will I see again?'

But he was scared to see. What had become of him? What monster would greet him on the other side?

There was a pause, before: 'None of us knows what's going to happen.'

Eve got up. He heard her move away. No warmth. She was a stranger to him. They all were. People he would once have charmed—women he might once have bedded—turned from him, an empty hole into which communication evaporated.

Of all the eyes in all the bedrooms he had set up in the world, the only two Jacob Lyle cared for were his own. Without them, there was nothing.

***

Angela stopped. 'Are you OK? You're slowing back there.'

In the dappled jungle shadows her companions shifted in and out of light, crisply visible one instant and mottled dark the next. Mitch hauled on, his complexion pallid with sweat and dirt, and he kept his eyes on the ground and never looked up.

'Ugh!' Tawny's cry blasted from the rear. 'I stepped in shit! I skidded in shit!'

Angela tramped back. The model had slipped, landing on her ass. A fetid pat, bearing the mark of Tawny's shoe-print, had been flattened, attracting a wave of flies.

'Am I sitting in it?' She shot up, swiping her ass. 'Is it on me?'

Angela knelt to the heap. 'What do you think made this?'

'Who cares? Shit's shit—and it stinks.'

'Pigs,' said Angela, answering her own question. 'Nothing bigger than that.'

Tawny's eyes bugged. 'Like farmyard pigs?'

'The tracks we saw would suggest hooves,' she said, 'rather than paws.'

'*Paws?*'

'Big cats: tigers, leopards, I guess. Like Celeste said.'

Tawny squawked: 'But all we've seen evidence of is pigs. Right?'

The forest twitched. It was hot and potent.

'Let's keep moving all the same.'

'Hang on.' Tawny stopped. 'I need the bathroom.'

'Can't it wait?'

'What's the difference between going in the trees down there and going in the trees up here? They're the same fucking trees and it sucks either way.'

'Fine.'

'Come with me.'

'No,' said Angela. 'We stay together.'

'With him checking me out?'

Mitch turned, embarrassed.

'Mitch has got more on his mind right now than you taking your knickers off.'

'Can't. Stage fright.'

'I'm staying here,' said Angela.

'And leaving me alone to get my hundred-million-dollar-insured ass chewed off by an alligator?'

'You're being ridiculous.'

'Am I?'

Angela looked into the murky trees.

'Fine. Let's get it over with.'

They took just a few paces from the pig run, but it was so snarled underfoot it might as well have been a hike. Tawny tried not to think about all the things she might be stepping on—snakes and creepy-crawlies, beetles and rats, not to mention the reeking manure that was still caked to the underside of her shoe.

She squatted uncomfortably on the mulchy ground. Peeing in this sick tropical nightmare was peculiar, an ordinary necessity in the most extraordinary of places. She wondered if she was the first person ever to pee on the island. Was she disrupting some finely balanced eco-system? Maybe she would be responsible for extinguishing all life on this godforsaken hell-hole—starting, she thought grimly, with herself.

As she hauled up her pants, she spied what appeared to be a flat expanse of clay running parallel to the route they had been on. It was scattered with green, reedy shoots, and looked quicker and easier to navigate.

'I'm going this way,' she yelled back.

Tawny shot off before Angela could stop her, deciding she

had had quite enough of struggling through the undergrowth for one day, thank you very much.

As soon as she stepped onto it, she knew she had made a big mistake.

The clay gave way. Her foot sank.

The ground turned to mush, sucking and binding and slurping. Tawny's leg was quick to follow, first her ankle, then her calf, then her thigh, vanishing with queasy efficiency into the peat, as if the maw of some great beast was devouring it.

She toppled forwards, putting her hands out to break the fall, and the gulping, lapping mess swallowed them too. Horror ambushed her. 'HELP ME!'

A snap of branches and Angela's voice surfaced from behind: 'It's a swamp.'

'Get me out of it! For God's sake, get me out of it!'

She tried to turn, but the gloop was too thick, caked to her waist like cement.

'Don't move.' Angela stepped round to the rim, crouched on a bed of shoots, and held her arms out. Her eyes met Tawny's at an angle that suggested if they didn't think fast Tawny wouldn't be moving anywhere again any time soon.

'If you struggle,' she said, 'it will make it worse. I'm going to find something to pull you out. Breathe. Nice and easy, Tawny. Try to stay calm—'

Tawny's stomach plunged into the bog. '*Don't you dare leave me!*'

Insects buzzed on the recking surface, midges and flies crawling up her nose and across her lips. Tawny honked a sob. The swamp burped.

'Listen to me. Are you listening?'

'*I'm listening!*'

'Make yourself as flat as possible. Lean forward. Lean into it, like this—'

'You're trying to kill me!'

'Pretend you're swimming. Now take the end of this, it's strong, OK? Take it.'

The mud bubbled and belched. Tawny felt it creeping up around her breasts. Moving an inch was like trying to lift a car. She let the mud claim her.

I'm going to die. I'm going to die in a horrible stinking bog and no one will ever find me. No one will know what happened to me because we'll never be found.

This wasn't meant to happen. She was Tawny Lascelles. She was beautiful.

She had wound up no better than a pig—a pig with painted toenails!

'Got it? Now take a deep breath, as deep as you can.'

Tawny shook her head, the only part of her still free. No. No, she couldn't!

'I won't let you go. You're going under and once you're under you need to stay as flat as possible so I can draw you towards me.'

'I can't. I can't! I can't do it!'

'You have to.'

The trouble was that she couldn't relax her breath enough to get a lungful. Air was coming short and quick, blood burning in her chest. If she held it for more than two seconds she would pass out. The sludge sucked.

The first things it filled were her nostrils. The mud was surprisingly cold, and stank of rotten eggs and decomposition. It leached into every orifice, syrupy, gelatinous, barely liquid. Even through her closed lids she sensed the absolute dark of this macabre underground and gripped as tight as she could to her lifeline, the flimsy wire, terrified it would break, on the end of which she pictured Angela Silvers in that heavenly sphere called daylight, the jungle, anything to be back in the jungle...

Oxygen was running out. Her heart smacked against her ribs. Her ears plugged with mud. It leaked between her lips.

The cord was running between her fingers; she was losing it, she was fading...

Images reared, hideous as gargoyles. Cruel images she had locked away for fear their resurrection would choke her. She couldn't die here.

I'm a survivor...remember? Remember what happened, Tawny Linden?

Yes, she remembered.

She remembered escaping the dancing bar that chill January night, boarding the bus, her make-up smudged as she shivered in her borrowed coat. She remembered fleeing back to Sunnydale, a poor little small-town girl ready to admit defeat, to accept that the life she'd dreamed of would never come to fruition. She remembered weeping in expectancy of the reunion, a safe place, finally, after all she'd endured, but it wasn't to be. Her family, bitter and blank, as if she were a stranger, telling her she had betrayed them and was no longer their daughter, their sister, she was *nothing* to them; and her hot, stinging tears, begging them to take her back, *please, please, please take me back...*

You're dead to us, her family said. *Never come here again.* Oh, she remembered that.

She had sought refuge on the streets, hitching her way upstate as fast as she hitched her skirt. Men found her pretty; she lived to see another day.

Then one night, three of them, high on crack, their heavy boots tripping across her sleeping rough and she closed her mind and soul to their clawing hands but she could not close her body. She had endured it before; all through the Rams she had endured it. But this was different. Fierce. Endless. At the end of her road, desolate and alone and utterly without hope, Tawny Linden passed out…and woke up in a hospital bed.

She never told staff what had brought her there. Could not admit the shame and humiliation of the years. But, at her lowest point, she found her deepest strength: a kernel that refused to back down, that had to triumph whatever it took. Tawny could not sink any more, and if that didn't mean heart-ache then it meant freedom. *Ambition*. She could become anything she wanted—but what? In the mirror she spied her bruised reflection, pretty but torn—and a light in her eyes, a savage light that made her extraordinary.

One day, flicking through a magazine, she locked on a world-famous model. That was it. That was her destiny. She would become the most ravishing, successful catwalk kit-ten in the history of fashion. She would seek revenge on all the people who had wronged her—her family, Nathan, the guys at the Rams, the freak with a stammer, the men who'd assaulted her—by defying them all.

A trip to LA and a queue of castings and that was it: the rise had begun. She would never forget the first thing the owner at Thunder Models had said:

You're the most incredible girl I've ever seen.

She had come so far. If she could survive that, she wasn't dying now.

No way.

This wasn't Tawny Linden any more: this was Tawny Las-celles.

Fresh air hit her lungs. Tawny slumped onto the earth, gasping and coughing the rancid peat from her mouth and nostrils. She heaved for breath, her body weighted with what felt like half a ton of mud.

She lay on her back, arms cast wide, her chest rising and falling.

'What's going on?'

Mitch's voice broke out of the forest. Tawny wrestled onto her elbows, her eyes gleaming blue from the crusted, black grime of her face. Her hair was matted in thick, glooping tendrils, Medusa-like, a creature emerged from the deep.

'Tawny went for a swim,' said Angela.

She helped the model to her feet, smothered in muck from top to toe.

'Come on,' she led the way, 'and let's stick to the trees this time.'

Little sleep was had that night. By the time the trio returned to the wreck, it was getting dark. Hulking shadows pooled beneath the trees.

Water sustained them, though all were aware it was a dwindling source. At twilight Eve found three coconuts pitted into the sand, which they prised open with the knife, thirstily devouring their contents and carving the fruit up between them.

Nobody objected to the beach relocation. The darkness in the jungle reminded them all of the crash, and with a new vista came revived hope.

All night they watched the far-off horizon, searching for the light of a boat or an approaching plane. The black canvas, swirling towards dawn into a palette of purple and orange, seemed an artificial sky that smelted in the climbing sun.

No one came.

38

America

'Calm down, Joanie! They'll find him; they will!'

Sketch Falkner watched Kevin's mother rampage through the Bel Air mansion, her face wild and tear-stained and her hair a ravaged nest.

The TV droned on in the background, a terrible harbinger and a flashing circus of despair. Search planes were being sent over the region. Boats had been dispatched. The aircraft's final communications were being analysed.

Out on the street, photographers and reporters teemed. Sketch had almost run a gang of them down on his way through, their clamouring and battering relentless and frightening. The tragedy had made monsters of them. This was a Hollywood movie sprung gruesomely to life, a genuine icon for every starring role. On the fringes of the calamity, the press grappled for their part in the story, the biggest the century would see. All across the world similar scenes played out. Families of the missing—managers, lovers, husbands, wives—were being hounded for a comment, and against those closed doors the media assailed the next rung: distant cousins, ex-boyfriends, old bosses, classmates, anyone and everyone who could give it that punch of emotion, who could speak of the despair and disbelief assailing the nation.

Sketch was in shock. Disasters on this scale just didn't happen. Not to people like them. Not to Kevin. Kevin, his boy wonder, his protégé, his surrogate son…

'This is your fault!' Joan was bawling. 'You made him go!'

Kevin's puck face danced in front of his eyes. The last time they had seen him.

'Joanie—'

'How could you do it?' She was frantic. 'I said to him at the airport, I said, *Kevin, baby, are you sure you want to go through with this?* And he said you were on his back about it, and what choice did he have? *You made him go!*'

Sketch grabbed her wrists as she thrashed and writhed. Joan was manic.

'Now look what's happened! My prince is dead!'

'Kevin isn't dead, do you hear me? *Kevin isn't dead.*' Sketch calmed her sufficiently to proffer a glass of water, but Joan slapped it away, causing it to jettison across a priceless Spanish suede futon he had picked out for Christmas. She launched the tumbler after it, smashing it against a trophy showcase.

'We have to remain calm,' Sketch said.

'*Calm?*' Joan's face was a twisted mask. 'Don't you see what's staring us in the face? They're gone! They're drowned!'

'We don't know that.'

'I don't care what the news says—they're lying to us; it's all lies!'

Sketch drew her close. Joan's strength sapped out of her and she collapsed.

'We don't know the facts,' he said. 'They're doing every-thing they can.'

'I want my baby!' Joan sobbed. '*I want my baby back!*'

'I know you do—but, Joanie, this will all be over in a matter of hours. They'll bring Kevin home; you'll see. Right now he's probably in a lifeboat someplace, catching a suntan! He'll tell us everything when he gets here—and he'll need you to be strong for him, OK? He'll need you to look after him.'

Joan pulled back, sodden with grief, her red eyes wide.

'You swear?' she gulped. 'You promise?'

'It's an ocean,' Sketch said, with a damn sight more confi-dence than he felt, 'and some freaking islands. How hard can it be?'

Noah Lawson hadn't seen Orlando Silvers since he was sev-enteen.

Physically, Angela's brother was as he remembered—the thick black hair, the richly tanned skin, the regal features and the air of riches untold—but never had Orlando been asso-ciated with this kind of fear. Unshaven and hollow-eyed, he paced the kitchen in the Boston house Noah had last set foot in nine years ago.

Noah remembered being here, upstairs, in her bedroom: the scent of the evening, her hand in his, her smile and her kiss, how it had felt to look deep into her eyes. He could not accept she was gone.

'I came to tell you I'm going. Angela's still alive.'

Orlando shook his head. 'It's useless,' he said emptily. 'They're already looking.'

'Not fast enough.'

'You think you stand a better chance?'

'I'm not letting her go.'

Noah had done that once. On a porch in Boston almost a decade ago, guilt in his heart and cash in his hand, and he was damned if he was doing it again.

'Quit playing the hero, Lawson. What's Angela to you anyway?'

'You know. She always said you knew. About us.'

Orlando looked up. 'It didn't take a genius to figure it out,' he said. 'Only time she seemed happy was after she saw you—same as when we were teenagers. She had me down as the enemy. She never realised I was her friend.'

'I would die for her,' said Noah.

'So would I. She was my little sister.'

Orlando thought of the bodies and for a second he could not breathe. Angela wasn't the only person that had mattered to him on that jet.

Not just Angela.

Eve. Stupid, stubborn, brilliant, exasperating, maddening Eve; Eve who refused to tell him the secrets of her heart but it didn't matter, she didn't need to, he could already see them, he could feel them, he knew it when they lay together, pretending it was nothing but sex, he knew it when he touched her beating blood and with it the fire in her soul, if only she would let him in…

The last words they had spoken had been in anger.

He could not let that be it.

'Whatever you thought in the old days,' said Noah, 'I never stopped loving Angela. I'm not going to stand by and watch this get held up by a load of suits and bureaucrats. It's still open. Nothing's been found. Nothing's confirmed.'

Orlando tried to push it away, but each time it sprang to the surface.

Eve…

My child…

'Where will you start?' he asked.

'The islands,' said Noah. 'There are thousands of rocks out there.'

'What makes you think they came down on land?'

'What makes you think they didn't?'

'And if you do find them?' Orlando dared allow himself the possibility. 'And what if they're...?' He didn't need to finish.

'I'd rather know,' said Noah. 'Wouldn't you?'

39

Szolsvár Castle, Gemenc Forest, Hungary

'Here we are, Mr Cane.'

Janika brought his lunch in on a tray. 'It's your favourite—salmon sandwiches and pickled cucumber.' She smiled, setting down the platter, and clasped her hands. 'After all, we're celebrating!'

So why didn't her boss look happier?

Voldan was seated in his wheelchair at the head of the dining room's grand mahogany table. His eyes flitted across the luncheon. In the adjacent Great Hall, news screens blared their perpetual memorial. 'Where is the mayonnaise?' he demanded.

'Oh!' Janika was crushed at the omission. 'My mistake, Mr Cane.'

She cursed herself as she shot off to the scullery. Lemon and tarragon cream was his preference. How could she have forgotten? Every distress Mr Cane suffered wounded her deeply. She was here to look after him, and look after him she must.

Moments later she was back, bearing a silver pot.

'Do you need anything else?'

His thumb was twitching. Janika knew how to read the

signs. Mr Cane's thumb only twitched like that when there was something on his mind.

He would tell her in his own time.

'Feed me,' he droned.

Janika adored mealtimes. It gave her a sense of power, to be the mother figure that brought fresh worms to the nest. Voldan parted his lips. Onto his tongue she placed the succulent chunks, sweet and salty pickles and the crustless squares of rye with their light spread of butter. She dabbed spots from the corners of his mouth.

The cordial he had requested was cloudy and sweet, and she offered it to him through a straw, watching as his poor, damaged skin closed meekly around it.

'Did you like that?' She smiled tenderly.

He indicated he had finished with a pursed, shut-tight mouth.

'Something troubles you,' Janika pressed. 'Tell me what it is.'

Voldan's eyes were fixed on the opposite wall. On it hung a portrait of his wife, her arm around a young Grigori. Two greyhounds nestled at their feet, and in the background the Gemenc Forest spread wide. Of course the likeness was imagined, she had never lived to see her son take his first steps, and had been drawn from Voldan's brief: how Grigori's mother might have looked, how she would have tended to and cared for her son, and, best of all, Grigori's unfettered joy at her company.

'Fetch me the telephone,' Voldan bleated. 'Now.'

Janika darted off, her footsteps echoing around the cavernous chamber.

Voldan traced circles on the arm of the wheelchair.

The maggot had come for him.

It had crawled beneath his skin while he slept, burrowing

deep and planting its seed of doubt. Each hour it buried further, digging a thin black hole in his heart.

Grigori's ghost had visited. Voldan had woken in the middle of the night.

They live on, his son had told him. *Our mission has failed.*

Strapped helpless to his bed, Voldan had longed to reach out and touch him. That beautiful face he had tried to conjure so many times. The cheeks he had kissed tears from when Grigori was a boy. He longed to hold his son. He longed to ask why Grigori had never come to him for help. He would have done anything.

Our mission has failed...

No stammer. In death, Grigori had been spared.

Doubt emaciated Voldan, rotting him like an apple on the winter ground.

It could not be—and yet the possibility, however faint, gnawed.

Janika wheeled in the walnut desk, empty apart from the handsome telephone at its centre. She lifted the receiver and dialled the number. The line rang.

Voldan spoke into it. Minutes later, he was finished.

His instructions had been heard.

Instantly, he felt revived. Grigori's work would yet be completed.

His eyes rested greedily on Janika, who had learned a long time ago not to ask questions. The maid's mousy hair was scragged back in a ponytail: a silent clue that she was eager to perform. Voldan had no sensation down there any longer, but it excited him to watch. Janika understood what he wanted. She wanted it, too.

Wordlessly, she trundled his chair back from the table.

Unzipping his trousers, she knelt.

Watching her was like watching a porno, a situation

removed, unfolding in a time and place with which Voldan would never be engaged.

His brain registered arousal yet he had no feeling to go with it.

He tried to imagine the warmth of her tongue, remember what it felt like to grow against the back of a woman's throat, but it was no good. Those days were gone.

Still, the ritual fascinated him. Janika took pleasure in the task, her moans becoming louder and her breasts smothering his knees, until seconds later she shuddered and cried, burying her face in his lap as her back shook and spasmed.

It was over.

Voldan fixed his eyes through the dining room door and into the Great Hall, where the crash reports continued their grisly eulogy.

In a way, they had both met their climax.

40

Day 2

Morning came.

Angela woke at dawn, sand in her hair and beneath her fingernails. The sweep of beach was as idyllic as it had appeared from up on the granite rock, under other circumstances a private slice of paradise: the clear, turquoise lagoon and the yawning ocean a seamless blue. The expanse was unchanged, the horizon still empty.

She had dreamed of him. At home in Boston, sixteen again, the day Angela had discovered the ring he put through her door, and slipped it on, a perfect fit.

'*Why d'you wear that thing for?*' Dino had asked.

'*It's personal.*'

'*So's your marriage.*'

Behind her, a wall of leaves whispered.

The beach was separated from the jungle by an abundance of palms. Their shafts were thick and coarse, rising to bulbous knots that were sprung with hair, and stalks that gave way to bursts of brilliant lime-green fronds. The leaves were wide, strong and stiff, a foot long and tapered at their ends to a dry, sharp point.

She found Eve alone further down the beach. Her clothes

were grimy and her legs were bare. She looked like she hadn't slept.

'Were you telling the truth yesterday?' said Angela.

Eve blinked. 'About what?'

'What you said to me in the plane.' Angela sat down. 'I knew before that, too. You're pregnant.'

Eve turned on her. Where the rest of the group was dazed and stumbling, like drawings from a shipwreck, Eve was sharp. Switched on. 'Don't say it again.'

'What do you want me to say?'

'This is my business. Only mine. I don't have to justify it to anyone.'

'I'm not asking you to.'

'I don't want anyone else to know.'

'They'll find out sooner or later.'

'Everyone here just cares about themselves. We're nothing to each other. Let's keep it that way.'

'I don't feel like that.'

'I'll remind them to saint you when we get home.'

Against the other woman's resolve, Angela found she could express the fear she had been keeping in check.

'We don't know if we're going home,' she said.

'We are. They'll come.'

'They might not.'

'They will.'

'Are you scared?'

'No.'

The sea washed in. The sun blazed down. The skyline gave them nothing.

'I thought I'd lost him,' said Eve, after a moment. She didn't look at Angela directly. 'I feel it's a boy. I don't know why. Just a feeling.'

Angela waited. 'Who's the father?'

'Nobody important.'

'Someone from England?'

'One of those things... A stupid thing.'

'But not a mistake.'

'Maybe a mistake.'

'Did you tell him?'

'Yes.'

'Jesus.' Angela exhaled. 'Poor guy must be going out of his mind.'

'Oh, he made his position perfectly clear,' said Eve. 'I was always on my own.'

'I'm sorry. That's hard.'

But Eve was quick to qualify, as if she'd said something she hadn't really meant. 'It wasn't like that. It's how I wanted it.'

The women squinted through the rising light. A bank of clouds was gathered on the horizon, shot through with pink and yellow. It could almost be beautiful.

'You know what I think?' said Angela.

'What?'

'I think your baby made it for a reason. I think we all did.'

'If it makes you feel better.'

'I'm guessing you're not the sentimental type.'

Eve threw her a short glance. 'Anyway, if you're so sure, what's the big reason? Why did we survive?'

But Angela didn't know. Not yet.

'I'll tell you once I've figured that out.'

She called a meeting. It was an effort to drag everyone together, literally and figuratively, resigned as some of the group were to gazing out at the ocean, as if by sheer force of will they could prompt a rescue to appear.

The sun shone down from an endless arc. Where the sand

banked against the palms was a raised stone slab. Angela stepped onto it.

'Today we split up,' she said. 'Kevin and Mitch, you return to the hold. Bring back everything you can. Water. Food. Supplies. All that's left of the luggage.' She nodded to Jacob. 'Anything we can use to help him—lotions, moisturisers, sun creams…'

'A bit late for that, isn't it?' Tawny snorted. 'A shame he wasn't wearing SPF when he caught fire!' She regretted it instantly. The rest of the group stared at her in appalled silence—even Kevin, whom she sensed was her safest ally.

But at the possibility of reclaiming their possessions, the mood lifted slightly. Kevin was thinking about his pills. Celeste was thinking about her soap. Tawny was thinking about her Gucci shades, her cherry-red FrenchFifty bikini, and, oh, her Chantecaille make-up bag, which after yesterday's swamp ordeal was top on her list of priorities. Only a pity she couldn't plug in her beloved straighteners.

Kevin asked: 'What about the bodies?' He and Celeste had located the first officer late last night: he, too, had perished. 'It's rank. They stink.'

'We've got to get rid of them,' agreed Celeste.

'Well duh,' said Tawny bitchily. 'Anything helpful to add?'

'How?' Angela asked. Celeste was right, and the sooner the better: they didn't want to attract animals. She scanned the faces looking up at her and offered herself:

'I'll do it.'

Celeste raised her hand. 'I'll help.'

Tawny rolled her eyes. The friction between these two had been instant. Angela had noticed the way the model clocked Celeste back at Jakarta, a swift glance up and down, as if assessing the competition. Of course Tawny was the more gorgeous, it went without saying—but where Tawny's beauty was enhanced by elaborate make-up and the finishing school of styling tongs, Celeste's look thrived on the opposite. Of all the assembled here today, the Italian, it had to be said, shone out as the prettiest. Her white skin and brown eyes were fragile and appealing. She oozed culture, sophistication and intelligence. Tawny couldn't stand it.

'We should put them out to sea,' said Eve. 'Keep them down with rocks. We'll need to build a raft—logs, something we can use as rope…'

Kevin pulled a face. 'Won't they wash back in?'

'How about a pyre?' Celeste suggested.

Tawny shot her a nasty look. 'A what?'

'A funeral pyre—we set fire to them and send them out that way.'

'Don't you think we've set fire to enough?' Tawny lowered her voice, as if Jacob had lost not just his sight but also the ability to hear when other people were talking about him. She made a point by taking his hand, managing to contain her revulsion at his injuries. Yesterday she wouldn't even have contemplated such a move—she could hardly imagine hitting downtown New York with a guy on her arm holding a white stick. Hopefully Jacob would be back to normal soon, and hopefully he would stop being blind as well, because if she was going to channel shipwreck chic (and if anyone could pull it off, Tawny could), then there had to be at least one hot guy around to witness it.

'Same problem,' said Angela. 'Unless we get right out into the ocean.'

'Then we go right out into the ocean,' said Eve.

'We shouldn't do that.'

'Why?' Tawny pouted. 'I went in the water yesterday.'

'The lagoon, yes—so long as we stay close to the shore.'

'What's the big deal?'

Nobody wanted to say it.

'Sharks,' said Angela.

Tawny's mouth fell open.

'I'll come with you,' offered Kevin, inflating his chest. 'If you're scared.'

'No offence,' snapped Tawny, 'but how much help would *you* be?' Kevin going up against a shark would be like a tadpole going up against, well, a shark.

'It's given me an idea, though,' said Angela. 'We need to make fire—for warmth, but also as a signal. Sooner or later, a ship's got to pass on that horizon.'

'We'll rub sticks,' said Kevin. 'I saw it on *Intense Survival*. You make this nest of twigs and leaves and things and then pile the sticks on top. We need a mirror, and glass to catch the sunlight, then we build it up and make a spark—'

'We'll use a lighter,' interjected Eve. 'I've got one in my purse.'

'That doesn't solve the problem of the pilots,' said Celeste.

'Why not?' Tawny yawned. 'Burn them.'

'You could do that?'

'Of course,' Tawny lied. 'We're not all pathetic like you.'

'Don't be like that, Tawny,' said Angela.

'What? It's true. Celeste shouldn't even *be* here; she's hardly in the same league. And what's she done to help out anyway? Oh yeah, she prayed—fat lot of good that did. Hello, God? What, nobody there? Big surprise. Meanwhile poor Jacob was risking his life, trying to save ours—'

'I wish I hadn't been on that plane,' said Celeste.

'Wow, no shit, I'm enlightened.'

'And I might speak more if you didn't criticise everything I say.'

'So it's my fault now, is it?'

'I never said that.'

'Whatever, bitch.'

'Enough!' said Angela. 'We turn against each other and we lose everything. We're all each other has right now, do you understand?'

Tawny sulked. Celeste looked away.

'We'll take the bodies over the mountain,' said Angela. 'The same route we walked yesterday. There's a highland at the top. We'll carry them over the ridge.'

'What about the woman?' said Eve.

Nobody wanted to think about the flight attendant. She was still out there. They hadn't been able to find her, had scoured the jungle and the crash site. Nothing.

'I can't promise she wasn't left in the hold,' Angela said. 'When we got out, I wasn't thinking... It was a blur. I panicked. There was heaps of rubble, and I...' She spoke the sad truth. 'She didn't even cross my mind.'

'We'll look,' said Mitch. 'She has to be somewhere.'

The senator seemed to think twice about it, before asking: 'Did anyone take a walk on the beach yesterday? Round by the bluff, towards the caves?'

'We only came down to the beach at night.' Angela frowned. 'Why?'

'No reason.'

'Did you see something?'

'Only I wondered if we'd explored that part of the coastline yet. We should.'

The rest of the group was disbanding.

'OK,' said Angela, as she stepped off the rock. 'Good idea.'

Mitch went off across the sand.

She watched the statesman go, her eyes narrowed against the heat.

The rear fuselage was a mangled chaos. Its plummet from the canopy had destroyed what form it managed to maintain through impact, rendering it a wreck of metal and plastic. Shards of aluminum, molten at their edges, were strewn like abstract sculptures. Everything was a crumpled heap. It was impossible to believe that this thing had once been airborne, and that they had been inside it.

Kevin was rummaging through the remains. He had ripped strips off his T-shirt to wrap around his forehead. His torso was slick with sweat that gathered in his sternum and trickled into the waistband of his jeans. His shoulders were burned, the skin there flaking, and his hairless legs were pimpled with insect bites.

'What happened?' he asked. 'What started it?'

Mitch Corrigan was tearing through the burst cabin, pulling his way to the back. His wig was skewed to one side and Kevin figured he had lost whatever pins were responsible for holding that road kill in place.

'I don't know,' the senator replied.

'The thing is,' said Kevin, 'I dreamed this. I dreamed the whole thing.'

'Mm.'

'Don't you think that's messed up? It's like I knew it was

going to happen or something... I should have said, but like anyone would have believed me...'

Mitch surfaced, swiping his forehead. He leaned over to catch his breath.

'You OK, man?' Kevin said. 'You look kinda sick.'

'I'm fine.'

'Is it that flight attendant? Did you find her?'

'Just leave me alone, would you?'

'Hey,' Kevin held his hands up, 'sorry for asking...'

They worked in silence and that suited Kevin fine because Mitch Corrigan was psycho. He came across on TV so confident and together, with his career in movies and the White House and everything, but in person it was like he was jumped up on something. They were all freaking, but the senator was next level. Getting to the wreck had been nuts, with Mitch tensing and checking behind him at every crack of a twig, every snap of a branch. Kevin didn't mind so much because it made *him* feel like the big man, which was funny since he cried at a spider in his room at home.

Home.

He thought of Joan, and Sketch, and the guys at Cut N Dry. He thought of his Little Chasers.

What were they going through? What did they think had happened to him?

The backlash would be unreal. Hard to believe that all those miles away the tragedy was coming to light. Kevin half expected to be able to hear it, a distant explosion. This was part of the same earth, but it didn't feel like it. Here, it didn't matter that he was Kevin Chase. It didn't matter that any of them was anyone.

Those familiar things he had raged against were now impossible indulgences. Kevin had been a dick. He saw it plain as day. He had taken it for granted, every adoring fan, every one of his mom's perfumed cuddles, every superstar he had met in his whirlwind social calendar on a power trip that half the globe would happily have given their right arms for, and all he wanted now was every part of it back.

All the bitching he had done, in the face of all he had. Those people in Salimanta, whose lives were reduced to nothing, no possessions but the clothes on their backs: they were the ones to feel sorry for. Kevin's gut cramped with guilt.

He and Mitch unearthed the crate of water: thirty bottles; warm as a bath and it wouldn't last long but, for now, it was better than nothing. Mitch tore the cap off one and downed half. He held the remainder out to Kevin and Kevin guessed they should save it for the others but he was thirsty and they'd been working so he took it.

The luggage Angela had hoped for was a lost cause. Part of her bag was intact, together with a satchel containing Eve's smashed iPad, but that was it. The rest was a mangle of charred garbage. Kevin and Mitch clambered through it, victorious when they turned up something new—a phone charger, a half-demolished sneaker, a face towel, Kevin's set of headphones, the only thing he had left—

His pills!

Fuck!

Kevin's lungs constricted. His fingers went tingly. His breath was strangled. He was about to topple over into a panic attack.

What was he going to do without his pills?

'You got asthma or something?' asked Mitch.

'I—no—my medication—'

'Where?'

'In my bag,' Kevin gasped, 'it's gone.'

'Christ, kid, what are we looking for? A bottle? An inhaler?'

'Pills.'

'Pills?' Mitch stopped. 'Can you do without them?'

'I don't know.'

'What do you mean, you don't know? What are they?'

'Vitamins.' Kevin heard how lame that sounded, even through the jangling chords of his hysteria. 'Special vitamins.'

'What for?'

At a loss for his own words, he echoed Sketch's. 'To keep me at the top of my game!' Then he added pointlessly, 'It's hard being me, you know!'

'Keep calm. You'll be fine. It's just vitamins.'

'It's not *just vitamins*—I've been taking them my whole life!'

'Doctor prescribe them?'

'No.' Kevin realised a doctor had never told him to take any pills—only Sketch and the board at Cut N Dry. 'My management.'

'I'm sure they'll understand,' said Mitch.

But it wasn't that. Right now Kevin couldn't give two shits whether Sketch understood or not. It was that without his pills he didn't know which way was fucking up. He had been tripping on a high wire for long enough—and now this?

To be stranded out here, of all places, without his precious capsules?

What was going to become of him?

Celeste started a fire. She piled the kindling close to camp and used Eve's light to catch the flame. Blowing the flint, she watched as a thin stream of smoke danced like ribbon, wrap-

ping round the nearest twig, snaking up its length and crack-
ling to life.

The fire must smoke non-stop. It was their best—their
only—chance.

Celeste understood their place on the map, and it didn't
fill her with courage. This was a vast ocean dotted with clusters of islands, archipelagos made up of scores, perhaps hundreds, of rocks, and theirs was a tiny speck.

Help could be a long time coming. Had they been near
civilisation, it would have arrived by now. Seaplanes would
have been sent. Helicopters. Lifeboats.

They had to be cast out on their own. Their island was
invisible. From what the others had said, it was unlikely to
ever have been visited.

Marooned. A word that belonged with Robinson Crusoe:
silly and fictional.

But that was what they were.

The flames fizzed and spat, too hot to be near, and Celeste
went to the lagoon to rinse the dirt from her hands. The water
was cool and clear, light enough to be silver, and tiny fish
zigzagged through the shallows. She submerged her cupped
hands and caught one, feeling it tickle the skin on her palms
before letting it go.

'You stupid woman,' Carl had told her once, when they
had holidayed in the South of France. They had taken a boat
out, deep-sea fishing: Carl's favourite pastime though he was
yet to have success. Celeste had tried her luck, and on her first
attempt the line had snagged, resulting in the biggest reel of
the day. Immediately she had unhooked and released the fish
into the water. She hadn't been able to bear its gasping mouth
and straining gills, the way it flipped gracelessly on the deck,
and how Carl had staked claim to it, this bewildered creature
that ought to be free.

'*You stupid, sentimental woman.*'

She pictured Carl now in the Venice apartment. It was dull, the weather bad, and he was in his chair at the window. He wouldn't cry. Carl wasn't a man who cried. Instead, he would think. About what he could do to get her back—because wherever Celeste went, however far and for however long, she would always go back to him.

It seemed a long way away, that drizzly Venice apartment. Here, the sun blazed. The water glittered. She was marooned. Nobody was getting her back.

She turned to the forest, and saw something move.

Just a slip between the trees: a black, liquid shape, gone as soon as it was there.

Celeste froze.

The jungle wall remained still.

She searched for movement but the shape was gone.

The heat played tricks: she must have imagined it. But firm as she told it, she didn't believe. Last night she had witnessed the same thing, a shadow in the dusk, close to the camp, watching them. Like now, the second she turned, it had vanished.

When the jet had gone down, Celeste had thought of one thing. One person.

The person she had killed.

This is your punishment, a voice had said.

You deserve this. No one can save you now.

There were no such things as ghosts.

She made her way up the beach towards Jacob. He was resting in the shade of a palm, a bandage wrapped round his eyes. Celeste remembered him at Jakarta: confident, arrogant, full of bravado. That man was gone.

They found antiseptic cream in the first aid. Celeste had

been swabbing his chest and face. Thankfully the burns were
surface wounds, and looked far worse than they were. She
could already see new skin emerging, smooth and intact. The
key was to avoid infection. If she could keep the damage
clean and hydrated, he might just pull through. She prayed he
would. She couldn't imagine what Jacob must be enduring:
for all the terribleness of their ordeal, it would be nothing
compared with his.

The first time she had tended to him, he had grabbed her
wrists.

'Tawny? Is that you?' He had been delirious, confused.
'Who is that?'

'Celeste.'

'Where's Tawny? Is she here?'

'Yes, she's here.'

Tawny had come rushing. The supermodel refused to care
for his wounds, but neither did she like it when Celeste took
charge. Were Tawny and Jacob lovers? At Jakarta there had
been a definite frisson, equal parts desire and dislike. But for
all Tawny's proclamations, Celeste had seen the way she'd
flinched from him in the beginning, recoiling from an attractive thing gone ugly, as if the disease were contagious and
her own loveliness could be put at risk; the fear that her rosy,
glossy fruit would become pitted and withered, because there
was nothing left without it.

Then again, Tawny didn't much like anything Celeste did,
so there was no way of winning. Celeste didn't know what
she had done to garner such animosity. She wasn't the sort
to make enemies, and it was a shock to find herself on the
receiving end of Tawny's barbed remarks.

Jacob stirred. Celeste touched his shoulder.

'Here,' she said. 'Water.'

She held the bottle to his lips. He drank from it. Droplets

ran down Jacob's neck and she caught them before they could soak the collar of his shirt.

'I'll get you more.'

'Don't,' Jacob reached out, 'wait. Stay. Stay and talk to me a while. Please. I can't... I don't want to be alone.'

Celeste sat back down. 'What do you want to talk about?' she said.

'Anything. You. Tell me about you.'

42

Eve sank beneath the surface of the water. It was a clear pool bordered by soaring rock, making it safer than the sea or the lagoon. The cliffs offered shade, but where they broke pockets of sunlight shone through and danced on the ripples. At one end a waterfall crashed lusciously into the glittering sheet, throwing up spray.

She floated on her back, listening to the sharp caw of tropical birds, the flutter of high branches as they swayed and bucked under the leaps and dives of wild things.

Her baby's heart was beating. A drum within a drum, a rhythm within a rhythm: a part of her. How strange that she had come close to extinguishing it. Even now, against the severity of this place, she would not retract that decision. It had been right then and it was right today.

Who's the father?

Perhaps she should tell. She and Angela had been through enough: what they had seen and heard and been forced to do over the last two days meant surely they could never be shocked again. What did it matter anyway? It wasn't as if she and Orlando were together. Angela would be surprised; maybe she'd be disappointed. Eve wasn't the sort of girl he normally went for. She might even be branded a liar.

Knowing Angela made better sense of Orlando. Arrogant,

selfish Orlando: Orlando who smelled of expensive cologne and wore suits that cost more than she earned in a year. Orlando who had challenged in her London flat and at their table the night they'd fought, and told her he wanted nothing to do with the life he had made. Orlando who had lost his father, and now his sister, and now the mother of his child, though how much he cared for the last was hard to say. Angela had that same streak of belligerence. She would be tough to argue with. Orlando was the only man against whom Eve's sharp tongue had been blunted: she sensed it ran in the genes.

What was going through his mind? What was going through any of their minds? Had the group been written off? Had they been deemed a lost cause? What if, for all their hopes and prayers, no one was looking for them?

No. Any second now, the boats would sweep in. They would return to their lives, the incident carried with them, and, in a year, maybe two, maybe ten, it would start to fade. It would become part of a long-forgotten dream. Imagined. Impossible.

Eve swam to the ridge, scooping her arms through the radiant lake. Opening her eyes underwater she saw shoals of brightly coloured fish—pink, purple, gold and green—darting this way and that, their metallic stripes shimmering.

Reaching the side, she hauled herself out. The jungle pulsated with hidden life.

She checked she was alone. Her bump was modest and beneath clothes could still be concealed, but naked there was no denial. Angela was right, the group would find out soon enough. Perhaps she had already told (though Angela didn't seem one to disclose other people's secrets). Eve could hear the accusations—why had she come? Why had she flown? How could she have been so irresponsible? She had already

thrown all she could at herself and didn't need anyone else's
input.

They would assume she had accepted for the bloodlust. All
they knew of Eve Harley was as a story-hungry jackal. The
lure of celebrity, another ego-fuelled set ripe for the pickings,
whose jaunt halfway across the world would make front-page
news.

They would assume she had put her job before her unborn
child.

Had she?

Tawny hated her. Kevin hated her. Mitch Corrigan hated
her worst of all.

She didn't care. These people meant nothing.

Before she left London, Eve had completed the Veroli
piece, sending it to her editor with one important omission:
Corrigan's name. If they could hold out just a few more
weeks, she promised, it would spell the ultimate exclusive.
After the trip to Indonesia, Eve would have the definitive
Senator Corrigan exposé, the kind of up close and personal
that money couldn't buy.

While the paper had been persuaded, they had insisted on
publishing parts of what they had. The item made no mention
of Corrigan, but it remained clear the writer knew exactly
whom *Mr X* was. Judging by Corrigan's reluctance to give
Eve a second of his time, she was confident he had seen
it.

Corrigan knew she was on to him. He knew it had been
her who'd trailed him in Italy. He would know better than to
think he had escaped. She would wait, that was what she did,
lying low in the grass. Angela Silvers might not be one to
disclose other people's secrets—but Eve was. She hadn't got
this far by nursing a conscience.

She was pulling on clothes when, from the corner of her

eye, she detected something move: an outline, solid yet liquid, pouring from a tree branch.

A fat black snake was coiled round the limb, about a foot from where she stood. Its scales were jet, apart from the rings of bright, fierce yellow that were splashed down its length. Against the foliage the serpent's marks were dagger-points, spooling and writhing. Its head, the underside a same vivid canary, dripped down to her level.

Its tongue darted out. It eyed her beadily, its tight reptilian skull leading a weapon of brutal muscle and fatal efficiency. She dared not move. The snake's head dipped from side to side, a queasy pendulum, before, silent and smooth, it slinked back onto the branch, unfurled itself and slipped soundlessly from sight.

43

Ten thousand miles away, on a terrace outside the Parisian, Dino Zenetti released an anguished shout and kicked the top of a mock-stone fountain.

He turned on his father.

'She's *my* prize!' he yelled. 'Get her back!'

'It ain't that easy, D,' Carmine Zenetti replied.

He let his only son play out the tantrum. Dino had always been hot-headed. He always reacted badly to news. Sometimes he needed just a little time to think it over, before he saw the advantages. For a man like Carmine, there were always advantages.

'We're supposed to be gettin' married! Holy crap, I waited long enough.' Dino's face was puce. Spit pellets flew from his mouth. Angela was a hot piece: he had been champing to nail her his whole life and, just as he got within reach, she went and got herself killed. 'She never even put out!' he complained.

Carmine took a seat. As usual, he waited for the penny to drop.

'An' what's that jackass Lawson thinking, jumpin' in on

my parade? Angela's mine, goddamnit! I oughtta floor the guy!'

'You would if he was worth it,' said Carmine.

'Fuckin' damn straight I would.' Though Dino had never been in a fight in his life. 'Acting like he's Indiana fuckin' Jones—y'know they're saying he got with Angela one time? Makin' out like it's a big fuckin' love story and what am I s'posed to do with that? Fuck him. Fact is she's *engaged*. To *me*.'

Carmine narrowed his eyes. He didn't give a crap whatever stories came out, except for the one where they all got found someplace, which, while nobody wanted to say so, was never going to happen. Jeez, it was getting boring! Nobody talked about anything else.

If just one VIP had carked it, the reaction would be bad enough, but stick a load of them at the bottom of the ocean and things got out of hand. After a time it became nothing but white noise, shock piled on shock piled on shock. There was no upward scale, no escalation. It reminded Carmine of his ex-wife, who had used to scream at him at equal volume whether he left a clump of hair in the shower drain or nailed six hookers in a night and blew three million dollars on the craps table.

Carmine tuned out. He had higher matters on his mind.

'Exactly,' he said.

'Exactly what?'

'You're engaged. You and Angela.'

'Yeah? What about it?'

'Think it through, D.' Carmine stood. 'The contract we signed entitles us to half the Silvers fortune. That sum's trebled since the engagement got announced.'

'And?'

'And in turn Angela gets half of the Zenettis'.' Carmine paused, licked his lips. 'But what if there is no Angela?'

'I don't get it.'

'Until the marriage got stamped, the whole deal rests with her, right? My little slice of insurance pie—in case she had a wise idea and decided to back out.'

'She wouldn't have.'

'It don't matter if she would or she wouldn't,' Carmine said. 'What matters is that *the Silvers don't see a dime*. Orlando, Gianluca, kaput. Now she's gone, it all comes to us, kid—the mother ship! That's what I've been tryin' to tell you…'

'But she *is* coming back. We're getting married.'

Carmine pursed his lips. He approached his son, held him by his shoulders and abruptly drew him into an embrace. Carmine was not a man who often showed affection, and Dino stood limply, his arms hanging down by his sides.

'Let it go,' Carmine murmured. 'It's over.'

'But—'

'But you and me are richer than we've ever been.' Carmine drew back, holding Dino at arm's length. 'Every business cloud has a silver lining, my friend.'

44

Day 3

Another day came. Nothing changed. No sign of home.

LA, Boston, San Fran, New York; London, Tokyo, Lagos… They flicked through Jacob's mind like shadows on a wall. Make-believe cities unfeasible in their light and sound, their movement. The clubs he had partied in, the music he had danced to, the shots he had drunk, the women he had kissed, the parties he had crashed, the sunsets he had seen: so much to see and so many colours.

Heat alone separated day from dusk. Behind his bandages, everything was dark. Celeste came to unwrap him. The red glow on his lids blazed. She held up fingers, asked him to count how many. He started to see glimmers, sometimes wrong, mostly wrong, but he tried and when he got it wrong they tried again.

Later, he went to the pool with Tawny. She kept charging off ahead and having to come back and haul him up when he stumbled. He hated it. He had never felt so powerless. Here was the woman he had spent weeks trying to impress, and this was the result.

Since they had no clothes to change into, the same set had to be washed. Jacob heard her undress, and pictured it: the material gathered at her feet, her skin brown, her blonde hair lightened in the sun. Of all his companions, hers was the face he remembered most clearly. Tawny's beauty had been etched onto his mind since the moment they had met. He pictured her breasts, the nipples pink and delicate. Her bush, honey-coloured, damp in the heat. Tawny's body was here, finally right next to him, close enough to touch—and Jacob couldn't see a thing.

He thought of the girls on his tapes, their eyes looking past the camera but never into it, glazed and vacant. Images played on a twisted loop. All of them, looking at him—and he couldn't look back.

Tawny was wringing her clothes. She didn't stop talking. She seemed to have two modes, verbal splurge or hysterical tears. They all had their way of dealing.

'…It was the freakiest thing,' Tawny was saying. 'Cacatra Island, you know? Reuben van der Meyde's place—that über-exclusive spa rehab; I was going to say you must have been, but then you probably haven't because *most* people haven't. Anyhow I went last summer—and when we came here I thought at first, Shit, this is it! Just a different bit… And when we went to the top, I don't know, maybe the sun fried my brain, but I could swear we were going over the hill and there it would be—all the huts dotted on the water and the helicopter pad and everything…but of course there wasn't—just more cliffs, and more sea, and more heat, and more jungle. Maybe the next ridge, I thought, maybe then, but we could see the whole island by then…'

Jacob imagined their position on a map, a giant map of Indonesia and the Banda Sea. If it were Jacob he would call it without hesitation: the passengers had died. The plane had crashed. Game over.

'...I guess Angela wants me to be grateful, and I mean don't get me wrong or anything, it's not like I'm *not* grateful, but then it *was* her fault in the first place that we went anywhere near that stupid swamp. Look, talk to me once you're in that position 'cause I'm telling you, it's like the worst thing ever. And I thought the mudpacks at the Monterey were bad! Anyhow now it's like she wants me to kiss her ass. It's like we have to do things *her* way because *she's* the only one who knows what she's talking about or whatever. Who made her chief? I didn't.'

There was a neat splash, and Jacob's face was spattered with water. He heard her swimming and inched towards the rim of the pool, hands discovering the earth, positioning himself on the ledge and dangling his legs in.

'Promise me you're not peeking?' said Tawny.

'I'm not.'

'Promise you can't see a thing?'

'Just a blur.'

'Can you see this?'

There was an upsurge of water. He envisaged her breasts on the surface.

'How about this?'

He wished he could.

'Celeste has got the hots for you, you know,' said Tawny. 'It's obvious. She's hardly had much practice with men—you can tell. Well, not *you*, because you can't see, but to me it's painful. Maybe she's got a thing for blind people. Ha! Sorry—lame joke.' She swam closer. Jacob felt her put her hands on his knees.

'Do you like Celeste?' said Tawny softly. 'Do you think she's pretty?'

'I don't remember what she looks like.'

'Liar.'

'I don't.' It was the truth. Celeste had been tending to him more than anyone else, but he couldn't even recall setting eyes on her in Jakarta. She must have been there, but he had been so wrapped up in Tawny he hadn't noticed.

'It's your turn,' said Tawny.

'For what?'

'To wash.' Her hands spread up his thighs. 'Take your clothes off.'

She helped him remove his shirt. As she peeled it open, she ran her hands across his muscled chest. The patch beneath his collarbone stung, the burn almost healed but still sore to touch.

Next came his jeans.

'And the rest,' she said.

Jacob could feel her cool breasts pressed against his shins. He took a risk and reached down, catching one in his hand. Tawny gasped in surprise or affront, but it lasted only a second before she sank closer. Her breast filled his palm, the nipple stiff and pronounced. She took his other hand and pressed it to her chest. He imagined her nakedness, her head thrown back and her hair trailing into the water...

Jacob's brain told him he was aroused, but his dick wouldn't work.

Tawny took a step out of the water, her chest level with his face, and he felt her fingers guiding his chin. Obediently he tasted, licking and biting her skin. He cupped her ass, slipping his touch into the moist slit. At the front she was completely hairless, not what he had expected, and it felt strange, alien, without being able to see.

His cock lay dormant. Tawny freed it. He felt her tongue engage and if anything was going to get him hard this was it.

She flicked across his penis, circling the head, and moaned, taking him in her mouth. Everything about this should have been turning him on, but every time he went to let go something stopped him.

Tawny after the crash; how she had recoiled from his injuries.

Get him away from me! She had yelped, as if he were a monster.

'What's the matter?' she asked now. The question came from a different mouth to the one that had moments ago been pleasuring his balls; it was the voice of his History teacher at school. *Pay attention, Jacob! What's the matter with you?*

'Nothing,' he said. 'Keep going.'

'Like hell I am. You want to screw, then try getting hard.'

'What do you think I'm doing?'

She laughed scornfully. Jacob heard the swish of water as she backed away.

'Sorry if I didn't realise it was going to be such an effort. The impression you gave me before we came out here, I thought you'd be spunking all over the place!'

'I guess I'm not in the best frame of mind. Go figure.'

A pause before she asked, 'Is it me?'

'No.'

'Is it because you can't see me?'

'I don't think so.'

'It must be. If you could see me you wouldn't be having this problem.'

'It isn't a problem.'

She snorted, confidence restored. 'It isn't anything.'

He fumbled for his clothes. Tawny didn't help.

'I'm not used to this,' he said.

'Believe me,' Tawny hauled herself from the pool, 'neither am I.'

He felt, rather than heard, her go.

Jacob dressed alone.

He put everything on the wrong way round, and had to wait for the next person to come to the pool and assist him before he could get back to camp.

45

Night fell. The fire flickered, red and gold, casting a glow across their sleeping bodies. The lagoon was a sheet of ink, creamy moonshine thrown across its surface. Flames leaped and sprang; and beyond the beach, behind the palms, the deep jungle trembled with nocturnal imaginings. Dark screams sprang from a dark place.

Celeste went to the shore. She listened to the wash of the sea as it kissed the sand and with it her toes. It was warm at night, soaking up the heat from the beach.

Serrated cliffs were visible, giant silhouettes above the silent indigo. In a spill of moonlight, a shape glided darkly through the water.

Another shark fin followed instantly.

The realisation of this prehistoric creature was incredible. Fear was dwarfed by awe, for in this context the animal seemed less terrifying than majestic.

Here, it belonged, and they were the imposters. This was its home, not theirs.

She daren't tell the others that she couldn't swim. She didn't want to be weak, or to be ruled out of things, the pathetic woman that Carl always told her she was.

Tawny had already targeted her for sticking to the shallows instead of the pool. '*You can't soap-dodge for ever, you know.*' If only she knew how Celeste scrubbed night and day, rinsing off her crime until the skin bled and tore. Then Tawny had added, maliciously, under her breath, '*Fucking Europeans.*'

Celeste returned to the fire, cracking and hissing as it spat orange gems into the night. Sleeping bodies were scattered on the sand. By the forgiving glow of the flames, Jacob looked young and vulnerable, like a child. Innocent.

A sparkle caught her eye, winking in the darkness. *Diamonds.*

Next to a gently snoring Tawny was a shallow, wide boulder, on which the chain was delicately laid. Celeste knew that Jacob had bought the necklace for her. Tawny hadn't stopped going on about it, making sure Celeste was in earshot every time she did. '*He pursued me like you wouldn't believe— flowers, jewellery, you name it! It's kind of cute. What sane girl says no to diamonds?*'

It had been months since Celeste had last stolen. She watched the gems, thinking of Jacob, and Tawny, and Carl, and how out of control the world had become.

She crept closer. Temptation beckoned.

She listened for Tawny's exhalations, a rhythmic murmur, and reached out.

Unseen, Celeste lifted the diamonds, her swift fingers pearl-white in the liquid sable. Her pulse slowed. Her blood calmed. She watched Tawny's face and wondered at how something so lovely could be so unkind.

All night she held the jewels in the palm of her hand, tight, as if someone already knew they were there and would come to take them from her.

***

A shriek erupted from the forest. It was met by a second, this one a shout, almost human. Kevin shivered. He turned his back on the trees that marked the limit of their territory.

The dividing wall was deep and inscrutable. It frightened him; in the pitch it crept closer, a faceless, nameless shroud behind which mad things flourished.

Everyone was asleep.

A solitary tear rolled out of Kevin's eye and plopped down to his ear. He sat up, swallowed his sobs, and traced into the sand the KC symbol that adorned all his album covers. Come the morning, when the tide washed in, the sign would dissolve. It felt significant.

At home, the world revolved around Kevin Chase. Out here, Kevin Chase ceased to be. All the petty grievances he had held against Sketch, how trivial they seemed now. All the times he had told his mom to staple her cake-hole shut, or sworn at his PR, or stomped off with Trey, or blasted Rusty for a pointless thing…

He wished Sketch were here to tell him what to do. Kevin had never decided on much himself—assistants were always on hand; hordes of his subjects grovelling to help—and who could blame him? He had lived like a god, and gods didn't need to look after themselves. Out here, he was no god. He was a castaway.

If he were back in LA, hearing this shit happen to someone else, he would figure they had all died. Of course he would. More bleak was the fact he would give it all of five minutes' thought before focusing on the next distraction: where to get a cookie milkshake, who was giving him most love on Twitter, where the label wanted to shoot his new kick-ass album cover…

Maybe the loss of his pills would bring about a quicker, merciful end.

The pills.

In living memory, Kevin had never let a day pass without them. Realising their loss had been like toppling from a skyscraper. He would keep falling, and only when he had fallen for long enough would he start to see the effects of the lapse. He was convinced that things were about to change.

Without his pills, he would start to transform.

Into what, he did not know.

Mitch checked the gold watch. Three a.m. Noiselessly he drew a log from the pile and held it to the fire. The end glowed, throwing off sparks that whispered and cracked. The fire betrayed their presence. It found them out. It made them conspicuous to anyone who cared to look. It was a single candle left to burn in a deserted house.

Angela stirred and moaned, turning in her sleep. Mitch stilled. He waited. He had to be sure. He didn't want anyone following, not where he was going.

The torch was lit. Mitch turned to the raven forest. It welcomed him, the noises deep inside calls to a dark and curious part of his soul.

With barely a ripple, the trees swallowed him.

Inside, the tropical air was singing. Animal cries whipped through the canopy, impossible to separate or identify. Monkey screams and livid birdcalls, a flutter of wings and the shake of a branch, vibrating undergrowth swarming round his feet—and, at a lower, more menacing pitch, a suffering yowl. It was caught in the throat, thick, mournful, melancholy, close to a growl but not quite. At intervals it seemed horribly close, at others far away, but then Mitch reminded himself there could be more than one creature making it. The forest was rife with nameless plagues.

Flame held aloft, he began the trek to the mountain. It was easier than the first day. Others had taken the route since, flattening the vegetation into a path. Though the night brought with it new menace, nothing could be as bad as the heat of high noon.

After a time he emerged on to the plateau. Up here the star-rich vault seemed close enough to touch, and the crisp, clear moon was dimpled with craters.

He crossed the plinth, without hesitation scrambling down the side of the mountain, gripping the holds and footings that broke up the lethal gradient. Several times he stumbled, slipping on loose dirt, and grabbed a clutch of weeds, careful not to drop his torch for fear of setting fire to the dry, sun-baked moss.

Finally he was spat out onto the beach.

It was an unfriendly shoreline; the crags were cruel and the sea bruised and heaving, swelling around clusters of hostile, skull-splitting rock and churning white froth against the cliffs. He remembered a movie he had shot in the eighties, his renegade character on a mission to rescue his lost love. Mitch had punched pirates, leaped into writhing breakers and abseiled down precipices. *Tony Gunn.* He hadn't thought of the character's name in years.

Across the sand, the mouth of the cave grinned back.

Mitch advanced. What footprints he had seen would have been washed away—unless a new set had been made. He felt fear, but he also felt deliverance. If they were here, he would find them. He could not be the hunted any more.

He had to become the hunter.

Even before Mitch entered the fissure, he could feel how freezing it was. Guided by torchlight, he stepped into its damp, slick interior. It smelled of salt. Stalagmites rose like witches' fingers from the pitted sand, lifeless yet organic,

the misshapen bulges that millennia had spawned, one lonely
drip at a time.

Drip, drip, drip...

Sound echoed through the cavern, ghostly and thin. It must
connect with another cavity further up, some flue where the
wind got in.

Drip, drip, drip...

Mitch moved deeper. To think of this hollow as unexplored
since the sun first warmed the Earth. To think that he was the
first person to enter...

Or was he?

A snake of sand, twisting between rocks, and there, illuminated by the glow, was a chain of footprints. Fright slid
under Mitch's skin. Ahead was darkness, into which the
prints meandered then disappeared. He held the flame high,
his knuckles tight, afraid to look further in, afraid as a child
of what might soar from the shadows.

Drip, drip, drip...

His torch was being extinguished. Dribbling stalactites pit-
patted on the stick, making it falter and fizz. The glow around
him shrunk, closer and closer, and died.

A sour lump rose in his throat.

Turning, Mitch saw he had been lured in deep. The
entrance to the cave was a remote pinch in a stifling canvas
and he dashed for it, stubbing his toe on the uneven ground
and tripping in his haste. The aperture of open beach trembled closer.

A cry of wings! Black terror. An explosion around his
head, hitting him, slapping his face, clawing his hairpiece, as
the cave sprang to frenzied life. A rush of air punched him
forward and knocked him flat. Fragments of black fog assailed him, leathery and swift and hectic, and beyond his own
cries of alarm wheeled a shrill, ceaseless squeak. Mitch buck-

led his arms over his head, his mouth filled with grit, as the stampede prickled and shivered across his back. With horror he realised that something had attached itself to his head. It whipped and pulled, twisted and tore, trying to break free. He could feel its claws rip through his toupee, tangled in the thick crown and yanking it free. A colony of bats shot out into the night and he reeled after them, yanking his rug with one hand and the other flailing its way in the dark.

Onto the beach he flew like a madman, thrashing his head until finally, disastrously, the rodent broke free, taking off into the night with a thick slap of wings.

Its silhouette flew against the moon, that heavenly orb as round and bald as the man now gazing up at it, for clasped in the fruit bat's toes was the senator's chestnut wig.

46

Angela found refuge in closed eyes. There, she could be with him.

She tried to capture every detail, the crease in Noah's cheeks and the way his eyes lit up when he laughed. The day he had picked her up in his friend's car, the first time they had gone to the lake, and she had spent the whole ride watching his hands on the wheel and wanting to hold one.

In her mind they were together. It didn't matter where they were, so long as they were together. She was buried in the warmth of his chest and could smell his skin, that safe, Noah smell. Sometimes she captured it so sharply that she could almost believe it were true, and when she woke in bursts to the eternal sky and remembered where she was and what had happened, her heart almost stopped.

A marble moon gazed down, watching them, curious, these creatures that didn't belong, childlike in their fumbling for answers.

Noah, where are you?

Angela was just a person, ordinary, average, unremarkable, and never more so than out here. They had all been stripped of their decorations. Now they had to see what was left.

Who could adapt, and who would survive?

I'll try, she thought. *I'll try for you.*
Always, his name flew back to her.
Noah.
It was sweet on her tongue, like a lullaby.

47

America

Noah Lawson arrived at LAX amid a stampede of photographers. Security did all they could to keep the paps at bay but it was no use: in the aftermath of the disaster the press had been hurtled into apocalypse—just one name on that doomed list would fuel ample stories for a lifetime. And it was one name they were concerned with.

'Noah, are you going for Angela? Are the rumours true?'

He lifted a hand to shield his face—partly because that was how he did things and partly as a promise to management. They had advised him against the expedition, of course: there was nothing to be gained from entering the fray except a load of speculative press. The authorities were doing all they could and the rescue effort had not waned, despite what Noah believed. But he hadn't budged. He hadn't given in. When they finally realised he could not be stopped, he undertook to stay closed on the matter: no comment, no sound-bites, nothing to toss the press. Let them make of his silence what they would. Fictions would be told in any case, inaccuracies blown up and supposition rife, so that any nugget of truth would soon be lost.

They wanted a love story. Given the reach of the crisis, it was hardly surprising that an old contact from Hank's, someone Noah hadn't spoken to or heard from in years, had crawled from the woodwork to disclose the friendship with Angela.

Despite her engagement to Dino Zenetti, which, if anything, only made the anecdote more exciting, Noah was tagged the love-struck hero.

Half of that was true. Angela Silvers had struck him like lightning when he was sixteen and he had never recovered from the bolt.

It was why he was here. It was why he had to act.

'Noah, do you think there's still a chance?'

He wouldn't be boarding a plane if he didn't.

Across town, closeted in her son's Bel Air mansion with the blinds drawn and the windows bolted, Joan Chase blubbed into her toffee popcorn bucket. She had taken refuge in Kevin's home movie theatre, spending her days (or nights, for the two had become indistinguishable) watching footage from his gigs and stuffing her face with junk and alcohol, until such a time came as she passed out for a few merciful hours.

Her prince stalked across the stage, reaching out to fans, spinning through his routines and crooning his number-one ballads. This was her personal favourite, a love song called 'Always With Me', which Joan privately thought was about her, not that Kevin had ever said so. She reassured herself of it now, with the dual effect of bolstering her spirits and scraping the scab off her torment so it bled afresh.

'I'm always with you and you're always with me; we're always together, how can it be any different, you know I want it too, I always want to be with you...'

Joan wailed. She tossed the bucket across the room and a confetti of kernels exploded against the screen. She couldn't go on. She couldn't do it!

She had considered driving out to the Sixth Street Bridge and tossing herself off, but there was a problem: Joan was too afraid to leave the house.

Hysterical Little Chasers camped at the mansion gates twenty-four-seven, clutching each other and sobbing. They left flowers and notes that declared their devotion: while Kevin might have been robbed from this life, he would always live on in their hearts, and their hearts, like their love, were indestructible. There had to be thousands, clinging to the railings, weeping and lashing and imploring the sky for Kevin's safe return, though anyone with half a brain knew that was wishful thinking.

If Joan were to step outside, she would be mobbed, if not by Little Chasers then by a legion of paparazzi. All on board the Challenger jet were mourned, but there was something about the youngest, the boy wonder, that struck the resounding chord.

His mother cut a tragic figure: shoulders stooped as she was glimpsed at the mansion, the one time she had dared to slip a toe onto the porch and the army had gushed like a tidal wave. Joan had been snapped peeking fearfully out from beneath a baseball cap bearing Kevin's name, clutching a dachshund in a trench coat.

She had taken to making Trey clothes from the ones left behind by her son, in the same style, with the matching accessories that Kevin had loved: belts and scarves, booties and chains. She would press Trey to her aching heart in the hope that wherever Kevin was, there might be a scrap of him still here, with her, in the life he had always known. Trey, unmoved, endured these ministrations with patience and dignity, but nevertheless refused to wear hi-tops, even if they were fur-trimmed.

Joan staggered up to the kitchen.

The buzz of the refrigerator drew her. Opening it, she helped herself to a packet of ham, unthinkingly folding layer after layer of the pink chiffon onto her tongue until the whole thing was finished. She glugged a carton of milk, then stuffed in a peanut chocolate bar. Was this what people did when they were grieving?

At first, Sketch didn't allow it—*'We're not grieving, Joanie; we don't know anything yet'*—but even he had since given up on that tired line. Nearly a week after the disaster, the language of tribute was subtly eclipsing any assurances of rescue.

Already it was becoming a cash cow. A charity single was getting fast-tracked. Talks were happening around a movie, possibly a TV series, and a chain of documentaries being commissioned. Conspiracy theories flourished. Publishers were signing book deals. Never before in the modern age had there been such an outpouring, Kevin himself by virtue of his youth immortalised as a quasi-religious figure, a saviour of sorts, martyred by his lost life and frozen in history for ever.

Joan closed the fridge door. Trey was on his bed in the corner, licking his ass.

'What am I going to do, Trey?' she asked him.

'What in God's name am I going to do?'

Melinda Corrigan took one look at her cell phone's text history and barfed into the porcelain bowl of her French-chateau-inspired bathroom.

Last night was hot. You're hot. Let's get hot again? G x

It was Gary's last message, sent minutes before the news broke.

To think she had been with him while her husband was… While he was…

She could not bring herself to say it, not even in her head.

Dying. That's the word you're looking for, you adulterous bitch.

Shaking all over, tendrils of her usually immaculate tresses clinging to her sick-soaked chin, Melinda crept on all fours back to the master suite. Since the impossible struck, she had alternated between states of extreme nausea, disabling sorrow, sheer incredulity and a paralysed, blood-freezing shock. Her husband. Mitch.

Yes, they had suffered their differences. No, their marriage wasn't perfect. But he was her partner, her friend, her ally…*the father of her children*.

Melinda groaned. The kids were in the play den, tended to by the nanny. They didn't understand. How could they? Mitch was away from home so often that they had become used to not seeing him. This absence was nothing new.

Some channels reported they were searching for survivors, others for wreckage. Melinda was no fool. Her husband's jet had vanished in the middle of the night. It had been lost over the ocean. One report alleged that signal had been abandoned way before they came down, because the captain's last missive betrayed nothing untoward. The chance of life prevailing was minimal. Mitch was never coming back.

Her phone rang. Melinda staggered up, collapsing onto the bed as she saw whom the call was from. *Gary.* What did he want: to say he was sorry he had been boning her up the ass while her husband choked? She couldn't contemplate speaking with him, let alone seeing him. At what point had

Mitch expired—as she was coming, as she had pumped up and down on Gary's hard cock? As she had lapped at their neighbour's balls? As she had rode her illicit lover like a jumped-up jockey?

Inconceivable. Mitch should be ensconced in his office downstairs, the kids playing outside and the sun streaming in through the conservatory window.

This was real life—not one of her husband's movies.

Melinda put her hands over her ears and screamed.

48

Day 7

Dawn broke and dawn faded. Night-time came and went. Hours slipped into days. There was no way of telling the date, how many suns had risen and fallen in the time they had been here, was it four, five, six, more? Flies buzzed over sleep-deprived bodies. Everyone lay limp in the heat, unable to move, watching the ocean and every so often roused to life when they thought they saw a boat or a beacon, running to the shore and screaming at the others to follow, only to find they'd been tricked.

The sun got hotter. The sea rolled on.

Once, an airplane passed overhead, far up, where the bright sky became a deeper blue: a tiny silver dagger on the cusp of the atmosphere. They had shot across the beach, waving their arms and shouting, realising afterwards the futility of their exertions. The plane was an unreachable totem from the old world, and a sign that the planet was still in operation. It was only their lives that had stopped.

Eve suggested a signal on the beach, as big as they could make it. Half a day was spent arranging rocks in three letters: a giant SOS. It was the kind of thing they had seen in the movies, some grim providence that assailed other people, ill-fated souls who had run to the ends of their ideas. But they had to do something.

Anything.

Or they would surely go mad.

Early afternoon. The sun tilted off its midday axis. Angela stepped onto the rock.

The group was transformed from the glamorous creatures that had met at Jakarta a week ago. Everyone had lost weight, their bones poking through in hard lines and nodules, elbows and ribs sharpened, shoulders and knees pronounced.

A diet of berries and coconuts was taking its toll. Their supply of the latter was endless, and despite Tawny's initial ecstasy that her LA health spa's beloved coconut water was being served here of all places, the group was soon sick of the dense, white, too-sweet harvest. Several had been ill, their stomachs unaccustomed to the new diet, and had shed half a stone in a day. The water supply was set to run dry.

Angela surveyed each of her companions. She wondered what she herself looked like. The kind of girl Noah would glance twice at in Hank's Hardware? The kind of girl Dino Zenetti would be proud to parade at the Parisian?

Or neither: a new person, nothing to do with them?

Tawny's hair was bleached and coarse, her nose and forehead pink, and her shoulders had turned a dark, nutty brown. Eve was pale and lethargic, though her green gaze still shone bright. Celeste, thin to begin with, was light enough to snap, and her eyes appeared even huger, peering out from beneath a fringe that to start with had been coal-black but was now warmer treacle.

Jacob was slowly healing, sheltered from the furious sun beneath a cover Celeste had fashioned of fronds and twine. Yesterday, Angela had taken him fruit and he had named her before she had spoken—the faintest shape, he said, but it was a start.

Mitch had lost his toupee in the jungle. He maintained it must have escaped when he bent to collect firewood, and now he was totally bald. Angela thought he looked better without it, but Mitch was understandably humiliated. He believed the piece had looked authentic and no one had suspected the fake—even when, in the heat, it had slipped halfway down the back of his head, or he had scratched it and the whole thing ramped back and forth like a mop on a kitchen floor.

Kevin, however, was the most puzzling. Unlike the others, the pop star seemed not to be losing weight but *gaining* it—or gaining muscle, at least. Kevin's bare chest was bulking out at an alarming rate, his calves thickening and his neck getting wider. Even his hands seemed bigger; his shoulders and back rippling. Angela couldn't fathom it: their diet thus far had been strictly vegetarian. It wasn't as if he had been doing much manual work, either: Kevin was second laziest in the group, eclipsed only by Tawny.

'We have to face facts,' she said. 'We might not be rescued for a while.'

Everyone had thought it, and everyone heard what she really meant.

We might not be rescued at all.

'We have to plan for what's ahead,' said Angela. 'Ways to live, how to get water… Finding proper food and shelter. Staying safe.'

'We've got a whole sea of water,' said Kevin. Angela swore his voice was deeper than it had been when they'd met.

'But we can't drink it,' she said. 'The salt will make you sick.'

'And dehydrated,' added Eve. 'You go twice as much to flush the saline out.'

'Boiled water is safe water,' agreed Angela. 'We find a source and bring it back.'

Celeste asked: 'Where?'

'Animal tracks on the way to the mountain—they're bound to reach a spring.'

'I'm not volunteering,' said Tawny, 'not after what I went through on that scummy pig run.' The model was squeezing dark berries between her fingers and applying the juice to her lips. Kevin caught her eye and smiled. She smiled back.

'This isn't a catwalk,' snapped Eve. 'No one cares what you look like.'

'What's wrong with taking a little pride in my appearance?' said Tawny, fluffing her hair. 'You could sure do with it, dressing in a tent like a fucking sad sack. Don't you get hot covered up all the time? No need to be frigid.'

'You're certainly not.'

'What's that supposed to mean?'

'Do you want me to spell it out?'

'You spelled out enough in that evil write-up of yours. You think you're smart but you know *nothing*—'

'I'm surprised you could read it.'

'Whatever, you fat cow.'

'Tawny, shut up,' said Angela.

'Why me? She started it.'

'I don't care who started it.' Angela shot Eve a pointed look. She had to own up to her pregnancy and it had to be soon. 'Moving on. Shelters. Celeste?'

'I can recreate what I did for Jacob.'

Tawny scowled. 'I can do that.'

'Great,' said Angela, 'then you can help.'

'I'm not doing it with *her*. I'll do it by myself.'

'It'll take forever,' said Eve.

The model shot her a glare. 'You got someplace else to be?'

'We'd need rope, an axe, proper things to build with,' said Eve, 'and if we had all that I'd be assembling a raft and sailing us out of here.'

'Shit,' said Jacob, 'rafts! Why didn't we think of that?'

Angela let the suggestion hang. In Jacob's state he wouldn't be putting a raft together any time soon, but he had to feel useful. The businessman she knew was a trailblazer. He took charge. He acted. He controlled. If things had been different, he would be leading this campaign and fighting every hour to get them home.

'If you didn't get eaten by sharks, you'd die of thirst,' Mitch spoke up, 'and that's assuming you could make the logs float in the first place.'

'We can always use you as a buoy,' said Tawny, smiling sweetly at his bald head.

'There aren't any sharks,' said Kevin, with a blasé shrug. 'I haven't seen any.'

'I saw a shark,' said Celeste, 'at night. Two of them.'

'Yeah, right,' said Tawny.

'I did.'

'Anyway,' said Kevin, 'if I saw one I'd just kill it.'

Eve laughed. 'I'd love to see that.'

'You'd love to vomit it up in your paper even more,' crabbed Tawny.

Bolstered by the model's defence, Kevin puffed out his chest. Angela noticed the light smattering of hairs there. She had a strong memory of the first time he had taken off his shirt—his torso had been less that of a nineteen-year-old and more that of a child. Now, it was transformed. Taller. Bigger. It looked like he was on steroids.

'Nobody's going in the ocean,' said Angela. 'Those rules still apply.'

'Fuck the rules,' said Kevin.

'And we're not building a raft until we've built shelters. Is anyone familiar with the weather systems out here?'

'Hot,' said Tawny, and Kevin sniggered.

'This island, wherever it is, has to have a rainy season,' Angela said. 'No way would this vegetation grow unless there was a counterpoint. Judging by the heat we have now, it's some downpour.'

'I'll get started,' said Celeste. Tawny pulled a face.

'The other thing is to avoid wounds. Scrapes and grazes, open cuts, soak them in salt water. Otherwise, it's common sense. Go carefully. Never venture into the jungle without shoes and never go in the sea without them, either.'

'In case a shark bites off our toes?' said Tawny.

'You never heard of jellyfish, anemones?'

'What shoes am I supposed to wear? All mine got frazzled to a crisp!'

'I'm sure you can take someone else's.'

'Yeah, well, whoever the thief is round here sure thinks so.'

'You're not still going on about that?' Eve said. 'You never brought that necklace in the first place, Tawny. I never even saw you wearing it.'

'I *did* bring the necklace,' argued Tawny, 'and it's not my fault you were too dumb to notice. Jacob knows it. I wore it at the airport, and I—'

'And it came off in the crash and you haven't had it since.'

'Bull. I had it after that swamp tried to eat me up. I took it off to wash, and then I took it off at night, and I had it *right here next to me—*'

'Except you bumped your head when the plane came down and now you can't be sure what's what.'

'But you can,' Tawny threw back, '*obviously*?'

'Obviously.'

Angela broke it up. 'Tawny, I don't know if you had the necklace with you or not and, frankly, I don't care. What I do care about is accusations flying around without proof. We make enemies of each other and we've had it. There is no thief.'

Tawny turned on Jacob. 'You saw me wearing it, didn't you? At Jakarta?'

'I don't remember.'

'Yes, you do. Of course you do. It was you who gave it to me.'

Kevin was sharpening the end of a stick. He glanced up.

'Help me look for it,' Tawny said. 'Now, Jacob, help me look!'

Jacob stared at her blankly. There was a long and awkward silence. Attempting to smooth over her gaffe, Tawny's blue eyes scanned the group.

'Whoever it is,' she said ominously, 'I'm on to you. I'll find you out.'

'Maybe it was her,' said Kevin.

'Who?'

'Her.' His voice was dark. 'The flight attendant.'

'Shut up, Kevin,' said Eve.

'I'm serious. She's out there.' Kevin planted his stick in the sand. 'There's something in that jungle. Every one of us feels it.'

If any of them had spoken out against him, it would have made it better. But nobody did. Mitch's face was sallow. Celeste wrapped her arms round herself.

'It's just us,' said Angela. 'That woman—she died. There's

no doubt in my mind that she died. It's just that we haven't found her yet.'

'Just like they're looking for us,' said Kevin. 'Only we're not dead.'

'We're not,' agreed Angela, 'but she is.'

'How do you know?'

'She would have come across us by now.'

'Who says she hasn't?'

The group fell silent.

'We've got enough to deal with in the world we can see,' said Angela, 'than to start freaking out about the one we can't. I'm not even going down that road.'

'We shouldn't walk out there alone,' said Celeste. 'Even so.'

Angela nodded. She held up a lipstick they had exhumed from the wreck. 'And if you absolutely have to, X marks the spot.'

'You want us to wear make-up?' Kevin squawked.

'We cross our path on the trees. That way we'll always know our way back.'

'What about food?' asked Jacob.

Tawny muttered: 'Why not throw your dick on the fire? A canapé before the main event.'

'Jacob's right,' said Angela. 'We have to get sustenance. Kevin, you tried fishing…'

'I could have a go,' Jacob said. 'I've always been good.'

'Er, maybe not…' said Tawny, with a mean laugh.

'Some things you don't need to be able to see,' Jacob explained. 'It's about feeling. Timing. Since this happened,' he faltered, 'since this happened it's like everything works in a new way. I can hear stuff. Feel stuff. Like my body works different to how it did before… Maybe I'm wrong, but it can't hurt to try.'

'Good,' said Angela, 'then that's settled. The other thing, of course, is meat.'

'That is too gross,' said Tawny. 'I am not eating a smelly old pig, especially one that's been shafted by that toothpick.'

Kevin brandished his stick. 'It's not a toothpick,' he said, in a thick, rough voice. There was a weird moment, gone as soon as it came, where he and Tawny exchanged glances and suddenly they weren't talking about the stick any more.

'We're all hungry,' said Angela, 'and we need to hunt.'

Hunt. The word was powerful. Savage.

If they could do that, what else would they be capable of?

'I'll do it,' said Kevin, baring his teeth. 'I'll hunt.'

49

Jakarta

The man did not like to be asked to complete a job twice. He fulfilled his role and then it was done. To suggest he had not finished the task was an insult.

Still, Voldan Cane paid the kind of money that helped to soften an insult.

The man flew into Jakarta airport early morning. It was a clear, hot day, and he was already thinking about the week he would spend on the beach once this hit was wrapped. Since his short-lived affair with Tawny Lascelles, he'd had a renewed appetite for beautiful women, and decided he would indulge in a few as a reward.

He passed through the airport unnoticed—Noah Lawson wouldn't have that luxury. Nor would Noah Lawson have an idea where to begin, unlike him.

The man's diligent calculations meant he had a target circle of just fifty miles.

That sure beat the authorities' sprawling search.

Admittedly, his boss's call had come as a surprise. The man had executed the plan according to instructions and he had succeeded. Even if the Challenger wreckage were found, there would be no way of returning it to Cane's door. Surely the fact it hadn't was a bonus: no black box to examine, no smelted straighteners to cast misgivings, no bodies to surrender clues. But Cane wanted more. He wanted proof.

Categorical proof.

He wanted those bodies photographed, and then disposed of.

Including Noah Lawson's.

Lawson was a nuisance, but he would be easy enough to eradicate.

And that was what the man was here to do.

50

Noah arrived on Maliki Island by boat. Clear green sea glistened in the sun, mottled with bursts of coral and pockets of deep khaki. The land was rugged and piratical. Towering cliffs reached right out into the water, and the beaches were wide swathes of crystal, applauded by swaying palms. The heat was intense.

This was where the ocean search was being launched, the closest inhabited island to the suspected crash site. Maliki was being kept strictly confidential as the hub of the rescue effort: Noah only knew about it thanks to a friend on the inside, a guy he had shadowed on one of his movies when he'd investigated the role of a government agent. They had stayed in touch, and the instant his decision was made Noah got straight on the phone, explained his interest and promised discretion.

His buddy had come through. It was a lead, and the best he was going to get.

The Maliki fisherman took his tip. A crowd of locals was gathered on the pier, wide-eyed, dark-skinned children, by now accustomed to the intrusion. For days they had watched the white men come and go about their operation, and regarded Noah with fascination and a pinch of distrust.

It was good to be somewhere he wasn't recognised. Transferring at Jakarta, he had fended off an onslaught of reporters from local news channels, as well as those who had followed him from the States.

'Noah, why are you here? What do you hope to achieve?'

It was simple.

People didn't just disappear.

Angela was out here somewhere.

Now all he had to do was find her.

Day 10

Kevin's nose twitched at the ripe, sour scent of pig drop-pings. He knelt to scoop up a handful. They were warm. Fresh. The animal was close.

You're not getting away from me this time...

He started to run. His body was filled with fuel, his mus-cles an engine, pistons pumping beneath his skin and his heart galloping fast and strong as a racehorse. Over creeks and logs he leaped, light as a nymph, through the under-growth that clawed and scratched at his bare back and shoul-ders, drawing thin lines of blood.

Up ahead he heard the thunder of frantic hooves. Twice he had come close to spearing a young sow: he would not let her elude him again.

Raising his spear, Kevin smashed through the bush, his sneakers too tight to contain his splurge from a size eight to twelve, but it didn't matter, the discomfort was secondary, a mere glitch against the adrenalin.

The pig came into view. Its rear end was massive, its haunches formidable, a swinging black tail swishing between sturdy legs. This was no sow, and it was no baby—this was an adult boar, and an angry one at that.

Kevin pulled back. He watched the animal disappear through a screen of jade, listening until the panicked thump had receded into the distance.

He narrowed his eyes at the still-shivering foliage.

Next time, he thought. *I'll get you next time.*

Something was happening to Kevin Chase.

And it was happening quickly.

His body was changing. His voice was deepening. Hair was sprouting in new, secret places: there was stubble on his chin, fuzz across his chest and on his arms and legs, and a bristly trail that ran into his shorts. He was *growing*—at least an inch or two taller from when they had arrived, his chest bulking and his biceps popping.

Tattoos that had once occupied the entire circumference of a spindly arm were now like paint flecks splashed on a wall. The clothes he had worn through the crash were too small, like clothes he had worn when he was thirteen. It was as if he had reacted to a chemical stimulus, bursting out of his shell, furious as the Hulk.

The thing was, it felt good.

It felt fucking good.

After years lagging behind in his girlish, weakened body, it felt unbelievable.

Kevin was becoming the man he had always wanted to be—a man like Jacob Lyle, and in such inverse correlation with Jacob's predicament it was as if he had robbed Jacob's status and made it all his own. As if they had swopped roles.

Yesterday, Kevin had taken a leak in the makeshift jungle latrine.

No way, man.

In the space of three days, his cock had grown by as many centimetres. He had blinked, awed, at the nest of pubic hair surrounding it—no longer the half-assed wisps of old, but a proper, thick covering, dense and matted, spreading down the insides of his thighs. His hands, as they cradled this new and incredible appendage, were broad and veined, the wrists smattered with fur that turned amber in the sun.

Kevin had peed proudly, spraying the shrubs with a mighty, virile jet, and laughing, throwing his head back and embracing the breadth of the sky.

Every second he could feel himself pushing at the boundaries of his new skin, primed to get bigger still, splitting through fibres like dental floss. Every hour he consulted the contents of his pants, and every hour it seemed to have lengthened.

It must be the island. Something in the air, or some fruit he had eaten, something that had magical, potent powers. But he could not think what he had been exposed to that the others had not. And it wasn't just a physical metamorphosis—it was mental, too. Kevin, on the cusp of twenty, had spent all his teens being thrust this way and that, all for the interests of another: Sketch, his management, his mom, the fans… Suddenly, it was about him. *He* was the powerful one, nobody else.

All the girls he had struggled with, all the rejections and taunts that Sandi had thrown his way—if only they could see him now!

Tawny had noticed. He had seen it in the supermodel's eyes. *Desire.*

The promise of that mystical prize called sex.

He had thought she and Jacob had something going, but the Casanova whom Kevin had held in such regard now seemed a smaller man than him. He bet Jacob's dick wasn't as big as his. He bet Jacob couldn't hunt pigs, even if he could see.

Whatever Jacob had, it wasn't enough to satisfy Tawny.
Kevin could satisfy her. He had no doubts about that.
Now, he could achieve anything.
He had arrived—and the world had better watch out.

52

Day 11

Jacob was knee-deep in the lagoon.

By now he could pick out the form of things, like concentrating on a developing photograph and figuring the shapes before they appeared: the mountains that climbed either side of the cove, and the difference between sea and sky.

If he stayed still long enough, he would feel a swish at his ankles, the flick of a tail or the fluid rush as something passed by his leg. The bigger fish caused vibrations when they were inches away: these were the ones to go for. He learned stealth, then with keen reflex to plunge his stick into the water. Hours passed between hooks, but it was worth the wait. Not just the promise of sleeping on a full belly, but the instant of triumph that accompanied a catch: the flipping, frippery body that was pulled from the water, held on the point of the harpoon, a silver, twitching trophy.

He sensed it was Celeste before she opened her mouth. The Italian woman had a definite scent, unlike any of the others.

'You've got the hang of this,' she commented.

'Want a go?'

'No.'

'Ever done it before?'

'Once.'

'Did you catch anything?'

'Yes.'

He smiled, lifting muscles that hadn't been used in days.

'You don't give away much, do you?' he said.

'It was an accident.'

'What was?'

'When I fished—just a fluke, I couldn't do it again.'

'Says who?'

'My boyfriend.'

Jacob was surprised, and a little disappointed. He didn't know why. He thought about all the girls he'd had sex with, and whether or not they'd had boyfriends. It had never occurred to him to ask. It hadn't mattered.

'Oh,' he said. 'I didn't know you had a boyfriend.'

'We've been together a long time.'

'What's his name?'

'Carl.'

Jacob ground his stick into the sand, twisting so it stayed upright. He crouched, unsteady, and she helped him. He splashed his chest with water.

'Does he make you happy?'

'That's a personal question.'

'I'm a personal guy.' But the question had surprised him, too. It was because Celeste had been so kind to him. He hoped that somebody was kind to her in return.

'He's good for me.'

'That isn't what I meant.'

She sat down next to him. 'What about you?'

'What about me?'

'Any special girl?'

'Lots of them.'

'Are you in love?'

He smiled again. 'Now who's being personal?'

'You don't have to answer.'

Jacob lifted his shoulders. 'Love's overrated. This soul-mates thing, I don't believe in it. Sexually compatibility, on the other hand…' But it felt like the old him talking.

'So the rumours are true.'

'Rumours?'

'You are a playboy.'

'I doubt you'll ever see me as that after what we've been through.' A pause, then: 'Thank you. I wanted to say that. I mean it, I really do. For what you've done. We don't know each other, Celeste—you didn't have to. Thank you.'

Jacob had never said anything like that before and meant it. Normally when he got sensitive with a girl it was because he wanted to get into her knickers.

Celeste was quiet a while, then said: 'It's nothing.'

'Carl's a lucky man.'

'He isn't, really.'

'He is. I know.'

'Some days I think this happened because of me… The crash. This.'

Jacob had felt it too. Perhaps they all had.

'I'd love to know how you work that one out,' he said.

'I've done things I'm ashamed of.'

'Who hasn't?'

'I'm not a good person.'

'Who is?'

'It was always going to happen. I deserved it.'

'For what?'

He heard her breathing.

'I killed my best friend.'

The words should have floored him, but, at that point, in

that particular place and at that particular time, they made absolute sense. He waited for her to go on.

'Until I met Sylvia,' Celeste began, 'I felt so lonely. My parents moved around a lot when I was small. I never made any friends. It was only when I went to college in England that all that changed. We were like sisters. She knew me better than my own family.'

A beat. 'What went wrong?'

'Nothing. That was just it. One day everything was perfect, the next it was ruined.'

'How old were you?'

'Twenty.'

'I'm sorry.'

'So am I.'

'You can tell me, you know.'

She shifted next to him. 'I know.'

And so she did.

From her first term at Oxford, she and Sylvia had been inseparable. Eight years had passed since the loss of her best friend, but it haunted Celeste as if it had been last week. Ever since then, she had struggled to regain control, to feel as if she had a say over anything that happened in her life. If something like that could ambush her, right out of nowhere, something unforeseen and until then unimaginable, how was it possible to govern a single day, an hour, a minute, let alone a lifetime?

She missed her. She missed her so much. Celeste had felt powerless since forever. Powerless to her parents' whim, powerless to the school, powerless when Sylvia died, powerless with men. She had to create her own power somehow…

Celeste had been driving that night. The girls had gone to a party, deep in the countryside, and the lanes home had been long and winding, the car's headlamps sweeping across the dark bulk of hedges. Celeste's decision to take the wheel, of opening the door and climbing in, of fastening her seatbelt: frozen snapshots. These moments that can change a life—or take one.

And Sylvia, with a whole world ahead of her, her hair streaming loose as they had rushed through the night; laughing, her neck thrown back, the radio blasting their favourite song. That was how Celeste kept her friend, moving, spirited, not in the coffin they had buried days later. The car had come from nowhere, from a hidden lane, its lights only just switched on, no time, no time, though she had swerved and they had hurtled towards the tree and after that nothing, only black.

Celeste hadn't been drunk, but she had been drinking. She should have made sure that Sylvia had her belt on. She should have seen the car before she did. She shouldn't have had the radio so loud, maybe then she would have heard it. She should have kept control when they went off-road. She should have accepted a ride off the boys who had left at midnight, and only hadn't because Sylvia had begged her not to since one of them had kissed her in the library and she didn't know if she liked him.

It didn't matter how many times Celeste post-rationalised it. Sylvia had been her friend, her confidante; the girl she had laughed and cried with, the keeper of her secrets, and the first place, really, she had truly belonged…and now she was gone.

'Believe me,' Celeste admitted, 'I'm no angel.'

The waves came up. They both sat alone with their thoughts.

'Do you know something?' said Celeste. 'Carl's the only person I ever told that to. And now I told you.'

'I'm flattered.'

'It helps that you can't see me.'

'I'd like to.'

'Carl said it was a mistake. But that we have to pay for our mistakes.'

'It seems like you've paid for yours.'

Jacob ran a hand through the sand. It was powder-soft and warm, every grain distinct and magnificent; things he didn't notice when he could see. Celeste's story reached into him in a way that would have been impossible had he the pictures to go with it. Had he seen her tears, her trembling lip, he might not have concentrated so hard on the words. As it was, the words touched his soul.

He hadn't known he had a soul.

'I've done things I'm not proud of either,' he said.

'I won't ask what they are.' There was warmth in Celeste's voice, easy and conspiratorial. Jacob wasn't used to having this sort of conversation with a woman, feeling they were on a level. Friends. It felt new, and good.

'Then I won't tell,' he said.

Tawny watched them from the shadows of the trees. The closeness of their shoulders, the elegant back of Celeste's neck, the way Jacob brushed against her when she spoke. Jealousy bit through her with tiny, stinging jaws.

She was mortified after their encounter by the pool. When had a guy *ever* failed to get it up for Tawny? It was ridiculous. A joke. An abomination.

If only Jacob could see! Then he would be reminded that she, Tawny, was indeed the fairest of all women and that there were no rivals worth a dime.

Yet even though she knew this, she accepted the disturbing truth: Celeste had flourished on the island. With her cool, artisan beauty, she brought to mind those haughty, above-it-all dancers with whom Tawny had worked at the Rams. The girls hadn't been ravishing, far from it, but they had carried a measure of dignity and poise that Tawny, to this day, felt had always eluded her. As if she had the package, the body, the face and the hair, but had never known quite what to do with it. She had never been able to take command of it in that way Celeste had—a quiet, contained control that needed no reassurance from others or guarantee that it existed.

She teetered on the edge of the void, from which a whistling query sailed up:

What else have you got, Tawny Linden?

Just a girl in a subway station, scrabbling for change.

A girl without a family, without a home. Rejected. A street whore.

You're dead to us.

Tawny's demons reared their heads, dancing like snakes from a wicker basket. She needed to be the one the men wanted. It was survival, and all the girls knew it.

She stepped backwards into the jungle. There was only room for one of them on this island, and it damn sure had to be her.

53

Dusk lengthened across the sand. Over the ocean the sun was a giant, melting disc, bleeding red and orange. Cliffs gleamed black and dense in the gloaming, and the first winking stars were starting to prick the sky.

The fish was sweet and salty, cooked on a spit over the fire so the skin was charred and crisp. The innards were white and moist, flaking apart, and the group devoured the meal in silence. Afterwards, full and tired, they surrendered to sleep.

All except Mitch Corrigan.

The senator lay awake, his heart shaking.

He was afraid to go back to the cave, but he knew he must.

He could hear them calling. *Come to us... Come to us...*

Infinite space, the universe more ancient and complex than he could fathom, and still there were those who believed that aliens belonged in the realm of movies: science fiction, a story, just a game. They couldn't see how much sense it made. On a rock hurtling through the cosmos, dwarfed by others in our solar system alone—what about other systems, other galaxies, the universe made up of hundreds of billions, more, an unlimited number? To assume solitude made no logic.

Before 2012, Mitch had held these beliefs, but in the vague and detached way of one who knows that in his lifetime, and the lifetime of his children, there would be no movement. It had been someone else's concern, and nothing to do with him.

Now, it was everything to do with him.

There was no doubt they had brought him here. Had he dared to step further into the cave over the mountain, he would have met them face to face—it was almost a relief, after all this time, the promise of closure. No more running and no more fear.

Would Melinda be there?

Come here, honey… Come on home…

His wife was in on it. She was one of them.

The transformation had been subtle. It had started with Melinda arriving home late, vanishing and reappearing, and refusing to meet his eye. She had been talking differently too, a weary, hollow drawl, so unlike her old voice that it seemed not to be Melinda speaking at all but a *voice inside her*, selecting the words, nothing but a ventriloquist's puppet. Next she had stopped cooking. She used to cook every day, whipping up feasts for the family at a moment's notice. These days she had no appetite. She drank endless glasses of water. He rarely saw a morsel pass her lips.

If she wasn't eating food, what the hell was she eating?

And so it came to this…

Had the pilots seen lights in the sky? Had the aircraft been guided towards its grisly fate by a beacon sent from another dimension?

Mitch walked down to the shore. Above the water hung a silver moon, a crescent slung in the sky, throwing silver glow. He could see the shadow of the Earth set across it, and thought as he always did how strange and fantastic it was that

that should be his own self reflected, however small: a tele-scopic mirror.

Stars abounded.

Maybe if he went to them, they would set the others free. The others had been a necessary appendage but there was no use for them now. It was Mitch they wanted. Thwarted at Veroli, smeared a hoax, the newcomers had a point to prove.

Would they lay claim to Eve Harley? Show her what was really going on?

'It's outrageous that someone in this person's position could have fallen for the fraud,' Eve's latest piece had read. *'We are asked to trust this man, one whose decisions might some day affect the world, and to entrust ourselves to him. Yet he believes the deception. He sought it out and he welcomed it...'*

She would see. She would repent.

The cave was calling. Those footprints didn't belong to the missing flight attendant—they belonged to the enemy. *Come to us...*

Mitch became aware of something thick and hairy pooled at his feet.

Stooping, he encountered a dark, coarse mass enveloping his toes. He had walked into it without noticing. Seaweed? A jellyfish? No, too furry.

Mitch lifted the thing out. At first he thought it was a washed-up creature, sodden and matted, before realising it wasn't. It was his hairpiece.

The bat must have dropped it.

Mitch held it aloft, dripping and sodden, before pressing it to his head. It seeped down his temples and the back of his neck. He took it off and hurled it back into the sand, where it landed with a wet squelch. Still not satisfied, he knelt and rummaged through the grains, digging a hole, slamming the wig in and covering it up.

The time for pretending was over.

Tasting the skin of his fear, Mitch gazed up to the forest and over the ridge.

If he went, he would not come back again.

54

Day 12

Kevin moved noiselessly through the forest.

He was deep in the trees, far in on his usual track.

The sound of hooves came across him diagonally this time, what couldn't be more than five metres in front. The molten air was charged. Kevin's spear was raised, his eyes alert, his ears pricked to any sound that might give away its whereabouts.

The animal had got clever to his advances—but not that clever.

Kevin stopped, sensing it close beyond the screen of leaves. He exhaled, the expelled air cool against the perspiration on his top lip. Nothing mattered more than this victory. A bead of sweat ran from his earlobe to his chin and fell to the earth.

It was an effort to hold back, everything primed for action and ready to spring, but he had to wait, he had to be patient...

In the end, it gave itself away.

A shuffle. A hot snort—

And then it was running, charging through the thicket but this time it was a done deal, this time it wasn't getting away, and Kevin's vision refined to a point as deadly as his weapon's as he launched the stick high into the air, his body propelled forward with the motion, watching as the javelin shivered in the steam before sailing towards its target on a fatal trajectory and impaling the boar through its neck.

He finished the job efficiently. In seconds it was over.

Kevin slit the knife, belly to throat, so the innards fell out. He butchered the head and the legs. With Jacob's help he skewered it. He had brought back the impossible: meat.

He thought of all the times Joan had brought mac and cheese to his bedroom while he was playing computer games, a knock at the door and a tray on the side: plastic containers, film lids and microwaves, knives and forks and a can of Pepsi.

An artificial world, a toy town, superstores packed with fakes and forgeries. Here was where reality set in.

Some days Kevin found it hard to remember all that. It was like a photo album whose images were disappearing one by one. He knew he should be crying for them, Joan and Sketch, just as he had at the start, but while his brain computed this message, he could not drag up the tears.

He told himself he couldn't afford to. The only way to make it was to throw away the key. Kevin had to change.

The old him would never survive.

Tawny gagged into a bush. 'My God,' she choked. 'You don't seriously expect me to eat that?'

'Makes more for the rest of us.'

'It's probably got rabies.'

Afterwards, Kevin went to wash in the pool. His naked body rose proud from the water and he surveyed the surrounding jungle with new eyes. Nothing here could defeat him. He had overpowered a beast. The others held him in reverence; even those who didn't admit it. He had hunted a wild thing and returned the victor.

55

Los Angeles

On Friday night, Sketch Faulkner arrived ahead of time, manoeuvring his BMW through the crowd of fans at Kevin's mansion gates. Agonised Chasers hollered for information, battering their fists, as grey, tear-streaked faces materialised like phantoms at the window. '*Where's Kevin? Have you found him?*'

If only Sketch had. Two weeks and nothing. Christ, Joan was in a state but it wasn't an easy ride for him either. He had loved the kid too, in his way.

Shame seared when he recalled giving Kevin his ultimatum—go to Salimanta or get out the door. How did he come to terms with that? He had sent Kevin to meet his maker. Sketch knew it. Joan knew it. Soon, no doubt, the fans would know it.

They screamed on. Mics lunged. Cameras loomed.

How had Kevin learned to live with this? The times Sketch had sat in the car with his client as they had passed through a post-gig fan pit hadn't been much different. Whether the Little Chasers were worshipping their idol or mourning him, it apparently spawned the same hysterical misery.

Past the gates, he relaxed a bit, and eased the car to a stop outside the porch.

The mansion was still shuttered, reams of mail and clusters of flowers heaped up at the door. Sketch began to sort through some of it before losing patience and kicking it to one side—then, on second thoughts, he lifted an attractive bouquet, tore off the message card and presented it just in time for Joan to open the door.

She looked awful. Fat and bloated, pale and yellow-eyed, and shoddily dressed in a pair of baggy lime-green sweat pants that Sketch had seen Kevin in once.

Inside, it was worse. Photos of Kevin were scattered across the floor, boxes of his belongings exploded in a kind of sprawling, shapeless shrine, and cartons of half-eaten takeout were tossed across counters and wedged under couches.

Sketch flicked the window blind and flooded the room with light, prompting Joan to dive onto a beanbag, shielding her face with her arms and crying for the dark.

'Joanie…' he coaxed, approaching with caution. 'Joanie, this can't go on…'

'*I can't go on!*' Joan spluttered, her blotched, angst-riddled face careening up at him, and the shock made him stumble back. Joan had always been a meek character, someone Sketch had regarded as a necessary if slightly irritating supplement to his client, but now she was demonic. She had lopped her hair off, the ends hacked and chewed, and it was stuck up at the back in a stiff nest, like a tuft of candyfloss.

Unexpectedly, she fell against him, weeping.

Sketch patted her through the worst of the sobs, and as she succumbed to more pedestrian tears looped an arm round her, gently stroking the ruined hair and telling her it was OK, things would work out, everything would be all right…

It was the worst thing to say. Joan clawed at it like a drowning woman.

'Is there news?' Her head knocked his chin on the way up. 'He's been found?'

Ruefully, Sketch shook his head. 'I'm sorry, Joanie. No news.'

Trey scampered in, sniffing at the takeout boxes.

Sketch took her hand. 'I think we have to accept facts, Joan.'

'*I don't!*' She scooped up the dog, dressed in a jumpsuit and baseball cap—Kevin's favourite outfit. Trey was licking sweet and sour sauce from his nose and didn't give a happy shit about Kevin. '*I can't!*'

'Even if they did make it through whatever happened up there,' said Sketch, 'it's over now.'

'I'm his mom,' she said, squeezing Trey so hard the dachshund's eyes bugged. 'I believe.'

'You're killing yourself.'

'Not fast enough.'

'You don't mean that.'

'Don't I? You think I don't wonder every second of the day what his final moments were like? How he died, and if he called for me, *his mommy*—and I couldn't be there? I've always been there for Kevin—always.'

'I know.'

'How could you know? You don't have kids.'

'It felt like I did.' Sketch splurged it, hadn't meant to. 'With Kevin, Joanie—I know it's not the same but sometimes Kevin felt like mine. The closest thing I had, anyway. I want him back just as much as you do. Every morning I wake up and I'm thinking, Maybe today's the day—yeah, maybe today—and I check the date in case I have to remember it: this special day they found him and brought him home.'

Joan blubbed.

'D'you know the worst thing?' she whispered. 'I did everything with Kevin. I did everything for him. Yet I don't know if I knew him at all.'

It wasn't like Joan to pose deep and meaningful questions. Sketch rode it out.

Bleakly she gazed up at him. 'He was my son…but he had so many secrets.'

Sketch didn't reply.

'I know he was sick, Sketch.'

'What?'

'All those pills.' Joan licked her lips. 'I'm not an idiot. You always thought I was, so did Kevin, but I'm not.'

'Joanie…'

'You were all too chicken to tell me—everyone at Cut N Dry. And yes, maybe I would have fallen apart, but I'd still have rather known. Whose decision was it? Yours? Kevin's? Who decided to keep it from me?'

Ice dripped down the back of Sketch's neck. He had thought it was over: that the tragedy of Kevin, appalling as it was, meant at least—at last—the sinking of the pills.

The pills…

'Well? I was his mother.'

'Joan—'

'When was *I* going to find out? When the pills stopped working, when my baby finally got poorly? The same time as the fans?' Her lip quivered. 'At first I believed you about the vitamins. Then I realised it was all a charade.'

Countless times Sketch had imagined this conversation. With whom he would have it, what the evidence would be, how it would play out… Now it was actually happening, he found he was stumped for words. Saying the truth was impossible. The facts were too absurd. The deception was too extreme. Joan could never grasp it.

'Now he's gone,' said Joan, 'and I never had the chance to comfort him. To tell him it was OK, *I knew*, and I would be there with him through it all, whatever it was and however it happened. He must have been so scared. He tried to protect me, even though he was the one that needed protection. I should have noticed. He was always small. What was it, Sketch? Something bone-wasting?'

A channel of sunlight fell across a framed picture of Kevin, mounted on the wall. In it the star was performing at the Olympics Closing Ceremony, fist raised to the sky like a warrior. Sketch stood. He crossed the room.

What did it matter any more? The boy wonder was gone. There were no more performances, no more tours, no more fragrance launches or book signings or red carpet junkets. No more protection. No more secrecy.

Joan Chase was a mother in mourning. How could he let her believe that her son had kept a terminal disease from her? He might be a coward, but he wasn't evil.

'The pills weren't because Kevin was sick, Joan.'

Sketch could feel her scrutiny on his back. He didn't look at her as he spoke.

As the truth unravelled, he kept his eyes fixed on Kevin in the frame—just Kevin.

'The pills weren't vitamins either,' he said. 'That was what we told Kevin, and that was what he accepted. We chose not to think of it as a lie—rather, a shield.'

Silence.

'The pills were hormones.'

Dense as lead, the admission heaved from Sketch's mouth.

'Kevin didn't know. They were hormones. Female hormones, Joan.'

He heard her sit down. *Collapse*—that was a better word.

The door swung open and the rest came free in a deranged rush.

'Picture it. We signed Kevin when he was twelve years old—this cute-as-a-button, candy-cane kid, with this butter-wouldn't-melt voice and little-boy dimples. We wanted him to stay that way. We wanted him to remain the boy we had found, and, for a couple of years, he did.' Sketch remembered when Kevin's voice had started to wobble, the deep notes creeping in. 'But by the time he turned fourteen, changes were starting to happen. The voice was about to drop. There were wisps round his chin. We had to take action.' Sketch was fired up by his own propaganda despite the fact it reeked of bullshit. *Did we? Did we really?* The question had haunted him for seven years—but once they had embarked on the campaign it was impossible to stop.

'It wasn't an easy decision,' he said. 'It was a mindfuck. But consider the evidence, Joanie, just for a second'—his own argument, the ideas that had been batted across the board at Cut N Dry—'child stars across history lose their appeal: Culkin, the two Coreys, Fred fucking Savage. Why? I'll tell you. *Puberty*, Joan. These guys lose their fan base because their fan base changes. It grows up, and the new fans that take their place are looking for the same thing, only those guys *aren't* the same any more. Enter a new king: a new Kevin. What we did was give Kevin the ability, the *right*, to keep that crown. We gave him immortality.'

Sketch turned. He was shaking.

Joan's lips formed around a word that made no sound.

'Oestrogen arrested his development,' he said. 'Not enough to give Kevin female assets, but enough to prevent the male ones: it stopped the hairs growing, it kept his voice young, it made him delicate, unthreatening, even pretty. It never hurt him and it never caused him pain. He was our star and we wanted to keep him—that was all. We did this in Kevin's best interests, Joanie. Remember how much he wanted this career? How much *both* of you did? Kevin knew what it took to succeed—and what it took to stay at the top. We enabled that to happen for him.'

This was how he had convinced himself. All the arguments, all the post-rationalising, tripping off his tongue as if he had spoken it yesterday.

'Look at other stars' attempts: redirecting their image, going under the knife, turning to drugs. We defended Kevin against all of that. We tried the newest tack of all—and trust me, Joanie, five years from now they'll all be doing it. Age is a hell of a thing to unpick…but what if it never happens in the first place?'

Finally Joan found her voice. It was a changed voice.

'You sinful fucking bastard,' she said. 'You wicked, wicked man.'

Sketch took it. He deserved it. He would deserve it for the rest of his life.

'No wonder he was such a mess.' Joan's eyes were black. 'The mood swings. The panic attacks. The anger.'

'I know.'

'You punished him for it. And all along you were the one responsible.'

'We were protecting our investment. For all our benefits—'

'Don't you dare. Don't you dare make out that I was part of this.'

'—Kevin's benefit, and yours, even if right then it didn't seem obvious.'

'Get out of this house.'

'Joanie—'

'OUT!'

Trey shot from the room. Sketch gathered his things. He had expected Joan to leap at him, to attack him, to batter and to slap him. He hadn't expected this stark, chilling control. She terrified him. He opened the door, a broken man.

'I'm so sorry, Joan,' he choked. 'I'm so, so sorry.'

56

New York

Fit for NYC was shrouded in gloom. Couture treasures sparkled, going for tags that could have fed whole families for a
year, but instead were vanity prizes for a Hollywood socialite
who would bury them in the back of a Bel Air closet to be
worn once, shoes permitting, at a rival hostess's dinner party.
How pointless it all seemed.

Orlando put a hand on his brother's back. 'We mustn't give
up,' he said.

Luca slammed a fist on the glass. With a crack the cabinet
splintered, a diamond cobweb, but the impact wasn't enough,
he had more to burn, and he finished the job, smashing the
surface so it obliterated into thousands of gossamer shards.

'I don't know what's worse,' he said. 'Losing my mind
back here or doing a Noah Lawson and losing it on the other
side of the world.'

'We have to stay strong.'

'It's all right for you, isn't it?' Luca turned with a tortured
kind of pride. 'You don't have the same regrets as me.'

'Don't I?'

'Dad never knew me—neither did Angela. Now it's too
late.'

'Screw your self-pity.'

'You were always the golden child. You walked on water. Now all that's left is Mom and even she doesn't...' Luca's voice broke. 'I mean I can't even tell her...'

Orlando went to his brother. He and Luca had never been close, but if there was ever a time to remedy that, it had arrived. Luca thought none of them knew he had a boyfriend. Truth was, they had known he was gay since he was a teenager. Orlando couldn't speak for his father—yes, there was a chance that Donald had been kept in the dark, and that Isabella hadn't discussed it with him, but even if she had, they wouldn't have known because Donald didn't speak about things like that.

Every evening for the past decade, when they had stayed up after hours, Orlando had waited for his brother to confess. Luca never did.

'I know, Luca,' Orlando said. 'It's OK.'

'You must think I'm some loser, huh. Some coward who parties so hard till he can't remember who he is. So he doesn't have to look himself in the mirror. Dad lied about the reason the hotels went under. It wasn't that he made a bad decision. It was that I flushed the whole fucking thing down the can because I fell apart. I lost the money. Me. Only Dad didn't want you to know that.' A teardrop ran down his cheek. 'I killed him. I made him sick and that sickness finished him off. My own father.'

'That's not true.'

'Course it fucking is.'

Orlando had always wondered about the reasons for their debt. It had never felt right. Donald Silvers hadn't made a bad business move in his life and he wouldn't have started now. It had been Luca all along.

'You think you're the only one who messed up?' said Orlando.

'As far as Dad was concerned, yeah.'

'You're not alone in carrying a burden. Angela isn't the only person I lost.' It hurt him like a physical wound. 'I knew Eve,' he said. 'Eve Harley.'

Luca was quiet a moment, then said: 'How?'

'She was carrying something of mine.'

'What?'

In the silence that followed, in Orlando's ashen face, Luca understood.

'Oh,' he said.

'Yeah. Oh.'

'How long?'

'Would've been six months.' Orlando's chest ached. 'I said I didn't want it. I told her she was on her own. She died knowing that. They both did.' Every baby he saw on the street, every picture in a magazine, every crawling infant in a bloody stupid TV commercial, squeezed him inside out. Becoming a father had been something he might do later, at some distant, invisible point, because life went on for ever, right? And there was always a more important job to be done, like cutting a deal or checking into a hotel or getting drunk with his cronies. None of it amounted to anything. Not like Eve's baby.

Not like my baby.

'Shit,' said Luca. 'I had no idea.'

'How could you? I didn't tell anyone.' How he wished now he had told Eve: that he wanted this child, that he wanted her, that he wanted the whole damn lot.

If only he'd put his pride aside and had the balls to admit it.

A siren screamed outside.

'Now I've told you,' said Orlando, 'and you've told me, for what it's worth, we're in it together—we're brothers,

Luca. My regret isn't fixable, but yours is. You can still make Dad proud. We can still buy out of the Zenetti deal and rebuild from scratch. We'll make it better than ever. It's what he would have wanted—Angela too.'

'You think we can?'

'I know we can. I'm letting Silvers go over my dead body.' Orlando tasted his resolve, sharp and intoxicating. 'It's everything to me. It's all I have left.'

His cell beeped.

'Carmine Zenetti wants us in Vegas,' he said, grabbing his keys. 'Says he's got some news—and we're gonna want to hear it, apparently.'

57

The Midwest

Melinda Corrigan entered her neighbour's garage and told him it was over.

She didn't dress it up and she didn't let him down gently. She had more on her mind than the frankly insignificant matter of hurting Gary's feelings.

He had been pestering her non-stop. If he didn't quit, she was getting a restraining order. *I have to see you*, his messages said. *Let me comfort you.*

'Why?' Gary begged now.

'I'll credit you with some intelligence,' said Melinda, 'and take that as a joke.'

'Of course it isn't a joke,' said Gary. He had transformed his garage into a gym and he slumped down onto one of his bench presses. 'I love you.'

'Don't you dare say that again.'

'I can't help it!'

'Bullshit you can't. You're married to Mandy, and I'm married to Mitch.'

'But Mitch is…'

'What?' Melinda saw herself in that moment, hair unwashed, face scrubbed clean, because what was the point of make-up when you cried it all off anyway?

'Mitch is what, Gary?'

Gary reached for her. She slapped him off. Call her an idiot to have come in the first place—sneaking like a thief from her basement into Gary's: imagine if the paps got hold of it! But fire had to be fought with fire. If Melinda didn't sort this today, the papers would surely catch a sniff. Gary was a leaky bucket. Any moment he would crumple under his wife's steely gaze and the whole charade would explode.

The kids. She could not risk them finding out.

What would the world think? Boffing her married neighbour while her senator husband was in the ocean somewhere with a mouthful of fish.

Once, when Melinda had been sitting at home with the children, attempting to explain what had happened to their father in any terms they, or indeed she, could understand, Gary had barged into the house and demanded to speak.

Mitch's disappearance was terrible, he conceded once they were alone, but it wasn't a deal-breaker.

A deal-breaker?

She had told him to get lost. He hadn't listened. He had come back again, and again, as if Mitch's disappearance was a fucking aphrodisiac.

'Well?' she pushed. '*What is he?* Go on, Gary—say it!'

Gary stumbled. 'Mitch is dead.'

The words hit her like a punch, despite the number of times she had experimented with them in her head. *My husband is dead.*

The president's latest delivery said as much. Melinda had heard it so many times since its release, played on a loop, she could remember it verbatim:

> *'As a nation and a world, we are distressed and shocked by the events that took place over the*

Indian Ocean on July 1st, 2014. Those who have been lost to the sea were known the world over—but they were also regular people. People like you and me. Husbands and wives, sons and daughters, friends and colleagues: their loss cannot be measured against the box office or the billboard, it is measured in the hearts of those they have left behind...'

What a heap of horseshit. Melinda respected that man, but the tripe he got asked to churn out was beyond the pale. Naturally, the White House was doing all it could to extend the arm of comfort. Mitch had been 'a supreme human being', 'a fine leader' and 'an exemplary father'. Anything they could do to ease her pain...

They could start by bringing back the bodies.

She needed to see. She needed to know.

The search had thrown up nothing. After a passionate mission in those early days, they were now engaged in a lacklustre limp to recover corpses.

'Don't ever let me hear you speak Mitch's name again,' Melinda said.

'But there's nothing to stop us being together now! I'll tell Mandy—'

'Are you *insane*?'

'I've never been thinking so clearly.'

'Then think on this. You and I are over, Gary. Finished.'

'Can't you see how it's all worked out?'

'You think I would have *chosen* this? Haven't you a shred of decency?'

Gary stood. His muscles bulged and Melinda caught him sneak a sidelong glance into the gym mirror to check out his guns. All of a sudden he was repulsive, a giant inflatable sex toy she had reached for in her hour of loneliness.

'I didn't hear you crying out for decency while I was nailing you to the wall,' he said.

Melinda couldn't bear to hear any more. She rushed for the door but he seized her arm. Filled with rage and regret, she spun round and spat in his face.

Gary staggered backwards. Numb, he wiped his cheek.

'You psychotic bitch!'

'Come near me again and you'll see just how right you are.'

She didn't hang around for an answer.

58

Day 15

Mitch Corrigan had been missing three days.

'This is crazy,' said Angela. 'He can't have vanished into thin air.'

'He has,' said Kevin, gutting one of Jacob's fish. 'He's gone.'

'People don't just disappear.' Angela paced the camp. 'What about the forest?'

'Nothing,' said Eve.

'The mountain?'

'We've been all over. Kevin's right.'

Angela looked out to sea. She had thought it strange when Mitch had asked if anyone had been down on the bluff. As if he'd seen something he shouldn't have.

'I think he's snuffed it,' said Kevin.

'Shut up.'

'This place'll kill you unless you know what you're doing.'

Of course, that was the logical thing. Mitch had gone for a swim, neglected to tell anyone, and had been taken by a shark. Mitch had gone exploring in the heat and tumbled down a rock. Mitch had toppled into a swamp and drowned.

'He's depressed,' said Eve. 'I don't blame him for what he did.'

Her suggestion didn't need to be voiced.

Mitch wouldn't be the first of them to contemplate a quick way out.

The shelters were crude, but gave the illusion of an organised society. They consisted of woven branches cracked and bent to a curve, rooted in the sand and forming a half-tunnel in which it was possible to feel, even for a short time, alone. The need for privacy, however thrown together, was acute.

Eve was resting on the heap of moss she called a bed. It was draped in material scavenged from the cabin, raised from the sand, and used one of the jet's life jackets as a bolster. Sunlight filtered through the cracks in shimmering ribbons.

Kevin's meat loot had sustained them for days. Eve remembered when the pop star had brought it back, the mouth-watering aromas as it started to cook, salty skin and the tempting pop and frazzle. Angela had advised they fill up slowly because their systems were out of practice, but it hadn't been easy: the instinct to feed and be filled was primitive. Eve had eaten until she could stomach no more, with every mouthful imagining it travelling into her baby. Even Tawny, who had vowed to abstain, had eventually been enticed, her reluctant, supermodel-squeamish pickings giving way to a devoted campaign—juice on their fingers, shredding with their bare hands.

Ever since the senator lost his wig, more than his hair had gone AWOL. Nights ago, while the others had been asleep and the sun edged over the lip of the world, Eve had caught him by the pool, naked in the violet light, his hands lifted to the sky. It had been a strangely religious pose. Another time she had startled him at the forest perimeter, just as it was getting dark. 'I thought I was alone,' Mitch had said, once he caught his breath. 'I thought you were… You could have been…'

Eve knew what he had meant. It was as if the mask had come down, as if the veneer had been wiped, leaving only…fear.

Eve turned over. The ocean ran blue to the ends of the earth.

She tried not to think of a worst-case scenario. Corrigan would be back soon. He was an intelligent man, a family man, despite his hare-brained beliefs.

A niggling voice said: *You drove him to this. You hounded him to it.*

Wasn't that what she did? Wasn't that her job? Hounded people, for a story, for a buck, for a byline—in a way, for her own warped version of fame.

Eve Harley: persecutor.

It didn't quite have the ring of her early ambitions, working to change the world. Bringing people down and exposing their secrets—there *had* been a reason behind it, and that reason was her father. Her tormentor.

In turn Eve had become the tormentor, and people had run from her.

At first, Eve been distraught at her iPad smashing—it was too much to wish for a connection in as remote a place as this, but the idea of reviving her documents, of having something to focus on, became an obsession. As a result she had broken the habit of reaching for it whenever she had a twist of poison to drain.

At home, whenever she thought of her father, she would pick up her piece and embark on a new theory. Whenever she remembered his cruelty, she would hit on a new target and pitch it to her editor. Whenever injustice flourished, she would polish a text from a new and obliterating angle. Every bad thing Eve had written had come from a bad place. And yet, the less she indulged that place, the less she fed it, the quieter it became. She never thought she would say it, but she did not miss her work.

Eve sat up. She knocked her head on the roof of the shelter and swore.

Celeste's legs appeared in the square of daylight. The Italian ducked under, and Eve just had time to adjust her shirt, parted to reveal her gently rounded tummy.

'We know that you're pregnant,' Celeste said, sitting down. The woman who appraised Eve was not the meek specimen she had met at Jakarta. She matched Eve's eye plainly, and did not look away.

'It's that obvious, huh.'

'Why didn't you say?'

'Why should I?'

'You'd have had to eventually.'

Eve wasn't used to being the one questioned. 'I guess you think I'm stupid for agreeing to this in the first place,' she said.

'None of us agreed to this.'

'You know what I mean.'

Celeste shook her head. 'I don't think you're stupid. Anyway, we'll get rescued soon, and you'll have your baby at home.'

'Maybe.'

'You sound like you don't believe it.'

'Do you?'

'I'm trying.'

Celeste stared out of the shelter. Jacob was at the lagoon, splashing his face and shoulders. Eve saw her expression and surprised herself with a smile.

'You wouldn't want to stay, by any chance?' she said. 'Only that a deserted paradise with a guy you've got the hots for could be worse.'

Celeste went red. 'What?'

'Have you got a boyfriend at home? A husband?'

'What difference does that make?'

'I'm guessing a lot, to him.'

'To Jacob?'

Eve sat back. 'I meant your boyfriend.'

'Oh.'

They sat in companionable quiet, listening to the waves.

'What do you think happened to Mitch?' Celeste asked. Her voice was cautious, reverent, as if they were speaking of the already dead.

'Angela and I are going out later, once it cools.'

'I don't like not knowing. I feel like these people are watching us.'

'People?'

'Mitch. The flight attendant.' Celeste's dark eyes met hers. 'I feel like I'm being watched. Do you know? Every shadow, every sound…'

Eve did know, but she didn't want to admit it.

'There's no way that woman could have lived,' she said instead, 'and if she had, she would have found us by now. Corrigan will come back. You'll see.'

'I keep thinking of his wife. He has children, hasn't he?'

Eve nodded. Had she thought for a second about those children while she was writing up her piece on Veroli? Had she thought about any of the children, or the relatives, or anyone impacted, when she had been set on pulling apart those lives?

She had been a child once. Ruined differently, but ruined all the same.

'We've all got someone we need to live for, don't we?' said Celeste.

Eve nodded. Her baby. Orlando...

'We do,' Eve said, and prayed it was true. 'Someone is waiting for us.'

59

Noah used Maliki Island as a base. Every dawn he woke to a sky-splitting sunrise, a pink and red explosion as if the earth had been set on fire, and took a boat out to sea. The area was large as a continent, studded with landmasses but mostly swallowed by water. Wherever he was, on whatever rock that looked like another rock that looked like another, he would scan the horizon, hazy with distance and heat, and decipher a chain of islets, knuckle-sharp and primeval, and beyond those a further chain, and beyond that another. The task was daunting.

The official search was disbanding. Noah saw in their expressions the acceptance of failure, that this last push was a formality, a case of ticking the boxes.

'You're wasting your time,' he was told, days after he had arrived.

Noah didn't see it as a waste. Coming out here might be dumb, it might be the dumbest thing he ever did, but it sure beat sitting around waiting for a miracle to happen. And maybe he did have a better chance. Maybe for all the power of the White House, for all the muscle of the media, they were doing it for image, not heart. Noah had Angela to do it for and he wasn't giving her up, not today, not ever.

It helped to be near her. Regardless of whether he was

searching for her kiss or her body, it was still her body, and he was not leaving it behind.

Early evening. The sun was setting, a syrupy arc softening into marmalade. The ocean shone black and the line of cliffs were frayed across the dusky mauve sky.

Noah smoothed the map in his hands, a chequered mess of probabilities and possibilities, where he had understood from the locals in fits and starts if they had seen a fire in the sky that night, or woken in the small hours with a sound in their ears. He didn't know how much sense it made, if he was taking down information back to front, upside down, if there was any point to it at all. One boy had nodded when questioned about lights—yes, he had said, he knew what lights were; yes, he had seen them overhead; and yes, the lights would have been around that time—and then he had pointed to Noah's shoes and used the same word for them.

Logic told him it was a losing battle. And yet…

Twisting between the rocks was an area Noah hadn't explored: the furthest outreach of the archipelago, where the islands looped into a curve like a chain on a velvet cushion, tens of miles between them and leagues of bottomless sea.

The search had ruled it out as too far from the flight path. Was it?

He had to find out—because after that his ideas dried up.

Tomorrow he would set sail, take enough food and fuel to sustain him, and he wouldn't return until he had something. He would go it alone and it would push him to the limits of endurance, but, unless he did, he would never be able to sleep again.

He sat on the sand. He was tired, and the days ahead of him long.

He did not hear the footsteps approach.

***

The man pinched the fabric of his T-shirt, peeling it away from his chest. It soldered to his skin before yielding. He scanned the jetty, and set off across the beach.

Beyond the crags, he emerged into a cove. A fishing boat was bobbing on the water, and there, on the shore, was the person he had come for.

Noah Lawson was studying a map, at intervals looking up and out to sea with an expression, as much as could be deciphered side-on, of simultaneous optimism and despair. He was taller and broader than the man had expected.

The man advanced, emerging from the trees, a dark shape on the pale sand, the weapon glinting in his belt.

He put a hand on Noah Lawson's shoulder.

'Hello,' he said. 'We've been looking for you.'

60

Day 16

Jacob learned the number of steps it took to reach the jungle wall. He drew himself up on the skin of a tree trunk, hands in front, feet hesitant, and walked into the forest. Shapes burgeoned and dissolved behind the bandages. The shade was fresh, layers of flavour hitting his senses. Every sound he picked up, the squawk in a tree, the buzz of insects, the shiver of a branch.

Alone, he crouched. His bandage was knotted at the back, the ends frayed and set with sweat, and it was a struggle to loosen it. At last it came free.

Days it had been on, and the outcome was a shock.

Jacob blinked. It wasn't perfect. A little fuzzy round the edges, like waking from an intense sleep, but the outlines were there—and, yes, the more he pushed through, his eyes growing accustomed to light after so long in the dark, he didn't know how long, the more the scene in front of him sharpened into focus.

Golden sunlight spilled on the crusted floor. A pea-green lizard shot across a rock, stopping to warm its armoured back. Flies twitched on a stagnant slop of water. Twisted roots thick as his arm knotted into the musty earth, and an emerald parrot with a pastel-blue head called from the canopy, flying low between the trees with its green wings spread. Colour, light, shape—how perfect the world looked!

He wanted to see the beach. He wanted to see more.

Jacob moved fast, his vision refining by the second to something hyper-real.

Sky had never been so blue. Sand had never been so dazzling. Sea had never been so clear. His wits were amplified, inhaling the salt breeze and catching the chalk from the rocks in the distance. He rushed down to the lagoon, scooping up handfuls and dousing himself in silver.

The beach was deserted. Fire smouldered by the rock platform. Jacob plunged back into the jungle, pushing through fronds until he reached the path the others had trodden. Vision was like water after the desert. His eyes wanted more—to see it all, to drink it in, an unquenchable thirst. As if he were meeting it for the first time.

How hopeless he had felt. Unable to act for himself, a burden to the group, following where he was led and trusting in people he did not know. Sight was power—and fear had made a man of him. In the ordinary world he never felt that emotion. Why should he? Jacob Lyle always called the shots. Having that authority wrenched from him had thrown him on the mercy of others.

Through a shield of creepers he came to the bathing pool. It was not how he had imagined: his mind had only been able to capture it as a still life. Here, life was moving. The waterfall rushed, spilling from a high platform and cascading onto the rocks, filling the air with a suspended, glittering spray. The pool was aquamarine, white sand visible from the surface. Sheer rock walls contained it, a paradise suntrap.

He knelt at the lip of the lake and peered over the edge.

His appearance was less important to him than he thought it would be.

Even so, it was better than he'd feared. His face was badly sunburned, nothing better, nothing worse, and across his forehead and down the line of his nose was a colourless strip of skin. Jacob removed his shirt, his neck and chest delicate, but it was almost healed, patches of white blossoming through. His chest remained muscled where he had thought it would have faded away. Where he hadn't been scorched, on forearms, shoulders and legs, he had turned a rich, honey brown.

His hair was long, curling round his ears, and he had a beard.

The woman who had made it possible: *Celeste*.

Jacob knew how much worse it might have been. Celeste had looked after him. She had been his eyes when his own had failed.

He caught a new sound beneath the drum of the waterfall, a faint, humming tune. He looked up and in an instant he remembered: Celeste at Jakarta, in the pencil skirt and the smart blouse, the dark hair and the soulful eyes...

And there she was now.

He dashed behind a rock.

Celeste was naked, singing softly as she showered beneath the waterfall. She was a nymph; her cropped black hair slick and boyish. When she climbed out to dry herself, Jacob's breath caught at the sight of her body. It was petite and pale, perfectly proportioned, her arms and legs slender and her breasts high and small. The bush between her thighs was soft and abundant. Jacob's cock sprang to attention.

Never had he noticed the shape of someone's ankles. Never had he noticed the cuppable flesh where her ass met her thighs. Never had he noticed the swan-like line of her neck as she bent to the ground—and then come up abruptly, sensing his scrutiny, huge eyes scanning the pool. Jacob stayed hidden, holding his breath.

His erection strained. Not being able to get it up for Tawny, he'd thought that was it. Not any more. For all the tapes he had watched, all the women with their legs apart and their come-to-bed faces, all the times he had got horny watching a harem of beauties writhe, never before had he felt as aroused as he did right now.

He wanted Celeste Cavalieri more than he had ever wanted anyone.

Had she seen him? He couldn't be sure. Celeste was looking in his direction, her eyes stilled on the spot where he was, but she didn't move. She didn't cover up.

She stood, dripping, her breasts rising and falling with her breath.

Jacob stared back from his hiding place.

At last, she slipped into the forest and disappeared from sight.

Jacob put his forehead against the rock and exhaled.

61

Day 17

The meat did strange things.

For the first time since arriving on Koloku, the group were using their teeth. They tore into flesh, tearing and ripping and shredding before sucking the skin off their fingers. They had exercised the right of man over beast.

Possibilities of rescue came in fits and starts. Once they had considered it every minute; now it was possible for hours to pass without it being mentioned.

Appetite claimed them in different ways: physical, emotional and sexual. They felt themselves changing, past selves and past lives abandoned.

Still there was no sign of Mitch. Angela led the search. They scoped the island. With Jacob's vision renewed, he scoured the coastline and thrashed through the jungle. Nothing. The senator was nowhere to be found.

Against the afternoon sun, Kevin's silhouette was long and wide on the lagoon. It was stretched and refracted in god-like proportions, like a biblical drawing of man.

He had discarded his shirt. Kevin's shoulders were russet brown, peeled and chapped where they met his collarbone, revealing cauliflower patches of hot red. His pecs were wide as plates and his legs were strong, his haunches mighty. When he caught his reflection in the ripples he scarcely knew the man looking back.

In his fist he carried a harpoon. Kevin directed his spear into the water with cut-throat precision. He felt the slipping body yield and collapse, and when he raised it and held it to the sun it jerked blindly, tail whipping.

Kevin brought the prey close and studied it. A trickle of blood escaped at the point of impact, and the fish's mouth was open. He flung the catch to shore and returned to the task, darting shadows tempting his lance into another one-sided battle.

Deeper in, beyond the spinach-green seaweed, Tawny was bathing. Kevin squinted to see better, because the rules said they weren't allowed to swim out that far. He liked that Tawny had gone against the rules. Rules were boring. Rules were pointless. Kevin Chase had lived by other people's rules his whole life, and now he was free of them he was finally coming alive.

In a few short strokes he was with her. Close to, he saw she was topless, and made no effort to conceal herself. Tawny was a goddess; there was no doubt about it. Her hair was tangled blonde and her eyes were the exact colour of his swimming pool back in Bel Air. Her tanned breasts bobbed at the surface of the water. There was a cute mole where her cleavage would have been had she had bigger tits. Kevin stared at them brazenly. He felt no shame, only arousal. At long, long last, *arousal*…

It was futile to deny his attraction. He wanted her. He wanted *anyone*.

Kevin was horny beyond his wildest dreams. He had so much horn he didn't know what to do with it. Twice an hour he was vanishing into the jungle for a desperate jerk-off, irrigating the fronds with a seemingly endless supply of silky white semen. But no matter how hard he pumped or how fiercely he ejaculated, inside the next thirty minutes the impulse overtook him again.

'I've seen you looking at me,' said Tawny. She lifted her arms and her tits rose enticingly, capped by buds that were pink as candy. Kevin couldn't keep his eyes off them. So many years he had stared at women's tits in magazines, hidden behind designer blouses or red carpet gowns, or in his mom's panty catalogue, and now they were here, begging to be touched. Sandi's tits had been the tits of a girl; the tits of that fan he'd almost had backstage at *The Craig Winston Show* had been the tits of a girl—but Tawny Lascelles was all woman. Which was just as well, because he was all man.

On cue, Tawny said: 'You've changed.'

'Yeah?'

'Yeah.' She licked her lips. 'You're hot.'

Christ, he was ready to explode!

'Do you think they can see us?' Tawny looked over his shoulder. Back on the beach, Angela and Celeste were tending to the fire. Eve was asleep in the shade. Jacob was gutting fish at the shore. Tawny's eyes rested on the entrepreneur.

'Who cares?' said Kevin.

'Maybe we should swim in a little,' said Tawny.

'Why?'

'In case it's not safe.'

Kevin raised his spear. 'You're safe with me.'

She giggled. On the beach, Jacob heard the sound and looked up. Satisfied she now had his attention, Tawny returned to Kevin and looped her arms around his neck.

'Whatever's happened to you, I like it. I like it a lot.

Y'know, all this sitting around gets me kinda frustrated; it makes me wanna…let off some steam.'

Kevin knew how that felt. Boy, he did.

He wedged the harpoon in the sand, just possible to touch with the tips of his toes. Moving towards her, he fed his hand beneath the surface. Tawny was so close he could feel her breath, and the irresistible slurp of her skin touching his.

'Whoa,' she said, as her fingers clasped round his cock. Kevin spilled into her grip, choking with lust.

'You're big,' she said, shocked. 'Seriously big.'

'Let me put it in you,' Kevin grunted.

Tawny stepped out of her knickers, holding them just a moment too long above her head, in case anyone on the shore should care to look, before discarding them in the water. Kevin grabbed her round the waist.

'To think you were such a kid…' she began, her lips about to touch his, her breasts grazing his chest, her pussy about to slide over him when—

There was a commotion coming from the shore.

The figures were distant. All were waving frantically.

Tawny smirked.

'Looks like they want us back in,' she said, drawing away. 'Hey—!'

'I guess Jacob's finally jealous… Come on, Kevin: you seriously thought I was going to fuck you? Right here, in front of everyone? Dream on.'

The uproar from the beach got louder. The group was shouting now, arms high, signalling violently. Kevin spun round. Angela, or at least he thought it was Angela, was holding two sticks in the air, crossed at their tips. What the…?

All the fucking rules…

Fuck 'em.

And then it happened. Curdling terror. Kevin reached for

Tawny, growling, 'Come here,' at the same time as Tawny shrieked: 'SHARK!'

Kevin's brain clotted. Blood filled his head.

He whipped round. Tawny was swimming, her arms churning the water and in the distance the yells were louder and they were all chanting the same thing:

'SWIM! SWIM! SWIM!'

Angela's sign: the triangle.

Quietly the shark's fin slipped behind him. Kevin saw the steel-grey shape glide beneath the surface before re-emerging several feet away, and moments later there was a sharp bump against his leg, the grind and thump of undiluted muscle.

He remembered a fan grabbing him after a gig, sometime back in the early days. It had been Seattle. His first sell-out show and he'd been beat. The fan had snatched him out of nowhere, evading security, and had pushed him down to the floor, pinning him with her knees and planting kisses all over his face. He'd been scared—properly scared. Persecuted against his will. Bullied into submission.

Not any more, sucker.

Kevin dived beneath the surface. He yanked the harpoon from its mooring.

Underwater, the shark moved more quick and fatal than ever. One minute it was obscured by the fog of a few metres away, the next whipping past, tail flashing, eyes beady and cold. Its prehistoric snout was butting and evil, hiding jagged rows of lethal zipper teeth.

Kevin was not about to be defeated. This shark had chosen the wrong fucking battle with the wrong fucking guy.

In his periphery he could see Tawny's manically flailing legs making for a swift getaway. It gave him pleasure to register her pearly-white butt in the context of this life-or-death situation.

Come on, you sonofabitch...

The shark was circling him. Every few seconds it receded into the ultramarine and then returned with a vengeance, darting for him, hard as a bullet, and if he swung away he could dodge it. Excited by the motion, the shark was fixed on its bait. Its gills were as long as his hands. Vaguely, Kevin knew this was no basking shark or tiger shark. This was the mother of them all: the Great White Motherfucker.

'FUCK YEAH!'

Drawing the spear from behind his back at the last possible moment, Kevin angled it into the animal's undercarriage, right at its throat. The monster boosted forward, ever more potent in the throes of the attack, a juggernaut propelling him through the water. Kevin seized its nose and jammed the harpoon in place.

The shark did the rest. Every inch the beast travelled was another inch of its gut slit. Clouds of red filled the lagoon. Confused as to where the blood was coming from, the Great White turned on itself, snapping aimlessly, until Kevin, with a final drive that came from within, thrust the spear so it lodged fast.

With that the light in the shark's eyes dimmed, glazed, and died.

Kevin surfaced. He had drifted in, was close now to the shore.

The water here was crimson. The beach had assumed the worst. Angela was stunned. Eve was on her knees. Tawny, splendid in her nakedness, watched open-mouthed as Kevin dragged the shark's carcass in behind him. His muscles rippled, his shoulders and back straining at this unfeasible triumph.

The group watched in awe until Jacob ran down to help him.

62

They gorged themselves that night. The shark-meat wouldn't keep and they would have to burn what was left. The creature was massive, beached and terrifying. They had never seen a shark that close up before. It seemed sacrilege to tear it apart.

Kevin sat separately from the group. He was restless, and claimed to have no appetite. He carved sticks into points, lining them up on the sand.

The others were wary of him. When he'd brought back the pig they'd been impressed, grateful, but this time it was different. This was an incredible feat.

It wasn't natural. The natural thing would be if Kevin hadn't come back in.

They realised they didn't want to be surprised. The island threw enough their way: they could not handle one of their own transforming.

63

The moon hung like a bell in the sky, whole and alone.

Celeste wondered that this was the same moon as the one she knew: the one she had seen from her Venice apartment, or on train journeys cross-country, travelling with her parents from one city to the next, or from the window of the college dorm she had shared with Sylvia.

She turned on her bed. The moon-balm shone directly onto Jacob, his eyelashes long and his hair swept across his fore-head. She watched him a while.

Making a decision, she got up and padded across the sand.

Wrapped in a nest of leaves and weighted down by a stone, she found what she was looking for: Tawny's diamond neck-lace. The jewels sparkled so violently that she feared some-one would notice, but when she turned back they all remained still.

Celeste pooled the necklace in her palm and crept towards Tawny. The model was on her side. Quietly, carefully, Celeste leaned over.

The fist that grabbed hers was quick as lightning.

'I knew you took it,' Tawny hissed. The women's faces

were inches from each other and Celeste could feel Tawny's hot, furious breath against her skin.

'You're a thief. I knew it. I *knew* you were a thief.'

'I'm sorry,' Celeste gasped.

'Too late.'

Angela woke. 'What's going on?'

Celeste panicked. Stupid as it was, she didn't want Jacob to hear.

'It was because *he* gave it to me, wasn't it?' lashed Tawny. 'He wanted me before you, and now he has to settle for second best.'

'No—'

'I've seen the way you look at him. It's desperate. It's embarrassing.'

Tawny's words hit her like a slap. She was right, of course; Celeste was nobody's first choice—Carl told her often enough. Carl said he was only with her because he felt sorry for her. He knew that no one else would look twice at her.

She had been crazy to imagine that Jacob might.

Tawny snatched the necklace back. 'Look, everyone! I was right all along. Celeste here's a thieving *bitch*.'

'Please, don't—'

'What do you think about that, Jacob?'

Jacob rubbed his eyes. He sat up. In the firelight his chest was golden. Celeste wanted to run her fingers across it and knew right then it was forever beyond her reach. She didn't want Jacob thinking badly of her. For once in her life, here was a man who believed she was good, who didn't judge her by the things she had done.

It had been idiotic of her to think, if only for a second, that she stood a chance. Against Tawny she was nothing.

'What?'

'Celeste stole my necklace. The necklace *you* bought me.'

'Tawny, leave it,' said Angela. 'She tried to give it back.'

'Like hell I will. She's not getting away with this.'

'I'm sorry,' said Celeste again. 'I'm really, truly sorry.'

'You can be sorry all you like, sweetheart. It doesn't change anything.'

She remembered what Sylvia's mother had said to her at the funeral: *Saying sorry doesn't change anything. It doesn't bring her back.*

'Calm down,' said Angela. 'Let's talk about this sensibly.'

'Jacob bought it for me and you had to have it, didn't you?' snarled Tawny. 'You had to play pretend, act like he got it for you instead of me because that's the kind of loser you are. Can't find a decent man of your own so you steal that too—'

'I bought that necklace when I liked you,' said Jacob.

'Liked me?' Tawny snorted. 'That's an understatement.'

'It's an overstatement,' he said, 'because I don't like you any more. As far as I'm concerned, Celeste can keep the necklace. She deserves it more than you.'

Tawny's expression was blank. 'What?'

'You heard.'

Tawny swayed a little on the spot, as if she'd been struck. Then she rounded on Celeste and in a mad flash went for her, hands tearing through her hair, nails ripping her skin. Celeste was thrown to the sand, winded.

Jacob hauled Tawny off. Celeste tasted blood on her lip. Tawny was writhing in his arms like a madwoman, striking to break free.

'Let me go!' she raged. 'Let me go!'

Jacob secured her arms behind her back. Celeste watched as Tawny's pretty blue eyes surveyed the scene, elected a trusted route and then broke out sobbing.

She turned and buried her face in Jacob's chest. 'She stole from me!' Tawny blubbed. 'She's a thief!'

Celeste was shaking. She blotted her lip on the back of her hand.

'We're not ourselves,' said Angela. 'None of us are.'

'I am!' Tawny wailed. She clutched Jacob's bulk like it was a rock in a stormy sea. 'I'm the same! I'm still the same as I always was!'

The affirmation didn't come to Celeste immediately, rather it swam up slowly, set in motion by Tawny's lavish protestations, the scorn the model had poured on her since the moment they had been introduced, deriding her at every opportunity and eclipsing her in the mighty shadow of her celebrity—and now in the claiming of Jacob, who had stepped up in her defence.

I'm not the same, thought Celeste.

She was sick of it. She was sick of Carl pushing her and hitting her. She was sick of being told what to do. She was sick of being bullied. She was sick of being weak. She was sick of regretting. She was sick of being the one they all trampled over because she didn't believe she was anything worth taking care of.

'I'm glad I took it,' she said.

The group stopped their squabbling.

'I might be a thief, but do you know what you are, Tawny Lascelles? You're vain, spoiled and selfish and I couldn't care less what you think of me. I took your necklace because I wanted a piece of you. I wanted to be a tiny bit like you, just for a day. And do you know what? Now, I can't think of anything worse. I don't want to be you, and any woman who does needs their head examined. You might be pretty on the outside but you're ugly in your soul. You make yourself feel good by making other people feel bad, and the sad thing is you've been doing it for so long and you do it so well that you've forgotten how to stop. I'm not going to be the other person any more.'

She pushed past, knocking Tawny on the shoulder. The supermodel's mouth was open.

'Oh, and one more thing.' Celeste stopped. She turned, and slapped Tawny clean across her cheek. 'That's for making me bleed.'

64

Day 21

Morning was slow to arrive.

Eve didn't want to remain at camp. Since Kevin's attack on the shark, their behaviour had been raw and unpredictable, as if the pretence no longer needed to be upheld. The pretence of what: society? Humanity?

Days after the event, the beast's scent still filled the air, a bitter reminder of their lost selves—and the new frontiers of their capability.

Angela would never let her go alone, so Eve hung back until the moment came when she could slip into the forest unnoticed. She would be back before dark.

And, with any luck, she would bring Mitch Corrigan with her.

It was a bold claim, she accepted, as she followed the pig run up the side of the mountain. Eve feared that to bring him back alive was no longer an option, but to bury him would put all their minds at peace. It might give the group what they needed, a sense of closure, of starting afresh. After last night, they needed it.

She hadn't wanted to admit her anxieties when Kevin had

raised them, but she felt it too. She felt like someone was watching them.

Her legs dripped with sweat and her shirt was heavy. Her belly was swollen now, the navel distended. She stopped for breath, drinking thirstily.

When she reached the plateau, she looked out to the west. It was darker this side. The sea churned and the rocks were craggy and sharp. A thin line of sand snaked along the base of the cliffs and she was about to turn away and shout his name when something new registered: something she had not noticed before.

At the furthest reach was a cluster of caves. She had observed these during previous excursions, gouged out nubs whose innards were dark and dripping—but the biggest, an almost vertical slit in a face of hard grey rock, had eluded her until now.

The cave seemed to live and breathe. It seemed to stare back.

Eve lowered herself onto the beach, careful to hold the shoots and sprays that broke the descent. Down on the sand, the cave seemed bigger.

Leading into it was a trail of footprints.

Eve stopped. It was strange to see the mark of a person anywhere except at camp. Unease climbed in her stomach.

Corrigan? But another possibility surfaced.

The woman they had lost, the flight attendant. She had become magical and threatening in Eve's mind, polished and smiling when they had boarded at Jakarta, then a terror-stamped mask when they had fallen from the skies. She was the dark shake of the trees, the whisper of the wind, the question mark they could not face.

Eve pulled herself together. She was no longer that frightened little girl, afraid of the dark and the monsters it could bring. Her monster was locked up in jail. He was gone. He couldn't hurt her again. There were no other monsters.

Closer to, she saw the prints were big, the size of a man's, and couldn't decide if this was a comfort or not. Their trajectory was unusual: they didn't go direct into the mouth of the cave but, rather, seemed to step around it, changing direction.

If only Angela were with her. Angela would apply reason and sense, not let her imagination run away. It was a Silvers trait, Eve realised, and what had attracted her to Orlando in the first place. You just felt they knew how to handle things.

'Corrigan?' She stepped inside.

His name sounded weird in the dark, throwing itself back at her. She felt as if she were disturbing a creature that had been slumbering a thousand years.

The walls of the cave were damp and freezing. Water pooled at her feet. A crab scuttled over her toes and she put her hands in front of her to feel the way.

Something shifted in the dark. 'Who's there?'

No response. She had not come prepared—no light, no defence. Alone.

'Who's there?' she echoed, staring into the chasm.

Again, something moved. Eve felt the wall behind her, fingers touching daylight, and stayed where she was. The shape came closer. She could sense its approach in the dark.

'Corrigan, is that you…?'

But the sight that met her eyes was not Mitch Corrigan.

It was something else entirely.

All morning, Tawny refused to stir. She lay on her bunk, clutching the diamond chain around her neck as if it were the last vestige of a familiar world.

She thought of LA, of New York, of glamorous fashion galas and starry-eyed fans, of margaritas at Nobu and dancing at the Barrio, of runway shows and make-up chairs, of sharing a penthouse with her croupier lover and screwing until dawn, of photographers who eyed her ravenously even though they saw dozens of models a week, because she, Tawny, was the ultimate.

She wanted her manager. She wanted her car and her Security. She wanted Minty and JP. She wanted her hairdresser.

Angela tried to rouse her, but she barked at her to get lost. Celeste attempted an olive branch, but Tawny blanked it. Why should she play nice?

That witch had stolen from her, humiliated her—and, as if that hadn't been bad enough, she had seduced her man...

I don't like you any more.

Tawny could spew when she remembered Jacob's words.

No man had ever said that to her—as far back as she could recall, no man, married or divorced, single or attached, old or young or tall or short, had been able to resist her. And now Jacob had shunned her in favour of...of that *thieving cow*?

Tawny would not—could not—accept it. A long time ago, in a distant hospital bed, she had pledged that her days of being the victim were over.

She wasn't about to start again now.

She would find a way to deal with Celeste Cavalieri.

No one crossed Tawny Lascelles and got away with it.

65

Over a week in the cave had left him ravaged and delirious. He was emaciated, his eyes sunken and his lips cracked. His ribcage strained. He was naked save for a pair of underpants, blotted now with sand and grit.

Eve went to touch him and he flinched out of reach. The Mitch Corrigan who glared back at her was part animal, part man. His skin was bleached from the darkness of his hideout. He hunched beneath the dripping arches.

'Corrigan…' She held out water. 'I'm here to help.'

As her eyes became accustomed to the dark, she could make out the pit of his lair. Fish bones littered the sand; and the remains of a fire, chalky and black.

He regarded the liquid suspiciously.

'Come with me,' she urged. 'We'll look after you, Corrigan.'

He didn't trust her. Why should he?

'Get out.' His voice was rusty, like a car engine spluttering to a start.

Eve held her hands up, to show she meant no harm. 'Not unless you come with me.'

'Never.'

'You can't stay here.'

'I can't stay anywhere.'

A flash of the old senator—on TV or at the White House, his pristine smile and the smooth cap of his hairpiece. All decorations had been stripped.

'Come outside,' she said. 'Into the sun.'

He coughed, hacking and grisly. 'No. They're waiting.'

'Who?'

'*They're here.* I feel it.'

Eve took a chance. 'I feel it too.'

His hands were shaking, the fingernails blackened and torn. 'You lie.'

'It's with us,' she said. 'Something in the trees.'

'No. Here.'

'In the cave?'

'In the sky.'

'What are they waiting for?'

'Me. And I've been waiting for them. I've seen their footprints.'

'Those are your footprints.'

'They weren't the first time.'

Eve swallowed. 'The first time?'

'I saw them, on day one. From the mountain.'

Your eyes must have tricked you.

Eve wanted to say it but didn't, partly because it would break his confidence and partly because she didn't know if it was true. She hoped to God it was true.

'If I come back, they'll know where to find us.'

'We've got a better chance together, haven't we?'

He laughed. 'You mock me, Eve Harley. Do you think I don't know it was you who followed me to Italy? I know. You think you're clever but you're not. You all do, but you're the ones in the dark.'

'Corrigan…'

'And now I'm here, so why don't they take me?'

Without warning he ran past her, out onto the beach, imploring the empty sky.

'*Take me, you bastards!*' He punched the air; his arms aloft, pleading with such savage abandon that for a moment Eve half believed the dome was about to part, revealing a shaft of light through which Signor Rossetti's bizarre creation sprang forth.

Nothing happened.

Corrigan buckled to his knees at the altar of his faith.

'Put me out of my misery! *Take me!*'

Eve watched as the desperation of the last nine days, and all the days that had gone before, came pouring out. At last, unanswered, he wilted.

The storm passed. Eve came to him. This time he endured her touch. 'Please come back,' she said again.

Corrigan was defeated. 'It's too late.'

'It's never too late.'

He glanced at her. For the first time, his eyes were engaged. He regarded her differently, softly, almost human again.

'You're pregnant,' he said, out of the blue.

'Yes,' Eve said, smiling. 'I am.'

66

Every bone in Noah's body hurt. There was a shooting pain in his side. He hadn't dreamed, nor had he been aware of time passing—just a big black gulf between then and now.

What was then?

What was now?

Where was he?

He opened his eyes and saw he was on a stretcher, the white cotton beneath him starched and clean. A basic arrangement, a square cabin, and other beds like his, rigged up to saline drips and sachets of liquid. Noah thought of war films he had seen. Ailing soldiers.

The throb in his head didn't help, the kind of throb that made him conscious of the shape of his sockets and the dips and troughs of his skull: all that mechanical stuff he wasn't supposed to think about. It was hot: inescapable heat that filled the nostrils and the ears, and he recognised the heat, sort of, at least the smell of it, dense and tropical with a shave of lime peel. He could hear the ocean. A band of sunlight eased through a crack and he tried to sit up but the sting in his side was too much.

He needed water.

A face hovered over his. The nurse smiled, and brought

a bottle to his lips. 'Don't move,' she said in English. 'Stay here.'

'Where am I?'

He wasn't sure if he asked it, if the words came out. They must have, because she replied: 'You were hurt. We brought you back.'

A spread of crimson bloomed at his waist, staining the sheet, and he groaned, went to sit again but the pain forced him back. His knuckles were split and cracked. His lower lip was bust. The skin around his eye was shiny to touch, grape-smooth, and when he closed his other eye he could barely see at all.

He peeled back the sheet. The knife had gone deep. Surrounding a thick white compress was a livid purple welt, and the tail end of a trail of stitches.

'How long have I been here?'

'One week,' said the nurse.

A week! Despair crashed over him.

And then he remembered.

We can help each other, the man had said, *I have a lead, let's talk…*

The man had introduced himself as a friend of Angela's… How could Noah have been so careless?

He had wanted to believe it. A friend of Angela's, someone to help: someone who trusted as strongly as he did that they lived. He remembered the liquor, sour and salty. His senses fading, his reactions slowing…

The fight.

Flashes of the brawl assailed him in bursts, beaten up and left for dead.

MOVIE STAR NOAH LAWSON FOUND SLAIN IN ISLAND PARADISE.

They would say it was his fault. Trying to play the hero.

Come on, come on, come on. No time to waste. *Think!*

Noah had known the man's face, had seen it in a paper sometime. Who was he?

The Angela connection had thrown him. It had directed him off the scent and he hadn't thought to associate the man with anyone else. But that was it.

Of course, that was it.

Tawny Lascelles.

Definitely the same man, Noah was sure. He had been Tawny's boyfriend, for a time, in the weeks before the party disappeared. They had posed together, been snapped in the weeklies—some guy from Vegas.

What was he doing here?

Did he have something to do with the crash?

Why did he want to get rid of Noah?

Realisation struck. Suddenly, it was clear. The man knew, like he did, that the passengers on board that jet bound for Salimanta were still breathing.

Noah tore the bandage off. A bolt shot through his abdomen.

'No,' the nurse saw, 'you mustn't—'

They would have to kill him before they stopped him.

He could rest when he died for real. Right now, Noah was alive. And he had to find Angela before somebody else did.

67

Day 25

It was a day of the week but nobody knew its name. The sun beat down, spilling lava between the glades. The forest floor was arid; leaves turned to brittle crunch, while up above the canopy thronged with life. Monkeys sprang from branches, tagging each other and hanging from their tails, howling against their course of ropes and plummets.

They prayed for rain. The stream had dried up and the heat was unreal. Action was impossible at the height of the day and the group slumped beneath palm trees, torn between the temptation of the water and the threat of the blazing sun.

Jungle creatures, semi-naked, their hair grown and their skin turned brown; the line between their old world and the acceptance of this new, feral state was obliterated.

Mitch's return seemed to have carried a curse—the sun brighter than ever, the sky closer, the heat hotter. Salt caked on their skin and around their mouths.

On the molten horizon they thought they saw a ship, a cruel mirage, or heard on the thermals the engine of a plane.

They were wrong. It was over.

They would be here until they died. Some wished for an

ending, something quick and painless; others still dreamed of home.

Thirst made them mad. They needed water.

The scorching day gave way to evening shadows. Tawny volunteered to set out to find a new source—anything but to be stuck with them.

Much to her dismay, Jacob insisted on coming with her.

They worked through the jungle, brandishing torches of fire, orange glow darting between the trees. Tawny didn't speak to him. She couldn't look at him. Celeste's words swamped her mind, with every recollection growing larger and more horrible.

You're ugly in your soul.

'Slow down,' Jacob called from behind. 'Wait up.'

Tawny could leave him right here for all she cared, hope he got snatched and devoured by some awful creature. What had happened to the Jacob who had cornered her at the Rieux? Who had pursued her at the Tower Club and sent her flowers and jewellery and flooded her PA with messages? What had happened to that Jacob?

He had lost more than his sight when the plane came down. He had lost his fucking mind.

Jacob tripped and swore, but Tawny didn't turn back. She would give him nothing. He and Celeste had been flirting ever since that shameful night. The way Jacob looked at her... No one had ever looked at Tawny like that. Sure, they lusted after her. They told her what a hot body she had and how much they wanted to nail her. But they never looked at her like she was the last woman on Earth, never looked into her soul—her *ugly* soul—and accepted and loved what was there.

Maybe she had never given herself a chance. Shedding

her old skin had meant absolute denial: a mystery siren with no past, no story, no family and no friends, and in a way it had been the making of her, the enhanced allure, the implied goldmine that had kept reporters like Eve Harley on her tail for so long. But at what cost?

In burying the bad things about Tawny Linden, she had also buried the good. All those loveable parts that the woman she was today would never know.

Tawny's eyes filled with tears. Fleetingly she considered beginning an affair with Kevin—he was certainly the last viable option, what with Jacob losing his balls and old man Mitch's crab breath—but there was no point. They would all be dead soon. And she would die alone…and ugly.

Jacob wouldn't care even if she did bone Kevin. For the first time since her reinvention, Tawny was ordinary: she had no power and no secret. In Jacob's eyes she was just a girl, nothing more, nothing else, and that scared her more than anything.

The further they went, the darker it became.

Tawny hated the dark. When it was light she could still think of those bursts of brilliance: the flash of the paparazzo's camera, the spot-glow on the runway as she flaunted the look of the season, or the spark of a magazine shoot when all she had to wear was a plastic bikini and a slash of red lipstick.

When it was dark, bad thoughts crept in.

Perhaps she had died. Sometimes she persuaded herself that she had perished in that crash, they all had, and this was nothing but some limbo before their fates got decided. Who was there to say otherwise? They only had each other, and each was as deluded as the next. Who knew if her companions were even real? They could be figments of her addled imagination, or some residual flicker from the life she had departed when she flew out of Jakarta that day.

A chill raced, quick-legged, up her spine.

But wait. That wasn't a chill.

'ARGHHHH!'

Frantically Tawny began slapping her back, tearing her vest off, her face a grimace of terror. 'Get it off me, get it off me!'

'What is it?'

Tawny panted, gasping, and pointed shakily at the undergrowth, to where a dark shape was picking its way languidly through the bramble.

Spider.

The word didn't do it justice. This wasn't a teeny-weeny creepy-crawly she sometimes found in the corner of her Jacuzzi bathroom (and even then she got the maid to remove it): this was a *monster*. She had seen pictures of spiders like this, heard tales of their existence, witnessed them starring in their own fucking horror movie, but had never thought she would encounter one for real. It was huge and brown and furry. Its body was the size of a tennis ball and its legs were twig-thick limbs, bent at the knee in that revolting upturned V shape, and sprung with coarse hair.

Its eyes were out on stalks. *Stalks!*

Untroubled by Tawny's screams, the spider navigated its way through the dry leaves and vanished from sight.

'You're OK,' said Jacob, putting a hand on her back. 'It's gone.'

She shrugged him off.

'Touch me again and I'll fucking kill you.'

They walked on.

***

At last they came to a creek and filled the bottles. Jacob was so thirsty he scooped handfuls of water into his mouth, not caring if it made him sick. She hoped it did.

They loaded as many as they could carry. It would be enough to see them through until dawn, when the others would return for more.

Guided by the sound of the ocean, they decided to take a different route back. Jacob's torch had gone out and Tawny led the way. She heard him stagger and didn't hold up: it gave her pleasure to hear him struggle. Once, on a night like tonight, she would have seduced him. Had sex with him right here on the jungle floor. Instead he had chosen that scrawny doe-eyed flake. Tawny wondered if they'd had sex yet, if Jacob had been able to get it up for *her*, and died a little at the possibility.

Through a shield of foliage, they stepped into a clearing.

Moonlight flooded the glade, and in the centre was the tube of fuselage they had abandoned on the first day. It was pale and glowing. Eerie. A bird shot out of one of the windows and the front was crumpled where the cockpit should have been.

They stood for a while in silence, thinking of the captain and his first officer, buried over the mountain, and the flight attendant who was still at large. It seemed wrong to speak, disrespectful, as if this were more of a grave to those men than the one they had been given.

Eventually Jacob said: 'I never saw this before.' The last time he had laid eyes on this craft was in Jakarta, before they had boarded. 'What do you think happened?'

'We crashed, asshole.'

He stepped closer. 'How? Why? Do we know?'

Tawny couldn't be bothered to think of the reasons. It didn't change anything. It was too late to go back and do it again. They were here and that was the end of it.

As Jacob explored the cabin she crouched, planting her torch in the ground. A heap of detritus was gathered along the wing. Curious, she advanced towards it: stuff that had been brought from the hold, useless and abandoned.

She rifled through it. Ash stained her fingers, death and dust.

Her grip fastened around something familiar. The shape was so accustomed, the memory so firm and so wonderful that she let out a sob.

'Everything OK?' came Jacob's voice.

She did not want him to see. This was just for her.

Tawny wept as she fell across the residue of her beloved hair straighteners. There wasn't much to them, melted plastic, not yellow any more but bone-white and grey, the cable twisted and the handle morphed and a great hole in the middle where they had softened completely. A relic in a deserted house: a trace of someone who used to exist.

Did she used to be so beautiful? Who was that girl?

'TO THE FAIREST OF THEM ALL, WITH LOVE & ADMIRATION.'

Now it read: 'T HE F IRE T F H M AL W V & DMIR TION.'

It seemed to Tawny a symbolic sort of horror.

68

She kept the straighteners from Jacob, securing them in the waistband of her shorts.

Some time later, they emerged onto the beach. Those still awake were relieved at the find. Kevin was sharpening a spear, his eyes reflecting the flames.

'We need more meat,' he said. 'It's better at night.'

But it wasn't a question of needing—it was a question of wanting. Kevin had become consumed by the hunt, stalking the beasts and baiting them, from boldness to recklessness, as if the Great White wasn't enough, and he could and would slay anything that crossed his path. His growth was in defiance of everything they endured, the wasting away, the weakness, and it could not be understood. He showed no signs of slowing. Day on day, week on week, he just got bigger.

Tawny held the treasure out to Angela.

'What are they?'

'My hair straighteners.'

'Oh.'

Tawny had expected a more gratifying response, not so much for the object itself, but for the world it elicited. She had hoped it would serve as a reminder of who she was.

Despite how Celeste had ruined her, she was still one to be revered.

Eve joined them. 'Where did you find them?'

'In the wreck.'

The reporter took them. Tawny saw her scepticism—a woman like Eve didn't care for such vanity. She would make a mockery of them, and in turn a mockery of Tawny. But Tawny was made up of these things: they were what defined her.

'Careful—' said Tawny.

Eve fingered the middle section, where the gas would have been. Its contours were molten, smooth as wax where the plastic had bent out of shape.

Eve looked at Angela. Something was exchanged.

'What?' Tawny said.

'Was there a canister in here?' said Eve.

Tawny shrugged. She had no idea how her straighteners worked. They got heated and they made her pretty—there was nothing more to say.

'What's that got to do with anything?'

In the jungle, a vicious shriek burst out of the trees. She pictured Kevin, triumphant, his spear raised.

'Tawny,' said Eve, 'these are what caught fire.'

The night fell away.

'Oh no, Tawny,' Angela whispered. 'Oh no.'

69

Los Angeles

It had been two weeks since Sketch Falkner's heinous reveal.

In that time Joan Chase had barely let a morsel pass her lips. She slept all day. She dosed up on Ambien, zonking herself out so she wouldn't have to dream.

Every accusation she threw at herself: a barrage of loathing and shame. She was a terrible mother. She should have noticed. She should have stepped in. She should never have let Kevin get involved with Cut N Dry in the first place.

She should have *known*, because wasn't that what moms did? All that time, Kevin had been suffering under a noxious regime, and she hadn't had a clue.

If she had, they would have got Kevin away from the industry years ago. None of this would have happened. He would never have been on that fated jet.

Joan could not forgive the men who had done it. Sketch had committed an abominable crime: the worst betrayal of a boy who had looked up to and respected him; who had obeyed in ignorance of the machine that controlled his every move.

She hated Sketch. She would put ten Sketches on that

plane over her vulnerable son. Half son, half daughter, what was he?

She didn't know.

Sketch tried to see her. He came to the house, pleading at the door, but she did not let him in. He left messages on her voicemail, begging and wheedling:

'*You won't tell the police, will you, Joanie?*'

'*Answer my calls, I'm going out of my mind.*'

'*Please can I see you? Let me explain...*'

There was nothing to explain. Sketch had done all the explaining he needed to, and nothing he could say or do in the aftermath could possibly lessen the blow.

Joan ignored his attempts with stoicism. She hoped he was in distress. She hoped the Cut N Dry execs were in hell.

However bad they were feeling, it couldn't be a drop in the ocean of her suffering. *The pills, one red, one blue...*

She couldn't believe it.

One morning, something changed. Joan woke up and the sun was shining. As usual her body was sluggish, but her mind was awake. She felt alert, unusually engaged, and the clock by her bed read ten—the earliest she had been up in weeks.

She made her way to the bathroom. Trey sniffed at her heels, watching seriously at the door while she took a pee. On autopilot, she opened the cabinet for Xanax, and when she closed it again she caught her reflection.

A woman she did not recognise stared back at her. The time since Sketch's bombshell had taken pounds off her. Her face was thinner than it had been in years, her eyes wider and her lips fuller. Her roots could do with a touch-up, but on the whole she had an Olsen-twin thing going on and, despite her mood, she liked it.

'Hello,' she said, to no one in particular.

***

Over the next forty-eight hours, Joan came to a decision. She began, methodically, to sort through Kevin's belongings. She wasn't fighting it any longer.

She started answering the phone, cataloguing messages from reporters and deleting the ones from Sketch. It was strange to hear such a powerful man reduced to tatters. Sketch had always been the one to impress, the guy with the muscle, but all he had become was a mid-life crisis with a fuckload on his conscience.

Now Joan was the one in charge. That made her important. Over the years Kevin had eclipsed his mother as an accessory to his cash and success, offering her a snack but never the full feast, which seemed grossly unjust since she was the one who had brought him into this world. So when the phone calls changed tack, a splurge of agents and managers seeking to back Joan 'through this heart-wrenching time', she paused to consider what a month ago would have been impossible.

Why *shouldn't* she claim some of Kevin's legacy?

Didn't she deserve it, after the years of struggle and toil?

All the encouragement she had given him, putting her life on hold, tidying away her own concerns and desires—wasn't she entitled to her share?

What could her life have been without Kevin? What might *she* have become?

The decision was made easier by the fact that she no longer recognised memories of her son. The Kevin she grieved had been lost to her way before the Challenger jet disaster. For years Sketch and his cronies had stunted their protégé as one would a Bonsai: no wonder they had borne so many tears and tantrums, as Kevin chased the eternal carrot of puberty. No one could deny the treason—yet somehow, it became a fringe of comfort. The Kevin who had used to crawl around her hallway carpet and giggle as she tickled him in the tub was not the same as the one she had lost: that Kevin had been twisted by hormones, pumped full of pills and switched into a circus freak. All in the pursuit of fame, to appease generation upon generation of Little Chasers—the ultimate prince who would never grow old, who would always be their boyfriend, cute and playful and safe.

What would have happened had he lived? In what state would he have ended up? Would Kevin have been doing the same when he was forty, fifty, older? What kind of a mutant would they have raised by then?

Perhaps Kevin's death had been merciful, in its way. Joan clung to that hope because she needed to believe it. She couldn't accept that his loss had been in vain.

On Thursday morning she signed with an agency on Sunset. Within hours, they were inundated with offers for talk shows, magazine interviews, panel appearances, a book about Kevin, an autobiography, a film script of the crash in which Joan would play herself, a commercial, even her own reality TV show. Every party affiliated with the victims had juice that was ripe to be squeezed—and, in her capacity as mother of one of the biggest heart-throb pop players of the twenty-first century, none more so than Joan. She was given a stylist and an assistant, and was pledged a new woman.

Joan Chase was ready to become a star—this time in her own right.

At the weekend she stepped out of the mansion for the first time. Her hair was piled high on her head and her killer heels struck the drive. In her arms was Trey, nude except for a studded diamond collar whose tag bore the words: KEVIN RIP.

She was heading to her first ever TV show.

The paps leaped to life, frantic to snap the money shot

they had been waiting for weeks to secure. Joan's name was shouted from the ranks. The fans rushed at her, their hands grasping through the gate, begging for a word or a glance.

She gave them neither.

Joan climbed into her BMW and slammed the door, negotiating a path through the photographers, their cameras pressed up against the window.

It couldn't help but be a sign when she hit the radio and one of Kevin's songs blared out of the speakers. This was what her son would have wanted.

70

Las Vegas

'You can't do this to us. She's not even been declared dead yet, Zenetti, and you're making this call. This screwed-up, soulless, *sonofabitch* call…'

Carmine Zenetti had expected the brothers to kick off. After all, this was the glittering Silvers fortune they were talking about. Orlando and Gianluca had found themselves destitute, from heroes to zeros in less than a week.

'I won't accept it.' Orlando leaned in, his palms splayed across Carmine's mahogany desk and his eyes full of fire. 'Even if Angela never returns, you're not getting your dirty hands on a cent of our money and that's the end of it.'

Carmine tried to be patient. Naturally, it was a shock. The brothers had arrived in town full of ideas for growth and progress, for recouping their share of the business and putting their father's legacy back on the map. But Lady Luck hadn't been smiling down that day. Orlando had raged; that faggot Gianluca trailing him out of here like a sick pup. There had been threats of lawyers.

Carmine wasn't concerned. The deal was in black and white.

'Orlando, Orlando,' Carmine smiled, 'you keep forgetting.

Why do you keep forgetting? We have a contract. One your sister *and* your father signed.'

'Screw the damn contract.'

'That kind of defeats the point, doncha think?'

'So that's it: Angela's gone and we don't see a penny.'

'Got it in one.'

'I swear to God, Zenetti—you and me, right now, outside.'

Carmine laughed. Orlando went to strike.

'You're through,' he growled, as Luca drew him off. 'Do you get that?' Rage he had kept in check since the plane went down—since before, since the night he had walked out on Eve and said all those things he didn't mean—made him want to smash and smash until there was nothing left of Carmine Zenetti but a shivering pulp. He had lost his sister and his lover and the promise of his child. Protecting their dynasty was his final hope, the only thing that stood a chance of keeping him afloat.

'Don't you care?' Luca said. 'Aren't you hurt that Angela's gone?'

Carmine sat back. The tycoon thought it a moot point in light of their exchange before realising it was his son being addressed, not him. Dino was sitting on his father's cream couch and picking his thumbs. 'Sure I do,' he grumbled. 'But we gotta face facts, don't we? There ain't no point wishing for something that can't happen.'

Carmine smiled.

'Angela *is* coming back,' said Orlando. He was adamant, as deluded as the rest. It was tragic to see. Carmine would have wept if he were a crying man; as it was, he hadn't shed a tear since Juliet Caretta had stood him up by the bike sheds in fifth grade.

'How long's it gonna take,' said Carmine, wondering the

same about this rendezvous, 'a week, a month, before it sinks in? You gotta start makin' plans.'

'It's our money.'

'Not what my papers say.'

'Fuck your papers—and fuck you.'

'This, my friend, is business.' Carmine stood, the pumping heart of the Strip rolling out behind him. 'And this is the end of our meeting. Goodbye, boys, and good luck. Something tells me you're going to need it.'

71

Washington, D.C.

Paparazzi circled her husband's apartment like scavengers. They had heard Melinda Corrigan was coming. At last, friends and relatives of the deceased were crawling from the woodwork: a dream for those savvy enough to know where to find them.

Melinda had already attended the Farley Senate to pack up his office, where she'd encountered the usual stricken faces. 'Are you sure it isn't too soon?'

Like hell was it too soon. The weeks since the incident had spelled purgatory. Time abandoned its usual order, morphing and dissolving until the days and nights became inseparable, part of the endless cycle of her grief. The sooner she could clear Mitch away, the sooner she could come to terms. She had been widowed.

She missed him. God, she missed him.

'How are you, Melinda? How are the kids?' Photographers bleated their frivolous questions, assailing her as she fumbled the key code. 'What do you make of Noah Lawson's rescue expedition? Do you intend to join him out there?'

Melinda hurried inside the building and closed the door.

Shaking, she located the card to Mitch's opulent quarters and took the elevator to the penthouse.

Yes, she had been tempted to follow Noah. Yes, she had considered it. And then she had hit her face with cold water, slammed to her senses and instructed herself not to be so god-damn ridiculous. It was all well and good imagining Mitch setting up shop on a desert island somewhere and finding a cow or two to milk, or to picture him growing a beard in a cave, indulging in home dentistry and winding up nam-ing a fucking basketball, but the reality was here. It was in this phantom of an apartment. It was at home, with her two kids who had no daddy. It was in bed, where his side remained cold. It was at Thanksgiving, when there would be no Mitch to carve the turkey and toast marshmallows by the fire.

Melinda worked through his belongings, stacking them in boxes and gathering them in bags. Each time the tears brimmed, she swiped them away.

The last time they had been in Washington she had been a bitch. Saddened by his lack of interest in her sexually, Melinda had thrown out cruel ultimatums. No wonder he didn't get turned on. For all the ways in which Mitch had changed over the years, she had changed too. For starters, she had begun fucking Gary Stewart.

It was a release to get away from her neighbour. Since their confrontation in Gary's gym, he had eased off, but that didn't mean she was immune to the occasional revolting message. *I miss your pussy*, the last one said. She had promptly changed her number.

After an hour, Melinda fell onto the bed. Her bones were weary. Her heart was tired. Her head was sick of wondering. She lay on the side where Mitch used to sleep, trailing a fin-ger across the pillow before lifting it and pressing it to her face, inhaling it in the hope that his scent would still be there. It smelled of detergent.

When she put her head back down, it met with something hard.

Melinda sat up. Beneath Mitch's pillow was a book. It was narrow and leather-bound. A diary? A journal? She frowned and picked it up. What was it?

It felt wrong opening it, without Mitch here to defend himself—for what lay in these pages was clearly private. It was reams and reams long, scattered with capital letters and explanation marks and hectically underlined passages. She flipped to the front.

The first line read: *August 4, 2012 was when it all began...*

Melinda sat back and started to read.

72

Day 30

Blame landed at her door like a sack of coal and there was nothing she could do to lift it. Tawny had brought them to this island. The fire in the hold had been her fault.

She saw it in their eyes: umbrage, bitterness, wrath.

Finally their misery had a name, something to attach itself to, something they could touch and see and throw it all on: something to hate.

She could hardly hold it against them. She would feel the same. She *did* feel the same. To think of her cherished appliance being responsible for the crash was the biggest mind-fuck of the century. How had it happened? Had she left them switched on?

It made no difference. The facts were there. They had overheated, started a flame…

The rest was history.

'You stupid bitch!' Eve had pounced. 'What were you thinking?'

Angela had pulled her off. 'Stay calm. Let's think about this. Get it straight before we jump to conclusions—'

'This is pretty conclusive, don't you think?'

Kevin had been nonplussed. 'No point freaking about it

now,' he'd said. 'We're here, aren't we? Who cares whose fault it was.'

That magic word: *fault*. It gave them permission to assign guilt; it told them there was a reason. The existential questions died. Why them? Why now? How was this part of the grand design? Was it a divine intervention, intended to teach them a lesson?

No—because now it was someone's fault.

Eve raged, restrained by Jacob, whose look had been one of a healthy man staring into the eyes of another with a terminal illness: pity, disbelief, sadness, fear.

Thank God that isn't me.

'I didn't mean to!' Tawny threw back. 'How was I supposed to know? It's not like I did it on purpose!'

'We're on Death Row, all of us,' Eve had said. 'If you hadn't been so fucking obsessed with what you look like, if you hadn't come in the first—'

'If *you* hadn't come we wouldn't even be having this conversation so shut your face up, slut. You should have stayed at home anyway.'

'What did you call me?'

'You heard. Coming out here knocked up because you couldn't resist a chance to wreck another person's life. Let me tell you, you've done a great job already with your baby, that kid's sure gonna thank you for this—'

That time it had taken both Angela and Jacob to wrench them apart.

The discovery laid them bare. Words were pretend blades, tools on which to sharpen their anger. When those ran dry, they would reach for the real thing.

Dusk crept in. Across a high purple sky swam a screen of light clouds, the first they had seen. It was too much to hope for rain, but still they did. The horizon appeared thicker than normal, and more defined. There was change in the air.

Celeste was gathering firewood. A breeze skittered across her arms. So unused was she to the sensation that she clasped it, thinking it an insect or the wings of a bird.

She looked out to sea. A churn of pink slashed in the distance, a new palette. The leaves on the palms began to quiver. As she stepped through the tree line, she heard a woman crying. Tawny was behind the rock, arms round her knees and her toes in a trembling gutter of water. Her hair was lank and dull. Bites riddled her legs.

'What do you want?' She heard Celeste approach and furiously wiped her eyes. 'Go away. Just leave me alone.'

Celeste put the wood on the sand. Tentatively, she rested a hand on Tawny's shoulder, but the model recoiled from her touch.

'Fuck off, I said!'

'You can't go on like this.'

'Like what?'

'Being the outcast.'

'I can do what I want.' Tawny sniffed, then added, 'What choice do I have? Nobody wants me around. Everybody hates me.'

'We don't hate you.'

'Liar!' Tawny's tear-streaked face popped up at her like a jack-in-the-box. Her blue eyes were puffy and bloated. 'You hate me more than anyone.'

'No, I don't.'

Tawny snorted.

Celeste sat down next to her. 'You can't survive on your own,' she said.

'I'm better off on my own. I always have been. I started

my life alone and I'll end it alone. When it comes to it, people don't care. You have to rely on yourself.'

'That's what I thought, too—but I was wrong.'

'But you found Jacob, you mean?'

'Finding out like we did,' Celeste said, 'it was bad. It was for you, too. But what Kevin said is right—'

'Kevin's a freak.'

'But what he said is right. We're here now. How the fire started doesn't change anything—we still need to live and we still need to get out of here.'

Celeste saw something in the model's eyes: a kind of longing.

'D'you know what it's like to be hated?'

'Yes.'

'You can't. Not like this. All my life I've been adored.'

Celeste watched this broken woman and thought of the night they had first met, of Tawny's sniffed dismissal, and all the times she had seen the supermodel since, at some glamorous runway show or Hollywood premiere, and had wanted to be just like her.

'I feel so lonely,' said Tawny. 'And so...' she sobbed, 'so *grotesque*!'

'You're not grotesque.'

'I am compared with you. At least, that's what Jacob thinks.'

Tawny turned to face her. Her expression was alive with curiosity and she was beautiful with it, a new kind of beauty to the one she sold, childlike and open.

White froth washed up on the beach, harsh and spitting. Tawny leaned in and kissed her. Her lips crushed against Celeste's, her warm tongue slipping into her mouth, linking with hers and gently exploring. Pleasure shot through Celeste, primal and reflex, and she pulled back. For so long she had lusted after Jacob, a hot, nagging desire, and the shock of intimacy was intoxicating. Reckless.

Tawny took Celeste's hand and drew it to her breast. Celeste cupped the soft shape, concealed beneath a layer of cotton. She knew she had to pull away, yet her mind wasn't computing. The stiffened bud fascinated her, so like her own. She wanted to know if other parts of Tawny were just like her own, but that was crazy.

'We both want this,' whispered Tawny.

Celeste couldn't deny it. She did. Kissing a woman, the idea of being with a woman, it didn't freak her out like it might have. Every part of her screamed to be with someone, the warmth of another human body, limbs entwined, parts interlinked, hands clasped and mouths locked. With Carl it had never been like that. Carl did not make love to her: he fucked her and then he went to sleep. Cold sheets in a cold room.

Here, the sand was hot.

'I can't.'

Tawny pulled her down. Celeste tried to resist, but her resistance was only half-hearted, and when Tawny grabbed her hand and fed it between her legs she let herself be guided. Tawny seemed to open up and spill on to her, her back arched and her mouth open. Celeste's mouth opened too, in amazement.

She drew back as if she'd been scalded. 'I can't,' she fumbled. 'I'm sorry.'

Tawny began to cry.

'Please don't,' said Celeste. 'It's not you, it's—'

'Sure it is. It's always me.'

And before she could stop her, Tawny got up and ran off into the dark. Celeste watched her go, confused and helpless, as the first spots of rain began to fall.

73

Day 33

The deluge lasted for days. Rain battered and sliced through the choking heat. What had begun as a faint, barely believed patter had built to a relentless, longed-for downpour. They had danced on the beach, arms raised to the sky in praise of its gift, bathing in the water as it ran down their necks and arms and legs. The drops fell plump, plopping onto leaves and dripping off their ends. They collected it to drink, siphoning off the liquid and sipping at the petal points of great waxy teardrops.

Tawny was in the trees. The rain came so hard that it pooled with her sobs and it became impossible to tell the difference between the two. Here, in the forest, her misery ran free. She slumped against a tree, directionless in her mania and sadness.

Against the rules, she ventured into the jungle alone, tripping through slushy ground that days before had been hard enough to crack. Mud splashed up her legs and caked between her toes. Her ankle caught on a shoot and she tumbled into the dirt, landing on her knees and putting her fists out to break her fall. On all fours she was rendered a creature from the deep, tendrils of sodden hair stuck to her cheeks, drips pouring off her nose and chin. She carried on that way, sloshing through the soaked, sticky earth and tangled, wet roots. Wildlife retreated. The sound of the rain was thunderous, drumming on the canopy and coursing through the trees, each leaf a steel pan that threw back sound. What scant clothes she wore were soaked to the skin.

She came to the pool, hauled herself over the rim and peered into the water.

The surface was pockmarked, drops bouncing and splashing, but she could just make out her shivering reflection. Gone was the appearance she had built a career on. Gone was the woman she had seen in that hospital mirror a lifetime ago, whose beauty promised the future she had always longed for. Gone was the supermodel pronounced Loveliest in the World. Gone was the girl whose appeal had secured hundreds of clients at the Rams.

Even Celeste had turned her away.

Who was the fairest of them all?

Not her, not any more. Kevin was the only one who had paid her that kind of attention and he was a man-child. Tawny had lost her powers. The usual ways she had of making people fall for her—men, always men, who collapsed at her shrine in devotion—had deserted her. She put a hand to her matted hair and bawled.

'Tawny?'

The sound of her name took her by surprise.

Desolate, she raised her head.

Eve was in the water.

Tawny peered through the thick rain at the other woman's gently rounded belly, the expression of concern that the reporter wore, and couldn't decide which was the more astonishing. She was yet to make a decision when her eyes were drawn to a nearby rock, two of them, close to Eve: a pair of dark nodules breaking the surface.

Rocks themselves were nothing to observe, but there was something unusual about these ones, something *organic*. Tawny just had time to question why before the rocks sank in a silent stroke and then she understood. Terror filled her head.

'Eve,' she said. 'Get out.'

But Eve couldn't hear above the sound of the rain. 'What?'

'Get out of the water. Now.'

Then Eve saw.

Her scream was disembodied. Feral. Her arms flailed. Her legs kicked. Tawny reached for her, grasping at fingers only to feel them slip away as Eve scrambled to the side, delirious with dread and horror, and Tawny pulled as hard as she could, the pregnant woman sliding back down the bank, the water frothing and churning, their hands clasped and then ripped apart and Eve's cry like nothing she had heard in her life.

'Help me!' Eve rasped, as her feet fought for solid ground and the mud kept giving way. Tawny could see the whites of her eyes. She could smell her fear.

The animal was right behind her. Tawny saw its shell hunker beneath the water, silently moving in, drawn by the agitation as Eve clutched her shoulders, almost dragging her over and begging not to be let go.

'Help me! HELP ME!'

Tawny gripped her arm, above her elbow, and from deep within accessed a final shard of strength that delivered Eve from the water. In an upsurge Eve was brought to shore, staggering and stumbling into the trees.

In that instant Tawny turned back and the dark lake broke. All she saw was the inside of its mouth: teeth, jagged and copious, Jurassic and brutal; and the smooth cream leather of its tongue, like the upholstery in an ex-boyfriend's Porsche.

The crocodile cracked its jaws, a sharp, dead-wood blow like two oak doors banging together. Tawny's throat was bloated beyond the ability to scream and she reeled back, blank with fright, thinking she had got away, when the monster crawled out of the water, massive and lumbering, its armoured skin glistening, and began tossing its head, wrestling a chew toy and thrashing from side to side.

Only that was no chew toy...

Tawny felt no pain. She looked down and saw her bloody chest, one of her tits all but swiped clean, but she felt no pain. Shock, horror, white terror—and a limp, foreign, burbling moan that travelled up her oesophagus and escaped through her lips as she realised what the crocodile was holding in its mouth.

She thought: *I'll never be able to do swimwear again.*

Her eyes rolled back in her head and she passed out.

Unconscious, Tawny Lascelles was at least spared the horror of her death. The crocodile advanced towards her, its giant muscular tail swishing in the driving rain.

74

It was a week before Noah got his hook—but what a hook it was.

By now the search was packing up. News was travelling home of its disintegration. Funerals for those on board would finally be the acceptable course.

'Go home, get some rest,' was the advice he was given.

They didn't believe his story. Nobody did, not even the hospital. There was no record of the man who had attacked him. Noah barely remembered the order of events and he couldn't supply a motive: all he knew was that the assassin had struck to win. There was no proof, no weapon. Noah saw their scepticism—too many weeks in the sun, the disorientating effects of grief and shock, an obsession that had spun out of control—and realised he was alone. They thought he was crazy for doing this in the first place, and here was the logical next step. Noah Lawson had got drunk and almost killed himself.

Only, he hadn't.

He would not go home. He would not rest. If ever he needed a reason to carry on, this was it. The man knew something Noah didn't.

Angela was alive.

He didn't dare think it, and yet there it was, a tiny, glowing light.

***

The attack came to him in bursts of clarity. Noah went to the beach, searching for clues, trying to re-live it.

Kneeling, he touched something hard. At first he thought it was a rock, before reaching to remove its square, smooth edges. It was a familiar shape, incongruous amid the desolate landscape, and he brought the cell phone up and swept it clean, golden grains around the plastic rim and a smear across the screen.

He switched it on. The display lit up.

Noah searched its folders: texts, call logs, email. Probably one of the search team's.

It was blank.

He was about to turn it off when the ringtone sounded, a clean, clear bell.

A message came in. It read:

News?

Noah frowned. The message was from two initials: VC. It was followed by a second:

I do not like to be kept waiting.

And this by another, the third containing a jumble of numbers and another question mark. Noah waited for more, but none came.

All three messages had been sent a fortnight ago—about the time, Noah guessed, of the assault. His mind raced. The man had struck him here…

It wasn't impossible. The man would have departed, only later realising his mistake, but by then it was too late to come back. He'd had to press on.

Where to?

Noah looked at the numbers again.

Who or what was VC?

The C troubled him.

Cane Enterprises.

Noah recalled the government's inquiries into the outfit. Cane Enterprises had appeared authentic. Both Kevin's manager and Mitch's PR had enjoyed contact in the run-up, but after the crash the website had folded and none of the team could be found. There was no record. The IP address could not be traced. Investigating authorities decided that to unleash conspiracy suspicions on the press was a bad idea, and, instead, in the interests of buying time, fed one-liners to the media on the organisation's behalf: '*We are deeply aggrieved by this distressing turn of events*', or '*Our thoughts and prayers are with the families of those lost.*'

Nobody had got close to the truth. Was this it?

Was this VC?

It was the only clue Noah had found. He might not get another.

He pocketed the phone. Mountains climbed to a pink and grey sky. The ocean was dark, and rain clouds were starting to gather.

It was a theory, and all action began with theory: the man who attacked him knew the cargo still lived, and at Cane's behest had come to finish the job.

The numbers were coordinates. It had to be worth a try.

Noah was going to stop this bastard—and this time, he would not lose.

75

Day 36

All that was left was a sparkling diamond necklace. Traumatised, the group returned to the pool to pay their respects: they were afraid, both of the beast at large and of confronting the space where Tawny had died. The wet made it difficult, the ground thick and slurping and the downpour bucketing off plate-sized leaves into rushing, intraversible gullies. Eve led the charge.

She told the others what had happened, the rescue and the sacrifice—but found that words, in a novel realisation for Eve, weren't enough. She found that, try as she might, she could not express the unyielding resolve in Tawny's eyes when she had reached down to save her. She could not express the model's unwillingness, against all odds and all assumptions, to leave her behind. She could not express the understanding that went between them that Eve wasn't the only one being saved. She could not express the belief that Tawny had given her own life for the preservation of another's; and the remorse that resounded as a result of that, of all the horrid things Eve had believed of her companion, was the least expressible of all.

Tawny's ostracisation made villains of all six. They had pushed her away, through anger, through shock, and now it didn't matter about the stupid straighteners or what had brought about the fire. What Angela had said in the beginning was right: the group was all that counted. They had turned their backs on the most important rule of all.

Kevin was first to see it. 'There,' he said, pointing.

In the mud, by the rim of the pool, shone a tell-tale glint. Angela went to fetch it. She lifted the necklace. The final fact settled.

The crestfallen group watched the still silver pool. Nobody spoke.

At last Eve said: 'I'm sorry, Tawny.'

Angela sank to the floor, folding the jewels in her fist. The rain fell.

They held Tawny's funeral at the beach, at sunset. The rain broke for a spell, a new sunlight spilling through the fractured clouds in fragile pastels.

There was no body to bury. No one wanted to speak the word out loud. Despite their time in this broken paradise, it was still too vicious a concept. Everyone knew that a crocodile was the worst way to go. It wasn't painless and it wasn't quick.

Eve refused to elaborate on what she had seen, it seemed prurient, a tragedy turned anecdote, but it wasn't even the images that clung on. It was the sound. Tawny's rattling cries would haunt her for ever.

Angela scooped a dip in the sand close to Tawny's shelter. 'Does anyone want to say anything?'

They had their private thoughts. Jacob remembered the supermodel he had met in an LA club. Angela remembered Tawny's hands in hers as she had helped her out of the swamp. Celeste remembered Tawny's lips, just days ago, vital and alive.

Eve remembered her arm, firm and constant, and her eyes full of bravery.

All shared the whisper of a common theme: that so far, they had been lucky. It was a miracle that they had survived this long. One of them was bound to die first, and if one could die, then the rest could soon follow. Thirst, twisted ankles, insect rash and sunstroke—that could all be fixed. Tawny's death was a game-changer.

'Tawny inspired a lot of people,' said Angela, as she dropped the necklace into the sand, a final rose on a watery coffin. 'We will miss her spirit and her personality, and commit her to peace in the next life.'

The others knelt to help pat the ground flat. Celeste started to weep.

Only one member hung back.

Kevin Chase observed the group through hooded eyes, familiar to him and yet distant, as if he had just arrived and stumbled across this strange, human ritual.

Behind him, the jungle called.

76

Celeste and Jacob were gathering fruit. Batches of black and purple berries filled their arms, stained on their hands like blood. Tiny hairs from the fruit clung and itched against the supple buoyancy of their flesh. The rain had slashed much of their spoils to the earth, a jumble of colour on the ground. They bent to collect them, juice seeping. The rules were simple: eat what they recognised, and nothing danger-red.

Celeste was soaked but she no longer cared—heat or wet, it made no difference. She wore knickers and a T-shirt, slashed above the navel.

It was difficult not to notice Jacob's bare, chiselled chest. Tawny's demise both discouraged and deepened her desire. The idea that Tawny's living, breathing, passionate body was now extinguished made her hungry for sensation.

'I keep expecting to see her,' she said.

Jacob stopped what he was doing. He turned, his eyes burning.

'Me too,' he said.

'Do you think we're next?'

He shook his head. 'Tawny's gone,' he said, 'but we're not. We're still here.'

On the return leg, laden down with fruit, Celeste tripped on a buttress root. She fell forward and stopped herself with a sharp, high, 'Oh!'

The fruit scattered. In front of her, inches away, was a deep well.

Jacob took her shoulders and helped her up. Both stared into the abyss into which she had nearly vanished. It was impossible to see right to the bottom, so dense and incalculable was the drop. Jacob could feel her heartbeat through her ribcage, moving into his heart, and through his back, like a chain of heartbeats that would go on for all time: *da-dum, da-dum, da-dum*.

'What is it?' she asked.

He didn't know if she was referring to the chasm or to something else. Jacob realised his hands were close to her breasts, encircling her waist but his thumbs were tracing her uppermost rib, where the bone met soft tissue.

'It looks like a well.'

They should have moved away, then—but Jacob did not want to let go. He remembered Celeste's body at the pool and felt himself go hard.

'Do you think there's anything down there?' she said.

He released her, watching as she moved to the rim and reached over the edge.

'Hello?' she called, and it flew back at her, up and out into the world like a flock of tropical birds: '—*lo, —lo, —lo...!*'

Jacob scooped up a rock and tossed it in. They waited seconds before hearing its impact clatter on the rocks below, and the soft *phush* of it hitting water.

He dropped down next to her. The fruit was piled, bountiful heaps of glistening ebony, sweating and dripping in the hot rain; bursting so that rivulets of sweet, sticky sap seeped and oozed onto the wet ground, streaking it mauve.

'Do you want to go down?' Celeste asked.

The question hung between them like a gold ribbon, waiting to be caught.

Her deer-like eyes turned to his. Jacob remembered the secret treasure between her legs and a need to make love hit him in a way that, in spite of his years of conquests, was new and debilitating. It was physical. Innate. Brutal. It pumped his stiffening cock until he thought he would detonate right then, right there, before anything had been said or done, draping him in this strange, euphoric jungle magic that forced him into the deepest and truest part of himself.

Together, one mouth moved to the other. There was no distinction between who acted first, whose hand or whose leg was clasped round the other's, whose sweat mingled or was mingled with, whose tongue caught whose. Jacob wanted to be inside her and not in the conjugal sense—he wanted to possess her, to climb through her and become her, forcing his tongue into her mouth, running it around her teeth, two small sharp points where her molars were and he thought she tasted of fire.

In seconds they were stripped. Jacob descended to her tits, hands kneading as he pushed her breasts together and pulled them apart, drawing the wine-red buds between his thumb and forefinger until the flesh beneath was pulled taut. Celeste moaned her rapture, and shit how he had missed this, he had missed fucking a woman, he had missed Celeste; all this time he had missed Celeste.

His tongue trailed a line from her belly button. Appetite overtook and he lapped the canvas of her perfect skin, up around her tits, taking one in his mouth and sucking it to the back of his throat, gathering the flesh with his fingers to fill his mouth more. A deep, guttural sound choked out of him, matched by her cries that sailed on the heady air like paper. Wetly the breast was released, flooded pink with blood and lust, the mark of his teeth around the puckered nipple, and then he took the other, harder this time, sucking and dragging like a man who had drunk nothing in a week, extracting water from the neck of a bottle.

Next his fingers found the place between her legs. She gave him a strangled shout, was dry at first but in seconds coated his touch with salty silk. Her bush was wild and it turned him on. When he bent his head, the glossy, soft hair engulfed him, saline on his tongue as he spread her wide open. She was thrashing now, out of her senses, and Jacob's face was smothered in the scent of her, rich and raw and female. Her clit shone huge amid the shock of hair, shyly emerged from its hood of tender skin, and he flicked the tip of his tongue across it, up and down, in delicious, delicate circles, getting her hotter and wetter and wetter and hotter until her bucking thighs were at risk of stealing the breath from him completely.

This was a new Celeste, a woman in control: a woman at one with her body.

'*Coming, coming, I'm coming…*' she gasped.

Jacob flipped her round. Celeste's arms were thrown over the rim of the well and he reached up to grab her hair, long now around the ears but still with that exposure of neck that made him want to fang her like a predator.

'You like being on the edge?' he rasped in her ear. 'You like it here?'

'I want to go over,' she begged, 'make me go over!'

'Not until you're ready.'

He slapped her ass with the full sting of his hand, marvelling at the way her buttocks rose to meet his punitive force, smarting red at the point of impact. She lifted them again, pleading, and this time the flower between her legs parted to reveal that red, wet rose and he slapped her right there, right on the nub that sent her crazy, and he pushed three fingers deep inside to make her come, his thumb working her neat spot. He felt her tighten and soak him so much that he slid almost instantly out, but she wasn't ready yet. She wasn't ready until he told her she was ready.

Jacob hauled her up by her hair so she was kneeling in front of him, her back pressed against his chest. Her neck was laid open like a calf to the slaughter. Grabbing a clump of the black fruits, he smeared her bare breasts, then her face, feeding them between her lips so they spilled down her chin, and he did the same to himself, painting his forehead and cheeks and his stomach. He wanted to enter the void, to discover what was hiding, into the deep, dark pit, into whatever was left of his soul, and become it utterly. He wanted disguise, because disguise gave him freedom and freedom gave him fantasy. Not the kind of fantasy he had pursued at home, not the kick of the videotapes: this was more, this was dangerous.

We're still alive...

You and me, we're still alive...

She turned to him, eyes ablaze with tormented arousal, and worked his dick through her palms, smothering it with fruit and cupping his balls in the hot, sticky resin. When the head of his penis was loaded and glistening, she bent to it and closed her mouth around the shaft, tongue working from root to tip. Immediately he ejaculated, howling as a burst of yellow wings flew from the elevated trees. Slumping in defeat across her arched back, Jacob slipped a finger through the valley between her thighs, thick and woven and damp, past the hot swell and into the resistant knot of her asshole. Once admitted, she came instantly in shuddering, knee-dissolving spasms, his finger braced in place.

He and Celeste were, for those moments, painted yet unmasked, shrouded yet unveiled, more visible beneath that rush of purple juice than they had ever been before. They were animals. They were lovers. They were savages. They were born.

77

Day 40

Mitch drifted in and out of sleep. Rain pattered and drummed on the awning that Jacob had erected—their sleep shelters were useless now, the leaves and sticks sodden and the fire put out. Still the air remained hot, this heat closer and sultrier than before, their sweat mingling with rain-drops.

Mitch dreamed in fitful, restless bursts.

In his dream, Tawny Lascelles was standing by the pool, her mouth ready to scream. But it wasn't the crocodile that took her, it was a shadow: a presence with them in the trees, the nameless creature that saw their every move.

In his dream, the scream never came. Instead, Tawny was engulfed in bright white light, the same light that had hovered over Mitch's home two years ago.

The same light that had led him to the cave…

Come back to us… Come back… They called for him.

If he did not go, they would take the others, one by one, until nobody was left.

He woke with a start, his heart belting.

Eve was on the sand, her arm curved under the spill of

her stomach: new life to replace the old. By her side were Tawny's ruined hair straighteners.

Mitch turned away.

'I know what you think happened...' Eve ventured.

He didn't reply.

'But you're wrong. I saw it. I was there.'

Eve thought he was nuts to consider that Tawny had been snatched. But Mitch believed she was lying. Too ashamed to admit she was wrong after all this time, she had to make up a story like that.

'What happened at Veroli, Corrigan?'

The question took him by surprise.

'Was it real?'

Water leaked through the wood. A trickle fell by his ear.

Yes, it was real. Mitch had seen the withered body, if it could be called that, shrouded beneath a white sheet in Signor Rossetti's outdoor cabin. The craft had burned up on entering the atmosphere; metallic fragments cast onto the protected parkland and collected beneath a tarpaulin-wrapped shack. As for the creature itself, its flesh had been scalded in the fire, a charred brick red. It was big, its head twice the size of his and its frame close to three metres tall. Its blood had been a rich, blackcurrant purple. Its toes and fingers had been webbed. Its eye sockets hung deep and long, almost joining with the nose cavity, and its mouth a puckered, stitched-on line. Mitch had stared at that mouth. What would it say, if only it could speak?

Others, too, had been invited to witness the spectacle at Veroli—those who could pay, who had a vested interest and were vowed to absolute secrecy. This was the greatest classified find since Roswell; the stuff Area 51 didn't want them to know about. It was proof that extra-terrestrial life existed, that it was here, that it had landed. Mitch wasn't crazy. The rest of the world was.

'You believe Rossetti, still? Even after it was proved a hoax?'

'Nothing was proved,' he said. 'I don't have to justify anything to you. Leave me alone.'

'I'll stay, if it's all the same to you.'

They listened to the thrum of the rain.

Mitch said: 'Even now, in the state we're in, you can't resist.'

'What?'

'Hurting people.'

'I'm not hurting people. Not this time. I'm interested, that's all.'

'Interested enough to write it up the second you get home?'

'I don't think we're going home.'

Mitch grit his teeth. 'You are. I'm not. They'll come when they're ready.'

'You're certain.'

'They came for Tawny. What more do you need?'

'Why didn't they come for you?'

'Tawny was a warning.'

'Of what?'

'That they're close.'

He heard her shift position. 'What does your wife think?' Eve asked.

Melinda's name swam at him like a stranger's. Mitch hadn't thought of her in so long. Three syllables, an empty word to fit an empty woman.

'Wouldn't you like to know,' he said.

'I'm not as shallow as you think I am.'

'Based on evidence, I find that hard to believe.'

'I'm a journalist,' Eve said. 'It's my job to expose people.'

'It's your job to report the truth.'

'That's the same thing.'

'Is it? The truth is something you'll never get your hands on. You see the Veroli stitch-up and you see your truth; I see mine in what doesn't come to light.'

'We aren't so different, then.'

Mitch faced her. 'Everyone on this island has secrets,' he said. 'What makes you immune? People build lies to protect themselves—not to injure, or cheat, whatever you might think. If you want a hook, I'll give you one. I miss my wife. There. Satisfied? I miss the person she used to be. I miss the person I married and it eats me up every day, and I will never get her back even if we do get out of here because she's already lost. I've got nothing to go back for. I don't even want to be saved. Put that in your precious paper, see if I care.'

'I do care. That's why I came to find you.'

'I'll bet that was a real coup.'

'Do you think anyone's going to give a crap about your story, even if we do make it off this island? The story's dead, Corrigan. Your name was never even attached.'

'More fool them if they don't see. The end is nigh.'

'Now you sound like a maniac with a sandwich board.'

'If that's what you think I am.'

Eve picked up the straighteners.

'You're smart, Corrigan. How else would you be where you are? And I'm not immune, far from it. We all end up where we do because of our past, and mine—well, it happened. But being here and going through this, we're all cut from the same, aren't we? It doesn't matter what labels you buy, how much money you have or how many records you sold, when the chips are down we're all the same. We're all flesh and we all bleed. What can I say? Bad spreads—but I believe that good spreads too.' She looked at her stomach. 'I have to, don't I?'

Ashamed, Eve fiddled with the charred tongs. 'Every bad thing I ever wrote about Tawny, I hate myself for it.'

'I know what my beliefs are,' Mitch said, but the edge to his voice had gone.

'That Tawny was taken by that thing you saw at Veroli...'

'Yes. Or something like it.'

'And our plane came down because of them?'

'Yes.'

But Eve was only half listening. She pulled the straighteners closer and frowned at them. She was deeply focused, her eyes narrowed.

'What is it?' Mitch asked.

With a wrench she snapped them open, splitting them at their hinge. She fingered the plastic inside, coming to rest on something fixed in the pivot.

Her voice sounded weird. 'And if you're wrong?'

Mitch reached out. 'What are you looking at?'

The cracked straighteners shook in Eve's hand.

'So much for your aliens, Corrigan,' she said. 'We've been set up.'

78

Szolsvár Castle, Gemenc Forest, Hungary

Voldan Cane's mechanical summons ricocheted through the castle vaults.

'*Janika!*'

The maid came running. Mr Cane was propped up in his four-poster bed, a drink by his side, out of which a long straw protruded. His question was immediate: 'Is there news?'

Janika shook her head, unable to meet her boss's eye. She couldn't bear his disappointment. For too long they had been unable to contact the source: it was as if their man had vanished into thin air. Voldan contained his anger, but she saw it in his twitching thumb, and in the tortured moans he emitted in his sleep.

Janika knew in her heart that Voldan's plan had worked: those people were long gone. But he needed evidence and he would not be content until he got it.

'Do you think he's come to harm?' asked Janika.

'A man like that doesn't know how,' bleated Voldan. He spat the straw away and it flicked back, forcing him to spit again. Janika hurried to remove it.

'What should we do?' she wheedled.

'We wait. He will return. And when he does, you know what you must do. Nobody ignores Voldan Cane. He who dares will pay a terrible price.'

79

Day 45

The rain stopped. It happened suddenly, the sky-flood turning off like a tap and the grey clouds parting to a chorus of burnished rays. In a matter of hours the ground was gasping again, as if the rains had never been. Everything smelled different, crucial and living. The air was so fresh it stung the throat.

Sunlight on the water refracted like fish scales; thin gold bands that trembled and danced on the surface. Angela kept to her depth, the dark shade of sea beyond the lagoon synonymous now with fear: of sharks, of the deep, of the unknown.

She swam underwater in brave, large strokes, her arms scooping through the green. Her hands belonged to someone else, the liquid distorting their shape, and the extreme brown of her tan was magnified. Only the silver ring that Noah had given her marked the skin as Angela's, tarnished though it was by sweat and sun.

Shoals of fish dashed in her vision, some bigger, the size of her forearm, in lurid yellows and blues. A starfish splayed lazy, and the brittle, pimpled shell of an urchin was half obscured in the powdery sand. She dived to collect a gleaming shell and a mousse-pink pincer twitched from one side.

Holding her breath was a skill. She had always been good at it, practising in the Boston pool with Orlando and Luca when she was a girl. Angela liked to count the seconds she was under, and found that now she could reach a full minute before her lungs began to strain. It was peaceful. Her favourite place was a channel between two rocks, where she could grab hold of a hollow in the stone and hold on, keeping her body down. She would close her eyes and think of nothing.

Sometimes, she would enter a waking dream.

She dreamed that when she surfaced she would be at her father's house, on a summer's afternoon. Not the world she had left behind, exactly—an altered version. Noah would be there. He would never have left... Right back to that summer when she was fifteen, she unpicked the threads and wove anew. Donald would have lived. She and Noah would have married. They might even have had a family of their own.

This was one of her mother's garden parties, and Angela was swimming, and if she concentrated hard she could hear the muffled hum of conversation above—Isabella, there she was, in a green sundress, and her *nonna*. The barbecue infused the air with perfumed, bitter smoke. A ball game unfolded, spiked by cries of victory, and the laughter of children, someone's children, maybe hers.

On rare days, good days, the fantasy was real. Angela would stare into the water, visibility lost after just a few feet so that the deeper distance was an obscured, murky veil out of which she could summon Noah. She dreamed that he jumped into the pool. There was no splash, no clue to give him away.

She willed him to come.

That summer, before the fall-out, they had gone to the lake. Noah had driven her in his friend's car. It had been late

in the day, one of those clear, wide-sky days that seemed
to last for ever, and the sunset was orange, a burned, warm
amber.

Noah stripped off his T-shirt and dived from the pier.

'Come on! Come in! It's beautiful!

'I can't!' she said, laughing. 'Look away!'

*He did as he was told, turning from her, his hands over his
eyes to make sure. The back of his neck was glittering. His
hair was golden, dripping on his skin.*

*She thought, then: Remember this. This is a moment.
Remember it.*

*She peeled her top over her head, then her jeans, taking
her sandals off first so she could drag them inside out. She
tripped while she did it, putting out a hand to steady herself
on the branch of a tree, and with her hands covering her
chest, even though she still wore a bra, she ran to the end of
the pier and leaped off.*

'It's freezing!'

*The cold was like being tickled. She had never felt so
urgent. The lake appeared black in the fading sun, inviting
and frightening. Firs encircled it, their private enclave, amid
which the shining red of the car was their lifeline back to the
real world. It seemed to Angela that everything else might
just as well have evaporated; this was their universe now, the
two of them.*

*She floated on her back, her breasts surging at the surface,
the bra now see-through but she wasn't embarrassed. She
was sick of comparing herself with the girls Noah may or may
not have slept with, wondering if he liked her and, if so, how
much. For now it was enough to be with him, her ears deaf-
ened by the thick lake, as the hot peach sun melted behind the
sweet-scented spikes.*

He pulled her under. They didn't kiss but the elusion of his lips only compounded her longing. He entwined his limbs with hers, swirling in the cold, alone apart from the teenage adrenalin of skin on skin, where parts fitted, the loops and dips and grooves of another person, a person with whom she yearned to lock those pieces in place. She could feel the hairs on Noah's arms, and the hard bulk of his chest. There was nothing to see, it was ink, and she felt for him, every inch a new discovery. She touched something solid. She knew what it was. She had seen Orlando's stand up once, inside his tennis shorts when he was seventeen and Martha Pravershall joined the doubles match.

Noah's was thick and warm. She wanted to hold onto it but she didn't know what to do, or if she should, or what would happen if she did.

They sprang to the surface and the sun was all but gone. In the blossoming dark Noah was a silhouette, drops of water on his top lip and lashes. Angela thought how obvious it all was, how plain and how pure, once the fooling around was taken away. Instinct.

She would never be satisfied until Noah Lawson met the ache in her stomach, the warm thing she had found underwater, and quenched it, and set it free.

'You're cold,' he said.

She didn't argue. She didn't say anything. She wanted to tell him she had never been warmer. Something had melted and it would never be cold again.

The moment flew away and he began to swim, and when he reached the pier he held his arms out. She clung to them longer than was necessary and they dressed in silence, aware that a line had been breached, and, beyond it, who knew. On the drive home, he held her hand—nothing more, not even when he said goodbye.

***

Survival kicked in and she released her grip on the rocks. Angela had considered ways to quash this, this pesky reflex for life, because wouldn't it be easier to stay down here with her fantasies, living elsewhere in the cool, quiet deep? She didn't want to return to shore, just as she hadn't wanted to return to the pier that day. She wanted to stay in the water, if for nothing else than to see what happened.

In being removed from him, she understood now what she should have done.

She should have chosen Noah.

She should always have chosen him. She should have chosen him over Dino, over the business, over Donald's wishes. She should have chosen him over her dumb pride. She should have chosen him when she was fifteen and her father discovered them, and talked to him and heard him out and tried to understand. When they had rekindled their relationship years later but she'd never got rid of the hurt. When Noah had made love to her at the FNYC launch and she had bundled him out the door. When the suggestion of marriage had been aired. When she had met Dino. When she had told him the truth at the Gold Court Theatre and the flame had gone out in his eyes. She should have chosen Noah. Every time she should have chosen him.

It was too late now. There was no going back. She would never see him again.

There was fire again on the beach, a bundle of smouldering sticks. Eve was tending to it, the half-hearted resurgence of a rescue hope. Angela had been counting the days with stones. Over a month they had been here.

Tawny was gone. Who next? Maybe she would be lucky and it would be her.

At night, alone with her thoughts, Angela prayed that when

it happened, it would happen quickly. Death didn't frighten her, but dying did.

The sun beat down. The earth turned on, oblivious and giantly indifferent.

She swam back in.

80

Patience was both agonising and necessary. Noah hung back and counted to his moment. He wasn't about to risk it now.

The coordinates had led him here. He had been tracking the man, moving from rock to rock in pursuit of the ripening scent and shadowing his target from afar.

Now he would follow him to the final frontier—whatever or wherever that was.

The man loaded a fishing boat, climbed in and gunned the engine, which after a guttural start began to chug. He stooped to roll and spark a cigarette, an act that was deftly completed in twenty seconds. Noah knew the man's habits. He had observed him long enough.

The man blew out smoke. He scratched the back of his neck, a nervous tic of increasing regularity, and unsurprising given the messages that had come in. VC was not happy. The cell phone had received two more communications, equally brief and cryptic: *You know what this means*, read the first. Then: *It's over for you.*

After that, the contact had dried up.

As usual, upon grinding out his smoke, the man knelt to check his supplies. Noah seized his chance. He slipped from the leaf-shield and down to the water, where, unseen, he ducked into the stern of the boat.

A khaki tarpaulin was heaped in a nest—the ready-made cover he had anticipated—and Noah crawled beneath, managing to conceal himself.

It was hot under here. The tarpaulin blistered after hours cooking in the sun, thick as the skin on an overdone baked potato. It smelled funny, of must and cloves. Parts were ridged where the salt water had dried, stiff and crumpled as a dried chamois cloth. Noah did not know how long he could stay down.

He fingered the switchblade in his waistband, flinching as he did against the pain in his side. Only when the boat began to move and Noah's eyes adjusted to the dim could he see the reason for the hefty tarpaulin—and it put his own blade to shame. A flash in the dark and his elbow struck against it: a box of weapons, knives and guns, ropes and, holy fuck, a crossbow.

Stay calm. Think of the facts.

This man was hunting the crash site. Why bring this arsenal if all he expected to find was a bunch of bodies?

Fear evaporated. Noah was consumed by hope; a rush that wasn't born of desperation or denial, it was real, valid, firm enough to hold on to.

Angela.

Noah understood what this man intended to do.

But not if he got there first.

Time passed. He did not know how much. If only for a glimpse of sky or sea, a crack in the tarpaulin through which he could breathe. The cloying heat held him in a vacant state, tolerable if he remained absolutely still, a kind of half-consciousness. Noah could feel the shuddering engine, punctuated by the slop beneath his left ear, where a pocket of water seeped in.

His head throbbed with thirst.

He had seen the man stack a box of water and he imagined the bottles, became possessed by their proximity. He counted the number of cigarettes lit, could smell the smoke beneath his cover. Typically the man sparked up every ten or fifteen minutes: by that logic they had been on the water two hours.

He envisaged the map, all the islands in this great azure expanse, and their tiny boat dropped somewhere in the middle. Their destination was drawing closer.

Noah licked his lip in the hope a bead of moisture might swim across his tongue. The movement drenched him in sweat and before he could stop himself he shifted position, revealing a sliver of light, through which he could detect the man's boots, heavy and black. He dared widen the aperture, drinking in new air. The man was sitting on the rim of the boat. He sucked dry a bottle of water and chucked the plastic onto the deck, where it rolled towards Noah, tantalisingly close but not close enough. Silver droplets shivered on the bottleneck.

He had to choose his moment. Wait until the man's back was turned, his attention drawn, his defences down—because, despite the man's extensive armoury, Noah had the best missile of all: ambush.

The man dropped his cigarette. He swore, and bent to retrieve it.

Now.

Noah sprang, quick as a cobra. The man was startled. He reeled backwards, his mouth an O of surprise.

He was quick to recover, but it was already too late. Noah propelled him onto the deck. He punched him hard, again and again, scarlet blood spilling, teeth cracking, a series of brutal pummels to the jaw. The boat tipped.

Noah was slammed. Stumbling, he put his hands out to

break his fall and landed against the tarpaulin. The men rolled and writhed, hands round each other's necks, locked in combat. The man grinned, engaged now in the sport, and grabbed him and flipped him round so that Noah's head was thrust directly above the churning motor. Lethal blades whirred inches from his throat, chopping slices of air, juddering closer, and a knee descended on his back and forced him down. Noah pushed, blood raging, filling his head with grit and fury. *No. Not yet.*

He grabbed the edge of the boat, coarse with sand; the wood caked and cracked. His knuckles were white, holding him up, staying him from certain execution.

Instinct saved him. His other fist remembered. It dived to his waistband and wrapped around the handle of his blade. Pulling it out, in the same motion he blasted back against his assailant and launched them both into the air. Winded, the man bent double. He looked up, met Noah's weapon, realised his own were trapped behind his adversary and his face leached of colour. The knife glinted in the tropical sun as the men circled each other.

Noah tasted blood.

The man pounced but Noah switched his dagger and then it happened: he felt it flick into the man's soft, yielding gut.

The man choked, a splurge of red gushing from his mouth.

Soundlessly, holding Noah's shoulders, eyes wide with fear and shock, he crumpled to the deck.

Noah killed the engine.

The boat sighed and slowed.

Above, a bird cawed.

It didn't take much to push the man over the side. His body plopped into the water, face to the sky, amid a cloud of leaking crimson.

Noah drank two bottles of water and re-started the motor.

81

San Francisco

In a coffee shop on 7th Street, Leith Friedman unplugged his computer, removed the buds from his ears and wiped his glasses on his T-shirt.

It was no good. He couldn't focus, and he couldn't work. He had not slept in forty-eight hours and his appetite was shot to shit. Things were falling apart.

'Can I get you anything else?' asked a smiling waitress.

He had been nursing the same cup of coffee all afternoon. 'No, thanks.'

'Shout if you need me.' She winked.

The wink made Leith paranoid. Did she know him? Over the years Leith had taken pains to be the invisible one: let Jacob do the talking and the deal-breaking; let him be the face. Not any more.

Leith felt sick.

He had never wanted in with the Russians in the first place. Now Jacob had gone and bitten it, it was him who was left to pick up the pieces.

He had *told* him no. He had said it was too much of a risk. Had Jacob listened? Had he hell.

Selfishly, the first thought that had occurred to Leith in

the hangover of the crash wasn't how much he would mourn his business ally, rather it was how in Holy Mother's name he was going to extricate himself from the MoveFriends surveillance deal. Jacob had been the one who pushed for these advances, pushed until he got his way, and Leith realised now he was gone that the car they had piloted had lost its engine. Leith was cowering in the back seat, just like always, just as he had three years ago before Jacob deigned to pull over and pick him up. The years of commerce might have taught him code, but they hadn't taught him courage.

Heads in the coffee shop turned. Eyes swept across him. The heat of their examination made him sweat. Leith was ever more detectable as the Challenger coverage limped on. As Jacob Lyle's professional partner, he had been approached for myriad interviews to discuss his loss. Leith had declined them all. Recently he had begun fantasising about being sixteen again, returning to his childhood home in Maine and sitting upstairs playing computer games in a darkened room all day long. That was the real Leith, not this one. The Maine kid was an ordinary, scrawny virgin, and Leith liked him. He preferred him. This Leith was an asshole. He was a man who sold his soul for money—to the Russian government.

Leith slotted his tablet into his satchel and pulled on his sweater, flicking up the hood.

Behind the bar, his waitress cashed up. The screen was on, playing out its usual carousel: a smiling Angela Silvers at her father's side; Tawny Lascelles on the Paris runway; a weedy Kevin Chase performing for his fans; and Jacob, that cocksure friend who had maddened Leith but also saved him, shaking hands with the president. It had become the default picture-track to summer 2014. Not a day passed when those missing faces did not appear.

Of course he had gone to call it off with the Russians, as much as Leith's limp approach to proceedings ever could. That made it sound so incidental, like cancelling a movie date, but five seconds in their company told him they were not backing down.

There was nobody else to help, nobody in whom they had confided.

We're on our own, Jacob had said, just a matter of weeks ago as he had brandished his glass for a toast, a lover of life and luck, *just the way I like it*.

Leith exited the shop. He started walking, with no idea where he was going.

82

Day 50

'**I**'m getting off this island,' said Jacob, dragging the raft down to the shore. 'We've waited long enough. We stay here, we die.'

He had been toiling on the float for days, dragging armfuls of wood from the forest and sweating in the high heat of the day. Finally, it was ready to go.

'You're crazy,' Angela told him. 'We should wait for rescue. Keep the fire going. Hope the SOS gets picked up.'

But the claims were hollow, even to her ears: the SOS was a silent scream.

Jacob surveyed the group. 'Who's with me?'

Eve shook her head. 'It's suicide.'

'Are you forgetting what happened to Tawny?' Jacob got behind the logs. They rolled forward, gouging a scar in the sand. A gentle lift as the shallows took some of the weight. 'Out there, at least we've got a shot.'

'We don't even know where we are.'

Jacob threw down his tools. He came so close that Eve could see herself reflected in his pupils.

'But somebody does, right? Somebody out there knows we're here *because they fixed us up.*'

'Sabotage,' said Kevin. 'Except they failed.'

'Damn right they failed. And I'm fucked if I'm letting them win now.'

'You go out there, it's guaranteed,' said Angela. 'It's a dumb idea, Jacob.'

Jacob rounded on his companions. It was a sorry sight. The island was killing them, slowly but surely. Mosquito craters pimpled their chapped, peeled skin, leaking itchy sap that caked in the heat. Burn had turned to dark, indigenous tan, and clothes were worn at whim, sometimes not at all. Jacob didn't recognise them as the people they had been, and that in turn made him fear for his own estrangement. He, too, was transformed. Meat and fish rotted in the heat, stinking and gathering flies. Fruit flushed their systems. Bacteria made it hard to hold on to nutrients long enough to have any benefit. Their bodies were telling them they had done all they could. This place wasn't and never would be survivable.

He came to rest on Celeste. Gently he claimed her hand; he had to make her see that getting away was their only option. Jacob wanted to live—and, for the first time, for all the right reasons. He wanted it because now there was someone he wanted to live for. His life up until now had been hedonistic and selfish, gunning for the next screw or the next deal, maybe both at once. Celeste had shown him another path. He could not see this end.

Losing his vision, the miracle of its return, made him realise. True power could only be understood when one had been powerless.

'The island isn't safe,' he said. 'I'm not talking about the obvious; I'm talking about…*it*. You know what it is. Everyone does. There's something here with us.'

The forest behind them shivered.

'Can we be sure the person who did this isn't already here?'

'That's impossible,' said Angela.

'Is it?'

'What if Jacob's right?' Celeste whispered. 'Whoever sabotaged that plane could have been watching all along.'

The group fell quiet. Since Eve had extracted the timer from Tawny's appliance, they had run through every possibility—lovers they had jilted, co-stars they had snubbed, acquaintances from long ago they might have wounded—anything and everything from each of their pasts that might account for the vendetta.

And what a vendetta it was. Attempting to bump off a list of names like that...

It wasn't just high profile; it was stratospheric.

This person had to have money: check. They had to have resources: check. They had to have ambition: check. Above all, they had to have hatred.

Who? Who despised them to such unimaginable lengths?

Was it a grudge against one person, or all seven? They sought a reason to connect them, the thread that had bound them to the same star-crossed fate.

'We have to stay rational,' said Angela. 'That isn't an option.'

'Why not?'

'What are we going on? Shadows at our backs, noises in the trees? It's ridiculous.'

'That flight attendant's still out there,' said Celeste. 'Why couldn't *they* be?'

'She isn't,' said Angela flatly. Looking round the circle, she continued: 'Show me evidence, hard evidence that this isn't based on nightmares or paranoia or hysteria and I'll consider it.' She folded her arms. 'There's nothing to support this theory. So forget about it, all right? Or else we'll drive ourselves mad.'

'We're already there,' said Jacob.

'It isn't big enough,' said Kevin from the shore. 'You won't be able to carry us all.'

The raft was four feet by five. Jacob pushed it further in. Pockets of liquid slurped against the sides and he held it down, testing the buoyancy. Water seeped between the logs but it stayed afloat. They would leave their belongings, bring as much water as they could and pray for salvation. Jacob did not know what lay ahead, but he was willing to test the unknown. He had always been willing to test it.

'You oughtta take me,' said Kevin, his torso rippling in the sun. 'Defence.' He delivered a sharp punch to the air, as if he were breaking through a wall. The move brought to Jacob's mind a video he had once seen the pop prince in, where Kevin had channelled a Rocky Balboa vibe and pounded a punch bag. He had looked so different then.

That made three, then. With Eve and her baby, four.

'Don't do this.' Angela tried once more. 'We have to stick together. It's the only way.'

'It's the only way you can see.'

'We're nothing if we're not together. Jacob, think about this—'

'You're saying I haven't thought about it? What else is there to do with my time, Angela, *except* for think? Celeste, Eve, let's go.'

'I'm begging you. We're in this as a group, we have been since the first day.'

'And what day are we now?'

'Too many—I know that. But we're just trying to survive.'

'So am I. You're living in a fantasy if you think they're

still searching. We've got a pregnant woman here and we're doing nothing about it. What's going to happen when that baby comes? Has anyone actually considered that? Has anyone planned for it? Wake up and smell the fucking coconuts, people: *we're on our own*. I don't know about the rest of you but I want to live. I want to go home. Seeing as that isn't a priority at this end, fine, you're by yourself.'

'I'm not coming.'

Eve's voice made him turn round. 'What?'

'It's too dangerous.'

Jacob stormed back, eyes ablaze. 'I might have been blind once but I can see pretty fucking clearly right now. If anyone should understand the urgency of getting back to civilisation, Eve, surely it's you.'

'I understand the urgency of living another day. We'll die out there.'

'We'll die if we stay.'

'I'm not coming either, Jacob.' Celeste bowed her head. 'I'm sorry.'

His face drained.

'I can't swim,' she said.

The admission took them all by surprise. Jacob disregarded it. Need for Celeste to agree overtook his common sense.

'You don't have to.' To prove the point he climbed aboard. The float submerged, tipping to one side before he corrected the balance and it righted itself. Pushing a stick into the sand, he anchored it in place. 'See?'

'I'm scared.'

'Come here,' he encouraged, 'you'll be fine; it's safe, I promise…'

Without warning, Kevin charged down the sand and threw himself on the raft.

Jacob's stick snapped with the impact and rushed them into reverse. The raft bucked. Water gushed up. One of the logs spun loose, and once one was freed the rest followed, tumbling like a spool of tree trunks from the back of a truck. Jacob went under, coughing and sputtering. Kevin laughed, held his nose, and toppled backwards.

Jacob went for him.

'*You idiot!*' he thundered, dragging Kevin from the water and thumping his chest. 'Look what you did; you dumb punk! You think this is funny?'

Kevin stopped laughing. The thump barely moved him. He squared up against Jacob. The men stood in conflict on the beach, brute against brute.

'I'll show you funny.' Jacob shoved him, but Kevin didn't move. It was like slamming into a brick wall.

Kevin looked down at him—*down*, since when? Jacob couldn't conceive that this was the same kid that had trawled him round Boston all those months before. For starters, this wasn't a kid. Kevin Chase was a *monster*.

Jacob launched a blow, but instead of flooring his target, Kevin didn't flinch. 'What the fuck is the matter with you, huh? You *freak*!'

Kevin drew back. For a moment it looked as if he was going to walk away, then at the last instant he turned, cracked his fist and landed it in Jacob's solar plexus.

Jacob collapsed onto the sand, gasping for breath. Kevin descended on him, bolting his fingers round his throat. Angela fought to intervene, but trying to haul off Kevin was like trying to move a mountain.

Jacob choked, his eyes bugging, his face turning red. Kevin's grip tightened. 'You'll kill him!' Celeste screamed. 'Get off him, let him go; you'll kill him!' Kevin stared down with amusement. His thumbs pressed deeper.

Jacob blacked out, blinking through clouds of gloom.

'*Let him go!*'

In the end it took all four of them to drag him away.

Violently Jacob coughed. Celeste rushed to his side.

'What is wrong with you?' she cried. 'Have you gone insane?'

Kevin stared back at them without remorse.

He shrugged, unbothered. 'Just messing.'

83

Night fell. Certain colours shone brighter in the dark. As Kevin emerged onto the plateau, sprays of fuchsia lit his way. The pink was extreme, the artificial pink of hard-shelled candy. Flowers were giant, each petal as big as a hand, and they carried a melting, sweet fragrance that emitted pockets of dizzying intensity.

He didn't need the others. Fuck them: they were a bunch of losers.

Kevin wasn't taking shit off anyone. The way they had reacted, as if he had actually killed the guy? Jacob was a pussy. To think Kevin had worshipped him was some trip. Now *he* was the don. He was the one to be admired.

He had only hung around because of Tawny being a hot piece, and now she was gone, well, why should he stay? He would set up a new camp, a better camp.

Kevin was a survivor—and the jungle belonged to him.

It was different this side of the island. Harsh. The ocean resented his presence. To the west lay the caves, dark and foreboding. Spray crashed against hostile rocks and angry currents whirled. No lagoon, just open water.

Kevin stood naked at the top of the mountain. He breathed the air, his feet set apart and his hands on his hips. Hair crackled down his forearms, and his cock hung heavy between his legs. A burst of fireflies erupted from a nearby bush.

He had the power. It felt good.

He walked on, embraced by darkness.

84

Dawn came. Noah floated in and out of consciousness.

The boat swayed. He lay sprawled in the orange shade, lips dry and skin cracked; his body sagged and his lungs were lumps of fire.

Two days he had been adrift on the water. The engine had choked. Hours passed, and determination turned to dejection. He had rowed a day and a night, chasing an empty horizon. Land was nowhere: only blue. Sky and sea were all he had, and the occasional passing turtle shell as it drifted beneath the surface.

The heat was unfeasible. His water supply had run dry and the sun blazed. He had rigged the tarpaulin into a shelter, but still it burned.

He imagined Angela was with him. Her face came with startling clarity, the splash of green in her eyes and the scatter of freckles on the bridge of her nose.

He loved her. He would never again get to tell her that.

It wasn't meant to happen this way. He had let her down. Just as he had let her down all those years ago, when he had walked away from their friendship, frightened to feel what he felt because Angela was too good for him. How could he have believed, even for a second, that she thought him unworthy? Angela had never made him feel inferior: of all the people who could have, who should have, she had never belittled or derided his upbringing. She had made him forget it.

Just as he had let her down at the theatre, not knowing then that her father was dying and what an impossible decision she might have been forced into. He hadn't let her explain. Hurt and anguish overtook and he had pushed her away, not even calling her up when Donald was laid to rest.

He was sorry for that, most of all. He couldn't bear to think of her alone, so sad, wishing for him.

The sun crept round, a spotlight on the stage of his sorrow. It bathed his feet, encroaching on the den of airless shade, and he darted from it like a lizard on a rock. His tongue was dry and fat in his mouth. If he didn't drink soon, he would die.

Waves lapped; a circle of wings overhead, flapping, heavy in the heat.

So accustomed was Noah to the soundtrack of the sea that at first he didn't notice the rumbling addition that wove itself in between.

The purr of an engine came closer. He tried to raise himself, but found his limbs would not budge.

There was a burst of aggressive foreign voices. He didn't know what they were saying. Lots of them, talking over each other, shouting, directing, and the nudge of wood against wood as the boat scraped alongside.

Shadows pooled across his lonely capsule. Strong arms hauled him up.

85

Day 53

With Kevin's departure, the dynamic on the beach changed.

Frictions dispelled. Arguments ceased. Hostilities died. But with the loss of passion settled a depression: a sense of giving up, of waiting for the time to pass because each hour was an hour closer to the inevitable.

At first they thought that Kevin would be back.

Three days later, there was still no return. Angela went to look for him, and found only a jumble of clothes on the peak. The ocean swallowed her call.

'Let him sulk it out,' Jacob said, his neck still bruised from Kevin's toxic grip. He was intent on building a new raft: rather than dissuading him, the confrontation had only cemented his resolve. 'The kid needs to cool it.'

'I don't like that he's out there,' said Angela. 'We don't know where he is.'

'He'll show up sooner or later.'

'He's changed—you've seen what he's become.'

'Then we're better off without him.'

Angela drew a cross in the sand. 'Not necessarily.'

'You're scared of him?'

'Aren't you?'

Jacob secured a knot, slicing the ends apart. 'Of course not,' he lied.

Eve lay in the shelter. The heat made her weak.

Angela came in and touched a hand to her forehead.

'Just checking,' she said.

'I'm going to have this baby here, aren't I?' said Eve. Her stomach was stretched, almost eight months gone. 'I want to go home.'

'So do I.'

'I can't think about it. Home. Can you?'

'I shouldn't, but I do.'

'We're so far away.' Eve thought of London, her flat, her kitchen with the red kettle and the magnets on her fridge. 'There'll be no doctors, no drugs, no one to hold my hand…' Before, she would have rejected the idea, insisted she was fine on her own.

'*Do you want me to come with you?*' Orlando had said when she'd told him she was pregnant. She had been adamant. No. She didn't want anything.

Why had she done it to herself? Why had she systematically removed everyone who cared about her from her life? Why had she insisted on self-sufficiency to the point of total isolation? When had people become projects to her, subjects she might write about, defined by how useful they were to her work?

Orlando had been useful, for a time. But it had been more than that. She knew that now.

She wished he could hold her hand.

'I'll be there,' said Angela. 'You won't be alone.'

Eve swallowed her tears. 'Thank you. I never said that, but you saved my life—and his. You know, when we first got out of that plane I wished I'd died.'

'You weren't the only one.'

'But now I'm glad we made it. We made it this far. Whatever happens, we lived a little longer. Thank you for not leaving us behind.'

'As if I could.' Angela smiled.

'How did you know?'

'About what?'

'The pregnancy.'

'Just a feeling.' Angela glanced down. 'You know, whoever the father is, he's crazy to turn you away. I always wanted to have kids some day.'

'Yeah?'

'Now I'll never get a shot.'

'You don't know that,' said Eve. Seeing her upset, she took her hand and laid it on her tummy. 'Feel the kick?'

Angela laughed. The thump felt good: strong and definite, new life fighting to get out. The world had to be worth living in—even their version of it.

'There's something I have to tell you,' said Eve.

'Yes?'

'It's about my baby's father.'

Angela waited.

'He's…'

Eve faltered. She closed her eyes.

'Just that maybe he was right,' she said. 'Maybe this baby was a mistake.'

Angela touched the bump. Again she felt it kick.

'That isn't a mistake, Eve,' she said. 'At least I'm fairly sure whoever's in there doesn't think so.'

86

Celeste watched Jacob at work on the float. Consumed by the task, his arms worked the ropes with brutal efficiency. A thrill shot through her at the memory of his fingers inside her: the intimate places she had allowed him to touch.

The heat, the blaze, the fear, the single shining quest for survival sharpened every desire to a spearhead. They wanted to live, and there was no better way of expressing it than the pleasure they had brought to each other. Celeste had given to him without limits. She craved it again.

Yet she knew in her heart that she could never venture out on that raft, whether Jacob went or not. Fear, then, was stronger than love. Was she in love?

She had thought herself in love with Carl, but in a way she witnessed rather than felt. Memories of her relationship became a moving disc at the end of a telescope, a long dark tunnel between her and it. Was that why she didn't want Jacob to complete the raft? Maybe it wasn't the water; it was the idea of return.

'We'll be together,' said Jacob. But it wasn't that easy. Carl would find her. Out here, he couldn't find her. He would never find her.

She picked up a shell, glistening pink, its frilled opening

polished and iridescent. If Kevin's attack had been allowed to continue, how would it have ended? Would Jacob still be here? She couldn't consider it.

Kevin frightened her. Gone were his narrow bones and slim build. Now he was unbreakable, a before and after shot where several years should have elapsed, not several weeks. *He's a kid, let him be*, Jacob had counselled before the assault. But that was precisely it—*was* he a kid? Celeste wasn't sure. He had the brains of a kid and the body of a weight-lifter. It made for a dense, brick-built dunce; a physical titan with neither sense nor reason. Now, naked and volatile, he was a loose cannon at large in the forest.

She stood, dusting off the backs of her legs.

There it was again. That feeling. *Someone was looking*.

As Celeste made her way to the cliffs, she recalled a museum she had visited with her parents. Her mother had told her she was about to see the greatest works in the world, and what a lucky girl she was, but when they got there all Celeste felt was hounded. The portraits eyed her beadily. Their gaze travelled with her across the room. The subjects seemed animate, scrutinising her every move. Minutes into the expedition she had pleaded to leave. The museum had not welcomed her.

It had been the same at that castle in Hungary—perhaps that was why she had taken so strongly against that billionaire's portrait. It had seemed to say: *Get out. We don't want you here. Leave now*.

If only they could.

There was a tremor in the undergrowth.

Celeste hung back. A pig was snuffling in the leaves, its dark tail switching flies. With a grunt it looked up, sensing its witness, and its ear, covered in coarse, dank fur that Kevin had removed from one a week before, with no more enquiry than if he had been peeling back the plastic film on a packet of ham, twitched at the sound.

She stilled in the trees, until at last it moved on.

87

Day 55

At dusk Angela harpooned a fish and they grilled it over the fire, a third for Eve and the rest split equally. Mitch had fashioned a method for drinking from the coconuts, a split in the hide into which he fed a hollowed-out stalk, acting as a straw. It was an odd taste, creamy and metallic, but was a change from the boiled and cooled stream.

Afterwards, gathered at the fire, Mitch said: 'I haven't been truthful with you.'

Angela's face flickered in the glow. 'About what?'

'You asked for evidence that we weren't alone. I have it.'

Angela stayed perfectly still. Mitch's voice was eerie.

'There *is* someone else.' He threw a glance to Eve. 'I thought what I thought at first, but now we know for sure that we were set up... Well, I've changed my mind. This is a person—a real, flesh and blood person.'

'Kevin,' Angela intervened quickly. 'On the south side.'

'No. At the cave, on the day we arrived.'

Angela remembered his question. *Did anyone take a walk on the beach yesterday? Round by the bluff, towards the caves?* The slash of fear widened.

'The prints were there. I know what I saw.'

'They were yours,' said Eve.

'How can they have been, on the first day?'

'Someone went exploring.'

'That soon? We three were the only ones on the mountain. There's no way any of the rest of you could have beaten us to it.'

'Then who?'

The question strummed in the heat, taut and appalling.

Jacob took Celeste's hand. 'It's no one. Mitch imagined it.'

The senator delivered a dry laugh. 'Mitch imagines everything, right?'

'The flight attendant,' said Angela. 'Maybe I was wrong.'

'We should go back,' said Eve. 'We should find out.'

The crash of the waves carried with it a ghostly, female sigh. Angela shivered. She felt truly, horribly afraid.

'Tomorrow, we go,' she said. 'As soon as it's light.'

'We don't know it's her,' said Mitch. 'What if it's someone else?'

'Who?' Angela didn't like the way she sounded: shrill, and hunted. 'There's nobody else on this island. *It's just us.* We saw the pilots' bodies. We dealt with them. It's just us. OK?'

The silence glowed with dread possibility, a looming question mark.

What if you're wrong?

'It's her,' said Angela. 'And I'll prove it.'

But she did not know any more. Purgatory had become permanence—and now the threat was close, it was real and different and horrifying. Beyond the palms, into the jungle, shapes and shadows dripped and crept, startled and sinister.

88

Moonshine seeped in, soaking his surroundings in milky light.

In flashes Noah made out a porthole window, through which the horizon lifted and sank. It smelled rotten, like passages in a dank cellar.

He slept in protracted, intoxicating bursts. Each time he woke the dark had changed, hours passing, days passing; he had no concept of time. Food was brought and he devoured it like an animal, crusts and leftovers but it didn't matter what it was, only that it gave him strength. He drank water, dirty and tasting of iron, what felt like gallons of it, every drop sucked into him for fear that any second he would find himself back on the fishing boat, rotting in the scorching sun.

He could hear voices, the same voices that had picked him up.

Visions came and went: dark-skinned and evil-eyed, with sweat-drenched headbands and lean, muscular torsos, their chests and arms crawling with ink. Knives and guns slung in their belts. Their teeth, rotten and black. Pirates.

He kept hearing one word, repeated over and over:
Koloku.

Noah's hands were tied behind his back. His ankles were

bound. He knew he was going to be killed. Why, then, had they saved him? Why did they want to make him better?

For another purpose: *Koloku.*

Was it a place? A person? What did it want?

Noah dragged his strength from within. All he knew was that he had to escape before they reached it—because whatever Koloku was, it spelled danger.

89

Day 56

The cave was cold. It leaked and stank. Through its narrow opening the cavern lost light quickly, a few slick rocks petering out into total dark.

Mitch shuddered at the memory of being here. He had blanked those days out, unable to re-live them. Even now it was like stepping into a dream. The roof and walls were slippery, twisted stalactites dripping from above, mottled and alien.

He had been so sure…and yet they had not come. He had waited, and waited, but they had not come.

He had been so convinced, believing beyond any doubt, and now he knew of Tawny's sabotage it cast fresh, uncertain light on all that had passed before.

They hadn't brought him here. Someone else had.

'This is where you saw the prints?' Angela knelt.

Mitch nodded. The snake of sand was unmarked, as he had known it would be. A scorpion darted between rocks, vanishing into the grain.

It was clear what Angela was thinking. If Mitch were anyone else he might have thought it too: the heat, the sun, the circumstances, a recipe for hallucination.

The sand was curiously, unnaturally, smooth.

'You were here a long time,' she said. Mitch could make out the shard of light in her irises but nothing more. 'And you saw nothing?'

'Just the prints—on the first day, and then…'

'Then what?'

'Some mornings, when I woke.'

'The same trail?'

'Like someone came in the night.'

Angela's silhouette was becoming clearer to him now, peeling away from the pitch, as delicate as a fingernail.

'OK,' she said, 'here's the deal. I can't hold things together with this hanging over us—not if it can't be proved.'

'We should go further in.'

'No.'

'So we can be sure.'

'No. I'm not chasing ghosts. I'm not looking for trouble. Fear is a disease. It infects. I'm not letting that happen to us. There's nothing here. No prints. It's over.'

Angela stepped out onto the beach. Beyond, in the distance, a trail of fire smoke could be seen coming from the south, a thin, creeping grey. *Kevin.*

Days ago she would have gone to confront him; now she just walked away.

Mitch stared back into the inky void of the cave.

A gust of cool seeped from the darkness.

90

Los Angeles

The limousine pulled up at the foot of the red carpet. Cameras snapped and paparazzi heaved. A driver came round to open the passenger door and a pair of sparkling Louboutins struck the tarmac: a glimpse of slender ankles, shapely calves, and the hem of a designer dress. Joan Chase faced her admirers with a winning smile.

Emerging from the vehicle, she waved to the fans. As the closest thing the Little Chasers had to Kevin, his mother was now revered. She was also an impossibly glamorous upgrade on the fatso she had once been. Grief agreed with her. Now a size 8, she had lost ten years. Make-up reinstated cheekbones and a fuller top lip. Her stylist nipped and tucked with the most svelte combinations.

Joan clutched Trey the dachshund, her scarlet-painted talons buried in his coarse fur. Trey wore a tux and sneakers: what Kevin would have worn.

'Joan! Over here! This way, Joan! Another smile, Joan!'

Graciously, she obliged. Tonight was the premiere of *Chasing Glory*, a short docu-movie of her son's life. Microphones craned for a comment.

'It's my duty to carry on for Kevin,' she told *Entertainment Now!* 'Don't get me wrong; it's been a nightmare. But Kevin and I spent years securing his place and it would be remiss of me to let that go. We're keeping the door ajar. I believe Kevin *will* come home, and when he does I want all this to be ready for him. As his mother, it's my calling and my responsibility.'

A blonde Rottweiler from *Buzz Weekly* snarled an enquiry: 'What do you say to critics who deem this film to be in bad taste? Isn't it too soon to cash in?'

Trey growled and yapped.

'We're not cashing in. All proceeds are poured back into the search.'

'But all this glamour and PR, is it appropriate?'

'No less than your questioning, sweetheart.' Joan cracked a smile. 'I'm a mother in mourning and I'm doing all I can to support my son's memory.'

'What about your record deal with Cut N Dry?'

'These are songs Kevin never got the chance to release. He would have wanted the fans to hear them.'

'Move on, please.' PR steered her through. Everywhere she turned, people were hysterical for her attention. Was this what it had been like for Kevin? In the later years, he had hated it. Joan couldn't ever imagine hating it.

Now was her time to shine, and she intended to make the most of it. Obviously, she would never have chosen this outcome. But since it was here…

'Joan—'

Sketch was in the foyer. He seized her arm.

'Please, let me talk to you,' he begged. 'Please, just two minutes of your time.'

She stopped to appraise him. Wow, he looked bad. While Joan had shed the years, Sketch had accumulated them. He looked sixty. The hair at his temples, once on the attractive cusp of grey, was a dingy, unwashed slate. His eyes bugged, rimmed with lack of sleep and carrying two saggy bags. He was twitchy and fretful.

A gang of Cut N Dry execs stood at his back. Oh, how afraid she used to be of them! And now they were the ones cowering: major players, powerful titans of the music industry, reduced in her presence to a bunch of pant-wetting schoolboys.

Joan knew what they were thinking: *Please don't tell on us!*

The men eyed her warily, like a creature about to strike. Indeed she could, at any moment and without warning. She knew their secret, and it was wicked.

How could Cut N Dry have refused her contract? And, once this album was done, how could they fail to sign for another three, four, five?

'What do you want to say?' she asked Sketch coldly.

'Only that,' he gulped, 'well, you look very nice.'

'Thank you.'

'And,' Sketch withered under her arched brow, 'we were thinking, well, you see the thing is, maybe it's not such a great idea getting Turquoise da Luca to voice on the new track; she's busy right now, her people said they couldn't—'

Joan cut in. 'But you'll make it happen, right?'

Sketch's Adam's apple bobbed in his throat. 'Er, Joanie…'

'Because it *is* a good idea, because *I* said so.'

Sketch bowed his head. 'Right, yes, of course. Of course we will, Joanie.'

Joan smiled, satisfied. They could refuse her nothing.

Before she was escorted into the theatre, Joan pressed her

body against Sketch's. Her pink lips came close. She grabbed him by the balls.

'I've got your nut-sac on a chopping block,' she purred. 'Remember that.'

And she vanished in the sparkle of studio lights.

Day 60

Clothes marked his last lifeline to civilisation. After years being trussed up in suits and bling, moulded and styled for shoots and junkets, Kevin's body yearned to break out. He went naked, and gloried in the spectacular.

Squatting in the sand gutting fish, he muttered the lyrics to his songs. His fingers were stained with blood and the tips smelled briny and rich.

Late afternoon, he slid into the forest. The canopy was high and humid. All around him shadows were lengthening. Kevin went deep. His dick was hard, as it always was, an iron shaft leading the way. Obediently, he followed, led by the potent desire that had lain still for so long, a constant, uncontrollable ache.

Nature worshipped him. Scampers in the undergrowth retreated to let him pass, and the inquisitive eye of a monkey on a branch told him he was feared.

The animals could smell it. The birds could sense it.

Kevin Chase was king of the jungle.

He wished he had another name. That one no longer belonged to him. His previous life faded a little more each day. By now it was a smudged image, hazy and bleached. He thought of no one from the old world. It was how he imagined reincarnation, to be born again, and in glimpses he might catch frayed snippets of the past—performing on stage, running an interview, filming a video, those lyrics that played on a loop in his mind—but as soon as they arrived they were gone. They held no significance for him any more.

He came to a circular glade, into which a shaft of golden sunlight poured like wine from a jug. At its centre, he knelt, dragging his hands through a pit of soft mud and smearing it richly over his body. He took his time, the charge through his groin sizzling by the second but he enjoyed the anticipation; he knew the release would be all the more satisfying. In long, smooth strokes, he caked his erection.

Spreading his knees wide, he thrust his hips forward. He wanted to fuck. Right now he would fuck anything. The mud melted, a kaleidoscope of bucking browns and greens, and frantically he searched for a hole to put it into, anything, and located a pit of sticky, fuzzy moss clinging to the side of a tree trunk. Flinging his arms around the column of bark, Kevin pounded his erection inside, breaking through the tangle of leaves and twigs until it met with something soft and springy.

He threw his head back, picturing the tree as a woman's body: the Little Chaser who had seduced him after *The Craig Winston Show*, Tawny, Celeste, Angela, anyone who would let him, and held on tight and rocked against it, fucking the life out of nature because nothing else was enough. His thighs pummelled the tree and he lifted his ass from the ground, clamping his legs around it, working like a piston, hanging helpless with his hands and feet bound.

He could feel the tide rising. The girl beneath him would be on all fours, screaming her orgasm, and he would make her come and then—

With a howl, Kevin ejaculated into the tree. The climax was so extreme that the sky shivered and shook in his glassy, lust-drugged perception. He fell against it as one lover to another, his cheek crumpled against the bark.

Slowly he withdrew, careful not to snag himself on the rough exterior.

Only then did he realise he was stuck.

Not his dick, thank fuck, but his arms and legs. The bark, whose stickiness had seemed to him so erotic mere moments before, was smothered in tacky, gluey gum.

The sap had him stuck fast.

He tried to tug loose. It pulled like the time he was a kid and had soldered his fingers together with superglue, and Joan had to douse them in vinegary nail varnish to set them free. Agony. He tugged, and tugged again.

'*Shit!*'

His cock, now limp, dangled forlornly between his legs. He looked like a giant peanut, sludged with mud, a pair of panicked eyes glittering from a dirt-caked face.

With horror Kevin realised that his dick was prickling with needles of fire. Daring to look down, he saw the skin there was covered in a rash of tiny red pimples.

Mouth open, eyes wide, he watched as an army of red ants swarmed out of the hole in the tree, antennae twitching as they spread across it like seeping paint.

I fucked an ants' nest!

Kevin was unable to contain his scream. Rearing violently, he thrashed against the gluey prison but his fingers and toes weren't budging.

He had to think straight.

I fucked an ants' nest!

The insects were in their thousands now, and still spilling out, the lip of the hole thick as an earthenware pot. Kevin focused on doing it one millimetre at a time. Gently he could prise one wrist off, then the other, then use his grip to help with the feet...

It took an eternity. Hell was refreshed when he discovered the ants could jump, driving up his arms with itchy speed, nipping his flesh with their miniature teeth and leaping to his face, where they wrapped a crawling scarf around his neck and shoulders and he hadn't the capability to swipe them off. *I fucked an ants' nest!*

It was prolonged torture, and when finally the glue released him and he broke free, nursing his bruised, pecked balls in the palms of his hands, he fell back on the ground and could have burst out laughing. Swatting his body, he managed to dust off the majority of the insistent, wriggling army, digging about in his ears, under his arms and between his legs. He examined his dick, which was a livid, angry pink.

I fucked an ants' nest!

Kevin collapsed onto his back, drained, his chest rising and falling and scattered with bites. His palms and the soles of his feet were sticky. Sitting up, he prised off some of the gunk, which came away in a clinging white web.

The presence at his back didn't alarm him, because it carried such weight and bulk that at first he thought it was a rock or a giant stone or something. Only when it grunted and moved, a thick, padded sound, a *thump-thump-drag*, did he pause in what he was doing and wonder what the fuck had just witnessed him nailing a tree.

The presence grunted, and expelled a rubbery wheeze not dissimilar to a horse. There was a smell of shit, and zoos. As Kevin turned, a shock of orange hair filled his vision. Long strands draped over the creature's arms and legs, tousled and swathed like the shawl of a hippy aunt, and its face was a wide grey plate, the rim tough and circular, in the middle of which lay an arrangement of very human-looking features, and an expression that reminded Kevin of his dead grandpa.

A peculiar knot of red curls capped the animal's head, and surrounding its nose and chin was a paprika moustache and beard. It was shovelling crunchy leaves into its mouth with lazy, languid appetite, its teeth churning like a cement mixer.

Its hands were enormous and grey, the colour and texture of elephant skin.

Kevin and the orangutan stared at each other. Once one mouthful was done, it reached out and snatched another, stripping the plant in a single swipe. It appeared weary, and faintly amused. Appetite sated, it began scratching its armpit. Still, it did not take its eyes from Kevin. Kevin found this disconcerting a) because he was naked, b) because he had just fucked a tree, c) because he had just fucked an ants' nest, and d) because the orangutan's eyes were not the eyes of a stupid pig, or an angry croc, or even the Great White he had slayed—these were the eyes of, well, it had to be said, a *person*. They were wise and knowing, maybe slightly depressed. They seemed to say: *You think I've got an easy ride here? Munching leaves, sleeping and shitting, what kind of a life is that?* Kevin had the wild notion of returning to LA with the orangutan, taking it to the Hollywood Bowl, throwing shapes at Supperclub, for lunch at the mall, and then whale-watching at Newport Beach. Maybe he could even slap on one of his stage outfits and have it perform on his behalf. That was all he had been reduced to in the latter days, anyhow—a strutting, idiot monkey.

Except, this monkey was no idiot. Its scrutiny drenched Kevin in shame. He pictured his bare ass rutting the tree, the shrieks he had released and then the indignity of his struggle to get away. Had there been a whole audience of them here?

Was this the one that had been left behind, finishing his pop-corn while the credits rolled?

It regarded him with an edge of pity, and Kevin did not like to be pitied.

Who should pity him? He was king!

Kevin stood and dusted himself off.

'What you looking at?' he challenged. 'Huh? What's the big fucking show?'

The orangutan continued to stare.

'Ah, screw you.'

Kevin went to go. Just as he did, the world exploded with an almighty, ear-splitting roar. There was a deafening *thump-thump-drag* as the orangutan's fists pounded the ground and dragged its body up. When Kevin turned, all he saw was the inside of a gigantic and terrifying mouth: the orangutan's entire head seemed to have opened up, like a game Kevin used to have where these plastic hippos' jaws sprang back on hinges to receive winning pellets. Its teeth were tombstone-big and dirty yellow, and on the top were two brutally sharp canines, protruding from a stippled, grey gum. Its tongue brought to mind slabs of unsavoury meat in the butcher's window.

The orangutan's face was shrivelled to a walnut. Its eyes had vanished.

Kevin started to run.

Thump-thump-drag... Thump-thump drag...

It was chasing him, and with surprising speed for an ani-mal that size.

Naked, Kevin broke through brambles and stalks, tearing in his stung, mud-caked, post-coitus state through an impene-trable jungle and, in doing so, flattening the way for his psycho persecutor. He tripped on knotted clumps and fell and staggered, but he could not stop. He considered mounting a tree and clambering to the top, but a faint image swam to mind of an orangutan hanging out in the branches and he decided against it. The weight of the animal seemed to shake the forest floor.

Thump-thump-drag…

Thump-thump-drag…

The creature was gaining on him, beats between rhythms narrowing to a slice.

Kevin kept going. He would keep going until he reached the sea. He didn't know what direction he was headed, but eventually he had to hit it—this was an island! Orangutans didn't go in the sea, did they? Water was its Kryptonite.

Through dense thickets and the heat of his pursuit, Kevin was aware that this was a part of the jungle he had never accessed before. He noticed it not because the sounds and smells were different, or that the ground had changed, or even that the forest was tougher than usual—in fact, it was the contrary. He noticed it because suddenly he was bombing down an already trampled route, not a route travelled by Angela or the others, not a month-old route but what appeared to be an ancient one, compacted like a proper path, smoothed by the passage of countless feet.

Thump-thump-drag…

Thump-thump-drag…

The hunt was growing fainter, but Kevin didn't slow. He didn't slow until he lost the sound completely. When he halted, he bent double, hands on his knees, his blood pumping. He absorbed the unfamiliar surroundings.

And the unfamiliar voices…

Kevin gasped.

He stepped closer.

Through a screen of leaves, two dark faces spoke. They were crouched, a pair of upright spears at their sides, over the carcass of a fresh kill. They wore jewellery made from bones, and grass belts that covered their groins. They delved into the animal hide to retrieve its organs, before hauling it on to their shoulders.

They started walking.

Kevin followed.

92

Day 61

In a matter of weeks there would be another life to take care of. What was inside would be out. Eve could protect her child while it was hers to keep, but once it was born she could not guarantee its safety. Beyond its arrival was a whistling blank. Raising an infant, here in this wilderness, for how long, and when would it end?

Orlando came to signify everything she yearned for, and everything her baby would be without: security, a home, a father who wore suits and aftershave, who had an education and read *The New York Times*.

Here, Eve had nothing to give except herself. She had visions of it turning into a wolf child, savage and unruly, a being she did not and would never recognise: socially and culturally alienated.

All this time she had feared having a child for the ghost of her father's crimes. Now, her reality was a different challenge entirely. Some days she wanted to despair at her fate. Others, the promise of new life was the only thing that kept her going.

The undergrowth panted and shivered. Emerging into the speckled glade, Eve spotted a sow, metres away, hidden in the trees and obscured by the hot shade. It stilled, hoofs stamping the ground. Eve saw that it was pregnant. Its stomach was bulbous, and its nipples long and drooping.

She stood, unclothed, looking back.

Water dripped from her long hair.

She and the sow locked glances. It didn't acknowledge her as human, just an animal, just the same, and all they were doing was living because they must.

93

Day 62

Jacob dragged the raft down to the water. His gold watch flashed in the sun and his hair was wild. Celeste, on the shore, watched the waves splash around the structure, knowing that come nightfall he would be gone.

'This is it,' he said. 'It's this or giving up.'

'I can't.' It broke her heart to say it. 'I'm too afraid.'

'More afraid than you are of what's here?'

'Yes.'

Jacob took her hand. He dipped his head in defeat.

'I never met anyone like you,' he said. 'We can't let this go.'

'Then stay,' she whispered. 'Stay and pray for home.'

Jacob kissed her. 'Do you think it would be the same?' he murmured. 'Back in our ordinary lives, you and me...?'

'I've forgotten what ordinary life feels like.'

'So have I. Since you.'

She put her head on his warm shoulder. He wrapped her in his arms.

'I do think it would be the same,' she said. 'We're not so different.'

'You wouldn't say that if you knew me before.'

Celeste pulled back. 'Nor would you.'

She ran her fingers across his cracked knuckles, chalky with salt and razored by wood. 'I stole from Tawny,' she confessed. 'I feel so guilty about it. I feel guilty about all the stuff I stole, and the reasons why I did it. I'm a thief, Jacob. I've been stealing my whole life and I don't know how to stop.'

She expected judgement, but the face he gave her was one of concern.

'The first thing I took, I still can't forget it. I wonder what would have happened if I'd resisted. If I'd said no then, maybe I'd never have taken anything else. My shrink's given me a thousand reasons why I did it, but none of them makes it right. Just a frail old man; I can picture his face like it was yesterday…'

She half frowned and half smiled when the name fell into place.

'Cane,' she said. 'Do you know, I've been trying to think of that for so long? There it is. Cane. His son. A castle in Europe; it was a bracelet, silver and ruby—'

'Wait,' said Jacob. 'What did you say?'

'It was a bracelet—'

'His name.'

'Cane,' Celeste repeated, and when she said it this time it sounded altered, a new shape on her tongue.

Cane.

'Jesus, Celeste, if this is what I think it is…'

Jacob grabbed her. 'Come on,' he said, 'we have to find the others.'

The motivation for punishing Celeste was clear. The group accepted the theft of the jewellery as the reason for their fate—if not a certainty then a possibility.

But Angela wasn't convinced. The punishment did not fit

the crime. What Celeste had done was wrong, but it wasn't wrong enough. Nowhere near.

There was more to Cane's story.

As Celeste broke down, bewildered and apologising—'But why put me on a plane with all of you? I'm not famous like you, why you, why choose you?'—Angela wondered if, just if, they all had a corruption to confess. On its own nothing to warrant an ordeal on this scale, but together, a one-size-fits-all penalty…

Supposing every one of them had crossed Cane's path?

'Hold on,' said Angela.

The disorder on the beach ceased. The sun was falling. Evening crawled in.

'This isn't it. Celeste's right. Why would Cane choose six of the biggest names in the world if he just wanted to take down one woman? It makes no sense.'

'He's a fucking maniac,' said Jacob. 'None of it makes sense because it's crazy and he's crazy. You can't apply sense to a psychopath like that.'

'Think,' she urged, 'just think for a minute. Celeste's offence was years ago; this could be something way in the past. The name. Does it mean anything?'

Eve had a creeping feeling in the pit of her stomach. She was first to speak.

'He had a son,' she said. 'Do you remember? The boy died. Suicide. He was only nineteen. It was horrible. The paper covered it—it got a column, just a short one.'

'And you wrote it?' swiped Mitch. 'Something nasty?' It wouldn't be the first occasion a victim had wished Ms Harley wiped off the face of the earth.

But Eve shook her head. No, this time she hadn't written it. She had done something much, much worse. She, in her way, had been responsible.

Grigori Cane.

She said the name out loud. It was an ugly name, like a mouthful of grit. He had been no ordinary boy. Eve recalled an allergy to sunlight, a debilitating stammer. As an only child and sole heir, his wealthy father doted on his every move and would have tried anything to see him succeed. That promise stood in death as well as life.

She hadn't thought of the matter in so long. Stumbling through corridors, each scene slotting with horrid clarity into their twisted puzzle, Eve recounted her tale, her companions' expressions falling as they listened, as they, too, applied the prospect to themselves. Grigori was the shadow behind the sun, the shape in the corner, the murmur in the trees… He had been here, in some small way, for all of them.

After the suicide, Eve had read his obituary. According to the article, the Cane boy's depression had been triggered after his young heart was crushed. She had been the one to make that happen.

Rewind. For once, nobody else's story but her own.

Hitting adolescence, Grigori Cane had fallen for a girl, his fourteen-year-old sweetheart Lotte. Lotte was the daughter of a high-profile German family, and Grigori believed her love might save him. He had opened his heart, possibly the first and only time, and his father had trusted it to be the start of a new phase. But Eve had sniffed a story and she had gone for it, gone for the jugular, as only she knew how.

Lotte had a criminal uncle. Even now Eve couldn't summon with absolute certainty the felony, a minor hit-and-run that might or might not have made the uncle a bad man, it might even have been better kept buried, but Eve had been unable to leave anything buried. The exposure forced young Lotte and her family into hiding. As a result Grigori was cast aside, heartbroken and damned. He never saw Lotte again.

For the rest of his days, he would blame this outcome on Eve.

She laid it all bare, telling the tale as carefully as she could, handling it this way and that so she could feel its weight and shape; unwrapping layer by layer the heinous gift they all recognised now as the truth.

The boy who hadn't dared speak was screaming now.

'Voldan Cane.' Angela was next. 'He knew my father. They came to our house. It was my tenth birthday party. I remember Grigori—he was a creepy kid. No one wanted to play with him. He wanted to join in and we didn't let him.'

Voldan would justify it in the same way he justified Eve, who had committed an unfortunate act but it was hardly a means to this end. Angela was the young girl at whose party Grigori had undergone his first scarring humiliation, by none less than a spoiled, dirty-rich princess. Voldan had been a consort of Donald Silvers—he would expect his child, like Angela, to have all the world. But Grigori had been different. Even aged five, he had been different. Angela had shunned him, cutting loose the rope to her tree house to stop him climbing up. He had been jeered at. Mocked.

How deep had the rejection run?

Had it set the tone for the rest of his unhappy life?

What did it say about her, that she hadn't thought of it since? What did it say about any of them?

Selfish, Voldan would claim. In their lives of power and privilege, these people knew no suffering on a scale with his son's: nothing mattered except themselves.

'It was so long ago,' she said. 'They must have exiled to Europe soon after.'

'And…?' said Eve.

'And nothing—that was it. We were mean, but we were

kids, just messing. It didn't mean anything. We didn't want to cause harm. For God's sake, we were ten.'

'This is bullshit,' said Jacob. 'I'm not buying this.'

But Jacob couldn't think of anything else, no other enlightenment that linked them in this senseless circumstance. Mitch stepped up to the stage.

'Grigori came to a workshop of mine,' he admitted, 'years ago, in Dallas. Intense-looking. Dark hair, dark eyes, didn't talk much. He had this stammer, it took him minutes to force out a sentence, the other kids didn't know what to make of it and, for the most part, he got left alone. Crazy that he wanted to break into the movie industry but I'm guessing that's where his father came in. Anything Grigori wanted, I'd hazard it got paid for. Connections got exploited. Favours pulled.'

'What did you do?'

Mitch fumbled for his wrongdoing, so minor to be barely there, and thought how strange it was that no one scene in a person's life is viewed the same from two angles.

'After the session we ran through some break-up tasks,' he said. 'There was a weight-lifting competition, something informal to wrap up the day, a few kettle bells and some improvised trophies. Grigori struggled. He dropped the bells. Jesus, I don't recall much about him but I do recall this: he was so thin he could hardly have lifted a cup of damn coffee. Anyway it was no big deal, the fact he lost. We teased him, but it was in good nature. I told him to get over it, stop being a baby, and he reacted, well, badly. Left in tears, shrieking he was a failure…' Mitch tried to draw up more details, something truly awful he had done to the boy, something to warrant this penance.

'It was just another day,' he finished, baffled, 'just what happened…'

'Voldan blames us,' said Angela, 'for what happened to Grigori. He blames us totally. He thinks we pushed Grigori to it…starting with me.'

'And ending with me.' Celeste looked up. 'It wasn't just the bracelet,' she said. 'When I went to Szolsvár Castle, it was to value a painting—a portrait of Cane's wife. Grigori's mother.'

The castle sprang up in her memory: the isolated turrets, the cavernous rooms, the strange, quiet boy hidden up in the attic…

Cane Enterprises.

How could it be?

'I visited weeks before Grigori's suicide…' The likeness above the Great Hall fireplace lived on as the ugliest Celeste had seen. When her superior called, she had described it over the phone. What were the words she had she used? *Gruesome. Wretched.* And heard the creak of a floorboard on the other side of the door.

Grigori must have crept down from his attic, listening in, and bled at her dismissal: the final twist in his spiral of depression, her appraisal a blasphemy to his mother.

Finally Angela asked: 'Jacob?'

The entrepreneur was hesitant. Jacob didn't want to engage with the theory but, even as he resisted, he was grasping at echoes. Sitting cocksure at his desk with Leith, drunk on power, dismissing dreams like switching channels on a remote.

'He came to see Leith and me,' said Jacob. 'Had some notion for building a product. We turned him down. It wasn't viable.'

'How old was he?'

'Eighteen, maybe.'

It wasn't hard to fill in the blanks. Grigori's last stake at success, a chance to finally make something of his life. Perhaps he had watched a documentary on business thinkers and had been inspired. Perhaps he had sincerely believed in it. Perhaps Voldan had advised him against the pitch, but his son had been adamant. Perhaps Voldan had loved seeing Grigori passionate about something again, and prayed it would bolster his confidence even if the blueprint were refused...

Alas, no. On pitching to Jacob and his cronies, Grigori had wound up being guffawed out of the building.

'Then what?' Eve pushed. 'What did you do?'

'We laughed him out of town. I mean, shit, you should see the kind of things we get pitched, it was no big deal, seriously it wasn't...'

But it was to Voldan Cane.

'We turn away people every day, it's part of the business. If you can't face rejection...'

And that was it. Grigori hadn't been able to face rejection, and they had all rejected him. So his father had avenged his rejected soul.

'I don't know about Tawny,' said Eve, 'but Kevin I can guess at. He got signed to Cut N Dry Records aged twelve. His final audition was up against another kid—I asked him about it once. Kevin described this kid, dark, small, with a stutter that made him difficult to understand. Don't get me wrong: Grigori Cane was never going to be a pop star. He didn't look the part, he didn't sound the part, but I guess Voldan wanted to buy him a shot if that's what it took to make him happy. Of course Grigori lost out. It was never going to be any other way.'

The group pictured the scene: Grigori craving love and respect, what up until then had been cruelly out of reach, then, at the last hurdle, a kid with buckteeth and a bad attitude beat him to it. Being forced to witness Kevin's rise over the years would have been torture. Months before his death, *Time* magazine had labelled Kevin 'Bigger than Jesus'. It was the final nail in Grigori's coffin.

'There's five of us here,' said Angela, 'and one more we're certain of. It's too much of a coincidence for it not to be connected.'

'This is why,' agreed Eve. 'Oh God, this is why…'

How bold the invitation had been, how brazen, assuming the party's ignorance and arrogance because they would not remember—and Voldan Cane had been right: they hadn't remembered. They hadn't given Cane's name a second thought because whatever pain they had inflicted on his son, however it had affected the boy in his leaden years, it had meant nothing to them. Absolutely nothing.

What a price they had paid for their mistake.

'Cane wanted us dead,' said Jacob, 'and he succeeded.'

'He failed,' Angela said. 'We're still here.'

'For how much longer?'

Eve pointed over the mountain. 'What's that?'

Beyond the ridge was a burst of billowing grey smoke. Another appeared behind the plateau.

Two fires.

'Kevin,' said Celeste, but her voice was thin and afraid.

'It can't be,' said Eve. 'Those fires are a mile apart.'

'Then what?'

Angela didn't want to say it. *Miles apart…*

Two fires. Two separate camps.

Jacob started to walk. Celeste followed. Like children to their parents' call, they trailed across the sand and into the forest, blindly approaching the unknown.

94

Inside the jungle, shadows closed in. Trees hulked. The forest hissed. Moans and howls they had heard from the beach moved alongside them now.

Angela led the way. She could not explain the urgency of needing to spearhead the mission, to be the first to encounter what was waiting.

Others.

The suspicion they had nursed privately for weeks.

Who were they? Where were they? What did they want? One moment she was convinced of the need to find them: people meant help, communication, even salvation. The next she questioned why they had stayed hidden.

Either way, she had to know.

They reached the foot of the mountain, a sheer grey wall, and could not go on. Moonlight trickled through the canopy, not enough to see by. They had no torches to light their way. They stopped for the night, burned a fire to keep warm.

'They'll see us,' said Celeste.

'It doesn't matter. They already know we're here.' Eve did not know if she meant it as a comfort or a warning. 'They have since the beginning.'

'We can't be sure there is a they,' Jacob said. 'It could still be Kevin.'

But they didn't believe it. The time for excuses was over. Until today there had been no answers, no full stop; only question marks. Now they had a reason for the crash, and it made them hungry for more. The three fires were an invitation. If they accepted, they knew that in some important way they would never come back.

The shrieks of the rainforest arrived from near and far. In the firelight their faces were older, wiser, changed fundamentally, as if years had been both gained and lost.

Mitch spoke. 'Do you remember what Tawny said?'

'Don't,' Angela warned.

'Cannibals.' Mitch's mouth formed around the exotic word. It was magical. Voodoo.

'We don't know what these people are,' said Angela.

'But they won't be like us.'

'They might be,' said Jacob. 'Besides, I thought your demons came from above.'

'People are the worst things to be afraid of,' said Mitch. 'Why have they stayed away? If they wanted to help us, they would have come forward.'

'Unless they're as afraid of us as we are of them.'

'We have to trust that they mean us no harm,' said Angela. 'They won't—not when they see Eve.'

'Or especially when they see Eve.'

'Go to hell, Corrigan.'

'The others are our final hope,' Angela said.

'It'll bring about an ending one way or another,' said Jacob.

His words hung in the steaming air.

None of them slept that night. In the dead hour, it began to rain.

95

Noah dreamed. He lapsed in and out of that heady escape, hot with fever and cold with fear, pockets of emptiness that hurtled him back to an unknown present.

Angela was walking in the dark; he could hear her breath and the sigh of leaves on her skin. Her hands were in front of her. Up ahead shone a dazzling light. She was reaching for it, getting close, but Noah had to stop her. The light was bad. It meant to hurt her. He shouted her name but she couldn't hear. She kept going, seduced by the glow. Noah was with her, right behind, near enough to touch and he went to do just that, a graze, a brush, anything to bring her back…but she was gone.

When he called, no sound came out. He screamed her name into silence.

It was raining. Hard.

Spots on his face were cold and harsh, yet gloriously fresh after days boxed up below deck. He tipped his neck back to meet them, mouth open, drinking the storm. The wide black sky churned and growled.

The boat rocked. Men held him beneath his arms. Noah's shoulders, elbows and wrists ached beyond the point of reasonable pain, numb in their sockets, trapped in place. The rope around his ankles was searing as wire.

The pirates spoke in short, hostile bursts.

That word again: *Koloku*.

Noah wished he understood what they were saying. He struggled to break free and a thump landed on his back, knocking him forward, his cheek slamming on the deck. A boot descended, holding him down.

A scuffle broke out. Their leader was angry. Noah saw why. It wouldn't do to damage him. They had to keep him well—it was why they had been feeding him, watering him, bringing him up on deck for air. Why they could not afford to beat him.

What for? *What did they plan to do?*

The scuffle turned into a brawl. Rain slashed across Noah's vision and this time when the boat tipped there was no one to hold him in place. He crashed into a heap of sacks, kicking his legs out in front of him, his chest pounding as he watched one of the men get thrown against the mast, the man's head cracking and a jet of blood leaping free, staining the wooden pole red.

Above, the sail whipped and flapped.

Adrenalin came from nowhere. Noah had thought his muscles wasted, his will shattered, but when he saw his chance he had to take it. His hands groped across deck, locating a rusted cleat, its point sharp.

Sharp enough.

He worked the rope against it. By the time they came to retrieve him, it was already undone. Noah sprang, catching them off guard. Pulling free the bind at his ankles, he jumped from the deck of the boat and hurtled towards the roiling sea.

The last thing he heard was gunfire, and then he hit the water.

***

The ocean was freezing and oil-dark. Noah ducked under, partly survival and partly lack of strength to stay afloat. Bursts of black lasted a second and an hour, stinging cold and yawning deep as the roar of bullets ripped into the night.

The pirates' beam flashed across the churning waves, searching, searching, then gradually moving further away, the pouring, churning rollers hiding him from sight. Ice paralysed. Air escaped. His arms flailed.

There was nothing around him, nothing below, only the bobbing light of the boat as it grew smaller and fainter, and the men's shouts diminished.

Noah tried to swim. He failed. His body would not work. He knew he would die now.

Drowning was meant to be kind. As the oxygen left his body he would start to hallucinate—he hoped he would see Angela, the first day they had met and he had fallen fast into her green eyes, a deeper shade of green than he had known existed...

She had been lost for too long now. He had to go and find her, someplace they could be together again.

Noah let go, and went under for the final time. The ocean closed over his head and pulled him into her arms.

96

Szolsvár Castle, Gemenc Forest, Hungary

Voldan Cane wheeled his chair into the library. He brought it to a halt beneath a gilt-framed mirror, the glass dappled and gloomy. No matter how many times he confronted his reflection, the horror never lessened.

He had to trust that the battle had not been in vain.

Still he had heard nothing from his contact.

It made his blood catch fire.

The explanation he kept returning to was that the man had been found, and forced. He had given himself away—and Voldan knew, no matter how impressive the man's track record, it was only a matter of time before Voldan himself was given away too.

The media was stumbling on from the tragedy—strange how in a matter of weeks a cataclysm could become the past, consumed by the tides of history. But once the perpetrator was found, interest would come rushing back. Voldan wasn't hanging around for that.

Janika materialised behind him.

'Finish me off,' he bleated. 'That's an order. I don't care how you do it.'

The maid emerged from the dusk. She bent to kiss him. 'You don't mean that.'

'I do,' said Voldan. 'It's over. My work is done.'

Janika knelt. She took his hand and pressed the pale, crepey skin to her cheek. She smiled up at him, her eyes filled with wonder.

'Never, Mr Cane,' she soothed. 'I'll never do that. I'll never let you go.'

97

Day 63

Dawn came. The fire was smouldering. Grey light seeped through the trees.

Weary, the band trooped on. The climb was slow. As they got higher, the tree shield parted and the sky was revealed, an angry, swirling ash. Thunder rolled across the clouds; crackles of light sparking between.

From the plateau they scanned for smoke. The sea was heaving; the pitted caves dimpled into sheer rock menacing and ominous. Everything told them to leave. Had it said the same to Kevin? Was Kevin here, camping in the jungle, facing those dangers alone? Angela regretted their fight. He was a kid, just as Grigori Cane had been. They had forced him to fend for himself.

Was Kevin still alive?

What if they had got him?

Mitch pointed. 'There it is.'

A single funnel of smoke: a beacon.

The group scrambled down the cliff, tired but indomitable. Finding the others had become an obsession; they couldn't think beyond breaking the mystery. Celeste and Jacob helped Eve, who groaned with the effort.

'Stop,' Angela said. 'She has to rest.'

'No,' Eve objected. 'Go on. Keep going. I'll catch up.'

'We have to follow the fire,' said Jacob, 'before it disappears.'

Angela nodded. 'We'll be behind you,' she said. 'Go.'

They watched their companions vanish into the trees.

They were close now. They could feel it.

Jacob, Mitch and Celeste were spat out onto the beach. It was raining heavily, drops that speckled the sand and pattered the water. White froth rolled on the ocean. A bundle of sticks burned in the cove, abandoned and dying.

'Whose is it?'

It was then they heard the sound. Chanting. A dreadful song that came at them through the forest, above and behind, growing all around. At the far end of the beach, a line of shadows crept towards them: black shapes moving, unfathomable through the pouring rain.

Angela left to find water. They needed it.

She said 'we' but she meant Eve. Her companion was bent double, her face grey, wincing through spasms.

It was happening. They had to be ready.

Alone, Eve released the cry she had been keeping in check since waking. She knew her baby was coming—and she wanted to be on her own. It wasn't an instinct she had counted on. Like an animal, she craved a dark place: quiet and dark, a private stage for this miracle that had been performed since the dawn of time.

Now, it was her turn.

Angela told her to stay put. Her body told her to go.

She crawled off the stump, panting, and moved on all

fours. Her back ached. Her bladder was swollen. Her womb tensed, each contraction rawer than the last. Each time it brought her to the point of passing out, the pain lapsed and she could see again. *You're coming.*

Through brambles and ribbons she found her way, skidding down a dirt bank and sloshing through puddles, rain pooling from the tips of leaves and turning the earth to sludge. Brown clay caked her arms, slick and greasy, and she slipped and landed on her front. Pain shot through her belly. A raging clap of thunder drowned her scream. Another contraction, this one devastating, and she moaned and panted, panted and moaned, as her palms gave way and she tumbled down a verge onto a bed of leaves. Her waters broke.

The sky reeled. She crawled into a hollow, the entrance draped in fronds. Inside, it was cool and silent.

Eve put her hands on the rock wall, hauling herself up on her knees.

Her cries shook the cave. Nobody else could hear.

98

America

Two months after a Challenger jet carrying seven celeb-rities disappeared over the Pacific Ocean and was never seen again, the world accepted the facts.

All across America, services were held. The funerals attracted rampant media attention; several lawsuits were brought against breach of privacy, though most acknowl-edged the rituals were in the public interest. Each name had been written about, each face recycled, each life story engin-eered: it was inevitable the mourning had to be shared. Denial offered no more comfort. Hope was over.

Joan Chase cut a glamorous silhouette at her son's memorial. In couture Valentino with a black birdcage veil, her slim fig-ure and pale, tear-blushed face was every inch the mourning beauty. Headshots of Kevin surrounded the empty grave: if they could not have him in person they would copy his image twenty-fold. From plump-cheeked, wide-eyed baby to the nineteen-year-old sensation he had latterly become, Kevin's posters were tacked to billboards that chronicled his too-short life.

Joan was stoic. Trey shivered in her arms. At the perimeter, fans wept openly.

A film crew taped the whole thing.

Sketch touched her arm. 'You OK, Joanie?'

Joan didn't reply, but was gratified when Trey released a low growl in the back of his throat. Sketch's stooped figure melted away.

It was bad, but while the priest went droning on she couldn't help going over the lyrics to her forthcoming single: '*You brought me right out of the wings, boy, and made me step into the light. All it took was a leap of faith, boy, and now I know I'm right...*' Cut N Dry had advised her against the use of 'boy'—they said it wasn't 'age-appropriate'. Age-appropriate her ass! Joan had slapped that concern away. They hadn't a leg to stand on when it came to telling her what to do.

One image of Kevin pinned her with its stare. It was a still from one of his videos. He had mounted a white tiger and was flexing a pea-small bicep. His expression seemed to say: *Thank you.* After all, she was doing it for him, and for the Kevin Chase he might have become.

Joan accepted her cue. She stepped forward, stopping at the grave to release a sob. Elegantly she pressed a tissue to her nose, and with the other hand threw in Kevin's beloved debut album sleeve, *Untouched*, along with Trey's studded-diamond collar. The priest dipped his head. The fans sobbed to the sky.

Goodbye, son.

It wasn't meant to end this way, but Joan accepted the cards she'd been dealt. While Kevin was alive, she had taken her place in his support act; now he was dead, she took her place on his stage. It was a stage they had both worked for and she was darned if she was letting it go.

Finally, Joan Chase possessed the celebrity she had always wanted.

***

Three hundred miles away, in a bar on the Las Vegas Strip, Dino and Carmine Zenetti watched Angela's procession unfold on TV.

Carmine popped the cork on a magnum of champagne.

'An' there it is,' he said, filling the flutes, the signet on his pinkie twinkling as bubbles crawled up the sides. His sometime girlfriend, a big-breasted lounge singer called Mufti, kissed him on his cheek. Carmine looped an arm round her waist and grinned lustily. 'All tied up.'

Dino's Cristal tasted sour. As images of Angela appeared onscreen, interspersed with those of her mourning brothers, he thought of her soft mouth and big eyes and the sexy curve of her hips, and, despite what his father said, would trade in this eventuality, however profitable, with one night in bed with a lady like that.

'You wanna go celebrate in private?' Mufti asked Carmine, brushing her tits against his arm and batting her eyelashes suggestively.

Trouble was, thought Dino, there *were* no ladies like that.

'Gimme a minute, baby.' Carmine drank, satisfied. 'Somethin' tells me you and me are gonna have a lot to celebrate for a lot of years. Ain't that right, son?'

Dino mustered an answering smile. Just as everything else that had been decided in his life, there his father was at the helm, the eternal orchestrator.

He drained the champagne and held his glass out for another.

Tawny Lascelles' mourners gathered in Central Park, where a plaque was being unveiled—GREAT BEAUTY SHINES FOR EVER—alongside a replica of her iconic pose on last summer's cover of *Vogue*. Fashionistas from around the globe huddled to pay their respects, designers and models, photographers and stylists.

All were troubled not just by Tawny's premature demise, but also by the idea that anyone as ravishing as she, indeed as them, could be mortal in the first place. Death was terribly unglamorous. If it had to be done, it should unfold in some serene setting, like Snow White in her glass box in the middle of an emerald-green glade—not crashing into a horrible sea in the depths of night, never to be seen again.

JP Baudin, Tawny's personal assistant of five years, lit a candle and held it up to the plaque. It felt like he was appealing to the Virgin Mary.

Tawny had been no virgin, and she had certainly been no saint.

It was a terrible thing to concede but, since Tawny's vanishing, JP had been liberated. He had started to see his friends again. He had been to visit his family back in France and hadn't had his superior barking commands down the phone every twenty minutes. He had rescued a floundering relationship with his actor boyfriend.

Of course he had been shocked, and sad, and all the rest of it, but now, suddenly, his life was his again. He hadn't even realised he'd lost it in the first place.

Minty Patrick stood next to him. For her, the sorrow was genuine. Tawny hadn't always been the easiest person to work with, but she had been a friend. Minty suspected that Tawny hadn't had any real friends—she'd had a tough start in life and it was no wonder she'd found it hard to open up. She had used the only power she felt she had and turned it into a commodity: her body and her beauty were, she believed, her only assets. If only she had seen the world differently.

In the crowd, Minty identified a clutch of Tawny's old boyfriends, some one-time lovers, others month-long fixtures.

She thought it strange that her last boyfriend wasn't here: the guy they had talked about that day in Milan, the Vegas croupier. Minty hadn't liked the look of him. There had been something she didn't trust, and it seemed she'd been right, if he couldn't be bothered to turn up on a day like this.

She thought it strange, but then she wondered no more about it.

In Washington, the procession following Mitch Corrigan's empty casket was a dismal one. Draped in the American flag, the coffin was shouldered by four soldiers in uniform. Melinda, his widow, led close behind.

She clasped her two children to her, smoothing their heads and whispering not to cry: admittedly this was advice she neglected to take herself. Surely a person only had so many tears? She had been crying for weeks, some days in ragged bursts that could only be sustained for minutes at a time; others a prolonged moan that went on for hours. Hadn't she run dry? When would it stop?

Maybe never. Since Melinda had found her husband's diaries, there would never again be anything to smile about.

Supporters lined their path, holding aloft banners for Mitch, fans of his movies and advocates of his politics. If only they had known his true nature.

But then Melinda hadn't known it either, had she? And she was his wife. It was the definition of a sham marriage: two strangers, unable to talk, unwilling to communicate, embroiling themselves in a web of deceit.

Melinda wasn't just mourning her husband. She was mourning a lifetime of misunderstandings, a decade of regrets, the industry that had fucked him to the point of no return; the catalogue of mind-altering shit Mitch had pumped into his system over the reckless Hollywood years and the delusions he must have suffered as a result.

She mourned his incapacity to share them with her.

When they had first met, it hadn't been an easy ride. He'd had affairs. Taken drugs. Drunk himself into a pit. Before finding stability in government, Mitch had been a drifting soul, hyped after his years in LA but now with nowhere to go. Melinda had stood by him through that.

And how had he repaid her?

A husband who thought she was… Who believed she had been…

It was a joke. A bad punchline.

Why, Mitch?

He had told her why. The diary went on to describe the growing distance between them, her suspicious behaviour and her reluctance to answer questions about where she had been…

Aliens didn't invade me, honey. Try the guy next door…

The president came to offer his condolences. Melinda was aware of cameras on them the whole time, and wished this circus could be over. It meant nothing. Her husband wasn't even in that coffin. They were giving it pomp and circumstance because it wasn't about burying Mitch; it was about burying the episode. They were doing it so that tomorrow the world could turn over with a clear conscience. The bodies were on the ocean bed, but their souls were here with their families.

It had to be good enough.

It wasn't.

Leith Friedman attended a night-time vigil for Jacob outside their San Francisco office. Despite being a key player, he kept to the back of the crowd and declined to speak when invited.

He prayed that after Jacob's memory was interned, the ordeal would be finished.

He didn't dare believe it.

To his immense relief, the Russians had backed off. Just like that, their contact had stopped. Leith couldn't explain it—surely now was the time to storm in, to push the settlement to signature. For some reason, they hadn't. They'd disappeared.

Leith didn't care for the reasons. All that mattered was that they stayed that way. Lesson learned. Never again was he playing with that kind of fire.

The CEO of a multinational electronics corporation took to the podium to speak of Jacob's 'considerable flair' and 'infectious charm'. Leith's palms were hot. Would he always have this menace dancing at his back?

He could not let it ruin him. Maybe the Russians had found a better offer elsewhere. Maybe they'd had an attack of conscience and decided to leave him be.

It sounded as false to Leith's ears as any dwindling hopes of recovering Jacob, but it was as good as he was going to get.

It was an uncertainty he would have to live with.

Orlando Silvers sat between his mother and brother on the back seat of the Mercedes. Today's parade running through Angela's hometown was for show: a public appeasement. The family had done their grieving in private and it had nothing to do with anyone else.

He wondered if the Zenettis were watching. He hoped they were making the most of their victory because it wasn't going to last. The time for gloating was over.

There was no loyalty in this business—Carmine Zenetti had proved it. It was dog eat dog, every man for himself, and Orlando would take no prisoners.

The car stopped and Isabella climbed out.

'We have to tell her,' said Luca. 'It has to be soon.'

'There's nothing to tell,' said Orlando. 'The Zenettis are dead men.'

Even if he had to do it with his bare hands.

Orlando wasn't just a man scorned. He had lost it all, and from that point the only way was forward, fuelled by certainty that there was nowhere further to fall; there was no risk left because there was nothing more to let go of. Orlando had lost his sister, his baby and the woman he loved. It made him powerful beyond his imagining.

Carmine Zenetti had picked the wrong battle.

Orlando hoped that wherever the women had wound up, however it had finished, Eve and Angela had been together and had found some comfort in that.

He hoped it had been the three of them, in the end.

99

Day 63

The pain was worse than the pain she had heard about—different, integral, her insides ripping, the sting and pull as her baby fought free in smashing waves that broke against an invisible shore. Eve crouched, her knees spread; she used her muscles in the way she'd been told, and when the urge overcame she gripped and pushed, filling the cave with stark and brutal sounds.

The rain came furiously. By the time Angela returned to the clearing, Eve had gone.

Angela called her name. It sounded spooky in the answering quiet. She looked between the trees, searching for a shape. The trees glared back, an immovable army. She listened, but heard nothing except the *pit-pat* of rain and the humming, sticky air.

'Eve!'

She shouted louder this time. A horrible sensation slipped over her, as if all of nature had turned. The jungle itself—not the creatures in it or the dangers it carried, but the leaves and the shrubs and the mud and the *fibre* of it—was against her.

One sound picked its way through: a rattling hiss.

Close. Right at her back.

Angela's heart fell to her toes.

Alone in the glade and soaked to her skin, she turned.

The baby's head engaged. Eve screamed. The pain was incredible—sharp, stabbing jolts chased by seconds of drawn-out torture as if her stomach was on a stretching rack. She grabbed a knot in the rock, strained against it and howled as long and loud as she could, as if the agony might retreat if she frightened it hard enough. She was going to pass out. She was going to die.

I can't do it.

The admission was a relief. A firm foothold. She knew it now—she could not do this, not in a cave in the middle of the jungle. She could not do it.

She'd die. It had been a long time coming. It would be better for her baby, this way. They would go together; what kind of life would this be anyhow?

But her body didn't agree. It forced her into a final, awful thrust and then in a warbling gush she felt the baby spill out. She waited for its cry but nothing came.

Luxuriously, slowly, the snake seeped from its branch.

Angela froze. A flick of a black forked tongue as it wound, silent, oil-smooth. The body, secured at the tail, was winding and slinky, led by the bullet of its head.

Two amber eyes locked on her fear.

The reptile rose up, streaked with lethal diamonds, and prepared to strike.

Her child's first whimper was the sweetest sound she had ever heard. Groping in the darkness, her fingers closed around Angela's knife. She cut the cord.

Collapsing, Eve held her baby in her arms. She could make out its tiny, perfect features: eyes screwed tight, lungs bursting, crying to be alive, this tiny distillation of human will. Its head rested perfectly in the palm of her hand.

A girl.

Her daughter. A beginning. This was where it started, the two of them together.

She had to get out of here, find Angela and get help.

Spilling tears of happiness and surprise and amazement, Eve crawled towards the mouth of the cave and the bright window of rain.

The growl stilled her in her tracks. It was deep in the throat, and savage: a half mewl, half roar.

Eve stopped, her breath raw. She knew straight away what it was.

This was no cave.

It was a lair.

Behind her, two yellow eyes gleamed in the dark.

The snake bit in a flash, tensing and releasing like a coiled spring, striking her on the arm.

It didn't hurt. It felt like a puff of air, quick and silent.

Angela dropped to her knees. The wound began to bleed; two fang-points seeping steady red.

Don't panic.

She was aware of her beating heart, channelling the venom through her body: her veins, arteries and all the tiny capillaries that kept her alive, calmly under attack.

How quiet a death sentence could be.

Get out.

Somebody was talking.

Move. Stand up. Get out.

The voice was her own, inside her head, but distant, like a

stranger's. Her brain felt diluted, a sponge between her ears, waterlogged and useless. Her arm was numb.

The trees turned to water, thin and drizzling. She could not feel the rain. Her vision started to blot.

She staggered up and started to run.

Eve backed out of the cave. The leopard followed, huge paws padding the ground. Its body was supple and exquisitely marked, the tail long, its end pricked and tipped with black.

Eve was close enough to see the flecked gold eyes, the broad, smooth plane of the animal's nose, and the tiny pores from which coarse whiskers sprang. Behind, in the entrance to the den, two cubs emerged.

Run fast. Run now.

But she couldn't move. She couldn't break away.

She held her daughter tight.

The leopardess yowled, a haunting, primitive cry, and bore its canines. Razor teeth were gigantic and blade-sharp, the jaws flawless and powerful.

Lowering onto its haunches, the cat braced its muscles, ready to pounce.

She roared again, this time louder. Birds scattered from trees. The animal's cry reverberated through the jungle, into the sky, shaking the roots in the earth.

Eve did not back away.

She did not scream.

She pulled her daughter to her beating heart and thought: *You'll have to kill me before you take what's mine.*

Angela stumbled to the beach. The coast shivered and shook in the rain.

She clutched her arm. She searched for life, for any-one—and, in the distance, by the caves, made out the blotch of her group: two men and one woman. She could not remember their names, these people she had lived and died with before today—random people, foreigners, family.

She fell, the sand coarse on her knees, the rain coming fast, mingling with the threads of blood that escaped her wound. Crawling, she tried to call but no sound came out. There were others with them. More people than there should have been. Her group was approaching a second group: dark forms, naked, spikes in the sand.

She tumbled down to the shore, the sky reeling.

White froth rushed in. She fell again, and this time she could not get up.

She turned her face to the ocean, and heard her name, called from afar, from out on the water…

'Angela…'

She knew that voice, from a life long ago.

'Angela…'

Seawater rushed up and stung her eyes. She bled tears from them, for all that was lost and all that would never be found again.

'*Angela!*'

There were such things as angels. She saw his face and closed her eyes.

100

Noah knew who she was, of course—but the figure on the beach looked nothing like Angela Silvers. Half naked, her hair long and scorched by sun, her skin dark brown, her clothes torn, and she was thin, so thin, just a bundle of sticks.

He thrashed through the shallows, scooping her up as she fell. Her eyes were half shut but when he looked into them he knew he had come home. He bent his head and kissed her lips; they were dry and cracked, tears carving clear lines down her mud-streaked face, but these were the only lips, the only face, he ever had or ever would want to kiss. A sound escaped her but he could not make it out.

Across the beach, a trio of figures advanced. Noah recognised them as Jacob Lyle, Mitch Corrigan and Celeste Cavalieri. They walked unsteadily, jungle children. Jacob's beard was thick and matted. Mitch was half the man he'd been. All were changed, Noah could see it: not just physically but at some core, central pivot.

Beyond the threesome, Noah spied a second band of people melting into the trees, gone as soon as there.

Behind, in the shallows, the Russians disembarked.

'Mr Lyle,' said the captain, 'are we pleased to see you.'

Noah saw the watch on Jacob's wrist, the one the Russians

had told him about: the one that had led them to Koloku. Solid gold.

Jacob saw it too. He blinked, like someone waking from a long, deep sleep.

'It wasn't easy,' said the captain, 'but we found you in the end. We keep track of our investments, Jacob—in more ways than one.'

The Russian put a hand on Noah's shoulder. 'And look what we picked up along the way?'

Noah could feel Angela's breath on his chest. He had come so close; the outcome could have been so different. He had been on the cusp of oblivion when the Russians had found him, in the storm, against all odds, their boat already on its way to this shore.

They had brought him back to her.

Noah didn't believe in God, but he had to believe in something.

'The others,' he said. 'Where are they?'

'Tawny's dead,' said Jacob. 'Kevin's gone.'

'And Eve, what about Eve?'

Angela moaned, trying to speak. Noah brushed the hair from her face. The movement pulled him back and he saw the unthinkable fact.

It wasn't exhaustion; it was poison.

Trickling onto the sand, blurred with the rain, was a gash of blood. Angela's arm was punctured by two bites, deep and sharp. The skin around the rupture was clotted and grey. He noticed the rim around her eyes, purple like a bruise, and the sheen of sweat on her forehead.

'Snakebite.'

'Get her on the boat,' the captain instructed, summoning his crew. 'We'll take her back to the mainland.'

Noah stripped off his shirt. 'We haven't got time. It'll be

too late.' He tore a sleeve and wrapped it round Angela's elbow. He had no training, didn't know if what he was doing was right, but he had to act. He couldn't watch her die—not now, after everything.

'Don't do it,' said Jacob. 'It doesn't work.'

'Every second on that boat's going to count.'

'You'll infect it. You'll take the venom yourself.'

'I want it out of her.'

Noah looked to the Russians. There were no other options. They gave him the blade.

Noah cut into the skin around the twin incisions. Bending his head, he sucked Angela's wrist. It tasted sour, a tangy steel. Urban myth, the stuff of movies, and maybe Jacob was right and it wouldn't make the slightest bit of difference. But if there was a chance…

Angela's body sagged. He gathered her to his chest.

'You're safe,' he soothed. 'You'll be all right.'

'We have to move,' urged the Russians. 'Fast.'

Noah lifted her in his arms and carried her aboard.

From the trees, they heard the sound of a baby crying.

EPILOGUE

**FOUND! MIRACLE! SURVIVORS!
IDOLS BACK FROM THE DEAD!
READ THEIR INCREDIBLE STORY!
HEAR THEIR AMAZING TALE!**

In the weeks that followed the rescue, no corner of the media escaped. Word trickled out slowly at first, rumours of the return and the walking wounded: a whisper of triumph. But nobody dared label it real.

Then came the photographs. Friends and family flew to Jakarta to meet the aircraft, managers and press quick in pursuit and then the inevitable wave of pilgrims.

As brittle stars climbed uncertainly onto the runway, the miracle was confirmed. Yes, it was true; far cries from the VIPs who had boarded here nearly three months ago, but them all the same. In seconds the images were multiplied, stealing every headline, every column, every inch of every paper and every blog and every show, the only thing worth talking about in every shopping mall, every store, around every family table in the land... The world was stunned.

Fictions abounded in that first stage. Eager to assemble a story, the media invented ever more elaborate fictions.

Eventually the account solidified. Noah Lawson had met a group of fishermen, vacationing off an island close to Koloku. On explaining his plight, the men had agreed to help. One night, returning from the search, a storm had blown them off course. They hit Koloku. The rest was history.

But not all had come back. Yes, there were survivors. Yes, their families rejoiced. But not all had made it. Some were never seen again.

Had Voldan Cane been capable of the slightest degree of movement, he would have wheeled himself out to Szolsvár's ornamental lake, tipped his chair forward and laid face down in the sludge until the oxygen was robbed from his lungs.

As it was, he heard the reports and absorbed them without reaction. Only his right thumb gave him away. His eyes watered. Otherwise, he remained still.

'Oh, Mr Cane...' wailed Janika. She extinguished the news channels and stood with her hands balled up in her apron. The Great Hall was fat with silence.

'Did you hear that, Janika?' he bleated mechanically.

'They didn't all live...' she ventured, trying to find the positive.

'They know about me.'

Voldan's thumb activated the lever and his chair spun round.

'They worked it out. They're coming for us.'

'We can't be sure!'

'You must get out of this house.'

Janika sobbed. She dropped to her knees, burying her mousy head in Voldan's lap. 'Mr Cane, I can't bear it! I can't bear to see you like this!'

Voldan wanted to smack her. *Get off!* he inwardly raged. *Get away from me!*

'I will pack our belongings,' said Janika, straightening and wiping her eyes. 'I must stay strong for us, Mr Cane. I can do it. I will take charge.'

'That's right,' said Voldan coldly, 'you pack. But I am going nowhere.'

Janika stopped in the doorway. 'What?'

'Leave me. I stay. This house is all I have.'

The maid's chin quivered. 'But what about—?'

'You must do the right thing, Janika. You must finish the job.'

She shook her head. Not this again. 'No, Mr Cane, I could never—'

'You can and you will. It is all I want. I keep a gun in the master bureau. You know what to do. I cannot operate it myself—'

'Never, Mr Cane! *Never!*'

'Do as I say.'

'I won't! I won't!'

The chair lurched forward. Janika backed away. The chair lurched again. Janika stepped back. But the third time Voldan lunged, Janika didn't move.

She looked down at him. Her expression shifted, new light falling across it, subtle and gentle, like sand collapsing. She smiled.

'Very well, Mr Cane,' she said. 'I will be right back.'

Minutes later, Janika returned. Voldan faced the gardens, expecting the cool barrel to press against his temple and after that the sweet steal into hell.

Grigori would be waiting. His wife would be waiting. His family. His home.

Instead he felt himself being dragged backwards. Janika

wheeled him round, towards the vestibule. There was a collection of bags gathered at the door.

'What are you doing?' he croaked.

Janika stroked the back of his head. 'Don't you worry, Mr Cane,' she said. 'Everything is going to be perfect.'

'Take me back. This instant. *What are you doing?*'

'We're taking a trip, Mr Cane. We've never been away together before, have we? This is going to be special.'

'Take me back! I will not ask you again!'

'Do you think I'm going to leave you here?' Janika crooned, as they emerged onto the gravel drive, sunlight scorching him after so long in the gloom. 'Oh no, Mr Cane, I'm going to look after you. I'm going to look after you for the rest of your life, just like I always have. My sister has a cabin in the forest. There's a cot for you to sleep in, and a tin bath for bath-time. We can *both* look after you! They'll never find us there.' She squeaked with delight. 'My sister will be so pleased. Helga hasn't been the same since her daughter's accident. We'll be like one big family. You're going to be so very happy…'

Voldan tried to activate the brakes on his chair, but it was no use. The wheels scraped in the gravel and he released a high-pitched squawk but Janika took no notice. She unlocked the rear doors of her car.

'There you go, Mr Cane,' she said, tipping him into the back. 'Or should I call you Voldan now?' She folded the chair in after him and slammed the door.

Climbing into the front, Janika clicked on the crackly radio.

'Cheer up,' she enthused, 'we'll soon be there!'

The engine started and they trundled down the drive.

Voldan watched his beloved castle recede in the rear-view mirror.

A teardrop coursed down his cheek. His heart stormed and his soul raged and his lungs burned, but all that moved was his thumb.

Senator Mitch Corrigan was the first to step off the plane.

He searched the gathered crowd for one face: his wife's.

Melinda broke through the security barrier. She tore off her heels and sprinted barefoot onto the runway. She fell into her husband's arms and wept against his chest.

Mitch stroked her. He kissed her again and again.

'I'm sorry,' he murmured. 'For everything.'

'No,' she held him, 'I am. Mitch, I was—'

'Don't. It's over now.'

'It is over. I promise you. It's all over.'

He looked into the eyes of the woman he had married years ago, and saw their change reflected. Melinda was Melinda. She had never been anyone else.

'Let's start again,' he said. 'Please. I want to.'

She smiled at him. 'I want to, too.'

The kids rushed to their parents' side. The family embraced and the cameras went wild. Mitch Corrigan, husband and father, was home.

The following week, Mitch quit politics. He shied from the spotlight, refusing to run interviews despite the call-a-second influx he employed a dedicated team to field. Shortly afterwards, he paid off Oliver and the rest of his people. He sold the mansion and moved to a ranch, where he and Melinda farmed the land, kept horses, and taught the kids to ride. Staying in the city was no longer an option. High rises and crowds overwhelmed him. He suffered panic attacks when he had to brave the streets, or when he heard a phone ring or when a radio was switched on too loud. Actions he had taken for granted became unfeasible. Some days he wore his clothes back to front. He put salt in his coffee instead of sugar. He couldn't tie a tie. He could no longer drive his car.

Recovery would take time. That was what the counsellors said. Mitch was encouraged to talk about his experiences—but, like the others, he found he could not put it into words. He didn't trust anyone sufficiently to confide.

Instead, he spoke to Melinda. Husband and wife, after years of not speaking, finally rediscovered the meaning of communication.

Mitch told her everything—and not just about the island of Koloku. He told her about the reasons he had gone in the first place, and everything that meant. He told her about August 4, 2012. He told her about Veroli.

He told her his suspicions.

In return, Melinda told him that she already knew.

One night, sitting on the veranda of their mountain farm, wind chimes tinkling in the evening breeze and a bottle of wine opened between them, she produced the diary she had found in the Washington apartment.

'Is this everything?' she asked softly.

Mitch nodded. 'Yes.' Above was a galaxy of stars—hard to believe these were the same that had looked down on him all those weeks on Koloku. The same universe: one big neighbourhood. 'I'm crazy, aren't I?'

'We've both done crazy things.'

'I know now,' Mitch said, 'that it isn't true. I was convinced they were the ones that brought us down.' In fits and starts he told her about the island cave and the footprints. 'I went there,' he said. 'I welcomed them and they didn't come. I was so sure I knew the reason, poured all my faith into it, and then we found out about Cane and the sabotage. The crash was rigged here, in the real world, and suddenly the myth exploded. I invented it. There *are* no UFOs, Melinda. Veroli was a hoax.'

Melinda squeezed his fingers. 'What about that night?'

Mitch shook his head. He searched for explanations for August 4, not yet sure of them but needing to believe.

'I was on the verge of a breakdown. All the things I did back in the day—Melinda, you know I was a mess. All those drugs. All that drink… Some mornings I'd never get out of bed. You saved me.'

'Because I loved you,' she whispered. 'And I still do.'

'When we started the presidency bid, it got worse. All the stuff I'd repressed because if I didn't think about it then I didn't have to deal—Christ! I should have hauled my ass into therapy sooner. Then 2012 happened and I forgot how to trust you. I thought you were involved. I was scared; I couldn't face it. Then Koloku—and I had to face myself. I realised *I* was the hoax.'

Melinda reached for him.

'I prefer you like this,' she said, stroking his head. 'I never liked the wig.'

'I thought you hated me bald.'

She kissed him. 'Just one of the things we never said.'

He drew her close. Their kiss deepened.

'No more lies,' he smiled, 'I promise.'

Taking her hand, Mitch led his wife indoors. He flicked off the light. They climbed the stairs, entwined, exploring each other after so long estranged.

Outside, the stars shone bright. A tiny light moved across the sky.

For a while, Jacob Lyle tried his old life on for size. The city still seduced him, she always would—the flashing lights, the dancing colours, the available women. He embraced the media and got swept up in the ride; he returned to business and dated a string of beauties. But all of it left him cold.

The world was the same as when Jacob had left it—but he wasn't.

He burned all his videotapes. He said sorry for every girl he had filmed and remembered the only one he hadn't: Celeste.

She hadn't joined him in the limelight; it wasn't in her nature. Instead, she had gone back to Italy. He had not heard from her since. In LA they had said their farewells, awkward and rushed, wildly inadequate, but how else to express their feelings in front of the world's press? Jacob had not said what he meant to. He had been whisked off by his entourage and had left her in his wake.

At the end of the year, he travelled to Europe. It was his fourth voyage over the Atlantic in as many weeks. Some were surprised that he still flew, but Jacob could not give in. It wasn't the plane that had let them down, it was a psychopath called Voldan Cane—a villain still at large, number one on the world's Most Wanted.

Cane was an evil, dangerous mastermind who deserved to be fried. If only they could find him.

And if it weren't for the Russians, Cane's vile plan could have succeeded. They would all have perished, if not by the island then by the hands of the tribe—that eerie, wordless encounter on the last day, mere seconds before the boats came in. All along, they hadn't been alone. Jacob shivered when he thought of it.

He knew how lucky they had been. That was why, despite Leith Friedman's best efforts, he could not renege on the MoveFriends sale.

'A tracking device?' Leith had baulked. 'In your watch?'

It wasn't so strange: a gift as collateral.

The world imagined the intervention to be a stroke of fortune. Fishermen had picked up Noah Lawson, and carried him in on their boat, a happy coincidence.

Funny what people would believe.

Jacob had never visited Venice before. Disembarking on the Piazza San Marco, his trench coat blowing about him, he set off across the famous square.

He felt for the tell-tale shape in his pocket, that small secret box with the diamond inside, and smiled. It spat with rain, and the air smelled fresh and living. He wondered if she would be in—maybe, maybe not, but if Jacob had to wait for her a month it made no odds. He would wait a year to ask this question.

Life was magic, and he was not about to waste another second.

Celeste Cavalieri took a series of backstreets to her Venice apartment, hurrying along rain-slicked alleys and through the hustling throng of tourists.

Not that people recognised her as much as they did the others, the household names. It was bizarre to see her group returned to their glittering pedestals: people, at the core of it, just people. People she had seen weeping, stranded in the sun, sweating and fighting, screaming for help. People she had shared that with.

She had no desire to become part of the media parade.

But while Celeste still hid from the world, she did not hide from herself.

The first thing she had done was to break it off with Carl. She had not done it for Jacob. She had done it for herself. She had done it for Sylvia, who would never have wanted this life for her friend. She had done it for her parents, who had taught her to be free. She had done it for all the people whose trust she had betrayed, those she had stolen from, because if she was going to learn to do the right thing then she had to start on her own doorstep.

'It's over, Carl.'

He had gone to strike her: the only communication he knew. But Celeste wasn't the weak, battered woman Carl had last seen. She had met the abyss and looked right in its core and she had survived.

It had made her strong. Stronger than him. Alert to the ambushes of the jungle, she had been quick. Seizing Carl's fist, she had bent it to the small of his back and applied her knee to his groin. Carl had buckled, wheezing, vowing to finish her off once and for all.

Not this time.

When he came for her, she floored him. Celeste had lost weight but every muscle that remained, every sinew and every tendon, was geared towards action.

'If you come near me again I will kill you. I swear it.'

The following day she collected every stolen item in her apartment, sorted them into parcels and returned them anonymously to every owner she could recall.

All those she couldn't place, she donated to charity: tens of thousands of dollars, but a priceless exchange for her conscience. It was time to start afresh.

She hadn't done that for Jacob, either.

But still she could not forget his name…

She knew they were from different worlds. Their time on Koloku had been a bizarre interlude before ordinary life resumed. He was a city-boy, a player. He wasn't the bearded savage who had made love to her over the forest well. There, they were other people. Here, they were impossible. They had both known it the second they landed in America. Neither knew an avenue back to their intimacy.

It all seemed so strange now, as if it hadn't really happened. Koloku, the beach, the camp, the hunting, the fire, the secrets… Another time, another universe.

So why couldn't she let him go?

Celeste rounded the corner to her street. Immediately, she slowed.

A figure was outside her door. Her first thought was that it was Carl—but no. She recognised this man's shoulders, his height and the back of his head.

I know you.

He turned. For a second they just looked at each other.

The rain sliced across the abandoned courtyard, the cobbles slick and a thrum of water as it gushed from a broken drain. Celeste dropped her bags and ran to him.

After the rescue, a recovery mission was sent to Koloku.

Night and day an elite team trawled for Tawny Lascelles. Fans refused to accept the account: a crocodile was too much to bear. But when the remaining survivors reported the same in their statements, the terrible fate of the supermodel was realised once and for all.

Unwilling to let her memory fade, those left behind set up a charity in her name—the TLFF, or Tawny Lascelles Face Foundation—that funded those in need of reparative surgery. Tawny's crusade to make all things beautiful lived on.

Three bodies, however, were located: the two pilots on the mountain, and the body of the female flight attendant. The team uncovered her in a concealed hollow close to the crash site. She had been thrown clear of the aircraft and had died on impact.

All were flown home and given a proper burial.

Only one remained unaccounted for. Kevin Chase.

***

Kevin had disappeared.

They scoured Koloku, not knowing what they were searching for. The survivors had not seen him since the fall-out, when Kevin had stormed from their camp and pledged to set up on his own. For a while, foul play was suspected. Were the others hiding something? Were they nursing a guilty conscience? But Joan, the boy's mother, was unwilling to pursue an inquiry.

'Don't you want to know what happened?' the media asked.

'I know my son,' said Joan. 'He was never coming home.'

Neither did they discover the tribe Jacob Lyle had told them about. On the third day, a small rowing boat was located in a pile of reeds to the west of the island. Unknown to the survivors, and given the natives' ability to evade detection all those weeks, it was suggested they had been coming and going from an adjacent rock.

Or did the boat belong to Kevin?

Was he dodging their search beam?

In the weeks that followed, and in the years to come, Kevin Chase would become one of the most talked-about and enthralling figures of the millennium. Shrouded in mystery, he grew into a mythical Kurtz-like figure, a fabled being on a far-flung landmass, as legendary as Bigfoot, the Abominable Snowman or the Loch Ness Monster. People would photograph him on vacation, spot him in a forest or by a lake, swimming in the ocean or homeless on the streets of New York...

T-shirts were printed: I SAW KEVIN CHASE. KEVIN CHASE WAS HERE. KEVIN CHASE LIVES ON. KEVIN—I'LL NEVER STOP SEARCHING.

It gave whole new significance to the words 'Little Chaser'.

Kevin became the new Elvis. The God of Pop—and for some, God Himself, or at the height of urban conspiracy some messenger from outer space, sent to spread the pop word. His lyrics were analysed in a new light. Could it be that '*Girl, I wanna take you out tonight, be your date tonight, be your fate tonight; girl, I wanna take you to my favourite place, buy you burger and fries, give you a tiny surprise*' was code for some deeper philosophical equation?

For those more rational, Kevin had died. His body had drifted out to sea, or been demolished like Tawny's. Either way, he was never found.

Meanwhile, Joan Chase's career soared from strength to strength. With Cut N Dry unreservedly at her back, Joan became a pop sensation, a business queen and a mourning mother: a potent combination. She launched her own fragrance—'Missing You'—and her own pooch fashion range, aided and abetted by Trey the dachshund.

Some days Joan looked at Kevin's photograph and wept for the son she had lost. She vowed that she would trade her success in a heartbeat, if it meant one more moment with him. Others, she did not think of him at all.

Eve Harley hauled her suitcase onto the bed and began packing. She had to make the most of these pockets of peace, savour each minute before the wailing demands resumed. She had gone past the point of tired, getting by on barely any sleep, and it was harder work than she had ever believed, but all the same she would not swop it for the world. Hope was the start of a new chapter.

After what she had been through, Eve could cope with anything. When she thought back now to the island, to Koloku, to the trauma of her giving birth, it was like it had happened to another person.

In a way, it had.

When she saw the others on TV, or heard their voices on the radio, she felt a necessary pull. They all felt it. It was an invisible tie that would for ever bind them in mutual understanding, for the experiences they shared could never be conveyed to or understood by another. Now, brought back, the context of home was both familiar and distant. As people, they were caught between two stages of existence: the one without boundaries, the group they had been on that island, dark and desperate and somehow free, and this one, who shopped online, who changed her baby's nappies, who took cabs to meetings and who ate cereal for breakfast.

Eve stood at the wardrobe and surveyed her clothes.

She touched the fabrics. Clothes seemed arbitrary, almost illogical. Fabrics to cover the body, the strange shape of socks, knickers, gloves with their fingers cut out. It was the same everywhere. So much was unnecessary. What humans needed to survive was basic: water, shelter, food, and above all resilience. Yesterday she had been queuing in a Soho café and the woman in front of her had ordered a grande decaf caramel non-fat no-foam whipped cream macchiato. Eve had to leave.

Generally she avoided going down to the city. Like the others, save perhaps for Jacob, she had blanked the attention. As a new mother she carried added allure: they were desperate for her story, but she had no words in which to give it to them. Nothing could describe Koloku. Nothing could describe Hope's birth. Nothing could describe what happened afterwards. So why try?

She had no need to share it, no desire to confess, and, contrary to what the doctors believed, she wasn't suffering from pent-up frustration or an urge to repress.

Simply, she did not want to talk about it.

Nor did she wish to return to work, even when Hope was older.

Her editor had been in touch, almost every day at first, promising that her position was open whenever she felt ready. Eve couldn't imagine ever feeling ready. When she looked around her at the journalists pleading for a comment, camping outside her door and ringing her phone off the hook so she had to change her number, she wondered that she had ever been one of them. She had thought she was putting the world to rights, but all she had been doing was wringing the scandal.

When it came to it, to a human being like Mitch Corrigan whom she had dealt with for so long as a case study, it was at best pointless and at worse damaging. Mitch was a husband and a father, beneath it all just a man, and he had been suffering.

Who was Eve to tear his world apart? Just as she had torn the world from Grigori Cane, unwittingly sealing her place aboard that thwarted Challenger jet.

She could never go back.

Besides, she had a new person to think about now.

Eve peeled items from her hangers and folded them into the bag. There was a snuffle on the baby monitor: Hope was stirring.

Eve smiled. Just minutes without her daughter and she couldn't wait to see her again: her blue eyes opening, her delicate mouth and her tiny fat hands. She had known straight away what to call her. In the context of Hope's birth, the choice had been obvious.

So, too, had the first thing she'd done when she got back.

Her baby in her arms, a week after the rescue, Eve had stepped into the visitors' room at HM Prison Pentonville. Though she had not seen him in years, she recognised her father straight away. The thing was, he seemed smaller. Terry Harley walked, stooped, towards the plastic chair like an old man, which, she supposed, these days he was. Gone was the tyrant who had used to climb her stairs, the giant all-seeing monster who had clawed through her nights and terrorised her days.

'This is your granddaughter,' she'd said. 'Hope.'

Terry's eyes were blank. His grey hair clung to his temples.

'I thought you were dead,' was all he said.

His voice betrayed nothing, as if he couldn't have minded either way. He barely looked at Hope.

What had Eve been expecting? The old Eve might have craved a grand, emotional reunion, a begging apology or a plea for forgiveness. The new Eve hadn't succumbed to wishful thinking. He hadn't changed.

The important thing was that she had. Looking into her father's eyes, just as she had looked into the yellow stare of that majestic leopardess, Eve knew she was more powerful and brilliant than he would ever be. She had defended her child against a beast, roaring back in defiance of her territory, for those few seconds becoming part of the jungle, as woman, as mother, as survivor.

In realising that, she had cut the binds that tied her.

Hope started to cry. Eve went to the bedroom and picked her daughter up. 'Hello, my darling,' she said, and kissed her soft, wispy head.

They had a long journey ahead of them, and Eve was filled with nerves. She was going to see Orlando Silvers again.

Given the context, it wouldn't be easy. But the day was for Angela, and she had resolved to go. Angela had become the friend she trusted most on that island and she had to be there to offer her wishes. If it weren't for Angela, she might never have made it out of that plane wreck in the first place.

Eve wished she could have repaid the kindness.

Orlando stepped into the Boston garden and felt the sunlight warm his face. At last, Angela was here. She had come home.

'Everything ready?' asked Luca, coming to join him. His boyfriend, a banker from Detroit, was at his side.

Orlando nodded. 'It feels right, doesn't it?'

Luca nodded. 'Mom's doing well,' he said. 'After the shock of it, God, I wondered if she would.'

'This is closure,' Orlando agreed. 'Now we can look to the future.'

Guests began to arrive, filtering through the arched gates and building the respectful murmur of conversation reserved for occasions like this. The garden had been decorated accordingly: it was the only place to host today, in the house where Angela had grown up. Nothing fancy, nothing fussy, it wasn't what she would have wanted. Light, free, out in the open, it felt a good fit.

Luca glanced over his brother's shoulder, to where a dark car was drawing up. 'You have to be kidding me,' he said. 'How did they get in?'

Orlando followed his gaze, narrowing his eyes as the Zenettis emerged from the blacked-out vehicle. It defied belief that the men should have come on a day like today: Carmine and Dino, the devils who had taken it all from them in the time of their greatest tragedy.

He signalled to Security. The Zenettis wouldn't be on the premises long.

'Hey,' Luca nudged his brother, 'you got another visitor.'

Orlando turned. Eve Harley was in a plain summer dress, her auburn hair long and loose.

She looked beautiful—more beautiful than he remembered, more beautiful than was possible. In her arms was a tiny blonde baby.

'Hello, Orlando,' she said.

He wanted to kiss her, this amazing, brave, magnificent woman, just take her in his arms and kiss her for the rest of time. 'This is Hope.'

Instead, he gave Eve a smile, and touched his lips to her cheek, and oh, how he had missed the feel and fragrance of her skin. They would take it slowly, whatever Eve wanted and whatever he could give her, because Orlando knew that the protection of his woman and his child was a rare and priceless fortune.

Orlando went to hold his daughter.

'So it is,' he said.

She was nervous, which was crazy. After all she had been through, this should be a cinch. Still, it was a big day and she wanted to do it right.

'I'm proud of you,' said Isabella, squeezing her arm. 'Are you ready?'

Angela nodded. She and her mother stepped out of the house. Guests were gathered on the lawn, the family she thought she would never see again, her *nonna*, her aunts and uncles and cousins—and her new family, too.

Eve. She felt like a sister to her now.

There she was with her daughter: Angela's niece. The child had been with them all that time, an eighth islander. She would always carry the jungle with her.

Angela had been shocked when she'd heard about Orlando—her brother and Eve? Why hadn't he said? Why hadn't she? But none if it mattered against the place they had come from. It was good. It was better than good. It was great.

Two figures caught her eye. Carmine and Dino Zenetti, at the gate, blocked by Security.

'Wait here,' she told her mom.

Clad in her wedding dress, Angela stalked through the gate. Carmine saw her approach. He backed up, holding out his hands. 'Angela—'

Without a word she punched his jaw. It made a sharp, cracking sound and caused her veil to dislodge. Calmly, she fixed it. Carmine toppled backwards, flailing against the hood of his car. His son stumbled to catch him.

'We came to apologise!' mumbled Carmine. 'Have you lost your mind?'

Angela hauled him up and grabbed him by the collar. Dino withered away.

'You can shove your apology up your ass,' she told him. 'You're only here because you heard I've got plans to buy you out. Newsflash, Carmine, I can now—your balls are on the line and they're mine to do with as I damn well please.'

She pushed him back. 'But do you know what?' He gaped up at her. 'I'm not like you. I'm decent. We've got our money back, so here's the deal: you take yours and you run far, far away. Never look round. Never slow down. Never turn back. If you so much as attempt to contact me or my family again I will tear your dick from between your legs and send it back to you in the mail. It'd be a cheap delivery.'

Carmine straightened his jacket. His face was bleached.

'Goodbye, Carmine.' She nodded to his son. 'Dino.'

Dino watched her go, a parallel wedding, the wife he should have had, and helplessly reached out to nothing.

***

Music filled the air. Her brothers stood at the front, pillars on either side of the leaf-strewn altar. At its centre was the man she adored.

Noah Lawson.

Love of her life. Man of her dreams.

Angela half expected, as she did every day, to wake up and find herself still on that sun-drenched beach, the heat beating down, the sea glittering and wide, and the ache for home beating hard in her chest. All those times she had been desperate for Noah and had tried to conjure the contours of his face, the blue of his eyes and the softness of his lips…after all that, here he was.

Here. Hers.

Never again would they be separated, never again would they part. They had wasted too many years.

Noah had come for her. In a feat of bravery beyond her most courageous imaginings, he had searched where others had feared to tread. And when he had found her, he had saved her life. The snakebite Angela had almost died from was still a wound on the inside of her wrist—a tattoo she wore, a reminder of all she had conquered.

Those final stages were a blur, pieced together from what people told her.

But she did remember him: Noah's arms lifting her into the boat; the sound of his voice above the hum of the motor, never stopping, always telling her he loved her and that she would live and that they would live together, a long, lovely life, his voice carrying her across leagues of ocean, towards death or towards home and at some points there wasn't even a line in between.

For a week she had lain in hospital, Noah keeping vigil at her bedside. When she was better, they had flown to America.

They had shunned the whirlwind spotlight, renting a house by the lake, miles from everything.

Angela heard what Noah had been through: the search, the journey to Maliki, the man working for Cane, the pirates, the escape from the boat and finally the Russians who had rescued him in the eye of the storm…

Only one doubt remained: why the pirates had wanted to take him to Koloku. To whom had they meant to deliver? What for? She had her suspicions about the tribe, and what that might have meant. Noah did, too. But to this day the natives defied discovery, or definition. They came from another place that Angela and her fellow survivors would probably never know.

Isabella kissed her cheek and let her go.

Angela stepped up to the altar. She took her true love's hands. All she could see was Noah: a man who had chased her across wild oceans and brought her back from the brink—but still, as well, the boy she had known as a teenager, working at Hank's, driving to the lake in the open-top car and calling up to her window.

'Angela,' said the minister, 'do you take Noah to be your lifelong partner, to love and support him, forsaking all others, as long as you both shall live?'

'I do.'

They did not wait to be told they could kiss.

***

Koloku Island, Southeast Asia, the Palaccas Archipelago

Kevin Chase crept naked out of the trees.

The natives stood ahead of him: eight uniform lines, patiently waiting, their faces bright with awe and worship.

When they saw him they raised their spears and emitted a yodelling cry. They were eager to get started—and so was he.

Kevin touched the crown of leaves atop his head, and flexed his muscles. Behind, the village of Haulo began to emerge. Children came to see their god; women to survey their emperor, men to admire their leader.

Slowly, Kevin began to move. The locals watched him, transfixed.

The tune in Kevin's brain had never left him. The music never would. He had been put on this earth to teach his melodies far and wide.

Here, he reigned supreme.

The jungle seemed to sing with him. Moving gracefully in shapes and rhythms both new and marvellous to the native troupe, they followed his lead. Kevin executed his dance routine to his debut single, 'Sweet Talk'.

He sang, crooning as he had on stage in another, faraway reality, shooting his arms to the sky and launching up on his toes. The locals imitated, perfectly in sync, echoing the foreign sounds and slave to the beat.

Kevin's was a new order. He was powerful. He was king. He was almighty.

The wilderness had fought him—and he had won.

Welcome to Paradise.

Only the rich are invited...only the strongest survive.

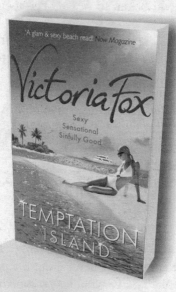

Three women drawn unwittingly to the shores
of Temptation Island, all looking for their own
truth, discover a secret so shocking there's no
turning back. It's wicked, it's sensational.
Are you ready to be told?

Is there such a thing as the *perfect* size?

Vivian Ward is in total control of her life. Actually, scrap that—she's thirty-five, estranged from her family, a failed actress and working in a London members' club to pay the bills. Truth is, the only thing she's in control of is what's on her plate…

But then she meets movie star Maximilian Fry, who's just as screwed up, and journeys into a world of celebrity even faker than the one she was already living in. Will image triumph, or will she realise that some of her answers lie within?